The Rhino Whisperer

A Crime Mystery set in South Africa

by

Evadeen Brickwood

EVADEEN BRICKWOOD

Another mystery novel set in modern South Africa. This time, the murders of a ranger and a rare black rhino in the idyllic Shangari Safari Park rattle the local community of Rutgersdrift. Sofia Helenius from Finland lives at the lodge with her boyfriend Tom Rutgers, the owner of Shangari. Sofia is tormented by a secret she yearns to share with Tom but the cruel events grab the limelight and put everything else in the shade. A native Khoi-San family is known to communicate with wild animals but what if the criminals get wind of this gift?

When another murder happens in the city of Johannesburg, smouldering secrets begin to unravel. How are the murders connected and will it be possible to halt a relentless crime-syndicate in order to save an African paradise?

<u>Other Titles by Evadeen Brickwood</u>

In the Youth Series:

"Children of the Moon" ("Remember the Future" 1)

"The Speaking Stone of Caradoc" ("Remember the Future" 2)

"The Secret of the Bird God" ("Remember the Future" 3)

In the German Edition:

"Kinder des Mondes" ("Erinnerung an die Zukunft" 1)

Novels:

"Singing Lizards" (A Mystery Adventure)

"Singende Eidechsen" (German Edition)

"Abenteuer Halbmond" (German Edition)

"A Half Moon Adventure" (A Mystery Adventure)

"Charlie Proudfoot Murder Mysteries" (Series)

Acknowledgements

I want to thank all my editors and test readers, especially Peter and Svenja Böttner, for their hard work and incredible input. A big thank-you also to the SanPark rangers who told me all about animal sanctuaries and the practice of soft release into the wild during the YeboGogga event at the University of the Witwatersrand in May 2017 and to all the wildlife conservation organisations, among them the International Rhino Foundation that are doing such an incredible job. My great appreciation to the Afrikaans-speaking side of our family for their valuable input regarding colloquial Afrikaans and last but not least Mannaka Productions for showing the Xnau documentary on TV, just when I needed to learn more about the Khoi-San culture in South Africa.

For Mari and Jonas

"It always seems impossible, until it is done."
Nelson Mandela

CHAPTER 1

There is a beautiful place in South Africa, between the Kalahari Desert and the Magaliesberg, where rocks and water and all living things pulse to the rhythm of nature. A place, where harmony reigns and the possession of money is not considered all-important.

It is here that you can find the Shangari Safari Lodge; a piece of paradise to many. The area hovers on the edge of the mighty Kalahari Desert and a whitewater stream churns past sandy beaches, hemming in woodland and bushveld and agave-covered hills.

If one follows directions, it is easy enough to find Shangari, as there is no need for street names in the countryside. All you have to do is take the new tar road north of Rutgersdrift and turn right by the great baobab tree. Two business-savvy women in traditional garb tend to their stall in the shade of the tree, selling avocados, macadamia nuts and delicious baobab jam.

If you are lucky, you'll catch a glimpse of baboons in the expansive branches or of a few inquisitive meerkats, scanning the road from the top of their burrow. The tar road carries on north, past avocado and citrus farms, over a bridge and through the village of Renosterspruit until a dirt road takes over all the way to the border with Botswana. Not much has changed here in many years and not much ever happens.

Rutgersdrift is the largest town in the district. It boasts streets in dappled shade, a small hospital and a sleepy police station next to the church steeple. Five minutes outside of town lies an airstrip; the frequent destination for small single-engine planes coming in from Johannesburg and Pretoria with their bellies full of tourists, hungry for the spectacle of nature.

It's half a mile down the dirt road to Shangari by car before gleaming-white gateposts come into sight. A farm hand in blue overalls repaints large letters overhead that spell "Shangari Safari Lodge" and two farmworkers sweep the road, waving at passing cars. Another minute past colourful flower beds and dusty cactuses, then the parking lot comes into sight. Made from natural stone, the lodge buildings can change their colours from ochre to pink to brown, depending on the angle of the sun.

Broad steps lead up to a cool double-story hall with its oversized African artworks and carved wooden pillars that support the lofty reed roof. It had to be one of the most-photographed hotel lobbies in South Africa, inviting visitors to take a well-deserved rest on pale sofas and upholstered wicker chairs.

Look to your left and the head of a Kudu with impressive corkscrew horns will grin down at you from behind the reception desk. Glass doors lead to a well-stocked curio shop. A small room with a whiteboard is used for briefings and lectures. Outside, a swimming pool beckons and a spacious wooden deck. Here you can enjoy a drink at the bar or tuck into a meal under shady umbrellas while spotting the occasional wildlife through your binoculars.

If you've booked one of the well-appointed rooms, you climb the wooden stairs after the porter with your luggage and settle with a happy sigh on a four-poster bed or a comfy chair on the private terrace, wowed by the magnificent view.

Shangari was by no means the only safari lodge in the district. In fact, many of the farms had converted to boutique hotels but Shangari offered something else apart from sheer luxury and unspoilt wilderness. It had become a secret tip among tourists who didn't mind the unreliable internet connection. Some even said Shangari had something magical about it.

Poachers who were targeting the magnificent rhinos on the border to Mozambique stayed thankfully far away - until a white rhino was shot and de-horned at the Lungile Game Park near Shangari. Shocked by the sudden act of violence, the game farmers in the area installed nightly ranger patrols and a deceptive sense of safety returned.

In February, with the crazy Christmas-season over, Shangari found itself once again in a dreamy state of self-content. It was so hot that the air above the road seemed to melt into shimmering waves and humans and animals slowed down to a lazy pace. But the poachers weren't quite done with this piece of paradise.

The night air was balmy; cicadas chirped their lullaby, rocking the people of Shangari to sleep in their beds under flimsy mosquito nets. A few guests were drunk after downing expensive liquor at the bar, others enjoyed the moonlit view from their rooms. A few farm workers had drunk too much of the popular sorghum beer at the shebeen and slept soundly, while the rangers kept Shangari safe from intruders.

Tom Rutgers, the owner of the lodge, rested next to his Finnish girlfriend, Sofia Helenius - the light of his life. He kissed her dark hair gently, not to wake her up. Sofia's cheeks were still flushed from their lovemaking. *How beautiful she looks*, he thought. She smiled in her sleep. Whenever she smiled, the dimple on her cheek and the one next to her mouth appeared and Sofia had a ready smile. They had enjoyed an hour of passion, yet troubling thoughts didn't let him rest. Tom and Sofia could be married by now, had she not turned him down back in Finland.

Their relationship had begun almost five years ago but whenever he wanted to talk about marriage, she dodged the subject. Was it time to ask her again? The small black box with the aquamarine ring was burning a hole into his sock drawer. A place Tom could be reasonably sure, she would never look. He knew that Sofia loved aquamarines but little did Tom Rutgers know about the secret that was pulling at her heartstrings, preventing her from fully committing. Soon, he drifted off into a pleasing dream and began to snore softly.

The farm hand slept blithely, having finished his paint-job before dusk. The cooks, the maids, the gardeners, the families of the workers, slept in the compound not far from the lodge. They dreamed dreams of wealth and glory after watching their favourite soapie on the large TV in the empty hall. Something they usually did before the weekend-guests arrived. Most of them wouldn't trade Shangari for any place on earth. Many of the Tswanas were related to the Bushmen who had lived in Shangari forever.

So were the seasoned rangers, keeping watch in the bushveld. The Khoi-San were unbeatable at tracking and some could even communicate with animals. Rangers knew not to confront the heavily armed poachers and to immediately inform the police via radio as soon as they detected suspicious movement. The balmy night promised to be as uneventful as the last. It should turn out very differently.

There was movement between the trees, shots were fired - and the unimaginable happened. The early rays of the sun found one of the brave rangers and a black rhino lying dead in pools of blood. The animal had lost its life because the horns, Mother Nature had bestowed on it, fetched higher prices than gold in Asia. The man because he had tried to intervene. The poachers didn't care. Filled with excitement over the promise of money for their deed, they made away with two grey lumps in a bloody bag.

A young calf sat next to the rhino, still in shock at what it had witnessed. It sat there waiting, crying softly, watching the life drain from its mother, while the ranger lay cold and alone in the thicket on the edge of the wood.

*

When Shangari awoke at sunrise, a tender dawn promised to melt into another blistering summer day. Tom Rutgers stirred as his pleasant dream gave way to practical thought. The lodge would be teeming with guests soon. They had booked to see the lunar eclipse on the weekend and there was much to do before their arrival. He fumbled for the alarm clock and before it had a chance to wake up Sofia, pressed the snooze button.

Four generations of Rutgers had lived in the sprawling farmhouse with its Cape-Dutch gables and broad verandas that enclosed a private garden with swimming pool. The house itself had been remodelled a few years ago with Tom's father supervising the building work.

Tom Rutgers was thirty-three and a trained civil engineer. He had made a name for himself, working for a prestigious firm in Cape Town. When his father suffered a sudden heart attack three years ago and died a few days later, Tom had returned to his rural home and Sofia had joined him after a few months to run the administration of the lodge. He had spent a happy childhood at Shangari and didn't mind taking over the reins of the business. His mother soon remarried and now lived in the Netherlands. Since her new husband didn't enjoy coming to Africa, Tom only spoke to his mother occasionally; and on Christmas and birthdays.

He had achieved most of his dreams. *Except...* Sofia, he thought and didn't understand. Better to get up than to think useless thoughts!

He was proud of the farm he had inherited from generations of Rutgers who had moved to South Africa from bonny England two centuries ago. In the sixties, his father had transformed the struggling citrus plantation into the Safari Park it was today. Each room at the lodge had linen curtains and wooden shutters for privacy and its individual African décor. Tom had added verandas with jacuzzis to the upstairs rooms, each with a view of the green hills or the savannah. He jumped out of bed and kissed a smiling Sofia on the forehead. She stretched and peeled herself with languid movements out of the bed covers.

"Morning," she breathed.

"Morning, Sofie."

They got dressed in the bedroom with the large four-poster bed, carved from valuable stinkwood. French doors opened onto the private garden with masses of red bougainvillea flowers and lemon trees greeting them every morning.

Tom didn't need long to get ready. A quick shower, a shave, sunblock, shorts and a simple cotton shirt. They both preferred casual clothes now and their smart city outfits kept each other company in the ancient walnut-wardrobe in the lounge. Tom's great-grandmother had brought the wardrobe with her from Belgium as part of her dowry. The smart clothes were reserved for formal events, like the cocktail party tonight.

His usual lack of fashion sense didn't harm Tom's rugged looks. Female guests often gave him admiring glances. Some tucked their phone number into his shirt pocket while batting their eyes at him, some made downright offers that he laughed off. Their efforts were wasted on Tom Rutgers. He was oblivious to the effect he had on women and had eyes only for Sofia. After five years, Tom was ready to commit. Would Sofia at twenty-nine also be ready at last?

He'd been told that twenty-nine was the magical age for most women, as far as marriage was concerned. Being-married-by-30 was apparently a big thing for women. Liesl, his pretty, blonde ex-girlfriend didn't leave any doubt that she expected to be married by twenty-five and to be taken care of by a husband. Tom resisted. They had met at high school and Tom had been in love for a few months but Liesl with the stunning body of a goddess, had no opinions of her own or any aspirations in life other than being a housewife and mother. Two years into their relationship, Tom had been so bored that he applied to study abroad. He was accepted and went to Finland. The relationship fizzled out and when headstrong Sofia came along, he was completely smitten.

They had met at Turku University. Sofia was in her third year, studying for a Bachelor of Commerce. She had noticed the charming, blond South African engineering-student with his clear hazel eyes from the word go, and her friend Milla introduced them at the International Student Club. His command of the Finnish language made her laugh but she could speak English rather well and they had talked until the early hours of the morning.

Sofia was as fresh as the cool sea air. Tom had told his friend Nikku back at the dorm that he would marry this amazing girl one day. It had been a wonderful summer. They couldn't wait to go on picnics and drives into the country with their friends. Then it was just the two of them who took strolls around the old harbour of Naantali, holding hands and kissing in dark corners. Soon they were like a house on fire. Tom impressed Sofia by rowing a boat out to one of the small islands for a sun-filled afternoon and Milla had probably told the others to leave them be because nobody had asked to come along.

During the students' traditional Glögi-run that winter, Tom had proposed against Nikku's advice after a few glasses of Finnish Glühwein. He must have been slurring his words a little because Sofia seemed stunned, declined and said that she wanted to get to know him better and see South Africa first. Get to know him better?

He'd swallowed his pride and agreed.

She had finished her degree in Cape Town, where Tom joined Sofia after a year-long internship in England. They had seen each other only once during that time and despite regular skyping and texting, it had been sheer torture for him.

He bent down to dry his legs, watching his girlfriend discreetly. Sofia stood in front of the mirror and put on simple makeup. She drew a black line above her blue eyes framed by long, dark lashes. Then a bit of sunblock and pink lip gloss. Done. The scar on her forehead didn't bother her. She pulled on the corner of her eye. Were there wrinkles, yet? No. Good.

Tom adored her even more for that hint of vanity. Her fresh, round face made her look younger than her years. If they could have a penny for every time someone had told her so, they'd be rich by now. At the age of 22, she had been barred from entering a nightclub in Turku for looking too young. Finnish genes, Sofia always said and winked.

She noticed Tom staring at her. "What?!" she asked the mirror and laughed. When she laughed, her eyes looked a bit slanted.

"Oh nothing, I just like looking at you. There won't be much time to do that later, with all the guests arriving." He wanted to distract from the awkwardness that threatened to drive him nuts.

"I know we never have time to ourselves these days," Sofia sighed. "But there's a silver lining: I'll see Gugu again."

Gugulethu Mbatha was one of Sofia's room-mates from her varsity days in Cape Town and still one of her best friends. Gugu worked for a large company in Johannesburg, where she had the position of PR manager and was very important. Her boss often invited key employees to spend a weekend at Shangari and the two of them always had a chat if they could.

Tom started to shave, wondering how he could arrange a proposal at such short notice. He had enough sense not to push Sofia into making a decision. He didn't want to drive her away, back to Cape Town or even back to Finland; didn't want to be away from her. Tonight would be a good time, at the cocktail party. Maybe he should ask her in front of everyone!

He lathered on shaving cream then ran a razor over his stubble. His blond beard was hardly showing but he liked his face clean and free of hair. The razor blade slipped on his chin and the white foam stained red. "Damn!" He cursed and wiped off the foam. That's what happened when you were deep in thought!

Sofia saw the bleeding cut. "Are you still half-asleep or what?" Her easy laughter warmed his heart. He pressed a tissue against the bleeding spot and Sofia handed him a tiny plaster.

"Are you surprised?" He asked in a provocative tone and enjoyed seeing her face take on a rosy colour. Tom grabbed her around the waist and pulled her close. "Don't you think it's time to..."

"Well, you know," she put her finger on his mouth. "Before you say anything, I have to tell you something..."

Tom looked at her in surprise. "Yes?" Why was she so serious? There was a loud crackle from the radio receiver on the bedside table. The intimacy of the moment passed.

'Shangari, Shangari…come in, Baas Tom. Crackle…come in…' It sounded urgent.

Tom Rutgers let go of Sofia and grabbed the radio. "What? What is it?" He barked. Everybody on the farms used radios and walkie-talkies to communicate. The mobile phone-network reached only as far as Rutgersdrift and even there, the reception was unreliable. Sofia went to the kitchen to make some coffee.

'So sorry, bad news Baas, Cornelius is dead,' Lebo, one of the farm workers, sounded rather upset.

"What? Who died?" Tom asked harshly. He struggled to focus on what Lebo was saying. "One of the elephants is dead?"

A dead elephant? That was bad news, indeed. Elephants were costly to replace and Tom loved every single one of his animals. 'No, Baas. No, no. Crackle. We are by the dry riverbed, cutting grass with pangas. Thando and Jackie and I,' Lebo choked.

"Yes, and?"

'We see Cornelius, the ranger, with a beeg hole in head from a gun. Crackle. So much blood. By the trees. I think last night, it happened. We look around. A rhino is also dead on the field. Ntombi. No horn left, cut off. Don't know. The poachers, they kill them. They are gone, Baas! Hai matata. Come quick and tell police! Please, Baas Tom, come quick!'

Tom felt the blood freeze in his veins. He had bought the pregnant black rhino only a few months ago at an auction at a nearby farm and paid a fortune for her. Black rhinos were rare and Ntombi had such a lovely nature. Now there were murderers in Shangari, poachers; and Ntombi was dead!

"Damn it all! Stay where you are. I'll be there as quickly as I can," Tom yelled. "Don't touch anything and watch the lions!" He swore and tossed the receiver on the rumpled bed. Sofia had wanted to say something. Something important. Tom knew it was important but he pushed the thought aside.

The poachers had come back and they had hit Shangari this time. Cornelius, the ranger... was dead. Murdered. A dead ranger, a dead rhino. Tom had to act but he needed a moment to get his bearings. "Damn it all!" He repeated and ran his fingers through his hair.

"What now?" Sofia asked faintly. "What's wrong?" She put the coffee cups down on the desk by the window.

"Lebo says, poachers killed Ntombi and cut her horns off. We have poachers on the farm. Down by the dried riverbed." Tom told her what Lebo had communicated over the radio.

"Rhino poachers, here? Murderers?" Sofia sat down on the bed. "No."

"Yes, in Shangari. They killed Cornelius as well."

Sofia sat down next to Tom. "What?! Cornelius? Oh no, that's awful! And Ntombi had her calf only a couple of months ago," she cried.

"Yes, little Oscar. Cornelius is one of my best men. I never thought they would go this far, those damned poachers. Damn it all!"

Sofia was rather upset. She had been the one to name the rhino calf after her father and like all the animals in the game park, the rhinos had become dear to her. "I hate them. Did they come from Mpumalanga? From Mozambique?"

Disturbing news was making the rounds that international gangs were paying poor Mozambicans to enter South Africa and kill rhinos and elephants. The poachers then disappeared with their loot across the border. "Greedy more like it," Tom grumbled.

"And poor Cornelius is dead... oh, poor Francina." Sofia wiped away a tear.

"The rangers must have confronted the poachers. Bliksem!" Tom felt shocked and angry at the same time. "They should've known better! Should have called it in. They can't stand up to a gang of armed poachers."

The rangers were armed as well but the poachers operated in large groups and game parks could not afford to spook its guests with wild gun battles on its grounds.

"I'm sure they tried." Sofia took a deep breath. "What should we do now?"

Tom zoomed in on the basics. "I'll call the police." That meant phoning Witbooi. He stood up and walked into the lounge. Witbooi was the nickname of Jacobus van Schalkwyk, the station commander of the Rutgersdrift police. He would inform the vet, secure evidence, take a report and notify the authorities. Witbooi also dealt with the border police. Perhaps, they could track the poachers across the border with Botswana. There was only so much Witbooi could do before the detectives of the Special Commission on Poaching took over.

Sofia heard Tom explain the situation on the phone. "The press will get wind of the matter. Especially, since Makaroff comes to stay this weekend..."

Stan Makaroff was Gugu Mbatha's boss. His secretary had booked him and five of his favoured employees into the best rooms for two nights. This time the occasion was the total eclipse of the moon tomorrow night.

Gugu was a feisty Xhosa-woman and as Makaroff's PR-expert, she had her hands full; spin-doctoring his reputation back into safe waters whenever his name came up in political scandals, was no mean task. Sofia accepted that it was Gugu's job and it had never come between the two friends. Makaroff had learned about Shangari through Gugu after all.

Stan Makaroff was a well-connected businessman and very rich. Stinking rich to be precise. The Makaroff empire included substantial shares in gold and platinum mines, import-export companies, various factories and a chain of sleazy strip-joints. He commanded political clout, thanks to his generous pay-offs and conniving charm.

His Russian parents had immigrated to South Africa in the sixties and his father had struck it rich as an entrepreneur in the import-export business. His mother kept out of the limelight and so did his South African wife.

"I think we should go." Tom walked back into the bedroom and put on his shoes. Sofia sighed. "Yes, yes of course..."

There was so much she wanted to say and had almost said

before the radio call came in. The true reason, why she had not agreed to marry Tom. Now she had to wait again and who knew for how long.

The dead ranger and the rhinos had become a priority and this murderous business was a lot to take in. Sofia understood that. Tom had to speak to Cornelius' wife, as soon as they got back. Sofia had no choice but to push everything else aside. For now.

"We must drive to the dry riverbed and check out what's going on."

"Sure. When we come back, I'll take care of the lodge, while you sort things out." Sofia tied her long, dark hair up into a silky ponytail. "The rooms should be ready by 9 o'clock. Frida can see to that. Cotton will fetch the German and Danish tourists at 11 o'clock from the airfield. So, that's sorted. The Makaroff-party arrives by helicopter in the afternoon. Gugu says, between 3 and 4 o'clock, after Makaroff's last Skype-conference of the day. Karen prepares the buffet lunch and the snacks for tonight. I hope everybody will do their job or we're in deep water." She hooked the mosquito net to the wall.

Tom barely listened. He waited, jingling the car keys and was out the door as soon as Sofia had slipped on her sandals.

Brutus, the Rhodesian Ridgeback, greeted them happily and jumped onto the back of the Nissan Sani, ready for action. They sped away from the lodge-buildings and down the bumpy dirt road toward the dried-out river bed.

Tom had decided not to take anybody else with them. He had to act fast before the news spread. They would manage with the help of the police and the vet and the workers already on location.

He took the radio receiver from the dashboard. "Lebo... Lebo come in." There was rustling then nothing. "Lebo... Lebo come in. Crackle."

"Yes, Baas!"

"Have you told anyone else about the poachers?"

"Baas... Crackle."

"Who did you tell?"

"Only... rustling... nobody else."

Tom switched the radio off. "We have to be quick before the news cause panic." He drove on, avoiding potholes and small rocks, dreading what they might find in the bushveld.

Tom Rutgers could only hope that murder didn't turn the tourists away. Their livelihood depended on a happy clientèle. An eclipse of the moon was a spectacular event and every last broom cupboard at the lodge was booked but poaching and murder was not part of the holiday-package.

They passed the luxury tents that had been erected to accommodate the South African weekend guests who preferred the cheaper camping option.

Then the compound of the park workers came into view. Two thin long wisps of smoke rose from the small houses, half-hidden by a sturdy wall. Breakfast was being prepared and kids needed to go to school. Tom stopped at the tall fence that separated the lodge from the game reserve and opened the gate. The sun rose higher and the colours around them changed as they drove on.

Sofia loved this time of day, had grown to love Shangari and accepted her new life away from city life. At first, it had been tough to be so far away from the ocean beaches, the shopping malls and quirky coffee shops. She'd missed her friends and the cooler climate of Cape Town. The farmers' wives had welcomed her with a mixture of curiosity and hostility. Sofia avoided the get-togethers on neighbouring farms, the local church women's group organised. She still didn't feel that she belonged there and often couldn't follow the discussions in Afrikaans.

The women seemed amazed by the fact that Sofia wasn't what they thought a typical Scandinavian woman should look like. Tom said she should ignore their silly remarks and that they would make someone else the centre of attention soon. Men were so naïve! She knew that the gossip continued behind her back but the lodge kept her busy. If she attended the meetings once or twice a year, it was more than enough.

Occasionally, Sofia dived into the pleasant anonymity of Pretoria or Johannesburg, where she ran errands, stocked up on supplies and went to the movies. Her cousin Astrid lived in Johannesburg and she could even speak in her mother tongue Suomi with her.

Tom was on the radio to his neighbour Barry Pienaar, while steering the bakkie with one hand. Barry was the local vet and pillar of rural society. He had spoken to Witbooi and wanted more details.

"Lebo says that Cornelius was shot dead in the thicket by the dry river bed. Bliksem! Yes, the ranger. Poor guy. They shot him in the head... ambushed. That's all I know," Tom shouted into the receiver. "When can you be here? Okay." He listened for a moment. "Yes. Yes, poachers. They also got Ntombi. You know she has a calf. Not three months old. Yes. I hope they left him alone. Will be difficult enough as it is." Barry Pienaar swore extensively on the other end and Tom handed the radio to Sofia. He had to use both hands to steer around a set of potholes.

"What?" It was Sofia's turn to shout into the receiver. "Yes exactly, not far from the dry river bed. We'll meet you there. Bye."

Tom's hair was blowing into his eyes and he pushed it back. Sofia handed him the radio receiver. "Bliksem," Tom grumbled and hooked it to the dashboard.

They sat quietly next to each other. There was no need for talk. She could have told Tom about her secret but now was simply not the time.

They carried on due east and the rising morning sun blinded her, despite the sunglasses. In the distance, vultures circled high up in the air. Tom pointed to the dark dots against the pinkish sky and Sofia nodded. On summer mornings, it didn't take long for the heat to set in by 8 o'clock tops, and soon lions and leopards would get wind of the cadavers. Trees came into sight.

"Baas, Baas!" Three men in blue work clothes waited in the shade of a thorn tree and waved wildly. They pointed to their right. Tom drove up to the spot and stopped the car and listened. There was the faint sound of sobbing in the tall grass. Animal sounds. Oscar, the baby rhinoceros was still alive, crying for his mother. "Where is he?" Sofia asked.

"Over there, behind the acacia trees. Let's approach carefully. He might bolt when we frighten him," Tom said and handed Sofia a loaded handgun. She held it gingerly as they crept forward, followed by Brutus the dog. Brutus was trained around wild animals and knew how to behave. The three farm workers stood at a distance beneath the thorn trees and watched.

"It's alright, alright…" Tom's voice was calming like a lullaby. The calf sat confused and sobbing next to the slaughtered rhino, its black eyes mournful. There was the scent of blood and the buzzing of flies. The sight of the bloated dead animal turned Sofia's stomach. She knew that Africa wasn't for sissies, but she was not from Africa after all. The nausea passed. Tom kept moving forward, cooing all the time in a soft voice. Sofia followed him reluctantly, while the three workers looked out for predators, holding up their shining pangas. What if a lion decided to have the dead rhino for breakfast?

Not to mention Cornelius… The little rhino sighed and lay down. Good. Tom waved the workers over. The sobbing started again but Tom could see that the little guy was not injured.

"Ja, Baas?" Lebo asked softly.

"We have to see to Cornelius…" He turned halfway around to Sofia. "Are you going with them?"

"You mean… no, oh no, definitely not!" Sofia had never seen a dead body. Seeing the dead rhino had been already too much for her.

"Alright then I'll go but you stay by the car." They crept back to the Nissan.

Tom took two shotguns out of their brackets and threw one of them to Thando. He knew how to handle weapons and caught the shotgun with ease. There was a slim chance that the poachers were hiding in the thicket but it was more likely that they had escaped across the river, taken the tar road to Renosterspruit and crossed the border. The Special Commission would probably try to find the perpetrators with the help of proper sniffer dogs; at least that's what they had done at Lungile Park.

He charged Thando with Sofia's safety and gave Brutus the 'stay' command. Then he waded with Jackie and Lebo in tow through the long grass down to the edge of the wood.

Sofia sat in the mud-encrusted car with Brutus at her feet. Thando did his best to calm the distraught calf by singing through the half-open window, while Sofia tried not to look at the grotesque, hulking body that had once been a handsome rhinoceros-lady. Brutus sniffed the air and whimpered a little. The baby kept sobbing. *Where is the vet, shouldn't he be here by now?* Sofia thought. *And what about Witbooi and his policemen?*

"Poor Cornelius. I hope Witbooi is on his way," she said and Thando gave her an encouraging nod. The friendly Tswana man could only speak Afrikaans and Setswana but he understood what she meant.

"Jaa." He smiled.

Afrikaans, this mixture of Dutch, African and European languages, was also spoken by the coloured people in Cape Town. People in the rural areas did not always speak English. Sofia had not mastered this language yet but she would support Cornelius' wife, whether she could speak Afrikaans or not. The funeral arrangements were done by Cornelius' family and the extended clan needed to pitch in.

An audience was gathering unnoticed beyond the trees. A herd of elephants were shifting from one leg to the other, the dignified leader trumpeting and flapping her ears. Baboons jumped restlessly from branch to branch and zebras, bucks and giraffes assembled. Just the predators stayed away for now.

Sofia watched the circling vultures. They came alarmingly close to Ntombi's carcass. A shot rang out. That was probably Tom, trying to keep the vultures at bay. A flock of birds rose from the treetops and Brutus started yelping, his ears pricked.

"Sit Brutus, sit. Good boy." The dog snuggled against her and sniffed the air through the half-open window. He could smell the unseen animals and knew he must stay in the car.

The three men came trudging back up the slope. They had seen dust clouds swirling in the distance. Somebody was coming down the dirt road.

Tom walked up to the Nissan. "And? What did you see down there?" Sofia asked and didn't really want to know.

"Those pigs got Cornelius from behind," Tom said. "One shot through the shoulder, one in the head. Must have been dead immediately. The poachers probably stalked the rangers to the woods when they were watching the dry riverbed. His walkie-talkie is missing and there's no trace of Mothusi, the other ranger. Wouldn't be surprised if they've abducted the poor guy. At least, I hope he's alive."

Sofia felt nauseous just listening to this. Dreadful, what they might have done to Mothusi. Poachers weren't known to be fair and gentle.

"Here, look at that... Cornelius was clutching this." Tom showed her a square pin made of blue enamel. He'd picked it up with a tissue. A golden circle with a V & S inside and an animal in every corner. It reminded Tom of the pin, Barry had received at a dinner function of the Veterinary Society in Pretoria. For long-standing membership. The vet had shown it around.

"What is it?" Sofia asked.

"We'll see."

"Should you take this away from the crime scene?"

"Probably not," Tom said and put the tissue with the pin in his pocket. "But I can't leave it down there."

Several cars approached. It was the vet's vehicle and Witbooi in his police car. Tom waved them over.

The slim, dark-haired woman in jeans and a pink shirt was the first thing Barry Pienaar saw against the tall grass as he drove toward the clearing. *Pretty thing*, he thought, as he'd thought many times before. *Tom is obviously serious about this one*. Barry Pienaar, the local veterinarian, knew Shangari as well as his own farm across the whitewater like the back of his hand. He had grown up here with Tom Rutgers and his younger brother.

Barry had studied in Pretoria and enjoyed himself during his years as a student. He'd never been further afield than Botswana and Namibia and the only other high point in his life had been meeting his wife Lorraine at their matric-dance in the Rutgersdrift-Hotel. Local girls were always in demand and Lorraine had been quite a looker. They got married after his studies and had settled on the Pienaar farm. Everything as it should be. When no children had made their appearance, Lorraine took to the bottle and their marriage had been crumbling ever since.

Barry wore his khaki vet-uniform and carried a suitcase with the tools of his trade. He was tall and muscular like most men in the country and used to the rigours of rural life. His greying hair framed a square face, permanently tanned by the relentless sun. He walked in long strides toward them.

"Morning, damn shit this!" he barked. There was no need to launch into unnecessary pleasantries. The portly station commander caught up with him. He had dressed in a hurry. The buttons of his shirt looked close to popping and his jacket seemed tight. More policemen followed a few paces behind.

Witbooi had phoned three of his constables before getting hold of Barry Pienaar and then informed the Special Commission on Poaching. Nobody had answered the office line at this time of day and Witbooi had left an urgent message on their voicemail. He could only hope that they would show up soon.

"Yes, damn shit!" Tom agreed. It felt good to swear in moments like this.

Barry held out a cautioning hand as the men approached the dead rhino and her calf. "Alright, alright, little one, we won't hurt you..." he said soothingly, just as Tom had done earlier. "Wonder what good this special commission will do," he mumbled. "Damn shame about the rhino."

International pressure on the government demanded that the slaughter of rhinos should be brought under control. 648 animals had died in South Africa last year alone and the smuggling rings were difficult to crack. Officials were tempted to cash in on the hot demand for rhino horn in Asia or they were simply too ignorant to care. To top it all, a handful of game farmers and rangers in the border areas had already been fingered for collaborating with the poachers. Witbooi and his honest colleagues did what they could but the Commission had yet to prove its worth. The sheer number of cases had proved overwhelming even for them.

Poaching was a danger to gameparks but so were rich tourists who fancied themselves sports-hunters with bows and arrows or hunting rifles. They often had their picture taken with their kill and posted it on social media. Hunting licenses were a lucrative business for corrupt officials who took their cut and couldn't remember a thing afterwards.

Even some game farmers and dodgy guides didn't scoff at the indecent sums but farmers like Tom Rutgers who cared more for the animals than the money, staunchly refused to allow these hunters on their land. The thought alone that one of his lions could end up as a hunting trophy on the expensive walls of London mansions or New York offices, gave Tom Rutgers the creeps. Poachers were not only after the big game and set traps in the bush that the gamekeepers had to clear on a daily basis.

A few months ago, they had rescued a young cheetah from an iron trap. His hind leg had to be amputated but his survival spirit had taken everybody by surprise. Sofia had named the cheetah Jethro. He was quite tame by now and the star of safari lodge. Jethro hobbled around on his three legs in his enclosure between the main building and the barn and loved being spoiled. There was no way, he could hunt ever again and survive in the wild.

Sofia felt tears running down her face. For a fleeting moment, she wished she could go back to Finland; to a cooler, well-ordered world without all this drama.

"Damn shit all that," he cursed again.

"Yes, total shit," Sofia said, sniffling.

The police station commander walked up to her window. "Morning, Sofia," Witbooi greeted her. "Everything okay?"

"Good morning, Witbooi. Everything's peachy," Sofia answered. "No, not really..."

Witbooi wiped his forehead with the sleeve of his jacket. "I know... damn mess all this. Tom shouldn't have brought you along."

"It's alright. Nerves, I guess," Sofia said.

The policeman grunted in sympathy. "Where is the dead man?" He asked Tom gruffly. "No predators around, that's good at least."

"Come, I'll show you," Tom said.

"Over here... and bring the blankets, the water and towels!" Barry Pienaar ordered his two assistants who carried big grey blankets, a water canister and wet towels. One blanket for covering the dead rhino, the other blanket and wet towels for the calf. They had to keep it cool, while it was under sedation, especially on a hot day like this. A third assistant steered the vet's bakkie right up to the two animals and sat with the young rhino.

"We'll have a look at Cornelius now," Witbooi said to Barry. "Come, let's go."

The policemen searched the edge of the woods, rifles at the ready, while Witbooi and Barry examined the dead ranger. Barry was the only available medical practitioner and had to do double duty. The poachers wouldn't dare attack so many armed men in broad daylight.

"Bliksem!" Witbooi said. "Fetch me the body bag, George!" The ranger's body was transported to the police van and one of the policemen got ready to drive back into town. Sofia felt a shiver go down her spine when she saw the body bag. This had been a living breathing human being and a really nice man.

Soon, Barry Pienaar took care of the calf. "Okay, okay..." he cooed and the sobbing subsided. Little Oscar allowed the human to touch him. "Do you need an injection, little one? Sorry about your mommy." The needle went in and out, without the baby even noticing.

Witbooi came stomping through the grass, somewhat out of breath. "We found an automatic rifle in the bushes and a few rounds of ammunition," he told Tom. "No idea why they left that behind. Impossible to say how big the gang was or if they took Mothusi with them. Possibly had a boat waiting on the beach by the whitewater. We walked all the way down to the shore and had a look. There are ropes lying around and a tangle of footprints in the mud." Brutus sniffed at his trousers and Witbooi patted the dog's head.

"My guess is that they are trying to flee across the green border," Tom said.

"Sure, it would be the easiest way if they get that far. Must contact the border guards. My guys are searching along the river. Who knows what they'll find!" He alluded to the missing ranger Mothusi, of course.

"George, take Cornelius to the morgue now. No point in waiting for the high and mighty detectives." Witbooi walked up to the police car and fumbled with the radio device. "You better take the calf to Gerda's animal sanctuary, Tom. Gerda's already looking after a couple of rhino calves. This little one is all right, just in shock," Barry Pienaar said. "We're still working on his mom. Best if the baby doesn't see it."

"Okay, we'll put him in the back. Grab the blanket over there. One, two, three!" Three of the men lifted the little rhino and heaved him onto the back of Tom's bakkie. Brutus jumped up next to him, sniffing the grey blanket.

"Sofia, can you please call Gerda and let her know, we're coming?"

"Sure," Sofia said and remembered why she felt queasy. They didn't even have their coffee this morning, never mind breakfast.

"Come here, Brutus." Tom whistled and his dog sat down by his feet. "Leave him, he's scared of you."

The sun was climbing higher by the minute and had

almost reached the top of the trees. Witbooi had finished speaking to the border guards and joined Tom. He nudged him, pointing to the whitewater. "Look at that."

Something was moving by the river. Out of nowhere, a string of small, half-naked men detached itself from the shore and came closer at a quick pace. They were Khoi-San. One of the short men up front wore the uniform of a ranger.

"Do you think that's Mothusi?" Sofia asked.

"Looks like it."

"Thank god, he's alive and kicking!" Witbooi said. "The Bushmen can help us track the poachers. With some luck, we'll find them before the detectives arrive with their sniffer dogs."

"Will you guys speak to Mothusi?" Tom asked. "I want to take the calf to the sanctuary and Sofia back to the lodge."

"Ja sure, Tom," Witbooi said. "I'll come over to your place later for statements. You go over to Gerda's so long."

"Okay, we'll see you at the house. Wear something decent. I don't want the guests to bolt when they see you in that uniform."

"Gee thanks, pal." Witbooi grinned. "Early afternoon?"

"Okay."

The Bushmen came closer.

"It's best if you sit next to the calf and hold him. That'll keep him calm," Barry Pienaar said to Sofia.

"But Barry," she protested and Brutus lifted his head. "What if he bites or jumps off the bakkie?"

"He won't. He's sedated. Just hold him and keep the wet towels in place. The sooner he gets a milk bottle, the better his chances of survival," the vet snapped at her and turned around to take care of other business.

Brutus didn't seem to share Sofia's concerns. He hopped onto the back of the bakkie, sniffed and snuggled up against the hulking baby. The Bushmen had almost reached the clearing when Tom pulled onto the dirt road. He would speak to Mothusi later. First things first. Two vehicles passed them in a cloud of dust. At last, the detectives from the Special Commission on Poaching were on their way to the crime scene.

CHAPTER 2

Sofia put her arm around the young animal under the blanket. "Alright, alright, there, there…" She felt nervous about touching the rhino.

Brutus placed his head on her thigh with a grunt, only to sit up straight again when the bakkie swerved around a rather deep pothole. They reached the game fence and then the gaily painted houses of the park workers behind the next slope. Women in the compound were now busy with domestic chores, hanging up washing and stomping mielies in hollowed-out tree trunks. They were getting as much done as possible before the heat of the day set in.

There were no signs of unrest or panic, so perhaps the bad news hadn't reached them yet. Rhythmic stomping and the monotonous melodies from Radio Bokspits mingled into a cheerful soundtrack that grew fainter as they moved closer to the rows of temporary tents. South Africans were already arriving by the scores and getting a headstart at the fireplaces. Braaing was part and parcel of a proper holiday and South African life in general. They left the tents behind and were accompanied by hibiscus bushes and blue agapanthus along the tarred road to the main building.

"I'll let you out at the lodge," Tom yelled against the headwind. He pulled up at the main entrance and Sofia jumped off the truck, followed by Brutus, the dog. A group of women came fluttering down the steps. So the people at the lodge were in the picture, after all. Brutus pricked his ears.

"What now?" Sofia asked Tom and stepped protectively in front of the hulking grey blanket, as the women marched toward the bakkie.

"Let me speak to them, then I'm off to Gerda's sanctuary and you take over here. Brutus comes with me." The dog whimpered when he heard his name.

"Alright," Sofia sighed.

The day ahead seemed to her like a mountain she had to climb. She still needed to speak to the chef about the cocktail party tonight... and a little breakfast would be good too. Cotton had to fetch guests from the airport and perhaps he could go past the liquor store in town. There was never enough water around in hot weather. Not only was Cotton the dedicated driver but also barman and safari guide all rolled into one. He usually shared his tasks with his younger brother who went by the name of Nelson.

After organising that, she had to greet the guests at the lodge and sort out the venue for the sundowners on the flat hill behind the barn.

Frida, the most senior of the maids, had been busy with the beds when the terrible news arrived. She was well-respected by the other workers because she was the wife of Obakeng, the gardener and local Sangoma or shaman. The rest of the staff waited at the top of the stairs.

The women stopped short in front of the driver's door. Right behind Frida were Fat Beauty and one of the kitchen ladies. "Dis verskriklik, Baas, wat met arm Cornelius gebeur het!" Frida blurted out and wagged her head. That's terrible, what happened to poor Cornelius!

Tom climbed out of the bakkie and addressed the women.

"Ja, Frida, verskriklik. Luister..." Listen. He spoke to them for a few minutes in Afrikaans, calmly describing the scene in the bushveld. He explained without divulging any critical details and told them that Mothusi was safe.

Sofia understood some of what was being said. "You should employ watchmen here, Baas, or we will all die!"

"The poachers are after the rhinos not our lives, Beauty."

"Oh, we are all going to die," Beauty cried and wrung her hands. "Look, what they did to Cornelius!"

Doing a great job at keeping them calm, Tom thought with

resignation.

Obakeng, the grey-haired sangoma walked down the stairs. Despite his grey hair, his face looked remarkably young. Even his eyes were unlined and his gaze alert. Nobody seemed to know his exact age, which was not unusual around here. In the absence of a tribal chief, Obakeng was the most important man in the compound. For more reasons than one.

His skill with the dowsing rod was legendary. Farmers sought him out if they were in need of finding new water veins. Obakeng's method was always the same: he placed a tiny bottle with water on his head, covered it with a hat, held another water bottle in his right hand and the forked dowsing rod in the left hand. Such equipped, he would walk around the area to be searched and usually found a source of water if there was one to be found. Many had tried to copy the wise Sangoma's method of dowsing but none of them had ever succeeded.

Obakeng came forward.

"Mr. Rutgers, the people are scared. They are deurmekaar," he reported. Deurmekaar meant confused. So they all knew by now, what had come to pass down by the river.

"I can see that. Maar die polisie doen hulle werk," Tom said. The police are doing their job. "Sê vir almal, hulle moet kalmeer." Tell everybody to stay calm.

Obakeng addressed Tom always as 'Mr.. Rutgers'. It was his way to ensure that he was regarded as an equal to his boss. For most of the rural Tswanas, it was unthinkable to see themselves as equals of higher-ranked individuals. They had been brought up in the strict hierarchy of their own tribal culture. But Obakeng was different.

"I have told Frida what I know. She will tell you the whole story and you must talk to the others. I'm relying on you, Obakeng."

Fat Beauty crossed her arms in from of her ample bosom and scoffed. Obakeng turned halfway around and she looked at the ground, suddenly shy. "I will do my best, Mr.. Rutgers."

"The last thing we need, is everybody running around in a panic. The poachers are long gone and Mothusi is back. Witbooi is talking to him right now. I have to go to Gerda Marais. Ntombi's baba survived. Madam will speak to Francina but I have to go now." Tom patted the Sangoma on the shoulder.

Francina was Cornelius' wife and she had to be informed of her husband's death as soon as possible. She would be inconsolable for sure, despite all the fighting and drunken arguments. Cornelius had been the sole provider of the family and was the father of her five children.

Frans, the eldest son was only fifteen.

"Francina does not understand any English," Obakeng said. He was remotely related to the late Cornelius and therefore family.

"Go with the Madam and translate, please. I'll be back in a couple of hours."

"Maybe reporters from the city will come. Who does something like that, Mr. Rutgers? Who needs these horns? I don't understand." Even a Sangoma like Obakeng, using who-knows-what for his potions, had no need for the horns of a rhino.

Obakeng did not read the newspapers and the news on Radio Bokspits was sketchy and mostly of a local nature.

"It's the money. We think they come from Mozambique. Some people with a lot of money pay them for the horns. In Asia, they pay even more money for the horns because they think it makes them stronger - you know, with women and such." Up north in the Kruger Park, the problem had increased, since the game fences at the border had been taken down to create a cross-border park.

"I understand. It's greed, Mr.. Rutgers."

"Yes, it's definitely greed. I don't have to explain to you, what that means. I will see you later. Totsiens." Tom jumped back into the driver seat of the bakkie. Soft crying came from the back and Brutus whimpered.

"Totsiens, Mr.. Rutgers. Take the baba to Gerda."

"Totsiens, Obakeng. Brutus!"

The dog jumped onto the back of the bakkie and Tom left, taking the little rhino to safety.

Sofia went to the kitchen to get herself a cup of coffee and some rusks. That made it easier to face the rest of the day. She washed up and put on a skirt out of respect for the older folks. Then she walked over to the workers' compound, flanked by Frida and Obakeng. Frida carried a bundle with gifts for the widow and stepped out with determined movements. She said little but when it came to community matters, Frida knew precisely what needed to be done.

The huts of the Khoi-San workers were set somewhat apart from those of the Tswanas. This practice was rooted in the tradition that the ancient Khoi-San were of a different heritage and culture. All huts were neat and the compound was clean. There was running water and electricity, unless there was a power outage, naturally. Tom looked well after the loyal families at Shangari.

Cornelius had painted his house red. It was Francina's favourite colour. There was loud wailing inside, which meant that the women had already gathered in the red home. A kettle with steaming tea stood on a grid above the hot embers in the fireplace outside.

They entered and it was as bad as Sofia had feared. She remembered the time when a little boy of three had played near a waterhole after a particularly bad thunderstorm and had fallen in. They had searched high and low for him before they'd found him drowned. The wailing, the tears and the grief had been raw. The family had mourned intensely for days until the tiny body had been buried and for weeks after that. This time Sofia knew how to guard herself.

Francina sat on the bed, covered in a blanket, staring into the distance. Her children were still at school. Frida and Obakeng took over and translated, what Sofia had to say about how Cornelius had come to meet his death.

As was customary, they took great care to embellish Cornelius' brave acts and his courage in the face of danger.

Later, Sofia walked back to the farmhouse feeling drained. She saw herself in the passage mirror. Her face smudged and her skirt covered in dust. There was just enough time for a shower and to put on a change of clothes.

When she returned to the main building, Cotton, the driver, had already collected the German and Danish tourists at the little airport in Rutgersdrift. The lodge filled up quickly and the newcomers moved into the shade by the bar to down cold beers. Local tourists used their own transport and there were so many cars in the parking lot that they had to use a field farther down the road.

At 15:10 pm on the dot, Stan Makaroff's helicopter landed on the helipad and Cotton took the VIP-party in the Shangari-minibus to the lodge building. Sofia saw that her friend Gugu was part of the group but they could only briefly greet each other with a nod of the head and a smile.

Sofia smiled and smiled all the time until she thought she must be getting lock jaw. "Welcome, sir." "Welcome to Shangari." "Yes, the air-conditioning is working." "We hope to see you at the cocktail party tonight..."

Nobody seemed to notice the strain she felt, how upset she still was. Good. Thanks to Obakeng's pep talk, the staff had themselves under control and she was proud of them for it.

Shangari squirmed under the scorching February sun, and the bartenders served cold beer and bottled water faster than you could say 'ice cube'. The kitchen staff had their hands full, cooling the bottles in the walk-in freezer and transferring them to the fridges outside. Cotton was sent off into town twice to buy more supplies from the bottle store.

Sofia spent some time in the kitchen, to go over lists with Karen, the chef.

"Did I tell you, that my brother Stephen is coming to visit?" Karen asked. "He's managing a hotel on the South Coast. I'm sure, the two of you will have lots to talk about."

"Oh, that's nice..." Sofia said. Her mind was still dwelling on the events in the bushveld and the other thing, she needed to talk to Tom about.

"Okay then... let's get to work on those canapés. How is my butternut soup doing? Turn down the heat - now please! No, I will do the tasting... thank you..." Some dishes crashed to the tiled floor, sending shards flying.

"Oh for goodness' sake, not the good china. No? Lucky duck!" Karen yelled and gave orders to clean up.

To Sofia's great relief, everything went without a hitch thereafter, apart from the usual niggles. One of the German guests complained that the towels in his room weren't soft enough and the air-conditioning not cool enough. Stan Makaroff demanded to change rooms with one guest of his own entourage. For some reason, he preferred the view from there today.

Tom had returned only an hour before the cocktail party was about to start and they ducked out to get ready for the event. He told her that it had taken a while for the little rhinoceros to settle in at his new home. One of the animal minders had eventually gone to lie down with him in one of the barns in the soft hay to give him a bottle and the exhausted baby had fallen asleep in the man's arms. Tom would check on him again tomorrow.

"It is so sad... all that because of sheer greed and stupidity. I hope they will find the poachers soon and punish them for what they did," Sofia said.

"They haven't found the criminals who killed the rhino at Lungile yet, so things don't look great. Special Commission my foot! But here's hoping. Tonight, five of the gamekeepers will be on patrol and everybody in the area is on alert. What more can we do?" Tom rolled his eyes.

"I don't know," Sofia sighed. "Hope, everything is going smoothly tonight."

"Yes, me too."

She fondly noted, how handsome Tom looked in his dark suit and brushed some fluff off his shoulder.

"I'll have to make an announcement to the guests before they hear the scary news from some unreliable source... you look stunning, by the way," Tom said in one breath and Sofia managed a wry smile.

She wore her black fifties-dress with capped sleeves and swinging skirt and large red poppies on it. She used to wear it so often in Cape Town whenever they went out to a dinner dance. Silky dark hair was dancing against her cheek but makeup belied the fact that she would rather have taken a nap than go to a party. "Thank you, kind sir," Sofia said and Tom offered her his arm.

"Madam, may I?"

Everybody with an invitation made their way in suits and elegant frocks to the top of the hill behind the barn. Here, a well-stocked buffet, expertly mixed cocktails and South African wines awaited them. Soft jazz music played in the background, while a colourful sunset drew admiring cries. The outdoor lights came on the minute the sun dipped below the hills in the west.

The guests were turning their attention to the buffet, which would surely please the palates of even the fussiest eaters. That came as no surprise since Karen MacAllister was a top South African chef with her own blog. She was blonde, stocky and without airs and graces but cooking was her absolute passion and she had worked at a few most impressive hotels abroad.

It had not been easy to lure her to the bushveld but Sofia could be rather persuasive. Finally, Karen had been adventurous enough to give notice in New York, where she cooked for a celebrity family and had signed with Shangari for a year. One year had turned into two and Karen still showed no signs of leaving. Right now, the famous chef stood in front of a buffet in her neat, black chef's uniform and introduced the dishes on the tables behind her.

"What are these interesting-looking brown thingies?" A woman asked in an American accent and pointed to small bowls with brown bits and pieces.

Karen answered such questions a dime a dozen. "That's biltong, madam. Traditionally dried and spiced meat. The farmers learned from the Bushmen how to make it." She pointed at the bowls one by one. "This one is made from Kudu and this one from ostrich meat. Biltong is a South African speciality."

"A Bushmen speciality..." someone murmured.

"Nothing for vegetarians then," said a woman with a haughty face, dressed in a dark-pink safari suit. She gave the biltong a disapproving glare and her remark drew unexpected laughter.

"No, that's not for vegetarians," Karen said patiently. "I can, however, recommend this vegetarian mango and avocado salad... over here... with pomegranate rubies. We grow our own avocados and pomegranates. We also grow lettuce, herbs and many other ingredients in the vegetable patch over there..."

Karen MacAllister had outdone herself again, conjuring up delicious canapés, fresh seafood from Namibia, curried butternut soup and chicken liver pâté to name but a few of her signature dishes. A selection of cocktails, beer and wine kept the guests happy at the bar and the mood was convivial, while a line began to form in front of the buffet.

Sofia was not in the mood for partying. She desperately wanted this day to end, wanted to be alone with Tom and talk to him. But Tom was busy entertaining his illustrious guests. He was their host after all.

Sofia decided to take a little time out on the veranda of their colonial farmhouse. Just for a few minutes...

As soon as she sank into her comfortable chair on the bougainvillea-shaded veranda, she closed her eyes and took a deep breath. She poured a glass of dark-red Merlot and her nerves began to ease. *I will get through this*, she thought, *I've been through worse than this after all.*

Steps grated on the white gravel and Sofia jumped with joy. Had Tom followed her to the farmhouse? Would they have a private moment away from the madding crowd? But it wasn't Tom who had followed her. There was the rustling of a silk dress.

"Hey, what's up with you?" It was a familiar voice. A voice that always cut to the chase. The woman in a lime-green dress staggered up the stairs in high heels. It was her good friend Gugulethu Mbatha.

Sofia sank back into her chair.

"Nothing much, Gugu. Just taking a break. I need a bit of peace after the day I had." Sofia took another sip of wine. "Want some?"

"Sure. Having a bad day?"

"You could say that." Sofia poured her friend a glass of Merlot and put the cork back in the bottle.

Gugu wore her hair in a short straight bob and only the right amount of expensive makeup. Her skin had a lovely bronze sheen and the lime-green silk dress enhanced the effect. The very picture of beauty and sophistication.

During their student days in Cape Town, Gugu had lived in jeans and casual tops but she'd been beautiful even then. After discovering the world of high-flying socialites and young professionals, Gugu's appearance had become nothing short of glamorous.

The girls had shared a flat in Seapoint with two other students. Lynette 'Nandi' Levenstein, a wannabe revolutionary with brunette dreadlocks, blue eyeshadow and expensive bohemian clothes, seemed to spend her time at political meetings rather than in classes at varsity. Carol Vlisma was the adopted Xhosa daughter of a wine farmer in Stellenbosch and had majored in Social Work. She had kept to herself and as far as Sofia knew, was now married to an Afrikaaner in Stellenbosch. Sofia and Gugu had completed the quartet. The two of them had clicked right from the start but even back in Cape Town, they'd moved in different circles. Sofia had been part of the rather serious BCom crowd, while outgoing Gugu studied Public Relations and loved nothing more than going out.

Gugu sometimes worked at a local radio station and had more fun than Sofia would ever have in a lifetime. In those days, she proudly dressed in colourful Xhosa outfits and heels - just to be different - and dragged Sofia to parties at expensive hotels. Gugu had introduced her to flamboyant friends but Sofia soon had enough of hot-air small talk and fashionable drunkenness. It simply wasn't her scene. Gugu called it networking. Through networking, she was put in touch with the Makaroff empire and eventually landed her current job as the PR manager.

"Has Stan already let you off the leash?" Sofia couldn't help sounding sarcastic. Her beautiful Xhosa-friend was working hard in the PR department of the Makaroff Corporation because Makaroff's questionable reputation had been in the news a lot lately.

"Oh, he'll barely know I'm not around," Gugu insisted. "He met this German guy who went holidaying in the Okavango Delta last year. Now the man is quite an expert, apart from my boss, of course. The two of them are swapping notes on what camp is best, what beer is best - stuff like that. Nothing I can contribute to, anyway. Surprising that he hasn't bought half of the Okavango Delta yet."

Sofia laughed at the thought. Stan Makaroff was also known for his grandiose gestures.

"But how about you, Sofie?" Gugu asked. "You look pale, my girl. I know something's up, so don't give me the duck and dive treatment."

Sofia patted the cushion on the empty wicker chair next to hers and indicated that Gugu should move closer, before pouring wine for her friend. "Okay, you caught me out," she sighed. "Tom and I need to sort things out. I have a feeling he's going to ask me to marry him again..."

"Are you still giving him the cold shoulder? That's not exactly fair."

"Well, you know why..."

"What I know is that he's just about the best man for you on this planet. And as for the other 'thing'... I thought it's all sorted by now."

"Well, yes, but I haven't told him... not yet. We were just too busy and I was about to tell him this morning, but... then he got this radio call and I didn't get a chance."

Of course, Gugulethu Mbatha already knew what the radio

call had been about. Impossible to keep something like that from one of the most capable PR boffs in the country. But the two women skirted the gory subject. They wanted to savour the rare moment together.

The moonlight lent Sofia's light skin an almost translucent glow. "You're a sight for sore eyes, Sofie," Gugu said. "No wonder he's so in love with you. My advice: don't keep the man dangling. I saw a few females eat him up with their eyes up there."

"Ha, just proves that I have good taste. You should wear lime-green more often, it's really your colour," Sofia said.

"Don't try to change the subject, sweetie."

She had been there when it happened, had supported Sofia through the whole thing. If anyone truly knew Sofia, it was Gugu Mbatha.

"I know," Sofia admitted. "You are right."

They sat quietly a few moments, sipping red wine, and watched the bright moon hoist itself up the sky. The stars of the Milky Way seemed so close as if you could touch them.

"I wish the night sky in Joburg was like that!" Gugu sighed. "Alas, the city lights... Listen here, I'm serious. You should talk to Tom soon or some hot chick will catch him right from under your nose. This one French woman..."

"Belgian."

"Okay, this one Belgian woman was straining at the bit."

"Thanks for putting it so vividly. I get it. I'll make a plan."

"You do that. Oh before I forget... Tom asked me to go fetch you. He wants to hold his speech with you being there."

The speech about what had happened last night! Tom had to put the guests in the picture before they learned it through the media.

"Thanks a lot, for not telling me sooner," Sofia mock-sulked.

"Listen, I'm not your nanny and I wanted to chat with you for a bit. Don't get much of a chance to do that these days."

"Well then, Miss Socialite. Let's go." The gravelled footpath didn't make it any easier to walk in high heels and Sofia's untrained ankles hurt. "Damn, I'm totally out of practice," she complained.

"You'll get back in the groove if you visit the city for a few weeks. I'll schlepp you everywhere in heels, I promise!"

"I take your word for it." Sofia grinned.

They passed the barn, where Tom Rutgers pursued his hobby of building a sailing boat. Just a small one whether they were close to the ocean or not. The project kept his memories of Cape Town and the ocean alive. Tom and Sofia had loved going to Muizenberg beach and cruising about in a sailing boat with friends. Naturally, it wasn't that easy to find the right tools and parts so close to the desert. His boat project didn't make much progress but it was his way of relaxing in his 'man cave'.

A lazy growl from the enclosure on the other side of the footpath made them listen up. Jethro, the three-legged cheetah, stretched himself half asleep on his favourite rock. His leg stump had healed well and didn't seem to bother him anymore. Although Jethro was quite tame by now, Tom only took him out of the enclosure when the cheetah had a full tummy and was in a good mood. The large cat was a big hit with the tourists who seemed to think of him as an overgrown kitten.

"Just a sec... I'll be right back." Sofia disappeared in the barn and returned with a glittering bracelet dangling from her hand.

"Wow, what do we have here?" Gugu whistled and Jethro answered with another growl.

"I forgot it here yesterday when I helped Tom glue on the slats," Sofia said.

"Holy moly, girlfriend. Are those sapphires?"

"That's Tanzanite. Tom gave me the bracelet for my birthday last year," Sofia explained.

"Tanzanite's not cheap stuff. I thought you don't care much for jewellery."

"I don't. I have exactly two pieces of jewellery: a pair of golden earrings from my mother and this bracelet."

"And you don't even bother to lock your doors at night around here! Aren't you worried that someone might walk in and take it?"

"Of course not," Sofia said. "This isn't Joburg, you know. The people who work here wouldn't dream of stealing from us, and everybody knows everything about everyone around here."

Gugu got distracted. "Crazy, how the lemon trees catch the moonlight. You can make out every single, silvery leaf."

"Don't go all psychedelic on me, Gugs," Sofia teased her. "The cactuses over there look almost like people, right?"

"You could've fooled me," Gugu laughed.

They teetered up the path to the top of the hill and arrived, just as the music stopped playing. Apparently, Tom had waited long enough and was ready to give his speech. There were a few morsels of biltong left but the canapés on the platters would last the rest of the evening. The guests were in high spirits.

"See you later," Gugu whispered and walked over to Stan Makaroff and his employees. Somebody held out a glass of wine for her and Gugu immersed herself in the crowd. Barry Pienaar took his, at least tenth, bottle of Castle Lager for a walk and declared with a booming voice that Tom was a good guy. The best he'd ever known. "Hey, Tom old chap…!" He toasted him with his beer bottle.

"Come on, Barry, haven't you had enough?" Tom said grinning but Sofia detected a note of embarrassment. Tom had to say something important and wasn't in the mood to deal with drunks. Not even his friend, the vet.

He usually didn't mind Barry having one too many. Lots of men did so on the weekend, standing around the braai, grilling steaks and sausages, drinking beer. Also, a vet was on call in the country, drunk or not. There was always an emergency operation on a giraffe to perform or diseases in cows and sheep to be kept under control, a difficult birth to be brought to a happy ending or a pride of lions to inoculate.

While Barry treated everyone to a cheesy joke at the bar, his wife Lorraine steadied herself against the counter and requested another Martini from Nelson, the young barkeeper. Martini was her favourite cocktail. Apple Martini. She watched him mixing the drink and asked all sorts of nonsense while playing seductively with her necklace. Nelson and his brother Cotton were always polite and patient with drunken guests. Tom looked around and when he saw Sofia, he lifted his hand.

"Everybody settle down, kids! My best friend here has something to say," Barry bellowed before Tom Rutgers could say a word. A couple of women tittered. The last conversation died down and the clinking of glasses.

"I can assure you, our Barry here is normally quite sober and the best veterinarian we could wish for." Restrained laughter and murmuring.

"Now may I have your attention, please. I'd like to say a few words - and what I have to tell you is not exactly easy for me."

Tom stood on the little stage they had built for the musicians and glanced down at the guests. He wanted to have it said and done with as quickly as possible. Sofia faced the Belgian beauty in a sexy red dress, Gugu had mentioned to her earlier. Long, blonde hair, a bejewelled neck and arms. No doubt, the woman looked at Tom with adoration.

"Some of you might have already heard what... what happened in Shangari last night." Tom continued without hesitation. "Unfortunately, terrible things do happen in our beautiful land. There was an incident here in the bush last night." Tom cleared his throat. "Let me get to the point. Poachers are at work in our area. Why they didn't stay in Mozambique and the Kruger Park... unfortunately... we don't know. A few weeks ago, it was a rhinoceros on a neighbouring game farm and last night... regrettably... a rhino and - very, very sadly a Shangari ranger - became their latest victims."

Loud murmuring. Tom tried to still the crowd with soothing hand movements and raised his voice over the murmur. "The police... the police are investigating and we would like to appeal to you, to stay calm and not to impede their work. We assure you that everything is being done to guarantee your safety. I sincerely hope that you will enjoy your weekend and the eclipse of the moon in..." Tom looked at his wristwatch, "... 23 hours and 42 minutes. Thank you."

He gave a sign and the music resumed, drowning out concerned calls. The last thing Sofia felt like doing, was fight through the crowd to get Tom's attention. A group of guests pelted him with questions and he tried his best to provide answers.

"Yes, we anticipate members of the press tomorrow morning. There will be a press conference at some stage."

"No, I can assure you that this has never happened before."

"I really don't have an answer to that yet, sir."

"Yes, we still have three rhinos on the grounds and with a bit of luck you will be able to see them in the morning during the safari-drive."

"Yes, we can assume that."

"A calf has survived. No, the place is kept secret and nobody is allowed to visit. No, no guided excursions, either." The Belgian woman in her plunging tomato-red dress definitely stood too close to him. Sofia had seen and heard enough and walked over to the bar.

"Couldn't care less about them damn poachers," a man said right next to her. "As long as I get value for my money - who cares? Let the police handle it."

He guffawed and downed his whisky on the rocks. Sofia bit her tongue.

"Hi Nelson, pour me a Rock Shandy, please," she sighed. The near alcohol-free drink, made with lemonade and Angostura bitters. Sofia needed a clear head and any more alcohol wouldn't do the trick.

"Of course, madam. Baas Tom has many problems now. Poor Cornelius. But not to worry, we all try and make the guests happy." The bartender put the glass on the counter.

"Thank you, Nelson, I appreciate that."

She sauntered toward the impressive buffet table with her glass. The mini-pitas with curried crab salad looked tantalizing and Sofia also helped herself to some Kalahari-Calamari. She began to eat and the hollow feeling in her tummy disappeared.

Tom was surrounded by a crowd, vying for his attention. She saw the vet order another beer at the bar, surprised that he was still able to stand upright.

Somebody grabbed Sofia's arm. It was Barry Pienaar's rather tipsy wife. Her coiffed bottle-blonde hair was a little out of shape and the sun-damaged skin made her appear older than 42. Lorraine and Sofia didn't like each other very much and Lorraine was unvaryingly cool towards the Finnish woman but she seemed in a talkative mood tonight.

Well, alright then, Sofia thought. Why not be nice to Lorraine? She had a lot of smiling-practice by now. Sofia placed the plate and her half-finished Rock Shandy on the bar counter and gave Lorraine a smile.

"You shoooold come 'round for a hair appointment, poppie," Lorraine said. She ran a beauty salon from the former dairy on the Pienaar farm. The farmer's wives frequented her salon because it cost less than the salon in town.

"I just had a haircut, Lorraine," Sofia said.

"Fine, shuit yourself, poppie. But my, that Tom looks good tonight. Your man's a handsome one," Lorraine slurred her words and winked at Sofia at the same time. The effort nearly made her fall over. "Not bad, how he'sh handling this... this thing. Good speesh. Not easy to play down someing like thaat." She lost her balance somewhat and the deep neckline of her leopard-print dress slipped, revealing a pale nipple. Lorraine adjusted the strap of her dress but the whisky-on-the-rocks guy had seen the mishap and cracked up laughing.

"Mind your own bloody business, you fool!" She snapped and the man walked away. His shirt had a large sweat stain at the back and smelled musty. Lorraine saw that Sofia's glass was empty. "Oh, budd you've noshing to drink, darling!" she cried and waved the barman over. "Cotton! Same again for my friend here."

"It's Nelson, madam."

"Waever..."

Sofia declined with a wave of her hand. "I don't think that

Tom's playing down the issue, Lorraine. He's trying to be open about the facts - as much as possible."

"Whaever... but why didn't he menshion how that rainshar died. Shot in da head... and all that."

Sofia flinched. How did Lorraine know about Cornelius' fatal head wound? The grisly details weren't public knowledge.

"Did Barry tell you that?" She asked.

"No, haven't shpoken to him," the vet's wife said and swayed a little. "Was in Renosdashpruit with my sishta. She'll swear to it that it was Mona who told 'er."

Pathetic! Was Lorraine trying to give herself an alibi? As if she had something to do with the crime. Sofia rejected the thought immediately. Lorraine had drunk a few Martinis too many, that's all. "I see... Why's Barry so sloshed tonight?"

Lorraine snorted with contempt. It was no secret that their marriage was on the rocks. "He'sh weak, Sofia." She leaned forward in a chummy gesture.

Sofia could smell the alcohol on her breath and took a step back.

"Why is he weak?" When she thought of Barry Pienaar, weak wasn't the word that sprang to mind.

"Has no shtomach for stuff like that." Lorraine shrugged her shoulders and slurped her next Martini. The toothpick with the olive tipped over the rim of the glass and the drink spilled onto her dress. She began to work on the stain with a paper serviette and Nelson offered her a fresh olive.

"No stomach for what? For murder?"

"Yes of coarsh, murder," Lorraine answered impatiently and vigorously rubbed the fabric with the serviette. "Barry sees dead and inshuad animals all day long but when he sees a dead person – he cannot shtomach that. Weak."

Sofia had enough of this senseless conversation. To hell with Lorraine and her drinking. She scanned the party. Tom was still surrounded by a group of eager female tourists and a few couples started dancing. *I give up*, she thought. *I'm tired and irritated and have no time for this.*

Oh, what the hell; tomorrow morning, Lorraine wouldn't

remember a thing, anyway. She decided to walk away before Lorraine could say another word and saw Tom working his way through the crowd towards her. He took Sofia's hand.

"Excuse us, Lorraine." He led her onto the dance floor. "May I ask this dance of you, madam? Haluaisitko tanssia kanssani?" It was one of the few Finnish phrases, he still remembered.

"But of course, good sir!" They laughed and Sofia forgot about Lorraine and her drunken talk. Tom pulled her toward him so that she could feel his warmth and smell his aftershave. Sofia sighed and pressed herself against his chest. "You did well," she whispered in his ear. "You just know, how to put things into words." Tom twirled her around and drew her close again.

"I hope they will all stay the weekend," Sofia said, meaning the tourists.

"They will. Where else are they supposed to go?"

"Hmm, let me see. Sinkhulu maybe or Lungile Lodge. The competition doesn't sleep," she said.

"We'll cross that bridge when we get there. Tomorrow's another day," Tom murmured.

"Yes, tomorrow's another day." She felt the muscles in his back relax as he held her so close. "It's the eclipse of the moon," Sofia said randomly.

"Yes it is, Love, yes it is," Tom said and closed his eyes.

Hours later, another morning announced itself with a flaming sky. The tourists stayed and day visitors started pouring in before noon. The poachers were apparently not enough of a deterrent to keep them away. They settled themselves under trees on the lawn and began asking for picnic baskets.

*

Sofia and Tom discussed food matters with Karen amid brisk activity in the kitchen. "... and parfaits for dessert tonight?" Tom asked. "That's probably best in this heat."

"Yes, we'll bring them out about half an hour before the eclipse starts."

"Good, timing's everything," Sofia said.

"Right. The day visitors can buy picnic baskets at the reception in about 10 minutes," Karen said. "Most of them will go into the fridge. Freshly baked bread, filled with all sorts of goodies, drumsticks, fruits... same price as the ones we had at Christmas."

There would be a braai on the hill and the braai-fires were already going by the tents. But with so many mouths to feed, picnic baskets were the most practical solution.

"Do we have enough champagne?" Sofia asked.

"We should. There's no time to get more, anyway. Bottle stores are closed on a Sunday afternoon. Beer and soft drinks we still have plenty of," Karen said. "Might run out of water but the supermarket should be open until 2 o'clock."

The kitchen doors swung open and waiters brought in the first breakfast dishes. The Danish tourists were early birds.

Cotton was dressed in a ranger's uniform and gave the first and only safari-talk of the day in the small classroom next to the reception. Six guests had put their names down for the 7 o'clock drive. Today, he wouldn't drive out in the afternoon. Eight people arrived and received a brief lesson in behaviour around wild animals: don't leave the open vehicle, unless you're told that it's safe, stay calm and listen to the guide's instructions at all times.

"Please do not pick any flowers or fruit or touch animals of any kind..."

Cotton pointed with a bamboo stick at colour charts and showed a two-minute film. Nelson who had done duty at the bar last night, would be the guide.

"Phone for you at the reception, Baas Tom," one of the waiters said.

It was Witbooi on the line. The commander of the local police station let Tom know that Cornelius' body would be transferred from the surgery of the village doctor to the coroner's office in town.

"Sorry, I couldn't take your statement yesterday," he said. "The special detectives kept me on my toes but I'll pop around after lunch and might bring one of them with me. If they work weekends that is."

It was bugging him that he had to deal with the big guns from the city and put up with their demanding ways. The detectives had dragged their feet in the Lungile Farm case, and whether they would be successful this time around was yet to be seen.

Witbooi was a special man. He had been born in the apartheid era as a dark-skinned son to white parents. A rare genetic anomaly that had caused quite a stir at the time. His parents came from well-to-do, salt-of the-earth farming families and somehow, his father had managed to get the smart little boy classified as white. Witbooi had attended school in Rutgersdrift and there was relative acceptance of the unusual child in the farming community.

The inevitable rumours of his mother's infidelity and bullying at school had been tough to deal with but nobody dared to exclude Witbooi due to his skin colour. The difference had become even less of an issue when the self-confident and well-liked Witbooi was appointed the highest police authority in the district.

"Okay Witbooi, let reception know when you're here," Tom said and gave his attention to the reporters of three TV stations who were arriving with their bulky equipment. After all, Shangari was a popular luxury-lodge and of some interest to TV viewers.

"No, you cannot film here and ask questions. Our guests deserve their privacy," Tom Rutgers warned one of the reporters. Cameramen started walking around the hall, taking shots of the giant vases and the carved pillars.

Cotton and Nelson were in the bush with the tourists by now and Tom led the reporters into the classroom, where the media briefing was being prepared. It went without a hitch. Tom wiped his brow and sat down with a bottle of cold water. An hour later, the interview was in the box and the TV crews were on their way back to the city.

At half past three, the heat relented somewhat. Lunch was

served and more picnic baskets were handed out. Many of the guests whiled the afternoon away in the swimming pool. Sofia strolled down to the farmhouse to take a dip in their own private pool.

The station commander arrived at the lodge with a special detective in tow, just as Tom Rutgers was in the middle of a lengthy discussion with Stan Makaroff on the upper-level gallery.

The well-known tycoon was a burly man. His bald head seemed polished and his dark eyes in the somewhat swollen face darted here and there. He wore casual-looking designer threads, the expensive linen shirt unbuttoned enough to allow his chest-hair to make an appearance. Tom tried not to stare at the shorts his celebrity-guest was wearing. Stan Makaroff was famous for his eccentric tastes but this looked as if he had been creative with a pair of scissors.

Apart from the chopped-off slacks, the fact that he poured Perrier over his head whenever he felt like cooling down, was a little distracting. The linen shirt looked worse for wear but the tycoon didn't seem to care one bit.

"Are you happy with everything, Mr. Makaroff?" Tom asked.

"Bull's eye, my man. The safari was top-shelf. We even saw lions up by the hills," Makaroff grunted. "Totally missed out on speaking to the reporters, though." *Grabbing every chance to market yourself,* Tom thought.

"I'm very glad to hear you had a good time, sir. The press were only here to cover the poaching incident yesterday. Any plans for today? "

"It's too damn hot. The moon thing tonight's sounds interesting. Almost made the 'Big Five' this weekend. Leopards, buffalo, elephants, lions... now all I need to see is a rhino. Perhaps, we'll have a bit of luck later."

"Yes perhaps," Tom frowned.

"I have a mind to do some hunting but you don't permit it here, do you?" Makaroff said in a taunting tone.

"No, we are not that type of game park. And in any case, you would need a license for that."

Tom tried not to let on, how much the topic irritated him but Makaroff thought it humorous. "I know, I know. Don't even have a rifle with me, ha-ha. You like to do the hunting yourself, right... right?!" He chortled and pointed to the Kudu head at the reception.

"I didn't say we don't hunt at all but not for sport. That head's been here longer than me," Tom said.

"One of these days, Rutgers... I'll buy this game park from you and then we'll organise one hunting party after the other. Breeding rhinos is also a good idea," Makaroff guffawed and let the pricey water run down his neck.

"I don't think so," Tom laughed the remark off. " You know I won't sell."

A burly bodyguard was leaning against the wooden railing, scanning the hall. Now he jumped to take the empty bottle off Makaroff's hands. Out of habit, he groped for his gun and remembered that it was locked away in the lodge's wall safe. The 'no gun' policy put him somewhat off balance, as his weapon felt like another limb to him. Tom gave the man a fleeting look.

"We'll see, Rutgers. One of these days, I'll make you an offer you can't refuse. I love a challenge, you know."

There was always a hint of danger under the jovial façade but Tom assumed that Makaroff simply enjoyed pushing his buttons. He certainly had the money to buy the entire area if he felt like it but Makaroff hadn't made any move to buy Shangari. And if Tom had anything to do with it, he would never get a chance.

"Yes, I know that," Tom answered good-naturedly.

"Don't look so serious, man. I'm joking." Makaroff slapped Tom's shoulder and laughed. The bodyguard chimed in. "I don't need all that stress. I'd rather just be a pampered guest here."

"And you are always a welcome guest at Shangari, sir. As long as you want to spend time with us, we'll be at your service."

"The water is so soft at Shangari," Makaroff said, changing the subject. "You should bottle the stuff and sell it for lots of money."

"We are in an arid area here, sir. You see, the desert and all. Every drop of water, the land is willing to provide counts." Tom tried to sound as polite as possible. The determined businessman, in his wet shirt and cut-off trousers, saluted him playfully, tipping his forehead with three fingers.

"Suit yourself, Rutgers, but give it some thought, please."

"I certainly will," Tom Rutgers lied and smiled.

Sofia came up the stairs. "Tom, Witbooi's here with somebody from the Special Commission. They're waiting for you down by the reception."

"Ah, beautiful lady... Lois Lane if I'm not mistaken." Makaroff's remark had something lewd about it but Sofia acknowledged him with a smile.

"Please excuse me, Mr. Makaroff, I have to go and take care of business."

"See you around, Rutgers. It would be a shame..." he pointed with his chin at a life-size bronze sculpture of a rhinoceros in the middle of the hall, "... if this was to become the only rhino in your fabulous game park."

"No, of course not. That would be a catastrophe. Enjoy your stay, sir." Tom walked down the stairs with Sofia.

He noticed Makaroff watching them from the gallery above. *Who knows what's going on in this bald, shiny head,* Tom thought. Makaroff turned around and addressed his bodyguard abruptly. "Well then, Bruno, let's have a cocktail or two at the bar, shall we?"

The bodyguard peeled away from the pillar, he was leaning against. "Cocktails for you and coca cola for me, sir."

"Where the hell is everybody? Enjoying themselves?" He referred to the members of his entourage who were making the most of their free luxury weekend.

"Yes sir, I think so. Last saw them by the pool."

"Excellent," Makaroff said and observed Tom and the visitors from the corner of his eye. "Let's join them."

Tom greeted Witbooi and the detective at the reception. Unsurprisingly, they felt hot and had taken their jackets off. The detective was admiring one of the oversized vases next to the entrance and couldn't help touching the smooth, cool surface.

"There you are Witb..." Tom caught himself in time. "...I mean station Commander van Schalkwyk." He didn't want to embarrass Witbooi in front of a detective from the city with too much familiarity. "I hope you didn't have to wait too long. I had to speak to one of our guests."

"I leave you guys to it. See you later, Tom," Sofia said and went to check on the picnic baskets in the kitchen.

"Ah, to be a guest at this wonderful lodge," the important detective mused.

"Tom, this is Captain Combrink from the Special Commission on Poaching in Johannesburg," Witbooi introduced the sweating man. "He is the detective in charge. He will also be investigating the murder."

"I see. Good day, Captain." The two men shook hands.

Makaroff walked past, his bodyguard following him closely. Outside, he grabbed a new bottle of Perrier from the pool bar and poured it over his head. The expensive water left more unattractive stains on his linen shirt, which none of his guests, lounging under red large umbrellas, seemed to notice.

"What did he want this time? Buy the farm again?" Witbooi asked.

"Yes, something like that."

Captain Combrink had a serious poker face if Tom had ever seen one. Perhaps, the policeman from the city had forgotten how to smile, considering the many crimes he's had to investigate during his career.

"Can we speak somewhere private, Mr.. Rutgers?" The captain asked with a stern expression. His investigators had been working under guard in the bushveld by the dry river bed in this goddam heat.

"Let's go over to the farmhouse, we'll have more privacy there." Tom Rutgers went ahead on the footpath past the cheetah enclosure and the vegetable garden. The three-legged cheetah purred amicably but the detective wasn't paying attention to the large feline. They took the stairs onto the veranda and navigated past wicker chairs to the French doors of the lounge. Sofia was taking another well-deserved break in the pool in the shade of a large bougainvillea bush.

"I would like to speak to your - hmm - girlfriend, Miss Helenius first if you don't mind. Alone if that's alright with you." Captain Combrink's thin lips didn't move much as he spoke but the sweaty brow belied his cool demeanour.

"Of course," Tom said. "We have nothing to hide."

Sofia had thrown on a robe and the interrogation was concluded quickly. By the time it was Tom's turn to be questioned, she had gone back to the lodge to oversee the sale of the picnic baskets.

There were still visitors arriving to watch the eclipse of the moon and they would soon be setting up the braais on the flat hilltop, where the glamorous cocktail party had been held the night before. Tonight, they would be roughing it up in casual clothes, on blankets and in camping chairs.

Tom Rutgers sat down between the two policemen at the dark dining room table. He answered the questions to his best ability, wishing, he could be somewhere else. Frida had put a jug with lemon water on the starched tablecloth and four glasses on coasters, then she left the room.

The ceiling fan swished round and round, beating the hot air, while Witbooi and Captain Combrink thirstily slurped the cool lemon water.

"So, the ranger you mentioned..." Captain Combrink put the glass down, pushed up his spectacles and looked at his notes. "Mothusi... isn't it? He had been on patrol with the deceased... Cornelius Grootman... and then disappeared from the scene... and returned only the morning after the incident..." He picked up his pen and twiddled it between his fingers.

"That's right," Tom said. "Rangers patrol Shangari and neighbouring farms every night, especially since poachers killed a rhino at Lungile Farm. They split up into small groups and are supposed to communicate with each other and the farms. Poaching is nothing new around here but the larger game, like our rhinos, have been spared up until now. Some of the rangers are Khoi-San or part Khoi-San. The clan has a homestead in the border area beyond Renosterspruit. I left the crime scene before Mothusi could be questioned. The rhino calf couldn't wait."

"Do you have any idea, where this... Mothusi... could have been until the next morning and why these two rangers may have been targeted?"

"No, I don't. Apart from the fact that Mothusi fled to his clan's homestead after Cornelius's murder - or so I've heard."

"You know that we arrested a number of rangers on the border to Mozambique a week ago who are - as we suspect - in cahoots with the poachers?"

"I did hear about that."

"This... Mothusi... said that the victim... Cornelius Grootman...had 'called' the rhino and her calf that night. To make sure they were okay." His voice took on a disparaging tone. "Afterwards, he meant to 'send them away' again... according to Mothusi. Just that it was too late and the poachers shot the mother rhino and sadly also Mr. Grootman."

"If he says so."

The detective's eyebrows shot up. "I beg your pardon, but 'calling' a rhino?! That's a cock-and-bull story if I ever heard one. Calling wild animals..."

"Why not? Bushmen live in unison with nature, as much as possible. I'm told that the Khoi-San communicate with animals. If Mothusi says, Cornelius 'called' the rhino, then that's what he did." Tom leaned back and took a sip of his lemon water. *Stay cool*, he reminded himself, *just stay cool.*

"I see." The detective took in Tom's answer. "I see. Is there any reason why we should treat any of the other farmworkers or rangers as suspects?"

"Hardly."

Lebo and the other workers had been questioned yesterday. He didn't exactly know what had been said but Tom Rutgers doubted that there was anything suspicious going on. He trusted them completely. Captain Combrink raised his eyebrows again and stared Tom right in the face.

"Oh, and why not?"

"They are related."

The detective leaned forward. "Let me tell you something, Mr.. Rutgers: Related or not - family bonds have their limits. Everyone involved in smuggling rhino horn is earning himself a bounty. One single horn is worth more than 3 million Rand and fetches much more in China, Thailand and especially in Vietnam."

He dropped the pen for an embarrassing second and bent down to pick it up from the floor. "Back to these other rangers," Combrink said and tidied his suit. "Perhaps Cornelius Grootman, the victim, was shot by accident during the cowardly deed... or the other poachers didn't want to share their loot with him."

"What are you trying to say? The Khoi-San cannot be bribed. They have no use for so much money. And in return for what? Killing the animals that are part of their world? If Mothusi says that poachers ambushed them, then that's what happened!" Tom was getting impatient with the city cop and Witbooi was observing them without saying a word.

The captain studied him from under the rim of his spectacles. "Does that make sense to you, Commander?"

"Well, Cornelius is part Tswana and to a large part Khoi-San," Witbooi said. "Old family line. Well-known in the area. You could just as well suspect Mr.. Rutgers here or our veterinarian Barry Pienaar. I could be wrong but weren't two local vets arrested on the Mozambican border?"

"The case is still under investigation. Are you saying that this vet had something to do with the poaching incident?"

"No, of course not. Just an example, sir," Witbooi said in an appeasing voice. Tom had wanted to tell the smug detective about the pin, he had picked up at the crime scene but perhaps he should give it to him after the interview and let him draw his own conclusions.

"Hmmm. I assume the rhino was insured."

"Now wait a minute..." Tom's eyes narrowed and Captain Combrink retracted.

"No offence, Mr.. Rutgers. It's my job to ask these questions."

"We all know that most poachers are henchmen, hired by international crime networks, apparently out to destroy our African wildlife to supply those with big pockets with whatever they want, are they not?" Tom snarled at the captain.

"I'm not at liberty to discuss the background of our cases with you, sir."

"No need, it's common knowledge that you guys are not getting anywhere with these so-called investigations." Tom took a sip of lemon water to stop himself from attacking the policeman outright.

"Come on, Tom," Witbooi tried to intervene. "Get a hold of yourself."

Tom Rutger's patience was wearing thin. He was hot and bothered and wanted cool off in the swimming pool before the evening rush.

"Was there anything else, Captain Combrink?"

The station commander cleared his throat and looked at Tom with a begging expression. Tom swallowed the words on the tip of his tongue. The detective grunted and said, "Yes... there was something else. I saw Stanislav Makaroff's name is in your guest register."

"Yes, he's one of our regular guests. Spending the weekend with some employees here to watch the eclipse of the moon tonight. Why is this relevant?"

"No particular reason. I think that's all for now. Thank you for your cooperation, Mr.. Rutgers," Captain Combrink said and pressed the upper end of his silver pen. Click click click. He got up and Witbooi followed suit. As soon as the two policemen had left, Tom drank another glass of lemon water. He walked out the French doors into the garden, opening his shirt. A swim would help him cool down. Perhaps, he shouldn't have reacted so hot-headed but that was difficult in this damned heat.

*

"How did it go?" Sofia stood by one of the long counters

amid the bedlam of the busy kitchen. Demand for the packed picnic baskets was extraordinary. A few tourists had already paid at the reception desk and were waiting in a line.

"Don't ask... I wanted to punch that smug face. He practically made fun of the Bushmen. If the police were only doing their job," Tom grumbled.

"Did you give it to him?" She gave him a meaningful look.

Tom looked at her with a puzzled expression.

"Give who what?"

"The blue pin Cornelius had in his hand, of course - to Witbooi..."

"Oh no!" He hit his forehead with the palm of his hand. "I totally forgot. Wanted to give it to this cop. I think I put it in my pocket. Witbooi's probably long gone. Will give it to him tomorrow."

Tom helped Sofia carry the picnic baskets to the main building. "Look who's there..." Sofia said and pointed with her chin at the bar by the swimming pool. Witbooi sat on a bar stool, tending to a glass of beer. "With some luck, the detective from the special commission is also still around..."

"Let me speak to him," Tom said.

"You can leave those here," Sofia laughed and looked at the picnic baskets he still carried in his hands. Tom Rutgers rolled his eyes, grinned and put the baskets on the counter.

"Hey, Witbooi!" He gave his friend a light slap on the shoulder and the station commander nearly jumped off his barstool.

"Gee Tom, you gave me a fright!" Witbooi growled. He held his tongue considering that there were tourists around.

"Sorry old guy!" Tom apologised. "Howzit? Growing a beer boep, are you?"

"Ja well, no fine. I'm off duty..."

"Never see you much these days, which is a good thing in a way," Tom said.

"I guess. Been busy lately. Drunken driving is on the increase. Three cases already this month."

"How is it going on the dating front?" Tom asked. "Het jy

'n roos al uit die dorings gekry? Did you find a rose among the thorns?"

"Hulle is maar skaars. They are rare. Not everybody is as lucky as you are, Tom. Sofia is a real treasure. I don't think I'll ever get married."

"Don't say that, broer. I'm not married yet, either."

"And why is that? You must get your act together and ask her, broer," Witbooi scolded.

"Ja well, I probably should..."

"Don't wait too long," Witbooi said and took a long swig of his beer.

"I just remembered something..." Tom scratched his head. "Damn heat's getting to me. I found a pin yesterday morning ..."

Captain Combrink approached them from the general direction of the ground floor toilets. "Ah, Captain Combrink. Good, you are still here," Tom said.

"Yes, where would I go in this heat?"

"Oh I don't know, the crime scene perhaps, searching for the poachers at the border or in your hotel in Renosterspruit?"

"Well, I'll have something cold to drink if you don't mind." He ordered himself a club soda - being on duty and all. "What is it, Mr.. Rutgers?"

His tone held a grumpy question like 'What do you want? I thought we were finished for now.' The lodge owner had seemed so keen for him to leave the farmhouse. Whether this was a sign of guilt, the detective would determine at a later stage.

"I forgot something earlier," Tom said. "It might be important or not."

Witbooi wanted to get up from his chair but the captain held him back. "I'll handle this, Commander van Schalkwyk." Witbooi shrugged his ample shoulders and returned his full attention to the cold draught beer in front of him. *Damn city folks*, he thought. Tom Rutgers and Captain Combrink went to a quiet corner of the hall to have their conversation.

"I remembered that... yesterday morning when we found Cornelius in the bushes by the dry riverbed, I saw that he was clutching something in his fist. It turned out to be a blue pin. You know, one of those you get at a company event or for membership in an organisation... I'm not sure," Tom explained.

"Yes?"

"Well, I still have it. Totally forgot that I'd put it in my pocket. Should I go get it for you?" He was ready to sprint back to the farmhouse but the detective held him back. "Let me handle the evidence, sir. Did you touch the pin?"

"Yes, unfortunately I did. Sorry, there was a lot of confusion at the time," Tom Rutgers apologised.

"Then we'll hardly be able to test it for fingerprints." The detective gave Tom an accusing look.

"I'm sorry," Tom repeated. This smug detective was beginning to get his hackles up again. Did he think Tom was withholding evidence?

"In the confusion, you say?" Captain Combrink asked.

"Yes, everybody was deurmekaar. We didn't know what to do."

"Then you simply forgot to hand the pin over to the police?"

"What are you trying to say?" Tom flared up, only to apologise a second later. "Sorry, it's been quite stressful. I better go and check the braai fires."

"Mr.. Rutgers, please don't mention the pin you found to anyone for now," the detective said unmoved, "...or anything else of importance for that matter..."

"Only the station commander and my girlfriend know."

"Then let's keep it like that."

"Whatever you say."

"I'm glad we understand each other. May I take possession of the pin in question?"

"Of course, let me take you."

Tom Rutgers escorted Captain Combrink to the farmhouse and then back to the hall. Tom was worried. Not because of the statement he'd made or that he might be considered a suspect. He was worried that Mothusi had given the Special Commission on Poaching too many details about Cornelius' abilities to call wild animals. If this fell on the wrong ears, whoever was behind the poaching operation might sooner or later harass the workers at Shangari. If someone could call the animals, he would be a much sought-after instrument for them.

Not only Cornelius had this particular gift, and public knowledge of this fact might lead to serious problems. Tom went over to the vegetable garden and looked up and down the lush green rows, where the plants thrived under dark shade nets. The helper watered one side of the garden and they nodded at each other. Then he spotted Obakeng. The dignified gardener stood bent over, weeding between heads of lettuce.

"Obakeng, there you are!"

Obakeng lifted his grey head, his eyes glinting.

"Yes, Mr.. Rutgers?"

"We must talk," Tom said and the grey-haired man nodded knowingly.

*

In the evening, Sofia watched the repeat of the interview, Tom Rutgers had given in the morning. Important news was up first: the South African government had chalked up another hair-raising corruption scandal and somewhere in North Africa, a power-hungry dictator had been found in his hiding place and assaulted by an angry crowd.

The pretty news presenter read with her usual cool expression off the teleprompter until she got to the Shangari-segment.

Where on earth is Tom? Sofia looked around, wondering. He had wanted to watch the news with her. She leaned back in her armchair and watched the spunky news presenter address Joanne Botha, the reporter who had come to Shangari to interview Tom. It was still morning on the smaller screen behind the news anchor when Joanne Botha had just arrived with her cameraman at Shangari Safari Lodge.

"Thank you, Lucinda." The smaller insert grew and took over the entire screen. Joanne Botha gave a brief introduction on the stairs in front of the lodge next to orange-flowering cannas. She waved at the building then turned around to face Tom.

"Mr. Rutgers, you are the owner of Shangari Safari Lodge, where a rhino was poached and one of your rangers was shot dead yesterday. Can you give us some information about the circumstances of this incident?"

The reporter held the microphone up, waiting for an answer.

"We are shocked and dismayed by the events that took one of our beloved community members, a ranger, doing his duty. We have been spared large-scale poaching so far and this will hopefully remain an isolated incident. Rhinos are valuable, ancient animals and in dire need of protection."

"Our deepest condolences to the family of the ranger who was killed. Isn't it true, though, that another such incident took place at a game farm not far from here a couple of weeks ago?"

"Thank you, Joanne. And yes, it is true. It happened on a game farm closer to the Kruger National Park," Tom said.

"What is being done to bring the guilty parties to book?"

"All I can say right now is that the police are doing their best to secure the evidence. The Special Commission on Poaching will surely address the media of the progress in due course."

The reporter ignored this. "Word has it that a rare rhinoceros was shot and killed for its horns."

"Yes, unfortunately, that is true. A rare black rhino. We hope that those responsible will be found and brought to book soon. Too many rhinos are being killed in South Africa."

"Yes, A ghastly crime. We all hope that the Special Commission on Poaching is able to give us an update soon," Joanne Botha agreed. "Is it true that a well-known businessman from Johannesburg is currently among the guests at Shangari?" She'd jumped the question on him but Tom was on his guard.

"We often welcome celebrity-guests here. There is, however, no connection to the event we discussed. Thank you very much, Joanne."

"Thank you for your time, Mr.. Rutgers. Back to the studio." The news anchor reappeared on the screen. "And thank you, Joanne Botha. We'll be back with market indicators after the break…" That was it.

The tragic murder of human and animal reduced to a 2-minute interview segment. Soon, the public would have forgotten even those 2 minutes and rhino poaching would disappear from the public radar once again.

"Well that was sufficiently elusive," Tom said and put his hand on Sofia's shoulder. He had come in quietly and seen the last bit of the interview.

"Where have you been?" Sofia switched the TV off and turned around.

"Needed to take care of something urgent. Want to go for a dip in the pool before dinner?"

"Sure. The eclipse of the moon starts at 21:17 pm. My guess is, it'll get hectic around eight o'clock."

At eight o'clock, the camping chairs on the hilltop were already occupied and most of the visitors were sitting on blankets with their picnic baskets. Everybody tucked into their food and the champagne flowed. Smoke from braai fires and faint Boere-music rose up from the large tents below.

Barry Pienaar and his wife Lorraine had also come over from their farm but stuck to Coke and fruit juice instead of hard liquor. Hopefully, there wouldn't be a repeat of the drunken scene yesterday.

The more planet Earth pushed between the moon and the sun, the more the dark disk in front of the moon seemed to grow in size. The great, bright moon first turned orange and then dark red.

All around them, nature ground to a standstill. The birds grew silent and even the chirping cicadas seemed in awe of the spectacle. All other sounds ceased and in the increasing darkness, one could barely make out the landscape surrounding the flat-top hill. Everybody stared at the darkening moon high up in the sky as if it was a revelation. A lion roared lazily in his sleep then there was only the rushing sound of the whitewater in the distance. Even the music had lapsed into silence. It was completely dark now, apart from the unimpressed stars in the broad stream of the Milky Way and a couple of blinking satellites that moved across the sky.

"You see the star sign up there? It looks like a reel of sewing cotton with a line of three stars in the middle," a strapping South African asked his rather thin wife in a whispering tone. In the stark silence, it seemed awfully loud.

"Over there, Greg?" The woman pointed at the star-covered firmament. "Yes, right there. That's Orion, you know." The woman took a sip from her champagne flute. Before the eclipse, she had given the people around her an account of her life story and nobody had been able to get a word in edgewise. She was quiet now and stared at the clear night sky.

"And that over there..."

"Quiet man..."

"...that's the Big Dipper." The South African man fell silent.

The view from the hill was priceless, especially when the dark-red disk gradually changed its colour back from red to a dark orange, light orange, then to yellow and white. Once again, bright moonlight lit up the sky and the hills and trees reappeared in their silver glory. Then the buildings and the people around them became visible and finally the birds and cicadas continued their nightly concert.

There was clapping as if the lunar eclipse had been a scheduled theatre show. People began to leave but a thinning crowd kept watching until the early hours of the morning when a fading moon sank below the hills and a grey stripe appeared on the horizon.

Many of the guests had gone to bed in their luxury rooms and tent houses after midnight but the die-hards were determined to savour every last moment of the rare spectacle. Sofia was asleep in her camping chair, resting her head against Tom's shoulder. Some people packed their blankets and baskets and picked up sleeping children. The mood was mellow when a jarring shot echoed off the tranquil hills.

A couple of women screamed.

"What the hell!" Tom Rutgers jumped up from his

camping chair and Sofia's head rolled off his shoulder, waking her with a jolt.

"What?" She yawned. "What is it?"

Had the shot come from the barn at the bottom of the slope? A group of men assembled and, led by Tom and a Danish tourist by the name of Torben, hastened down the path. Others followed. Such an unexpected thrill and they were right in the middle of it!

"Stay here," Tom called out to Sofia. "Quiet, Brutus!" The dog instantly obeyed and sat down whimpering next to Sofia's chair.

The men reached the barn in no time. Jethro, the cheetah, hissed and snarled all agitated and jumped around in his cage. Tom went over to the bakkie and took a rifle from inside the cabin. He noted that the other rifle was missing.

He released the safety catch. In the faint light, he spotted the lifeless body of a man on the gravel in front of the barn door.

"I don't believe it..." he mumbled and saw something move by the barn door. "Who is there?" He yelled and lunged forward, his weapon at the ready. The other men formed a half-circle, while two of them knelt by the man on the ground.

Brutus barked and there was more excited snarling in the cheetah enclosure.

"Ho, hold your horses! It's just me," Tom recognised the voice and the disturbing chuckle. "Be careful with that thing or you'll rub me out!"

Stan Makaroff appeared in front of the door, a glowing cigarette in his right hand. He held up his arms in an almost playful gesture, swaying slightly as if he were drunk. There was no sign of his ever-present bodyguard.

Tom's jaw dropped to the ground. "What on earth...?"

"That's Stan Makaroff, Greg," the please-eat-something thin woman said in a hissing whisper. "You should give him your card. He might need insurance."

"Shhhh, that's not the right time or place," her husband hissed back.

Stanislav Makaroff, the arrogant celebrity-businessman, stood in front of them. He carelessly threw his glowing cigarette butt down and ground it into the gravel with the heel of his designer tekkie. Then he blew the last bit of smoke from the corner of his mouth. Was that a grin on his face?

"What're you doing in the barn at this time of night?" Tom demanded to know.

Everybody held their breath. What would happen now?

"Can't you see?" He taunted Tom Rutgers and pointed to the tobacco crumbs by his foot. "I wanted to smoke my cigarette in peace. There was a shot. Pretty damn loud, I might add - and I ran for cover. Without thinking twice." At first blush, that sounded like a plausible explanation.

"Did you see what happened?" Tom probed.

"Not really... It was dark."

"Who's that man?"

They had almost forgotten about the man who had been shot. Everyone stared at the figure on the ground.

"Couldn't say. Now, will you please take that thing down?"

Tom secured the rifle and threw it to Cotton who caught it effortlessly. Then he knelt next to the unconscious man. Somebody had turned him around on his back. The first reluctant sun rays shone on his face and a dark patch in his hair became obvious. Tom stared in stunned silence.

The man on the ground was Barry Pienaar.

CHAPTER 3

"Dammit Barry, you could've been killed! What the hell were you thinking?" Tom Rutgers was reading his friend the riot act for the umpteenth time.

The Danish tourist had turned out to be a doctor. He'd just examined Barry again after they had carried him into the guest bedroom at the farmhouse half an hour ago. Somebody had given him a blow to the side of his head, but luckily, it was only a concussion and the blood loss was minimal.

"How often must I say it?" Barry Pienaar said dolefully and closed his eyes. He lay with his bandaged head against a pile of pillows. "I'm sorry."

His wife Lorraine sat at the foot of the bed and kept whispering "Domkop, domkop," with a perplexed expression. Domkop meant idiot in Afrikaans.

"I heard noises in the barn, Tom... and wanted to see who it was. Could've been you for all I care. It was too dark to see anything but there was definitely somebody in the barn. I called... but no answer. Light switch didn't work. That's why I went to the bakkie to fetch a torchlight and the rifle." He took a deep breath.

"Before I knew it, someone clocked me soundly over the head and my lights went out. I think that's when the shot went off. Sorry if the bullet ripped a hole in the boat. By the way, thanks for treating my head, colleague."

The Danish doctor nodded. "You were lucky, Mr. Pienaar."

"Yes, goddam lucky!" Tom was still in a fluster. "You should have come to me, not check the barn out all by yourself. Especially not after what happened on Friday!"

"Oh, come on. I can take care of myself. What the hell is

in that old barn anyway? Just some tools and the half-finished yacht that you want to sail in the desert one day." He tried to laugh, only to grab his head again when he began to see stars. "Ouch, that hurt!"

"Sure, you can take care of yourself," Lorraine began to scold her husband. "That's why you are here with a big fat bump on your head. If you weren't so..."

"We should let him have some rest," the doctor interrupted.

"Alright then, we will search the barn with your consent, Mr.. Rutgers." Captain Combrink said. He had been asleep in his hotel room in Rutgersdrift when Witbooi rang him. The station commander looked exhausted. A slaughtered rhino, murder and attempted murder in two days were just too much. Speeding tickets, the occasional domestic matter or a drunk sobering up in the cell at the station, were the usual order of the day.

The city detectives were also a handful. They didn't trust anyone, not even him, the station commander of the Rutgersdrift police! Witbooi took out another Rennies and put it in his mouth. All this nonsense made his ulcer flare up.

"Of course I give my consent," Tom said. "Please be careful around the boat. The spar varnish is not quite dry yet." This sounded so trivial in light of what had happened in the past few days. And Barry had blown a nice big hole into the stern that needed fixing.

"We will try to be careful, Mr.. Rutgers, you can count on it." There was this mocking tone again. "Thank you," Tom said and didn't think that the detective cared one bit. One of the detectives called Captain Combrink into the dining room.

"Please excuse me," he said and left the guest bedroom. They heard muffled voices and bits and pieces of a conversation coming from the dining room.

"Of course not... I've already told you, how I ended up being in the barn. I explained it to you... and I didn't see anybody else. It was too dark. Goldie...?"

"Sir..." Makaroff's trusted attorney, Alwin Goldsmith,

answered. His boss called him Goldie, in a partly condescending, partly affectionate way.

He was part of the Makaroff-entourage this weekend and felt somewhat flustered because Daisy de Bruin, a paralegal at the Sandton office, had been under his blanket when Bruno, the bodyguard, had called him. It was against company rules to fraternise with a lower-ranked employee and to top it off, the good attorney was a married man. Miss de Bruin had hidden in the bathroom and Alwin Goldsmith could only hope that she had managed to slip out unnoticed.

"Mr. Makaroff's bodyguard was not there because... he had to relieve himself. Even bodyguards are human, you know. Mr. Makaroff is trying to cooperate here. A perfectly acceptable explanation and you asked the man himself... Bruno..."

At this hour, Alwin Goldsmith didn't cut an impressive figure in his shorts and a blue t-shirt. Gold-rimmed glasses sat askew on his nose and his sparse hair was dishevelled. Another voice mumbled something. It was probably the bodyguard.

"There you have it. No reason to hold Mr. Makaroff... on suspicion of what? Smoking?" The lawyer was trying to regain his composure.

"Mr. Goldsmith - there are more questions. We must ask Mr. Makaroff to appear at the station tomorrow morning... Yes of course... no, of course not..." The usually so cool calm and collected detective stuttered.

"If there is nothing else right now, you will excuse us," Goldie added imperiously. "The helicopter is waiting. Mr. Makaroff is scheduled..."

The detective had no choice but to relent. One didn't just willy-nilly arrest some prominent person without proof. Especially not someone like Mr. Makaroff, with lots of money and connections.

"At least there are no reporters here," Sofia whispered in Tom's ear.

"I wouldn't be so surprised if they get wind of this and come back."

"Makaroff's leaving. What are we supposed to do?"

"There's nothing we can do. We'll go to sleep now and wait for the dust to settle. It's the job of this detective to do something."

More muffled talk next door, then some shuffling as the tycoon and his party were ushered out of the farmhouse. Minutes later the Makaroff helicopter started from the helipad with much clatter and whirring that soon subsided.

Meanwhile, the policemen and detectives were scouring the barn and didn't take long to find the bullet that had been fired from Barry Pienaar's rifle. It had smashed through the boat, ricocheted off a metal frame behind it and become stuck in the wooden barn wall. The shell was on the floor close to the door.

That in itself didn't give any clues: who had been in the barn, whether it had been one perpetrator or two and what the motive could have been.

The object used to attack Dr. Pienaar was possibly still somewhere in the barn. He had received the blow to the head, facing the boat and the shot had gone off, so the path of the bullet was more or less random. Just that there had to be a motive. They didn't have to wait long to find out.

In a toolbox not far from the entrance, the policemen found a rather heavy, bulky object under a pile of bent nails, tucked into a dirty cloth. On closer inspection, they saw that there were two dark objects inside.

Captain Combrink inspected the objects from every angle. There was no doubt about it: he was looking at two dark-grey rhino horns.

Bloody fingerprints were all over the horns and rough saw marks. So the poacher's booty had been hidden by someone right here in the barn! Why had they not taken it with them across the border? The detectives of the Special Commission on Poaching were stumped.

Captain Combrink would have preferred the arrest of at least one suspect and chalked the case up to success for once. And it didn't look good for Makaroff.

The problem was that they had to prove his involvement -

and get past that dreadful lawyer of his. They had fingerprints and those fingerprints were the vital clue. Then there was the blue pin they had found in the pocket of Tom Rutger's shorts. It was already being sent for testing to Pretoria but Captain Combrink doubted that the lab would find anything useful on that pin.

The owner of the game farm had removed it from the scene and contaminated the evidence. Had he done it on purpose? It was possible that the shock of it all had been responsible for his lack of good judgement but was it likely?

Captain Combrink drew up a suspect list, scribbled down name after name, crossed them out and made notes. They had leads and they had the rhino horns. He knew that somebody at the lodge must have worked with the poachers. But who? Just a few more puzzle pieces put in place and he would make an arrest soon.

The detective was so sure of his hunch that his thin lips cracked into a rare smile. This damn heat! He took off his jacket and hung it carefully over the back of the chair. His stay at Shangari would be shorter than anticipated and that was good news. Frida walked in and Captain Combrink asked her to bring him some breakfast. *Soon*, he thought and smiled.

But he didn't look up to see the expression on Frida's face as placed the dishes on the dining room table.

*

Just south of the Trans-Kalahari Park, the truck from up north dropped off a group of passengers in a small dusty Khoi-San village. They had travelled in the back of the truck between sacks of plaster sand and rolls of wire, together with a handful of other passengers who had paid a few bucks for the lift. Francina and her children were not far from the cattle post and her home now.

One of the men handed down bundles with Francina's modest belongings and the little ones, then the truck drove on in a cloud of swirling dust.

Francina had decided to save the money, Baas Tom had

71

given her for the bus. She had caught a lift with one of the government vehicles taking supplies to Pofadder. Her home village was so different from Shangari, where she had lived with her husband, Cornelius Grootman for many years. But it was home.

She waited on the dusty road for a while. Francina had written a brief letter to her brother but you never knew these days if letters arrived, with the post office being so unreliable. When nobody came to greet them, she picked up a large bundle, put it on her head and trudged up the sand road toward the complex and her house. It was at the end of April and as soon as the sun sank below the horizon, the temperatures would drop.

Her son Frans took the other heavier bundle and the younger children carried plastic bags. One of Francina's cousins looked after the family hut, while they stayed in Shangari but she couldn't be sure that he had received her message in time. The area was desolate and void of water but it was home.

They reached the small spaza-shop up the road and a handful of Khoi-San came walking toward them. They were all members of their clan, welcoming the small family back into their fold. Two women joined them from nearby huts.

Although Baas Tom had offered that she could stay at Shangari, Francina had decided otherwise. It would be unsafe for them for the time being. Frans could not stay in the village of her forefathers alone with the younger children without her. Obakeng, the sangoma, had agreed with her decision and she had spoken to Mothusi.

Heartbroken, as she was over her husband's death, she had to think of the living. Later perhaps, for the children's sake, she would return and work for Baas Tom again. Schooling would be better at Renosterspruit and Baas Tom was a generous man. He had always treated them well. Francina touched the pouch with the payout that would keep them for quite a while. She and Frans could do odd jobs in the area and they would make ends meet.

Since the funeral, there had been much talk about the poaching and what could be done about it. People like Baas Tom had the police and commissions and what not. Much good it would do them.

The Bushmen, on the other hand, had their own way of finding out such things and dealing with them. The Khoi-San were not vengeful by nature, they were taught to accept everything that came their way, good or bad. It was their custom and Francina's clan still followed the ancient ways, although their days as hunter-gatherers were a faint memory now; only kept alive in songs and stories.

Modern ways were too rough for their sensitive natures. They had their rituals and knew how to communicate with nature. As far as they were concerned, there would be justice for Cornelius. One way or the other.

The adults chatted away in the ancient language of the San with its many click sounds and effusive gestures. It hailed from the glorious times when the Khoi-San had roamed the land far and wide like the bucks they hunted. Nowadays, they were blocked by tall fences everywhere and the clan had stopped moving around so much.

Once in a while, they visited their relatives in Namibia and Botswana by donkey cart or hitch-hiking on trucks. All of them spoke Afrikaans but only a few still knew how to use their very own language properly.

Francina walked on, accompanied by her relatives who helped carry the bundles and supplies for her. The children followed them sad and quiet. They reached the homestead, her cousin had kept going, and sat down on their haunches, around the flickering fire in front of the small house.

Francina greeted her cousin affectionately. There was potije-kos cooking in a three-legged iron pot and everybody filled their hungry stomachs. One of the men began to sing and the others joined in an ancient song of sadness and how life would go on. Francina was home and the world didn't feel quite so lonely anymore.

*

One chilly morning on the last day of May, Sofia was driving on the highway to Johannesburg at a comfortable speed. She had negotiated the usual maze of country roads, passed a squatter camp and was now cruising south on a broad, near-empty highway, slowly approaching the capital city of Pretoria.

Much had happened since February.

An international tourism company had signed a contract with Shangari and they were welcoming more and more tourists to their neck of the woods. Even budget tourists who didn't mind the lack of amenities in large tents. Tom was busy with the extension of ablution facilities, adding more showers and toilets and even more picnic tables at the back.

Many of the tourists had booked tours of Namibia and Botswana and stopped over for a couple of days on their way to the international airport in Johannesburg.

Luckily, there had been no more poaching incidents in the area, albeit in other game parks, and they hadn't heard from the Special Commission on Poaching for some time now. Tom had eventually given up phoning to find out, whether there had been any progress and given their track-record and the sheer number of cases, it was a waste of time.

Apparently, the fingerprints on the enamel pin had been inconclusive. The rhino horns, the police had found in the barn, had also been tested but the results had inexplicably disappeared together with the horns and relevant documents, after being transferred to headquarters in Johannesburg.

The most promising evidence to date - and it was gone.

They had found other clues, of course, and shoe imprints but the tracks had stopped short at the shore of the whitewater and the sniffer dogs had come up with nothing beyond the whitewater.

Captain Combrink had made his arrest, however. Poor Mothusi tested positive for gunshot residue and had spent two terrifying weeks in a prison cell in Pretoria. Tom had hired a good lawyer who managed to convince the magistrate to drop the charges due to a lack of evidence. Of course,

Mothusi had fired a gun during the ambush!

The weapon, the police had found in the woods was his alright. He'd thrown it away and fled down to the river to save his life. The poachers had chased him to the shore until he'd disappeared from their view. He'd watched three of them take the boat and cross the shallow water to the other side into the Pienaar farm.

When the ballistic test results came back, the Special Commission's case against Mothusi had collapsed. The bullets that had been found in the rhino and Cornelius were no match to his rifle.

Since then, the Commission had come up empty-handed. Not that Tom and Sofia had expected a resounding success but everybody had hoped for more than nothing. None of the poachers had been caught and in the meantime, international smuggling rings caused unrelenting terror in other game farms and nature parks.

Farmers in the area were outraged and demanded that Interpol intervene and the military be deployed to protect these precious animals.

The government had other priorities. As a result, the game farmers tried to render the horns on living rhinos unusable, with dye and poison. Some even sawed the horns off to save their rhinos. Then the involvement of officials in bribery and lack of political will was suspected. More than 106 rhinos had been killed in South Africa in the new year alone and virtually no inroads into the problem had been made.

After the dreadful events in February, Sofia had started a campaign on social media, trying to draw attention to the problem of rhino poaching. Her endeavour was helped by the fact that they had better access to the internet.

When international organisations were beginning to take up the cause, Sofia was able to dedicate more of her time to the lodge again. But something had to be done. In Uganda, elephants were being slaughtered by the thousands and lions were hunted for sport but there was almost no reaction to those atrocities. In Europe and America, people seemed blissfully unaware or showed indifference. Even their guests from Australia and New Zealand knew very little about rhino-poaching. And why the government was dragging its feet was anyone's guess.

Finally, Sofia could plan her long overdue trip to Johannesburg to purchase supplies and visit her cousin Astrid but that was not the only reason she was looking forward to her trip. She had quarrelled with Tom yesterday about something so stupid, she couldn't even remember the reason. Sofia preferred not to think about it. She had other things to worry about.

It was nearly 10:00 am. Sofia switched the heater off and turned on the car radio for the news. Another political scandal involving the president... and then:

"... according to the Special Commission on Rhino Poaching, a crashed helicopter has been discovered in the border region with Botswana this morning..." She turned up the volume. "... the whereabouts of the pilot could not be established or whether he is still alive. A search and rescue mission was launched by local authorities. It is also unclear, why the skids of the helicopter were sawn off and why there was blood found inside and outside the cabin of the helicopter. The cabin was riddled with bullets. A bloodied saw and a rifle-silencer were found on the ground next to the helicopter and the site was scantily disguised with thorny branches. Investigations are continuing. In other news..."

Now, that's something! Sofia thought.

Local Authorities that involved Witbooi, police in other districts and rangers from adjoining game farms who knew the bush well.

These investigations are not going to lead anywhere anyway, Sofia thought bitterly. It must be like an invitation to these wretched criminals if nothing ever happened to them. This helicopter story most certainly smacked of a crime. Sofia changed the channel and a soothing ballad came on when an expensive 4x4 flashed his headlights at her, came far too close, then sped past her bakkie on the wrong side and zoomed ahead in zigzag lines. Sofia managed to swerve at the last minute.

"Bloody idiot! Aalio, Kusipää. Painu vittuun täältä!" Sofia felt always better, swearing in Suomi. "Can you believe it?! This guy must be high on something." She slowed down and peeled off her cardigan. Phew, it was getting warmer already, even though it was much cooler in the south.

One of her favourite songs 'Baker Street' started playing and Sofia belted out the words right to the end. She changed the channel again when listeners started calling into the radio station to discuss some political topic in Afrikaans.

Her cousin Astrid Rankin lived in a nice house in Linden with her South African husband and their two children Charlie and Jessie and Sofia would be staying with them. Grant worked in import-export and travelled often. He had a good income and Astrid didn't have to work. She took care of the house, the kids, the dogs, volunteered at the local primary school and spent entire afternoons on Ikebana arrangements and yoga classes.

Things had not always been so easy for her cousin. Beautiful, blonde Astrid had a past, working as an exotic dancer in a London strip club, to raise money for her studies. Not even Sofia had known about this.

Sofia had moved to Sweden at the age of 12, after the accident that left her mother dead. Sofia's father couldn't get over the shock and had been unable to look after his only daughter. Aunt Malin, her mother's sister, was married to a Swedish man, uncle Sven in Malmö, and they had taken Sofia in. They were kind people and aunt Malin and Astrid always spoke Suomi with Sofia.

There were four cousins: Astrid and her three younger brothers. The girls had grown close during that time, always ganging up on the boys whenever they became irritating.

Full of ambition, Astrid moved to London to do her undergraduate studies at a well-known business school. Sofia had been in her last year at high school and missed Astrid terribly. Astrid told her later that she was too proud to ask her parents for more money when she'd failed her first year.

She had met Grant Rankin at the strip club and he'd swept her off her feet, paid for the last semester, then took her to South Africa. They were married within a year and settled in Johannesburg. Sofia had gone back to Finland to study and the cousins had lost touch for a while.

Sofia didn't like Grant all that much. He could be rude when he was drunk and she thought that he should treat her cousin with more respect. For Astrid's sake, she tried not to criticise him in front of her, and he wasn't around that much anyway. Grant would hopefully be gone for the entire time, Sofia had planned to stay with Astrid.

Tom knew that Sofia sometimes craved the city lights and didn't mind her short absences. In Johannesburg, she could catch up with Gugu and Astrid every two or three months and purchase whatever they needed over and above their regular supplies at Shangari.

The flow of traffic slowed down abruptly. A building site lay ahead and rows of orange cones guided the car first to the left, then back to the right side of the highway. A man in a bright green waistcoat waved a red flag, then held it out two cars ahead of Sofia's bakkie to give oncoming traffic the right of way. She changed the radio channel again and turned up the volume. Rap wasn't really her thing. Classical music, why not? Better than listening to a discussion about some outrageous government scandal.

Two days ago, Gugu had told her on the phone that Goldie, Makaroff's attorney, had been demoted from his top position under a cloud of scandal and had been replaced with a young, well-connected and highly ambitious man who - despite his age - ran a tight ship. Some called him ruthless.

'Nobody knows what the exact reason is but Makaroff always has his reasons. Goldie still has a job. I'm not sure why... because if he embezzled money or something, then...'

'Gugu, I must go...' Sofia had interrupted her, '... still need to finish the entries from last week. I see you in Joburg then, okay?'

'Okay, Sofia. I shouldn't drive and talk on the phone either. So we get together when you tell me. Sort that guy out - you know who - and call me.'

'I'll do that. Drive safely!'

'Yes... bye.'

Sofia had received an e-mail from... her... well... ex-boyfriend. His name was Errol Botes. The 'you know who'. He had never really been her boyfriend, except... she could still kick herself for not staying away from him when they'd first met. Why he was still writing was a mystery to Sofia. They were ancient history.

Errol had found a job at a hip radio station in Bloemfontein and that was good news because Bloemfontein was far away in the Free State. As long as she knew him, he'd been a DJ and the farther away from her, the better. She hadn't seen Errol for quite some time. He'd sent a photo of himself. Long curly hair, wearing a black t-shirt and black pants, his arm around two models at some fancy party. She shook herself just thinking about that photo. Luckily, she'd deleted the e-mail.

They had met in Cape Town at a party that Gugu had dragged her to. Sofia couldn't remember, what she had seen in him at the time, couldn't remember how she'd felt when they had been together. She shouldn't have accepted all those cocktails, he kept bringing her but she'd missed Tom and poured her heart out to a complete stranger! A womaniser as it turned out. Unbelievable that they had once been so close... and... that they had...

There it was again - the STITCH.

Her whole being was filled with Tom. His fragrant smell, how soft his hair was, his smile, the way she felt when he held her close. Feelings that crowded out any memories of past relationships. There was no space in her heart for somebody else and she hated arguing with Tom. Damn, she had to square with him, tell Tom the whole story.

The man with the red flag began to wave again. Sofia started the bakkie and steered it slowly past a long column of oncoming cars that had stopped for another red flag. Third gear, fourth, fifth... The south-bound traffic flowed again.

Errol was in Johannesburg right now, attending some media conference. She had forgotten what it was all about, nor did she care. Sofia didn't really want to see Errol and be reminded of their brief affair. Come to think of it, she didn't know much about him or his family at all. They had never reached the point, where one's favourite colour was discussed or favourite food or music or family.

He knew that she had a boyfriend. That was it. It made her uncomfortable to know that he would be so close by in Johannesburg but if he wanted to see her, she wouldn't object. They were friends now. Well kind of.

She had almost reached Pretoria now. More and more cars kept feeding onto the long, grey ribbon of concrete highway in front of her. More and more billboards raced past, screaming their colourful messages at her:

"Buy Me... Drink Me... Drive Me... Look At Me!"

A radio jingle announced the news again. The helicopter, they had found in the bush was mentioned even before the president's new scandal. Nothing new had been found out about the mysterious crash. Then something made her listen up: '... two companies under the umbrella of the Makaroff-Corporation: Staroff and BrightRental said to be in violation of the tax regulation...' *Nothing new there either*, Sofia thought. Stan Makaroff was known to have connections in high places and would get off lightly again. She turned the radio off.

Scumbags, the lot of them! She had good reason to be annoyed with Stan Makaroff. As soon as Barry Pienaar had recovered from his head wound in March, his wife Lorraine had left him. The community was in total shock and tongues were wagging.

Rumour had it that Lorraine now worked in Johannesburg for the Makaroff-Corporation as who-knows-what and that she had become too big for her boots. Not even her sister, Charmaine, knew whether she had filed for a divorce or not. Truth be told, their marriage had been on rocky ground for a while... but this! And it was all Makaroff's fault!

As could be expected, Barry Pienaar was hard hit by his wife's actions. He'd started drinking heavily again, missed her being there with him, even missed their cantankerous arguments.

A newly qualified veterinarian from Pretoria, he had taken on as an assistant, did the bulk of the veterinarian duties and Barry came to Shangari more often than she liked. He wanted to see Tom and the two of them were often talking and drinking until late at night.

Oh yes, that's what the fight with Tom had been about! She had voiced her opinion and Tom had defended his old friend. She should have known better...

The cottage, where Lorraine had styled the rural womenfolk's hairdos and manicured their nails, was now being turned into an additional facility for the animal clinic. Tom was building, and Barry was building... they had lots to talk about.

Sofia had gone to Rutgersdrift last week to buy the rooibos night cream that Astrid had asked for. Lorraine's sister stood by the post boxes - and had already seen her. 'Ah, Sofia,' she had said in the lilting voice of a native Afrikaans speaker. 'Terrible business with the rhinos, isn't it?'

Charmaine looked a lot like Lorraine, a touch younger and less groomed maybe.

'Yes, yes. Absolutely dreadful,' Sofia had answered and thought of the best escape route from this tiring small talk.

'And then this whole business with Lorraine. Don't know what that girl is thinking! To run off like that. Barry's really down. Have you seen him lately?'

Charmaine was fishing but Sofia didn't fall for it. 'Ah... no, not really.'

'There's Hanli! Huhu... come over here,' Charmaine waved to a stout woman in her early forties. Hanli was the local gossip.

This was getting better by the minute!

'I was just saying to Sofia here, what a terrible business

about Lorraine it is. Leaving for the city like that!'

'Yes, I know! Where are we getting our hair done now? The girls at the hair salon in town always cut my hair too short and last time, Jacoba didn't get the colour right,' Hanli had said. 'I hear that Andrea Erasmus is thinking of opening a salon on their farm.'

'I wouldn't trust her with my hair if she paid me.' The two women had laughed and switched to Afrikaans. 'Jerre, hou jou oë op die horison, jy weet nooit wat wag om die draai.' All Sofia understood was that you had to keep your eyes on the horizon.

She had used a polite excuse to get away from Gossipville and they had graciously let her go. Sofia really didn't want to know all the seedy details of everybody's business.

She passed Midrand; then the upmarket suburb of Sandton came into sight. Traffic slowed again for some reason. The highway was rather crowded. It wasn't even rush-hour traffic yet but the weekend started early on a Friday afternoon. Sofia looked in the rear mirror and saw a new BMW skidding left and right, trying to slow down - right behind her.

She expected the impact but the driver green BMW regained control of his vehicle just in time. After weeks of living in the bush, it was difficult to get used to the pace of the city and speeding was one of those things.

Sofia took the Glenhove off-ramp. Astrid lived in Linden, a quiet leafy suburb in northern Johannesburg with a low crime rate. Another thing about the city was that at every intersection, there were beggars and people selling newspapers, clothes hangers and packs of garbage bags.

She had seen an Indian man drop off some women with babies once. They had taken up their positions at the large intersection of William Nicol Drive and Main Road, arguing with another beggar about their spot, then flashing bright smiles at the drivers.

The sight of the sheer beauty around her made Sofia breathe in deeply. The suburb exuded tranquility. When the jacaranda trees were blooming their hearts out in October, these streets were bathed in blue petals. She turned into one of the side roads. Almost there.

Now in winter, the air was dry and crisp. Most of the trees had already lost their leaves and the jacarandas in Astrid's street had pink fabric wrapped around their trunks, to raise awareness for breast cancer this month.

The garden wall of the house on the right was guarded by lollipop trees. A gardener was busy trimming the tops into round shapes and waved at Sofia when she stopped in front of the gate. *He's definitely not from the city*, she thought and waved back. To the left, bougainvillea branches were spilling their masses of red blooms over a green palisade fence.

It was already lunchtime, when Sofia rang the bell outside the gate and received an electric spark as soon as she touched the metal plate. "Ouch, dammit!" She had forgotten the effect of the dry Johannesburg winter air!

Astrid's garden was pretty even now. White roses lined the driveway right up to the house with its Cape-Dutch gables. All the gardens in the area were pretty.

"Oh hi, Sofia, you're here!" Astrid said on the intercom. She spoke with a more pronounced accent than Sofia.

"Are you going to let me in or what?" Sofia rubbed her smarting hand.

"Oh yes of course..."

"Let me do that, mom." Giggling. "Hi, Auntie Sofie!"

"Hi, Jessica! Where is Charlie?" More giggling.

An even younger voice piped up. "Did you bring me a giraffe?" The heavy iron-gate slowly opened with a humming sound.

"A giraffe?"

"Guys, you can carry on talking inside the house. Jessie, did you lock up the dogs in the backyard?" Astrid switched the intercom off with a loud crackle.

The two exuberant Labradors were only allowed in the kitchen and had to go into the back garden when visitors came around. As Sofia drove the bakkie up the driveway, the front door opened and two wheat-blond children ran out.

Six-year-old Charlie was the first one by the bakkie and tried to open the driver's door.

"Hey, young man, hold your horses. Give me a chance to get out first," Sofia laughed. Then Charlie's eleven-year-old sister Jessica caught up with him.

"Let me do that, Charlie!" She said all grown up and opened the car door.

"You guys, come here and give your old aunt a big hug!" Sofia laughed.

"You're not old!"

"Oh okay if you say so."

Sofia loved visiting Astrid and apparently, Grant was away on a business trip. They greeted each other in Suomi.

"Terve, Sofia! Pitkästä aikaa," Astrid said and hugged her cousin. Hi, long time no see.

"Kuinka voit?" How are you? Sofia asked, only to be interrupted by the two boisterous children.

"Did you bring something for me? What did you bring for me?" Charlie cried and fumbled with the big knitted bag, Sofia was lifting out of the car.

"Hey, stop it you little brat!" Jessica loosened Charlie's grip on the bag.

"Hey both of you, behave yourselves! Or do you want auntie Sofie to turn around and go back home?" The children settled down a little. Their mother usually didn't joke about stuff like that.

"No," Charlie mouthed.

"I brought something for each one of you," Sofia said and put the bags on the ground. Their faces lit up again

"Mitä uutta? What's new?" Astrid wanted to know.

"Ei mitään oikastaan. Nothing much." Apart from the changes at the lodge and her fight with Tom but Astrid knew about that. The cousins always started speaking Suomi out of habit, then switched to English for the children's sake. Nobody else could understand them.

The two women looked nothing alike. Astrid had light-blonde, straight hair and brown eyes with little green specks.

Sofia's hair was dark brown and she had blue eyes. Almost opposites but both had the same slim build, translucent skin and facial shape. That's why people often took them for sisters.

They all carried the luggage into the hallway with its light Scandinavian décor. Despite Jessie's disapproving comments, Charlie was already busy unpacking the colourful knitted bag, bulging with gifts from the countryside.

"Didn't you bring me a snake, auntie Sofie? A real one?" Charlie sounded disappointed and dug deeper into the bag.

"Charlie, it was a joke. I can't catch a snake on the farm and take it with me to Joburg. Or giraffes. You should know that," Sofia laughed.

"Okay... but Kevin has one. He keeps it in a glass box."

"There won't be any snakes in this house if I have anything to do with it," Astrid said and Charlie pouted a little. Astrid still wore her hair in a braid over one shoulder, as she had done back home when they were teenagers.

Charlie pulled out two ostrich eggs for Astrid, a small wooden sculpture of a springbok for Charlie and a carved, round box with a lid for Jessica's girlie odds and ends. Sofia had bought the gifts directly from the Khoi-San at Shangari. She had even brought a carved letter opener for Grant, they sold at the curio shop and handed it to Astrid.

"Wait, I nearly forgot the face cream you wanted," Sofia said and rummaged in her purse. "And a rooibos-soap."

"Ah, thank you, cousin. I love rooibos." Astrid gave Sofia another hug before they carried the luggage upstairs into the guest bedroom. "Come, let's have some coffee. You can unpack later."

The large windows in the lounge were overlooking the front lawn, the white roses and flower beds against the fence. And beyond the fence, gave way to a spectacular view of the roofs and tree-covered slopes of Emmarentia. Another beautiful suburb.

After the first flush of excitement, the children had gone to the TV room to watch a movie. Sofia knew that Astrid had chosen a neighbourhood school and not the posh private school, so popular in her circle of friends. Astrid had never regretted her decision and the school was so close that they could walk. It was one of the very few things, Sofia liked about Grant Rankin: that he let his wife make some rather important decisions.

They chatted over coffee in the lounge with its thick Persian carpets and solid birch furniture. Sofia sorted through a stack of letters that Astrid had put on the coffee table for her.

She usually stated Astrid's Linden address on forms for the receiver of revenue, the bank and such. The postal service in Rutgersdrift was unreliable at the best of times and even in Johannesburg, letters could take a week or more to arrive. There was a letter with a handwritten address on a light blue envelope among the usual mail. Sofia opened it and went pale.

"So what does he want now?" Astrid asked.

She was, of course, referring to Errol, Sofia's former lover. He had written a couple of letters lately and Astrid assumed that this letter was from him.

"It's actually from Damian's... parents." Sofia hesitated at the word *parents*. Damian's mother, Suzanne Daniels, had written directly for the first time. She was Damian's other mother.

The decision to have an open adoption had been quite reasonable but somehow Sofia still felt like Damian's mother after all this time. It had to be... wait... almost four years coming August. Yes, the 11th of August - she would never forget that day full of excitement and anxiety and pain. Then the pain, not being able to see him and to hold her son.

She kept a picture of the laughing little boy with milk-coffee skin and dark, curly hair that Suzanne Daniels had sent not long ago, hidden in her purse. They lived in Cape Town, the Daniels. The boy's eyes were so clear - a clear hazel colour. Almost like Tom's! Tom had never seen the picture... dear Tom... Will I ever be able to tell you?

She swallowed hard and began to play absent-mindedly with her Tanzanite bracelet - the one Tom had given her for her birthday. She had phoned him a minute ago, just to tell him that she'd arrived safely in Johannesburg. He'd been brief but there were relief and warmth in his voice. They could both be so stubborn sometimes!

"Well?"

Sofia looked up and saw Astrid staring at her. "Well... she says, Damian's in need of a liver transplant," she said bluntly.

"What?!" Astrid looked at her in shocked disbelief. "Why?"

"Some virus infection he had. Nobody knows exactly what kind of infection. He started getting better and then he became jaundiced. They took him to the hospital... his liver was packing up... oh Astrid, he's so little! Why didn't they just give me a call?" Sofia wiped a tear from the corner of her eye.

"Oh my god - you have to do something, Sofia! Phone them now, get tested... something."

"Right getting tested - yes, that's what the letter says I should do. What if I'm not a match?" Sofia felt confused.

"Then get... get Errol involved," Astrid said.

"Errol!" Sofia snorted. "I'll never be rid of him!"

"What? Who cares?"

"He sent me an e-mail, saying that he's in Joburg at some conference or other... Oh god, you're right - I must try to get hold of him. I hope it's not too late."

"Where is Errol? At which hotel or venue or whatever? Maybe one of you is a match. You have to give it a try." Thank god, Astrid was always so level-headed.

"I don't know. The e-mail printout is in my purse. There's a phone number somewhere."

"I'll get your purse, you phone Damian's parents so long."

"Okay, thank you, Astrid! Kiitos."

"Ole hyvä. It will be alright."

Sofia had never spoken to Damian's new family, had never heard his new mother's voice. She dialled the number in the letter and spoke to Suzanne Daniels. She seemed nice and explained the situation to her. It was pretty much the same as she had written in the letter.

An hour later, Sofia sat in a doctor's office in Randburg.

The medical centre, Damian's mom, had directed her to. It was open after hours and ready to do the tests over the weekend. The nurse pulled the needle expertly out of her arm and placed a plaster on the tiny, bleeding mark. On the table next to Sofia, three glass vials with her blood and marked with her name were placed in a plastic stand.

"So, that's it, Ms Helenius. We'll let your GP know the results."

"Yes, the one in Cape Town. Mrs. Daniels' GP."

"Of course. Don't worry, we've marked it *express*. He'll have the results first thing Monday morning."

"Good, thank you. Did Mr. Botes make an appointment?"

Before the nurse could answer, she saw Errol walk into the reception area. Her heart jumped a fraction. Maybe it was all the nervous tension and hectic activity of the past two hours.

"Never mind. He's already here."

Sofia had phoned Errol at his hotel in Sandton, where the media conference was held. Errol had been in some breakaway session and it had taken them ten long minutes to find him. Sofia had begun to pray that they would hurry up.

'Hi, this is Errol Botes,' he'd answered. There it was again: this undefinable thing that gnawed at her heart and needed to be controlled. She had resisted the urge to hang up.

'Hi Errol, it's Sofia,' she'd said as calmly as possible. *Think before you speak*, she reminded herself.

'Oh hi, Sofia, good to hear from you. Where are you?' He seemed genuinely pleased. "Want to get together?"

'No... Yes. I'm in Joburg. We have to talk, Errol.'

'Talk? Okay. I thought we could go to Melrose Arch and try one of their new restaurants, then paint the town red... I mean, this is Joburg...'

'No, Errol, we can't do that,' Sofia had said patiently.' We really have to talk. It's about Damian...' It had taken less than two minutes to explain to Errol, what danger their little boy was in and that they had to act quickly. And he'd seemed to get his priorities right. For once...

Errol saw Sofia through the glass window and nodded, his

jaw was set tightly.

"Rush hour traffic," he apologised when they met at the reception. While they waited for him to be called by the nurse, she explained Damian's condition, trying to use the same words that Suzanne Daniels had used.

"He's getting liver-dialysis every second day. He's stable but his liver is not in good shape. They'll have to do a transplant as soon as possible..." Her eyes filled with tears and she leaned her head against Errol's shoulder. The feeling was familiar. He was tall and skinny and wore a fashionable shirt. His shoulder got wet but it didn't seem to bother him.

Errol took her face in his hands. "It will be okay, Sofia. Our son will be okay."

It was rather corny but Sofia didn't mind that. She felt less tense; had never expected him to care so much. Astrid was watching them from across the room, with Charlie sitting on her lap, looking at the pictures in some magazine. Jessica was studying the cool drink display on the vending machine. Suddenly, Astrid stood next to them and Sofia moved away from Errol.

"Oh Astrid, let me introduce you. This is Errol Botes. Errol, this my cousin Astrid Rankin," she said a little embarrassed.

"Hi Errol, I've heard much about you," Astrid said in a frigid tone.

"My pleasure. Hope you only heard good things," Errol said innocently and smiled his toothy smile.

"Well, I can't really..."

"Mom, I have to go to the loo," Charlie interrupted the encounter and pulled Astrid's hand. She ignored him.

"Okay... did you give your name at the reception?" Sofia asked. "I'm sure they're already waiting for you over there."

"Yes, yes, you're right." Errol looked around. "Where must I go to get my blood taken?"

"To that cubicle." Sofia pointed to the room with the big glass window.

"Mom, I have to go to the loo! Now!"

"Just now, Charlie. I'm sure we'll see you again, Errol,"

Astrid said and walked her son to the toilets. Jessica seemed fascinated by a poster on the symptoms of diabetes.

"Will you be here when I get out?" Errol asked.

"I don't think so. I'm sure, Astrid wants to get takeaways and then we'll go straight home. I only arrived a few hours ago, you know."

"Well, can I call you tomorrow, then?"

"Sure, why not?" Sofia wiped a lingering tear from the corner of her eye and got up. Why was she so emotional?

"Good." Errol smiled again, a bit more woeful than before. "Wait..."

"Yes?" Sofia turned around.

"I don't have your phone number."

"Yes, right." She didn't want this contact, didn't want him to phone her at all hours. Just that these were serious circumstances, so she gave him the phone number. "Do you have a pen?"

"Here, write on my hand."

"You do it..." She gave him Astrid's home number.

At least her mobile number would still be private.

"Okay, thanks." Errol scribbled the last digit on the palm of his hand. "Speak to you then."

He turned around and went with the nurse to the glass cubicle, while Sofia joined Jessica in front of the poster and answered the girl's curious questions about diabetes as well as she could.

CHAPTER 4

An hour later, Astrid and Sofia were cooking dinner in the Quaker-style kitchen in Linden. They had decided against take-away food and were glad about the distraction. Sofia emptied the dishwasher, while Astrid cooked up a storm. Spaghetti with her special Napoletana sauce and a massive salad, one of her signature dishes. The two of them had always been a good team in the kitchen back in Malmö.

"Where does this go?" Sofia held up a fish-shaped platter.

"Over there, the second cupboard at the top. No, the one next to it."

"Here?"

"Yes." They had often done the dishes in aunt Malin's kitchen, listening to the radio, chatting about girls' stuff. It had felt reassuring for both of them.

"When's Grant coming back?" Sofia asked and closed the cupboard door.

"Oh, I think on Saturday next week."

"You think?"

"Well, you know how it goes. Sometimes he needs to take out a client or he's got a meeting, then he stays another day or two." Astrid shook the little glass bottle with the Puttanesca spice a little too vigorously.

"Where is he now, anyway?" Sofia closed the lower cupboard.

"This time... wait... he first went to Nairobi, then Mozambique. His company wants him to buy building materials for the new harbour project in Maputo."

"I see... do you love him?" The random question had slipped out but it was too late to take it back.

"Love?" Astrid thought for a moment. "I think love is a

big word. There used to be something like that. At least, that's what I think it was. We are comfortable. The house, this lifestyle... and we have two children. What more could I ask for?" Astrid looked out the window at the bare tree branches.

"You think love isn't necessary?"

Astrid pulled herself together. "He literally rescued me from the strip joint, where I was dancing, Sofia. I'm not sure, I could have left that life behind without his help." That was news to Sofia.

"What? I thought you were in your last semester and you did it just for tuition and to pay for accommodation and food."

"Yes, sure, but it can get addictive that lifestyle," Astrid said. "I mean, we girls made a lot of money at the club back then." She lowered her voice and checked that the children were out of earshot. "It's a sleazy lifestyle for sure and difficult to separate from your personal life."

The kids didn't know about their mom's past, about the long hours in the sparsely-lit club. She had spent these hours gyrating around a pole under a spotlight, taking off her clothes, giving lap dances to customers in a back room with only the manager watching.

Astrid had tried to help one of the other girls get off drugs. They were easily available from dealers outside the club - and she comforted her when her ugly boyfriend lashed out in a drunken rage again.

"The tips alone were seductive. And there was all this attention. I missed classes because of that job, you know."

"I see. So how was it different with Grant then?"

"Grant? He treated me like a queen; he said he didn't care what I was doing for a living. That I was special. He was my knight in shining armour and I loved him for that."

Astrid sighed.

"But you never finished your studies," Sofia objected.

"I know. That was stupid of me but Grant wanted to return to South Africa and he convinced me to go with him. He made it sound so wonderful - to live here - and for the most part, he didn't lie. It's a great country but I would like my own career, my own life. I have the children, of course, but they are growing up fast. I want to go back to varsity but it feels like I'm stuck in a time warp when the other moms criticise me for wanting to work at all. Tricia said the other day, I would take a man's job away if I worked."

"They say stuff like that? That's dumb."

"Yes, well most of them don't work or have an education - well, the ones I meet, anyway. There are some women with careers but they are also frowned upon and it's a conversation-stopper right there. A life that circles around cake sales and gossip afternoons, chatting about maids and husbands. Grrr..." Astrid shook herself. "Not my thing."

"Do you regret coming to South Africa?"

Astrid shrugged her shoulders. "Well, I do feel lonely sometimes. I mean, there's a price to pay for everything, right? Mine is loneliness. Grant isn't around that much and the rest of the family is far away in Scandinavia. You're my only family here and I love it when you come to visit. My mom visits once a year at most and sometimes she brings my dad or one of my brothers with her."

Astrid looked sad. "Grant doesn't like visiting Europe too much. He says, he'd seen enough bad weather when he lived in England. We went to Malmö and Stockholm only twice, to show off the babies. Grant's mother lives in Germiston, close to Joburg. She's nice enough, I suppose, but we can't exactly have deep conversations. I'm not one bit interested in reality shows."

"Would you do it again? I mean come to South Africa and marry Grant and all that?"

The radio blared a familiar jingle. "Can you turn that up, please? It's the news."

Sofia wondered if Astrid was dodging the question, but she didn't insist on an answer and turned up the volume.

'We bring you the news at the top of the hour...' It was a litany of the usual scandal involving the president and his friends, the murder case against a prominent sportsman and then a report about some earthquake in Turkey.

'... Johannesburg... the trial against five South Africans from Musina, including the owner of the Hoekom game farm Adriaan Koekemoer and his wife Sandrine, three Vietnamese nationals and one Mozambican national, suspected of poaching and smuggling rhino horns, is set to begin on June 28 in the South Gauteng High Court. 371 rhinos have fallen victim to poachers this year alone...'

"Good," Sofia said, "good - something is being done about it at last."

"Terrible thing, that poaching," Astrid said.

"I'm not giving up hope that this whole thing can be turned around. Perhaps, the police will still find out what had happened at Shangari in February."

Sadly, the public took more interest in the bizarre murder case of the well-known sportsman, so the news segment was quite short. The business news, the weather... 'Sunshine is expected for tomorrow with minimum temperatures of 5°C and maximum temperatures of 16°C in Johannesburg, 7°C in Pretoria...' Same old, same old.

Sofia would carry on posting messages on wildlife and rhino-poaching on Facebook, once she got back to Shangari. Whether it made a difference, she didn't know.

They heard shouting from the playroom. Something fell.

"I told you not to touch my doll's house, you idiot! Look what you did with your damn robot!" Jessica yelled.

"You and your stupid dolls. Where's my robot supposed to live?" Charlie cried.

Astrid rolled her eyes and threw the dish towel on the table. "Kids! Could you keep an eye on the sauce for me?" she asked and was out the door.

"Put that back and listen!" Astrid tried to settle the argument outside.

"No, I want to watch Beauty and the Beast. We watched Robots yesterday!"

"We'll be eating in five minutes. You can watch a movie after supper. Tidy up now. What's auntie Sofie supposed to think?"

Sofia didn't listen. She kept thinking about her own situation with Tom. Did she regret coming to South Africa? Hmm... in some ways, but not because of Tom. There was definitely love between them, that's why she had come to South Africa in the first place. She turned down the heat and stirred the blood-red sauce until it stopped bubbling. It smelled delicious, just like an Italian restaurant.

Must be all the spices, Astrid had added. Sofia picked up one of the little jars on the counter. Oregano...

Could she be just 'comfortable' in her relationship with a man? To have a nice house and kids and no financial problems? No, Sofia decided, definitely not. What she wanted was real love with all the ups and downs. She wanted Tom. So why did she have to mess things up so badly?

Astrid walked into the kitchen. "There's a fundraiser at school tomorrow if you want to come. It's about Saving the Rhinos. The PTA's been planning the event for months."

"Sure I'll come," Sofia said lightly and handed over the wooden spoon.

"Are you nervous about the blood tests?"

"Yes, sure I am. Did Errol phone?"

"No, I don't think so," Astrid said and added some salt to the tomato sauce.

They chatted about Damian and Errol and what options they had to save the boy's life. The questions of romantic love and why they had come to South Africa were soon forgotten.

Jessica had to be at school at 8 o'clock on Saturday morning to help set up the stand, her class had prepared. The grade-sevens were selling hot dogs with the help of a few parents who had volunteered to take turns every couple of hours. Astrid had also volunteered.

"Did you lock up Loki and Freya at the back, Jess?" Astrid called up the stairs.

The dogs would run out the front gate and into the park if given half a chance. Or worse even, into traffic on the main road.

"Yes mom, I did," Jessica said in a bored voice and she came down.

"Did you pack the aprons?"

Jessica had dolled herself up in a fancy top and miniskirt. On special occasions, the students didn't have to wear their school uniforms and it seemed incredibly important for girls to show off their fashion sense. Six-year-old Charlie was still untouched by the need to impress the opposite sex. His interests were limited to sports and playing computer games with his two best buddies. And playing with robots, of course.

"No, I forgot. Sorry, mom. I'll get them."

"The other moms will be very upset if I forget the aprons," Astrid said. "Charlie is faster, Jessie! Quickly, run to my room, Charlie and get the red aprons. They are on the bed." The little boy took off in a flash, glad to be doing something other than watching silly girls getting ready.

"Surely, the other moms aren't perfect either." Sofia zipped up her jacket. The morning sun was only just beginning to twinkle through the bare trees.

"They like to think that they are," Astrid said and pulled a face.

A familiar melody grew louder in the street and the dogs in the neighbourhood started howling. Even the neighbour's cat sat on the wall meowing her heart out.

"Mom, why is the ice-cream truck coming around all the time? Who wants to eat ice cream in winter?"

"You and Charlie, I suppose, just now at the school..."

The ice-cream truck drove slowly past the house until the melody faded. It took longer for the howling to settle down. Charlie came running out the front door with the aprons in hand and Astrid locked up. "Okay then, everyone into the car. Off we go."

The school wasn't far away and if it wasn't for all the equipment, they had to bring, they would have walked. The streets were lined with parked cars. Proof that the neighbourhood had come out in force to party. The high turnout was probably based on a rumour that made the rounds: celebrity guests were expected to be there and pose for selfies. Someone had decorated a length of white cloth with the picture of a smiling green rhinoceros and "SAVE OUR RHINOS" above the school gate. Astrid found parking on the grounds. They took the baskets out of the boot and Charlie carried the aprons in front of them like flags of honour. Jessica's friends walked past with their parents and the girls waved at each other.

"Mom, I'm going with Ayanda and Paige to the office to get the float for our stand," Jessie announced. "See you at the stand just now."

"Don't take too long, Jessie, I need you to help me."

"Sure Mom," her daughter said and went off with her giggling friends.

"I can't believe, how big she is getting," Astrid said astonished. "She's practically a teenager."

Visitors were spoilt for choice. A variety of home-made snacks and junk-food was on offer, and there were music shows and rehearsed plays on a makeshift stage. You could have your hair spray-painted or play games on the sports field, throwing balls at tins to win a teddy bear or football. The turnout exceeded all expectations. This caused the PTA moms to walk around giddy with success, checking on their offspring, nodding importantly at other parents.

Damian will be in a school just like this one if everything goes well, Sofia thought and swallowed a tear. She felt a tap on her shoulder, and expecting Astrid, she turned around smiling. What she didn't expect, was to see Stan Makaroff's face. He was dressed in expensive shorts and a striped Oxford shirt topped with a bow tie. Behind him followed two strapping bodyguards, her friend Gugu and a photographer.

"If it isn't Lois Lane!" He laughed jovially and the photographer took a picture of him holding her hand. She withdrew it awkwardly.

"Mr. Makaroff... what... what are *you* doing here?"

"Oh well, the cause of rhino poaching is close to my heart now, of course."

"But isn't this a bit..."

Gugu looked every inch the professional PR lady in her snazzy outfit and her upswept, intertwined hairdo. She stepped forward on high heels. "Mr. Makaroff is the patron of the 'Save Our Beloved Rhinos Now!' Foundation. He will be speaking on stage in about half an hour," she explained and lowered her voice. " He's here incognito..."

"Really?" Sofia whispered back. *How can he be incognito if he is a speaker?* She thought. That Stan Makaroff was some patron saint of an organisation that wanted to save the rhinos was news to her.

"I see," Sofia found her bearings. "Well, then we have something in common, don't we, Mr. Makaroff? It's always good to welcome you at the Shangari Safari Lodge, sir. The conservation of rhinos is a worthy cause, indeed."

"Indeed, indeed, young lady... and it's Stan, please. Lovely seeing you here." He patted her arm with a fatherly gesture, then kept staring at a spot behind her. "Isn't that Richard Wackman from Gauteng Radio, Gugu?"

"Sure is, Mr. Makaroff. Let me introduce you to him."

Stan Makaroff was so eager to endear himself to the chirpy reporter from Johannesburg's most popular radio station that he forgot to say goodbye to Sofia. Gugulethu Mbatha led the way and greeted the reporter. She looked gorgeous in her patterned dress with the matching fruit-coloured blazer. Even from behind.

Astrid came to join her, holding up two yummy chocolate cupcakes with lots of dark swirly icing. "What was that all about?" She stared after the tycoon who had honoured their little neighbourhood school with his exalted presence. The bodyguards and the photographer were a dead giveaway that he had to be the rumoured celebrity.

"Not sure, actually." Sofia took one of the cupcakes. "That was Stan Makaroff, he's one of our best customers. Recognised me somehow. He's got a new foundation to save the rhinos - and he wants to give a speech later."

"I thought I recognised him from the news. Has friends in

high places. Some tax scandal or other. Stinking rich," Astrid said.

"That's about the gist of it. He usually arrives with the whole royal household. Strange to see only four people stumbling after him today. He usually books the most expensive suites at Shangari, which is great for us. Not sure what to think of him. He's a bit creepy."

"Oh well. Better he throws his money at Shangari and a foundation to save the rhinos than hunting wild animals..." Astrid wiped her mouth with a serviette.

"That's where the creepy part comes in. Maybe he's serious but he keeps bugging Tom about buying Shangari and offering tours to hunters from overseas. You missed a spot of chocolate icing on your cheek. Wait, I got it."

"Oh, you must talk. Looks like you've got a button on your nose. Eating cupcakes is a messy business."

The cousins helped each other wipe the icing off their faces with serviettes. "I'm due for my shift at the hot dog stand in about an hour. Jessie's already there, thank god. Do you feel like eating a hot dog with mustard and the works?" Astrid said.

"Let's go and see if your daughter can cook hot dogs," Sofia laughed. "Tomorrow it's back to healthier foods." This was a fundraiser and cupcakes, hot dogs and snow cones had better make friends in her tummy.

They passed an animated crowd, yelling and stomping to wild music. A kwaito group was performing on stage to some song, fired up by all that cheering. Groups of older girls in risqué clothes were falling over each other with excitement, trying to copy the band's every move.

Sofia couldn't stop thinking about Damian. How he must be lying in his hospital bed, waiting for the results, whether his biological parents were a match for the life-saving transplant or not.

They had to do their best to help him. One day he would be healthy, having fun with his friends at a fundraiser just like this one. The results of the blood test would only be in on Monday and there was no other reason they should talk. They strolled back toward the stage, balancing hot dogs dripping with mustard and ketchup that a proud Jessica had served up.

The headmistress gave a sign to cut the deafening music and managed to produce shrill noises from the microphone. This caused much booing and whistling from the audience.

"Aaaahhh!" The crowd complained. A couple of stagehands came running to adjust the volume and the dignified, grey-haired woman announced the celebrity speaker.

"There will be more music later. Right now let's give Mr.. Stan Makaroff a warm welcome." She sounded all excited. "A renowned Johannesburg businessman and champion of our cause, patron of the foundation 'Save Our Beloved Rhinos Now!'. Put your hands together for Mr.. Stan Makaroff!"

The crowd clapped and cheered.

"Today's proceeds will go to this wonderful foundation, thank you all for your support." More clapping and whistling. Gugu was probably backstage, speaking to more reporters, keeping the publicity machine rolling.

"Mr.. Makaroff will also draw the winners of our raffle at 15:30 sharp. So you better be here if you've bought a ticket. And if you haven't, you can buy one now. There's still time... it's only 10 Rand a piece. Please welcome Mr. Stan Makaroff!"

The business tycoon appeared behind the headmistress and boomed into the mike. "Good morning everyone!" Wild applause and ululating. "Good afternoon!!!"

"Is it afternoon already? Yes, it is. Look at this..." He stared at his Rolex watch in mock-horror. "Gugu, where is my hot dog for lunch?" He padded his stomach and pulled a face. Everybody laughed.

Makaroff had the crowd eating out of his hand but Sofia refused to be drawn in by his charm. She had watched him do the same thing before, wrapping people around his little finger. Somehow, she didn't quite believe in his sudden interest in wildlife conservation, especially since Tom had told her about Makaroff's wild plans to turn Shangari into an African destination for hunters. The licenses alone would bring in a fortune and Makaroff was all about money.

She had read in the paper that one of his shady business friends owned a game farm in Mpumalanga, where he bred rhinos and other big game. For the sole purpose of allowing hunters to shoot them for lots of money, license or not!

Court cases against the friend were pending but lawyers like Alwin Goldsmith surely knew how to delay the proceedings. It was near impossible to make it this rich without the right connections. And connections Makaroff had. But if he harboured similar plans for Shangari, he wouldn't get very far. No doubt, his little stint at the school was intended to divert public attention. Away from the unsavoury tax scandal, he was involved in. Everybody knew that Makaroff would emerge from the corruption case as squeaky clean as he always did. But his influence surely had its limits.

"... my greatest role model is my mother, followed closely by Nelson Mandela," Makaroff lowered his voice in reverence. "He loved children and children are the future of this country..."

The crowd was in awe. Nelson Mandela was still the hero of the people and one of the few role models, school children could look up to. Makaroff held up his hand beseechingly and the crowd fell silent. "I want to thank you all... and I mean all of you as you stand before me... in the name of our rhinos... that we shall have rhinos in Africa for generations to come. Give yourselves some applause. You are saving lives today!"

Wild applause.

Sofia Helenius, however, was unconvinced. After the attack on Barry Pienaar, he couldn't get away in his private helicopter fast enough. He'd showed not the slightest sign of concern for rhino poaching or anybody's life, then. The man must have had a change of heart since. Or maybe it was all just an act.

The emphatic speech had come to an end. Makaroff handed the microphone back to the headmistress who curtsied and nearly knelt in awe.

"Didn't I promise you a celebrity?" She addressed the

clapping audience, egging them on.

"Yeah!!!" "Yeah!!!"

Sofia rolled her eyes. That's how you created a hype! She felt like leaving, felt her dislike of the business tycoon grow. But she couldn't do that to Astrid and the children. While her cousin was starting her shift, Sofia walked over to Charlie's stand. A giggling Charlie did the honours of spray-painting her long dark hair and Sofia paid a generous donation over to the attending mothers.

"You look funny, auntie Sofie!" Charlie spluttered, then elbowed his best friend who nearly dropped the green spray bottle.

"Show some respect for your elders," Sofia scolded him in jest and got up from the camping chair. The rebuke drew even more giggles from the boys.

"They are starting the big raffle draw," Astrid said when she returned. "Let's see if we've won something with our tickets."

"Maybe we'll win the first prize. A trip to Mauritius!" Charlie said with big eyes.

"Maybe we will. After spending ten Rand for a ticket, we'd better win something!" Astrid took the eight tickets she'd bought out of her purse and held them up like poker cards.

Together, they strolled back to the stage. It was a bit warmer now so close to lunchtime and many visitors, including Sofia, had taken their jackets off.

As if on cue, the headmistress took to the stage again. Behind her, young actors who had performed in a conservation-play by the Grade Fives, were jostling bulky papier-mâché rhinos down the stairs. The headmistress pressed the button on the microphone, triggering a shrill sound, drawing cries of pain from the audience once again.

"How does this work?" The problem was resolved and two girls, carrying a plastic fishbowl filled with folded paper slips, positioned themselves next to the grey-haired lady. Gugu followed them to the middle of the stage.

"Hello everyone, my name is Gugulethu Mbatha. I work

for Mr. Makaroff," she began. "Are you ready for..."

"Did you get him a hot dog for lunch?" Someone yelled and the audience shrieked with laughter.

"But of course, I did... and a hamburger and a cupcake," Gugu played along. "He is a hungry man. Mr. Makaroff is also a *very* busy man, so I'm afraid, he had to leave for an important meeting and I'm taking over from him. I'll be drawing the winners of the raffle if that's okay with you!"

"Yeah!" The audience cheered and Charlie air-punched with excitement. His mother put her hands on his shoulders to control the boy.

"Thank you, thank you very much!" Gugu bowed and everybody clapped.

Someone handed her a list. "So, let's get started. I've got lots of great prices for you. The three winners of a golf-shirt by Grand Bank are the following numbers..." She stuck her hand into the paper salad and selected three paper slips. "Numbers 98... 114 and... 25!"

Many more prizes were handed out and when ticket number 37 was called, Astrid jumped for joy as if she had won the first prize.

Charlie was sent to the stage and came back with one of the hampers, displayed at the front. Lots of chocolates and a bottle of champagne under purple cellophane; the basket would be re-gifted, no doubt. Not much later, the fundraiser ended on a high note, after a famous local singer made an appearance. She also gave an interview in front of TV cameras.

"... yes, it is a very important cause, Amanda," she said in a honeyed voice. "If you check out my new album, you'll see that the song 'Always in my Heart' is based on the story of a rhino that..." The reporter began to look bored but the kids were ecstatic. Phone cameras flashed and the star announced that she had just donated two thousand Rand to the cause.

A murmur went through the crowd. For many, that was a lot of money.

Jessica waited all excited in the queue to have her picture

taken with the singer and they left the school later than intended. Astrid accompanied Jessica to the school office with the money box and by the time they came back, only a few cars were still parked on the school grounds.

The children sat tired and content in the back of the car, sucking on sweets, laughing and admiring the basket, their mother had so cleverly won.

*

At about the same time, not far from the school, a much more sinister scene played itself out. In the posh neighbourhood of Northcliff, an orange sun just dipped below the horizon when a yellow 4x4 vehicle zigzagged down a steep serpentine road at increasing speed past stately homes with steep driveways. Thankfully, there were not many people around, and those who were, knew to jump out of harm's way. The car missed the watchman's hut under a rocky outcrop by an inch, then veered across the road and toward the edge of the cliff. A black motorcycle manoeuvered around the yellow vehicle just in time before the careless driver somehow managed, for a brief moment, to correct its course. The car screeched back onto the road but it was going too fast and didn't seem to step on the brakes at all.

Hearing the pandemonium, the residents ran out of their homes. Was there something wrong with this driver or with the brakes? The yellow 4x4 accelerated and mowed down the low fence, between the road and the steep cliff without the slightest effort.

The flimsy fence didn't stand a chance. To everybody's horror, the car skidded over the edge and started falling.

It hit the rocky ground below with a loud metallic thud, then another and another. The car turned like a cartwheel before it came to rest on its side. The spectators high up on the hill expected to see the car go up in flames at any moment but there was no explosion. The tank must have been near empty.

Emergency services found the driver, a well-groomed woman with sun-tanned skin, heavy makeup and bottle-blonde hair, outside the vehicle. She was possibly in her late thirties, lying unconscious in the dry grass, blood trickling from her nose and mouth. The woman must have been thrown through the windshield on impact. Her hair and skimpy dress were in a sorry state and one of her legs was twisted at an unnatural angle. High heels and a handbag lay scattered around. The paramedics gave her provisional treatment, then lifted the woman onto a stretcher and began to move her up the slope. The onlookers stared in horrified fascination as she was carried past. They had witnessed accidents before but this one was particularly gruesome. One man murmured something about women drivers. Was she drunk? Was she dead?

The woman was taken to hospital, still breathing but barely hanging on. Everyone knew that the serpentine that wound its way up the Northcliff hill was dangerous - even more so when drivers were intoxicated.

The evening grew darker and colder as it progressed but many lingered, spell-bound and glad that it wasn't them who'd been in that yellow car. By the time the police arrived, stories abounded with ever new, alluring details.

"She must have had a stroke. The car went forth and back between the right and left sides of the road as if she was trying to gain control of it," the man who had moaned about women drivers, declared.

"Lucky that the petrol tank didn't explode!" One of the neighbours in a dark grey jogging suit said, gesturing excitedly. "My property is just over there and a fire could have spelled disaster for my thatched roof." He looked the archetype of an accountant and had been out on his daily after-work run.

They watched how emergency personnel struggled through dry shrubs and high grass, while others tried to clear the scene of the accident. Police had cordoned off the road and a crane was brought into position. A large hook on a long steel cable was lowered into the abyss. Inch by inch, firemen lifted the 4x4 back up the side of the steep slope. The car set down with an ugly thump and was lifted onto a truck that took it to the Northcliff police station.

"I'm sure, I saw a black BMW sedan drive away from the scene." The man, still in a suit and tie looked into the distance as if he was witnessing the scene again. "I was turning the corner, coming up from Neroli Drive when I saw it happen. The men got into their BMW and drove off. It was black and the windows were tinted. They passed me on the way down... and... oh yes, the men wore dark sunglasses."

That was rather unlikely because the accident happened just before sundown. Then the man topped even this ridiculous piece of information with another.

"I saw one of the guys jump out from the passenger side of the yellow car before the 4x4 went haywire..." he said.

"Can you recall the license plate?" The policeman asked.

"No, I can't. I think the car actually didn't have one."

At that point, nobody gave his report much weight anymore and his neighbours avoided his intent gaze. *He must be making the whole thing up*, they thought and felt embarrassed on his behalf. "Maybe he should go easy on the liquor," somebody mumbled.

"Was she - you know - the driver... was she under the influence?" A woman in a silk dress and fine Melton wool coat asked. "Or on drugs, perhaps? She could have killed somebody. These young executives nowadays. They're under way too much pressure."

She took care not to step too close to the edge of the cliff as she peered down, holding onto her gold earrings to keep them from falling down. Her new boyfriend would be picking her up on the Lower Ridge Road for a night out at Montecasino.

Since the road was cordoned off, she teetered down the steep road on foot and climbed into her boyfriend's waiting car. Hopefully, by the time she got back, the scene would be cleared. Or maybe she should just sleep over at her boyfriend's house for the first time. A plan was forming in her head and the accident scene was soon forgotten.

A policeman asked around for witnesses, trying to find out more about the injured woman. "Do you know the driver?

Does she live around here?"

All the witnesses who had come forward, denied knowing her. The make of the crashed yellow 4x4 was common enough in the area but nobody could recall ever having seen the blonde driver before.

"Well, she must have had a reason to come here. Maybe she was visiting somebody or looking at property," the accountant said. "There's a new development going up on the hill. Maybe that's where she came from." He was shivering in the wintry air and all he wanted now, was to go home to a warm TV dinner and his three poodles.

"If you remember anything important or hear of anything that could help us, please give us a call." The policeman handed out business cards.

Lorraine Pienaar hadn't felt the impact of the crash. She couldn't remember, why she had been in her car as it went careening down the steep road. As she lay on the stretcher in the ambulance, she vaguely noticed streetlights moving by, vaguely heard the siren softly blaring, before losing consciousness again. What she was doing in Northcliff was at the far back of her mind.

She had been on her way to meet Wendy Fowler-Morris, an investigative journalist with one of the larger newspapers. They'd had an appointment at 18:30 at Miss Fowler-Morris' flat in Northcliff, right on top of the ridge. *What a beautiful place to live in*, Lorraine had thought as she left the noise and traffic of the city behind.

She had parked her car outside the flat building by a large flowering bush and, for a few moments, enjoyed the flaming sunset across the road. She could see the city below, the tiny cars and people, the blinking lights. Lorraine had turned around with a deep sigh when somebody grabbed her by the arm. Dear god, a mugging, shot through her mind. Then there was a prick in her back and things became fuzzy. Somebody picked her up and carried her.

Lorraine began to dream of happier times with her husband Barry. How they had gone for long hikes and milked a cow together at a farm while enjoying their honeymoon. She remembered how he had picked her up in her wedding dress and carried her over the threshold.

Barry was quite the catch, her mother had always said. She'd been proud of her eldest daughter for becoming a respectable, married woman at such a young age. Lorraine suspected her sister Charmaine of jealousy but she was too happy and excited to care about things like that.

She remembered only the good things and the times before Stanislav had entered her life and turned everything upside down with his promises of a glamorous life in the city. She wanted to meet somebody on top of a steep hill but who was it? Maybe it wasn't that important.

Lorraine Pienaar came to, just long enough to realise that she was back in her car, behind the steering wheel but not driving. Unable to drive because she was too sleepy for that.

She couldn't move a muscle, that's how tired she was.

A nice man with sunglasses had put her in the driver's seat and the car started rolling. That was nice of him to help her. It must have been daytime and rather sunny, why else would he wear sunglasses? Where was the nice man now?

Maybe, he wanted to take her somewhere nice, like back then when Barry had taken her to the beach in Hermanus and they went whale-watching on the viewing platform. How nice that would be, to be back in Hermanus.

Street lights were flashing overhead one by one. She lay on a stretcher and wondered why. Of course, it was time to sleep!

"Stay with us, madam, stay with us..."

Lorraine had regained consciousness for a brief moment, just in time to avoid a rock wall, her foot had somehow slid onto the brake, then things had gone wobbly again. She was thrown forward, then looked up from the ground into the face of another nice young man.

She tried to smile at him, wanted to tell him to look at her back. The prick from the injection under her shoulder blade was bothering her but she couldn't get a word out and had fallen asleep again almost instantly. Forgetting the pain in her leg and back. Ah, to sleep...

While Lorraine Pienaar was prepped for surgery, a black BMW sped along the M1 highway toward the shining lights of Sandton City.

Two men sat impassively next to each other. There was no need for speaking. They knew their job and had completed their task, had successfully carried out what they had come to do. That's all there was to it.

A half-empty syringe, tainted with Rohypnol, was tossed onto the smooth, tarred highway with only a sad moon for a witness. The heavy tyres of an oncoming truck crushed the syringe without the slightest effort and propelled it into the ditch. Like a needle in a haystack, it would never be discovered, never be associated with the accident in Northcliff.

The tinted window of the BMW slid up noiselessly and the stark silence inside the car returned. The streetlights overhead flashed by, one by one. It was never easy - afterwards - but they had done their job and would speak again only to give their report to the client.

The client who had given them money upfront in cash, would pay the balance as all the other times before. The client was good for it. That's all they needed to know. Compassion was not part of their job description. Neither was questioning, why the mark had been targeted. The woman's identity was none of their business.

What was their business was to keep the client happy.

A ring-bound map book lay open on the back seat. It was open on the page that showed the hill in the Northcliff section, they had been directed to.

They had gone early, had lain in wait.

Two pairs of sunglasses in the glove compartment looked innocent enough to the ignorant eye. So would the map book. Easy does it, was their motto and it paid off. A printed map could be removed from the car and closed again and their destination that evening became virtually untraceable. Far better than using the inbuilt GPS system or cellphones.

These details, one learnt with experience. And experience they had. They needed experience to carry out their job, were the best hitmen money could buy.

It was not always as easy as it had been tonight. Sometimes, they were in danger of being hurt or even killed.

Then the price went up.

The two men in the black car knew their craft and, as usual, their client didn't mind one bit the high price they demanded for their exclusive service.

CHAPTER 5

"So, you're enjoying the quiet life on the farm, then?" Errol asked, trying to sound interested without being snarky. They had never really discussed her current rustic life at Shangari.

"Well it's not so much of a farm as a safari park with a lodge. There are lots of wild animals. And then there's the mind-blowing landscape and fresh air," she said. "... and it's not exactly quiet at the lodge right now. Lots of tourists come on holiday from the northern hemisphere. It's interesting to always meet new people but keeping the lodge and land in ship-shape is no piece of cake, I can tell you. There are also the workers and staff at the lodge... but it's rewarding."

It was Monday morning and Astrid had dropped Sofia off at the seafood restaurant at Brightwater Commons. Sofia expected a call from Suzanne Daniel's GP and she was grateful that she didn't have to wait on her own.

There were only a few people around and the atmosphere was peaceful. Errol was supposed to attend some presentation or other but had decided to bunk. Tonight, the conference was going to wrap up in style at the ball room of the Convention Centre. What Errol would do then, Sofia didn't know. Probably go back to his DJ-lifestyle in Bloemfontein.

"What's the place called again?" Errol asked.

"Shangari." She was on her guard; not prepared to discuss any deeper issues with him, especially not her relationship with Tom. And especially not when it didn't go so well with Tom right now.

"Are you going to invite me there some time?" Errol

winked at her.

"Why? All you have to do is book a holiday and we can have a chat, while you're there. If I invite you, Tom's going to think..." Sofia played with her bracelet.

"What, that we are still involved?"

"Well you know, it simply wouldn't be appropriate." Why was he so insistent? She had almost forgotten how controlling Errol could be. He had been controlling during the ten days of their brief involvement.

"Why, what's wrong with that, you aren't married yet, are you?" He mocked her.

"No Errol, but that doesn't mean..." Sofia jumped. She hadn't seen the waitress standing right next to her.

"Hi folks, my name is Mandisa and I'm your waitress for today. Are you ready to order?" They ordered sushi from the menu, although it wasn't quite lunchtime yet.

"Do you remember how I composed a poem for you?" Errol grinned. "I was all lost in thought and bumped my car into a Golf. Damn thing had abruptly stopped in front of me... wanted to turn into some driveway or something and forgot to indicate."

Sofia couldn't help but laugh. "You bashed your forehead into the windscreen of your red beetle. That must have hurt. The windscreen was all cracked but you didn't have a scratch on you." Sofia stopped laughing. Their meeting began to feel more like a date and she didn't like it. Her phone played the familiar theme from 'Out of Africa'. Sofia held her breath for a moment. Would she get good news from Cape Town?

"I'm sorry, but neither of you are a match for a liver transplant." Sofia heard the GP on the other end say, and didn't comprehend what she was hearing. He read from some notes, an explanation about subgroups and enzymes.

"Oh okay, thank you." She put the phone back on the table.

"They say, we are not a match," she said simply and held back her tears.

Errol stared at her. "We aren't? Not even one of us?"

"But why not? How is that possible?" Sofia stammered.

"We are Damian's biological parents, are we not?"

"Are you sure about that?" Errol winked at her playfully.

Sofia felt flustered. "That's not the time to make dumb jokes! Do you think we would be sitting here if you weren't the father?"

"Sorry."

They stared at their drinks and Sofia's phone rang again. It was Suzanne Daniels. "Apparently, there are no guarantees. Parents are not necessarily a match. Don't you two have other relatives that could be tested?"

The voice on the other end of the line was less sophisticated than Sofia had expected. Sofia knew that Suzanne was white and a lecturer at a college. Her husband Drew was an accountant and what you would call 'Cape-Coloured'. He had a good job with the Western Cape Department of Education, and Mrs. Daniels had worked until Damian came along. She'd only recently started to work again. Theirs was a good, solid marriage or so she had been told by the social worker who'd handled the adoption at the time.

It was something she hadn't been able to offer her child. What Sofia had, was a non-existing relationship with the father and a long-distance relationship with her boyfriend Tom. Not ideal to bring a baby into that kind of scenario.

"I don't know about... about that... I only have a cousin here in Johannesburg. Yes, I could also ask him... He should have family in the Cape." The image of a little boy in his hospital bed flashed past Sofia's inner eye.

"Oh please do, we are running out of time," the woman begged in a plaintive voice.

"The chances are probably slim but I will try."

"You don't know his family?" That was a strange question.

"We didn't know each other very well when... when..."

"Look, I don't want to pry but I'm desperate, we're running out of time!"

"Yes, of course. I'll do what I can. I'll let you know." She stared at Errol who in turn stared at the large TV screen above the restaurant entrance.

They sat outside in the roofed-in area, next to a fishpond. The weather was glorious: 20°C and sunny. And that's what they called winter! Sofia took her cardigan off and hung it over the back of the chair. Shangari must be even warmer today. It was always warmer up north. Yesterday, Tom had phoned her.

'Hi Tom,' she'd said a little too brightly. "How are you?"

'What's wrong?' He'd asked immediately.

'Why do you think something's wrong?'

'I know you.'

Of course, he did. She loved him for that. That she didn't have to explain everything all the time. He could always tell. Right now, she desperately wished, she could just tell him the truth - but on the phone? No, not yet.

'It's Astrid,' she lied and hated herself for it. 'I'm taking her to the clinic to have some blood tests done.'

'That sounds serious.'

'No, it isn't. Astrid explained it to me but I can't really remember what it's for.' She'd launched into a description of the fundraiser on Saturday and that they'd had a picnic at the Emmarentia Dam Sunday morning.

'Mhmm.'

'I'll go and buy supplies today. Where do you think I can find that spiral cutter, you know the one Karen wants for vegetable spaghetti...'

'You sound funny.'

'What?'

'I don't know what it is but you have a funny tone in your voice,' Tom sighed.

'Probably just the phone line.'

'The line is fine.' He didn't give her an inch.

'Oh Tom, let's talk when I'm back home. I have to go now.'

She knew she would have to tell him about Damian, about Errol Botes and that whole short-lived, ill-considered episode when Tom had been away in England. That dreadful, lonely time in Cape Town. About the charming DJ who had been attentive for an awkward ten days after that drunken night.

She would regret this time for the rest of her life.

How could she not have told Tom sooner?

'Okay, Barry's here anyway,' Tom said. 'Jethro needs his injections.' The young cheetah was developing well even though having only three legs was an obvious handicap.

'Everything else okay?' She'd wanted to know.

'It was busy on the weekend. Well, nothing new there. Oh yes... I miss you!' He'd blurted out.

'I miss you, too Tom,' she'd said and felt tearing up. She didn't want to get all mushy now or she'd break down and talk. 'Sorry about the fight we had. It was stupid.'

'Yes, it was. Can't even remember what it was about.'

'About Barry and stuff,' Sofia reminded him. These things couldn't be discussed over the phone, either.

'Ah yes. Sorry if he gets on your nerves. Will have a word with him.'

'I must go and get some sleep.'

'We'll communicate better from now on, agreed?' Tom had offered.

'Agreed. I've really got to go now. Speak to you tomorrow.'

Sofia had blown her nose and wiped away the tears. She didn't like hanging up, feeling so close to Tom again. She loved the soothing timbre in his voice and so many other things. Why couldn't she just teleport herself to Shangari?

But that was yesterday and today was now.

Sofia found herself suddenly back in Johannesburg, at the restaurant where sushi was being served. She felt her bracelet and looked up at the waitress.

"Thank you," Errol said to the friendly woman and picked up a California roll with wooden chop sticks.

"Will you?" Sofia asked.

"Will I what?" He air-punched and kept watching the soundless soccer game, as he made short shrift of his sushi.

"Will you call your family in Cape Town and ask them to get tested?"

"Sure, already on it," Errol said and chewed but he didn't dial any numbers. "Let's quickly eat, then we can go. I'll phone them from the hotel later. Can't stay away for too long anyway. The afternoon session starts at 14:00 and I can't miss that." She noticed that he didn't seem to be taking this whole thing seriously enough. But that was impossible, wasn't it?

"Okay, I'll give you Suzanne Daniels' phone number, then you can call her directly. I'm sure, she'll appreciate that."

"Don't look at me like that.. I'll phone, I promise," Errol said.

The waitress approached. "Are you happy with everything?"

"Emm yes, thank you." Sofia smiled back at the eager young woman who went on to ask patrons two tables down the same question.

Sofia had barely touched her sushi when they decided to leave. Errol asked for a doggy bag and paid the bill. They walked over to look at the Koi in the pond just outside the restaurant. Watching the fish come up from under the small wooden bridge, popping their heads through the water, opening their mouths... watching them had something calming about it.

"Maybe you should join me at the function tonight. It's the 'Journalist of the Year' award. Not that I have a snowball's chance in hell to win anything in my category but it's probably great fun," Errol said.

Sofia threw a morsel of bread to the fish, from the slice she'd saved from the breadbasket on the table.

"There will be food and booze, and it's all free..."

"I don't know. I don't feel like partying... and I don't have anything to wear."

"Come on now, it'll distract you a bit. I'm sure, Astrid has a pretty frock in her wardrobe, you can borrow." Had he said frock? That sounded so old-fashioned.

"Well, I'll think about it." Sofia walked away from him.

"So, is that a yes?" He could be so charmingly insistent. "Let me handle the family in Cape Town and the tests and you go do your thing now, buying stuff for your farm and what not. Should I pick you up at about 7 o'clock?"

"I'll think about it, Errol. It's all a bit much to deal with right now." She threw the last of the bread to the fishes.

"Alright then. Can I give you at least a lift back?" Errol pouted playfully.

"Sure."

They didn't speak in the car, until Errol parked in front of the house in Linden but Sofia had noticed him looking at her furtively a few times.

"So, will you give me a call about tonight for sure?" He wanted to know.

"I can't promise anything. Depends on how I feel about it later," Sofia said slightly irritated.

"Come on, Sofia, what's the harm? I'll be out of your hair soon enough anyway." Errol seemed really keen for her to come.

"I wish," she said and grabbed her handbag. "Let me think about it, alright?"

Errol got out first to open the car's passenger door for her. Astrid's Labradors were in the front garden and sprang up against the fence, barking relentlessly at the strange rental car.

"Okay, calm down, calm down," Sofia said to the alert dogs, making sure that they wouldn't run out of the small side gate. Errol quickly jumped back into the driver seat and waited until Sofia had locked the gate behind her. He then gestured 'phone me' and drove off.

*

"Hey Tom," Barry Pienaar said and walked down the steps to the low-lying boma next to the lodge building. "Can I speak to you for a sec?"

"Hello Barry. Everyone - that's my friend Barry Pienaar, our local vet. Barry, this is Gwendolyn and Paul, Robert and Edith. They are here on holiday from the UK." Tom introduced his friend to the tourists who sat in comfortable wooden armchairs around the fireplace.

They were having drinks, relaxing after the afternoon safari drive, and discussed the incredible colours of the sunset and how the sounds of the bush seemed to grow softer late in the day. Brutus sat up when he heard the vet approaching, then went to lie down again with a deep groan when he recognised the man.

"Pleased to meet you all," Barry said in greeting and nodded at Tom. "Can I speak to you for a moment? It won't take long, I promise."

"Excuse me please," Tom apologised to his guests. "I'll be right back."

The two men walked along the gravelled path to the barn and sat down on a bench not far from the spot, where Barry had been attacked a few months earlier. Brutus trotted after the men and plunked himself onto the ground with a heartfelt yawn.

"You alright?" Tom asked his old friend.

"Sure, I'm okay. No sweat. Just needed to talk to you about something." Barry wriggled around, so Tom got the impression that he needed to get something off his chest. "Is it about Lorraine?"

"Lorraine? No why?" Barry seemed genuinely surprised.

"Why indeed. Last time you told me how much you missed her and that your drinking may have driven her away."

"Yes..." Barry Pienaar exhaled on a long note. "Sorry I offloaded onto you. There are many things I shouldn't have done but it's too late now. Can't be undone, can they? How are things around here? Cornelius' family settled down?"

"As much as can be expected. Francina took the kids home somewhere in the Northern Cape. At least for a while," Tom Rutgers said.

"Why did she do that? Isn't it better for her to be here?" Barry asked.

"That's what she wanted, Barry. I'm sure she knows that she can come back anytime."

"How old is Frans now - fourteen? Maybe, he could train as a ranger and bring some money in," Barry suggested. "I could take him off her hands."

"He's fifteen. Did you come to talk about Francina and her kids? Or was there something else?" Tom said.

"No, no, of course not. There's something else..."

"What is it? Something wrong with you?" Tom probed. "Come on, shoot."

"Don't tempt me, man. No, I wouldn't call it that. It's

something... you should know about."

"What? Come on, out with it." Tom had no idea what Barry was talking about. He leaned back on the bench and stretched out his legs. "Do I have to beat it out of you or what?" He laughed and punched Barry's thigh. "Stop wriggling, already. What are you so nervous about?" He heard laughter at the boma. At least the tourist were having a good time. Brutus the dog sat up and pricked his ears.

"Well, where do I start? Okay, I'll jump right in. Do you remember our cottage, where Lorraine had the beauty salon?"

Tom nodded and patted Brutus' head. "Sure, what about it?"

"Yes well, you know we cleaned the place out, since she doesn't care about the hair and beauty stuff anymore. I'm turning it into an extra surgery for..."

"I know all of that. Did you find a dead body under the floorboards or what?" Tom laughed uneasily.

"Close, but no. Well, I found something alright but it's - letters," Barry said and took a plastic folder out of his satchel.

"Really - letters? You're making such a fuss because of some old letters?"

"Not any old letters, Tom. They are your - wait - great-grandmother's letters, from the time she was a young girl."

"What? Which great-grandmother? The one from Belgium?"

"No, Hendrina Botha."

"Man, that's a long time ago. What was my great-grandmother Hendrina doing in your house?"

"She lived on the farm for a while. The paper is yellow and the writing's smudged here and there but you can still read it. Hendrina had a neat handwriting, a bit child-like perhaps. She was still young."

Tom sat up straight and Brutus did the same. "Okay, that's kind of interesting but hardly an emergency. Letters addressed to whom anyway?"

"Well, I think you should read them yourself," Barry said quickly. "In your own time. Let's just say, you may not have known some stuff about Hendrina's life that you should know about. She talks about it in her letters."

"So you've read them?"

"Well yeah sort of. Otherwise, I wouldn't know what they are about."

"Okay then, I'll read the letters if it makes you happy. Just leave them with me. Was that all?"

"What do you mean?"

"What do I mean? Can I go back to my guests now or do you want to talk about something else?" Tom took the folder with the yellowed pages carefully out of Barry's hand. "I'll put them on the dining room table and read them as soon as I get a chance."

"Sure you can do that - and you can go back to your guests. Just promise, you'll read them asap."

"Okay, I still don't know why but I'll promise," Tom said.

Barry got up and walked to his bakkie. "Alright, old man, I see you soon. Tell me what you think about the letters. Sofia okay?"

"Yes, she's fine. She's spending some time with her cousin in Joburg. We should drink less when she's here. I think our bro-mance is getting to her."

"Ay, women!" Barry Pienaar shook his head. "Sure thing, Tom. I'm okay with all that stuff now... you know... what Lorraine did to me."

"I know and I'm glad," Tom said.

As Barry Pienaar walked past Jethro's enclosure, the three-legged cheetah growled in recognition. "Hey Jethro my boy, am I forgiven for the injections?" Jethro growled some more and hissed at the vet. "There's a good boy."

Tom watched him drive off and wondered what his visit had been all about. Some old letters! But because Barry beat around the bush like that, Tom's curiosity had been piqued. Later that night, he sat down at the dark dining room table and looked over the brittle pages.

They didn't seem to be letters at all but rather a kind of diary, Hendrina had addressed to God. The first few pages were written in Afrikaans, carried on in English, then Afrikaans again. The cottage on the farm had been a dairy. Some of the maid servants worked there, making cheese and butter and the milk had been kept cool.

All Tom knew was that his great-grandmother Hendrina had been named in honour of her father Hendrik van Oosthuizen, one of the first farmers in the Renosterspruit area. She had married Pieter Rutgers and moved to Shangari as a teenager. The family hadn't been that fond of her for some stupid reason, thinking that she wasn't good enough. Not an unusual scenario. Most families around here were related and there was always some bone to pick.

Jacobus Marthinus Pienaar, Barry's father, had married a Clara van Oosthuizen in the 1960s. Barry and Marius were their sons. Marius had died in an accident as a young man. So technically the Rutgers and Pienaars were related at some level. Family history had never been particularly interesting to Tom, so he was in for a surprise when he began to read. The first entry was rather formal.

Renosterspruit, 10th April 1887

"My name is Hendrina, named after my father Hendrik van Oosthuizen. I am 16 years old. They say, I'm pretty. I'm not allowed to go to school, so father taught me how to write. I'm writing down my story and hope that nobody will ever read these letters. I've caused enough trouble as it is, by just being here. My mother would give me a hiding if she found out. But my heart feels lighter if I share this with you, God, so I found a good hiding place in the dairy. I go there to get the cream for the kitchen and to churn butter and I like to write when nobody else is around in the evenings. That's when I like to write. Then they are all helping in the main house and leave me alone. Mevrou is sickly again and now with the new baby, she won't hit me anymore, I hope.

My mother doesn't like it that I write. She works in the household of Mineer and Mevrou van Oosthuizen and wants me to do the same. The old Mineer is my father. My mom's name is Sina Botha and she was pretty too when she was younger. She doesn't know who her Daddy was, which is odd. I'm sure you know who he is, God. Now Mama has a thick waist but it doesn't matter, she says. Finished with all that business. She means men. I'm not finished. I like Pieter Rutgers. He spoke to me four days ago when I went to fetch firewood from the pile behind the barn. Old Thabelo saw us and said to stay away from the young master, no good will ever come of it. Pieter has that glow in his eyes. That's not good for girls like me. Girls like me! Girls who are bored with all that housework and want to go walk in the fields, pick flowers and sing songs once in a while? I really like Pieter. I saw him again in church today but he didn't even look at me because his parents and the whole family were there. He can't just look at a coloured girl like me in front of everyone, especially not in church..."

Tom took a deep breath and continued to read.

Renosterspruit, 24 August 1887

Thabelo must have told my mother. She clapped me soundly and said to stay away from master Pieter. Nothing good will come of it. Look at you, she said that's what will come of it, we don't need to feed another mouth and no husband. Yes, but I do like Pieter. There's this twinkle in his eyes when he speaks to me and his lips are so soft when he kisses. Can I have a child from kissing? Oh, why is this so difficult? The other girls turn their noses up at me because I'm stupid, they say. They have boyfriends and I don't. I look down and don't say anything back. Mama says, not to be haughty. But they cannot write and I can, and Pieter likes me. Mbuyelo is especially mean. She likes Eddie and she thinks that Eddie likes me. What do I care about him?...

The last few lines on the page were too smudged to read. The letter went on about the other girls and what they thought of Hendrina, the light-skinned Lekgoa.

Shangari, 13 October 1888

What's a scandal? Pieter's mother died in the winter of the ague and after the mourning period, his father had a stroke. Now Pieter is alone and he asked me to marry him. He needs a woman on the farm and he loves me. That's what he says. Yes, me! He really did. I am strong and know how to work and have a nice disposition. I know it's not done normally, that I'm not what they want for a wife, although my skin is almost white. Mbuyelo says, I'm a loose girl and Pieter only wants me because there are not many marriageable women around. But why should my father say no? I told Pieter to speak to my mother and to Mineer Oosthuizen but not to Mevrou Oosthuizen. She is not nice and would surely hurt me again. Pieter said he made up his mind and doesn't care what anyone says. I am not with child, although we've been kissing a lot. Don't smite me, Lord, but I like him so much. Now, people say, I am causing a scandal. I know I'm coloured but I'm really very light and my hair is straight. People will calm down, Pieter says...

The page was damaged by water and termites but Tom could make out the date on the next letter: 17 November 1888.

... wedding flowers. Pieter is happy, he says, we don't need much, especially no double-faced so-and-sos. Just need to work hard and keep our heads down and pray to God and everything will be fine... Mama comes to visit

sometimes but she can't afford to bring presents. Mevrou is not very nice to her, now that she's pregnant again. That woman always seems to be pregnant. It's against God's will, Mevrou says and means me and Pieter. Is that true, God? In church, we still have to sit apart. I don't know if you like that very much but the pastor had to marry us on the farm in Shangari and Pieter says that's just as good as a church wedding. I hope that's true, Lord, so we don't live in sin...

The last letter was short and rather damaged and crumbled in his hands, as he picked it up.

Shangari, 9 February 1889

We never ever went to a dance or anything but Pieter isn't much for socialising anyway and he dances with me at home, twirls me around until we both laugh. We can still have fun. He bought a gramophone and had it shipped from England. Nobody else has a gramophone and the other women are so jealous. But they are jealous anyway because we are happy. I don't have any friends. My father comes to visit secretly now and again, so Mevrou won't give him a hard time. He is still not very happy about the marriage but I know he'll come around more when he holds his first grandchild in his arms..."

Tom put the letter back on the pile. He had to think hard to remember, what his father had told him about his heritage when he was younger. His great-grandmother Hendrina Botha had been a local girl who'd died in childbirth during the First World War. She had been a beauty of note and his great-grandfather had grieved for her and never remarried. Tom knew that Hendrina had borne her husband five children but only two of them had survived infancy. Ethel and her younger brother Jacob. Jacob Rutgers had married a nice girl from Pretoria who had come to work as a teacher at the school in Rutgersdrift in 1912. She was Tom Rutger's grandmother Elisabeth. Charles, Tom's father was the eldest son and it was he who'd inherited the farm. His brother Theo Rutgers had gone to Johannesburg to make his luck but the family had lost touch with him.

Nobody had ever thought to mention that his great-grandmother Hendrina had been coloured. He wondered, how the family had kept it a secret for so long. Quite a remarkable fact, considering the stance of the white community with regard to skin colour at the time. Tom couldn't begin to imagine what that must have been like in those days. His heart went out to the young, spirited woman without friends who had still found happiness with his great-grandfather, despite all the hardship on the farm and the restrictive community she'd lived in.

Tom Rutgers sat there and looked at his tanned hands, then his arms. The fine hairs were bleached almost white from the sun. People often said that there was something Mediterranean about him and he'd laughed it off as nonsense. He stared at the yellowed, brittle pages and gently closed the plastic folder.

Tom got up and went over to the dresser, opened the bottom drawer and took out a tattered box with photographs. Old family photographs, he never ever looked at. There had to be a picture of Hendrina Rutgers in there somewhere!

How he wished that Sofia could share this moment with him but Sofia was in Johannesburg and he had to do this on his own. How would she react if she knew his family secret?

Would she mind if she found out that he had a coloured great-grandmother? Probably not.

Most people didn't seem to know or remember and Barry would keep quiet about it. Some people in the country were still dead-set against such things and he wouldn't want to have a discussion with them but Sofia was open-minded. One of the things he so loved about her.

He wasn't even sure, what to think of it himself, especially when the issue was treated with such secrecy.

Tom laid the sepia-coloured photographs out on the table

one by one and studied them intensely. Some of the faces had faded over time or were blurry. Most of them looked at him with a stern expression. Unsmiling.

The photographers of old had taken their sweet time with those big, clumsy cameras, while their subjects sat or stood stiffly, waiting for the flashlight. By the time the flash lit up, it was too late for them to smile. *How things have changed,* Tom thought. Nowadays, you could take selfies with your phone at any given moment.

He picked up one of the photographs. It showed a young Pieter Rutgers with his parents. Pieter Rutgers was his great-grandfather and Hendrina's husband. The one who had balked at the societal rules of their time. Tom turned the picture around and read 'Christmas 1884'.

His grandmother Elisabeth and her two sons were on another photo. His father looked rather serious, which belied his easy-going nature. Grandmother Elisabeth had been kind and liked to bounce Tom on her knee when he was little.

She'd made the best milk tart for her grandchildren. Tom missed having family around. Ironic that he should be the marrying type and not have a family of his own yet. He had no recollection of his grandfather; just knew that he had died in his fifties. There were many more photos and most of them had writing on the back but not what he was looking for.

Tom studied the faces. In one of the pictures, a beautiful brunette woman with full lips was holding a bunch of flowers. Her face was half-hidden behind some big hats in the front row. She was the only one who smiled. No, she beamed into the camera. This had to be Hendrina Rutgers, his great-grandmother. She was prettier than any of the other women in the photographs. The young girl, who had written those intriguing letters, addressed them to none other than God, detailing her bitter-sweet experiences.

She must have hidden those letters under the termite-eaten floorboards of the Pienaar farm dairy because nobody would have understood why she wanted to write at all, back then.

CHAPTER 6

Sofia walked up the garden path, feeling despondent. She barely noticed the beautiful flowers left and right of her. Oh, it just couldn't be true! Poor Damian.

Astrid opened the front door. "Loki, Freya, stop barking! What's all this noise? Come here... COME HERE! Oh hey, Sofia." She closed the door and put the dogs in the kitchen, then she walked ahead of Sofia into the lounge.

"You alright?" She asked when she noticed her cousin's sad expression.

"They phoned from Cape Town," Sofia blurted out, "with the results of the blood tests. We were at the restaurant at Brightwater when they phoned."

"And?"

"We are not a match, Astrid. Can you believe it? Suzanne Daniels wants me to get other family members tested." She took a deep breath and wiped a tear away. "But there's no time. What if it's too late for Damian?"

She sat down on the couch and took out a tissue. There were cookies and tea on the table. Astrid had obviously enjoyed some quiet time on her own.

"Oh dear. That's terrible news." Astrid poured some tea for Sofia. "Listen, Sofie, you cannot get so involved, for your own sake. You are legally not his mother anymore. Aren't his adoptive parents supposed to take care of all that? You're not a magician."

"I don't know what to do. Damian is so little, so ill. What if he dies?"

"You mustn't even think like that," Astrid scolded her. "We'll go past the clinic and have me tested. The kids are still at school. Forget about the tea, let's go right now." Sofia nodded and put the teacup down. She got up and hugged her cousin. "Thank you." She put her shoes back on and buttoned up her cardigan.

"Ready to go?" Her cousin jingled the keys in her hand. How did Astrid always manage to be ready before her?

The procedure at the clinic was over in no time.

"Thank you, Astrid, I really appreciate this!" Sofia said when they drove off the clinic's parking lot. "You are right, you know."

Astrid looked at her with knitted eyebrows. "Right about what?" She asked and turned into the road.

"That I'm not his mother anymore and I shouldn't get quite so emotional. How can I help Damian if I'm falling apart?"

"I hope they can find a donor as soon as possible. He is just a little boy who needs help. My kids are still too young but I could ask Grant when he's back soon..." Astrid offered.

"I don't think his blood group would even match Damian's," Sofia said.

"I guess not but we could still try."

"Damian's A, like me and you."

"Grant's blood group is O."

"Then it doesn't make sense to involve him. In any case, you said you don't know when he'll be back. It would be too late by then anyway."

"Maybe one of my friends..."

"That's unlikely if they are not blood relatives, even distant ones, the chances are slim." Sofia's heart sank as she said this.

"But you and Errol are not a match either. That's strange," Astrid said and stopped at a traffic light.

"I know." Sofia hadn't imagined things being so difficult. Either Errol or she should have been a match. That's all she wanted. She wished it could have been her, being able to do at least that for the son she had given away. At times like these, she was grateful that they had taken Damian before she could look at him, hold him in her arms... the memory alone would have made this unbearable.

"Should we go to Brightwater Commons?" Astrid asked. "It's around the corner. Didn't you say, you still need to buy stuff for the lodge?"

"Yes, you're right. I could use a shopping buddy."

"No problem, we could go to the flea market."

"I need to find all this stuff, Tom wants for the reception area at the lodge... and some bathroom accessories. Here's the list." She took a piece of paper out of her handbag and pushed it into Astrid's hand.

"Soap dishes made of metal and towel rings? I know a better place where we can get that. Most of the items we'll find at the hardware discount store. The Chinese supermarket should have the saffron and fish-sauce. My goodness, what does your chef need all that for?" Astrid handed her the list.

"Oh, I don't know. I'm just carrying out orders," Sofia smiled. "Totally forgot to make a plan but I wasn't thinking clearly, I guess."

"You had a lot on your mind," Astrid said. "Don't worry, we'll get it all done. Wait, I have to fetch the kids from school at one." She looked at the dashboard clock. "It's after eleven. What did you organise with your ex?" Ex sounded so brutal.

"Nothing much. It's the last day of this conference and Errol wants to take a plane back to Bloemfontein sometime this week. He asked me to go with him to a formal function at the Convention Centre tonight. I'm sitting with this problem and he's in the wind tomorrow. Same old, same old. As if I feel like going out tonight."

"And why not? It would probably do you good to do something else than brood. Did you phone Gugu at all after the fundraiser?"

"No, not yet," Sofia had clean forgotten to call her best friend. And Gugu was the one, she really wanted to speak to.

"Hmm. Okay, why don't you try to get hold of this Errol-guy and tell him, you're going to the function with him? Then you phone Gugu and make arrangements to meet her as well. You can't go back and not see her."

Sofia thought for a moment. "That's a good plan," she

decided. "What would I do without you, cousin? But it's awkward to sit next to Errol in the car. I'll drive myself."

"Yip, that's what I would do." Astrid smiled. "And Errol can ask around in his family if somebody else is blood group A. He can do his bit."

"Yes, he can." Sofia took out her phone and dialled Errol's number.

*

They arrived back at the house, laden with bags and boxes and two sullen children in school uniforms trudging behind them into the house. They were tired, having had afternoon sport and all they wanted was to watch TV.

"I'm just going to warm up supper," Astrid said and herded the children upstairs to their room.

"Do you have a dress I could borrow?" Sofia asked her later.

"Sure, you can take your pick."

Astrid possessed an astronomical number of 'frocks'. In fact, an entire wardrobe in the passage upstairs was dedicated to evening robes and festive tops and trousers. And shoes, of course. She led the way and opened the wardrobe.

"What takes your fancy?" Astrid took out a few dresses and laid them unto the sofa next to the mirror in the passage.

"I'm not sure." Sofia touched a slinky, green, sequin-dress and decided that it wasn't for her. "That's probably too much."

"Didn't you ask Errol about the dress code?" Astrid asked.

"No, I didn't think about it. All he told me was to wear something pretty. It can't be that difficult, though..." Astrid was already googling the event. "... Sandton Convention Centre... Journalist of the Year Award... cocktail function... there you are. You need a cocktail dress."

"Okay then." Sofia sifted through the clothes again. Charlie scooted past them, trying to catch some whirring flying-toy. "Charles Edgar Sven Rankin, no running in the house!" His mother reprimanded him. The boy sighed but obeyed. "Sorry, mom. Dresses are sooo boring."

"Yes well, you don't have to wear any. But auntie Sofie does."

"Okay..." Charlie trotted off to his room and the whirring

started again.

Astrid chose three dresses, one more beautiful than the other, and put them on the sofa. "There you are. Choose one. I'll bring you the matching shoes."

"Wow, when do you have the time to wear them?" Sofia asked in wide-eyed wonder.

"Oh, we don't go out as much anymore with the children being around but once in a while, we're invited and then they come in handy."

Sofia chose a cream-coloured, floaty number that went well with her skin tone. "Don't you think it's awkward that I'm going out with Errol tonight?" She asked and held the dress up to study herself in the mirror. "He is my ex, after all."

"I thought we went through that already..." Astrid sighed.

"Yes, I know... but I feel so guilty." Sofia put the cream-coloured dress back on the sofa. "There's nothing to celebrate, yet."

"Didn't you say, you spoke to Errol about his family in Cape Town and that they will get tested?"

"Yes, he told me that seven of them had their blood taken this afternoon."

"That's wonderful. Then what more do you want, Sofie, sit around and mope?"

"I'm just really anxious about... everything," Sofia said

"I understand that but going out for a while won't do any harm. Enough with the gloom. Put that dress on in my bedroom right now."

A short while later, Astrid gave her a side-hug. "You look stunning, Sofie. Now go and enjoy yourself."

"Hey, my makeup!" Sofia pulled away a little and laughed.

"Okay, nothing's smudged. Off you go," Astrid said in a motherly tone. "If you leave now, you'll make it on time." She opened the gate for Sofia, then she joined her children in the TV room to watch 'A Toy Story 3' - again.

In Sandton, Sofia circled the undercover parking to find a free spot, which made her somewhat late. She scanned the spacious lobby of the Convention Centre and tried to call

Errol on her phone. There were smartly dressed people mingling everywhere but no Errol.

He didn't answer his phone and she was trying again when a gaggle of shrieking girls by the broad stairs caught her attention. There was Errol Botes, surrounded by pretty, young things in miniskirts and heavy makeup. The girls were from Bloemfontein and had recognised the local celebrity-DJ. Errol seemed to enjoy the attention. He signed autographs on skin and t-shirts and one of the girls took a selfie with him, chattering and giggling all the time.

What am I doing here? Sofia thought, *perhaps I should just leave...*

"If it's not my old friend Lois Lane," a jovial voice said behind her. Sofia turned around. "You look marvellous, just marvellous my dear."

These days, Stan Makaroff always seemed to be creeping up on her. It was the first time, she saw the tycoon properly attired for the occasion, in a suit and tie and... red Italian shoes. Gugu, looking sexy in a clinging, blue dress, followed him closely as usual.

"Thank you, Mr. Makaroff," Sofia said and gave him a weak smile. There was no escaping this man! His eye caught the blue and gold bracelet, she was wearing.

"My word, what an exquisite piece of jewellery. Are those Tanzanites, young lady?" He asked with genuine interest.

"Yes, they are indeed," Sofia said, a little embarrassed.

"Whoever gave it to you must love you very much."

"Mr. Makaroff if jewellery were the mark of love, half the women in Sandton..." she waved her hand to point out the richly dressed and adorned women in the lobby, "... must be the most loved women in the country."

Gugu laughed.

"Touché," Makaroff chuckled. "Touché, Lois Lane." His attention jumped to a group of business people by the escalators and he waved to them. He took Sofia's arm and led her to his acquaintances in charcoal and navy business suits. "There is somebody I must introduce you to, darlings."

Pleasantries were exchanged and Gugu positioned herself protectively next to Sofia.

"Who are these people?" Sofia whispered in Gugu's ear.

"Sponsors, donating money to the arts and good causes," Gugu whispered back.

Sofia wondered, why she was supposed to meet them but maybe there was no particular reason. Stan Makaroff often did things on a whim. She forgot who these people were, the moment she'd been introduced. Some chit-chat about sponsoring charities followed and the eccentric tycoon grew increasingly inattentive. Stan Makaroff rocked forth and back in his expensive red shoes that didn't match his outfit, waving to acquaintances here and there.

Heel-toes, heel-toes.

"You must come and visit us at our offices, my dear," he said to Sofia. "What about tomorrow morning?"

She looked at Gugu who nodded encouragement. "Hmm, yes. Why not?" Sofia tried to smile. "Any particular reason?"

"We must discuss, how we can best invest in your safari lodge. Perhaps, your boyfriend has a change of heart and will allow hunting after all. In order to draw interest from overseas, I was thinking... we start off with a breeding programme for antelopes. Kudu, Eland, even Springbok, perhaps. Then we move onto lions and rhinos. Hunters have deep pockets and will love..."

Sofia was speechless. Had he really just said that?

"Mr. Makaroff, I hardly think it's appropriate for us to discuss such a..."

"It's Stan, please..."

"Mr. Makaroff. I don't think that I want to discuss this at all." Sofia threw her head back and tendrils of dark, glossy hair bounced around her face.

Stan Makaroff didn't listen to her objection. "So sorry, got to beetle. Gugu will make arrangements with you to come see me tomorrow, Sofia." He bowed a little, then addressed the group. "Enjoy yourselves, kids," he boomed in a strident voice. "Must say hello to someone over there and prepare my speech. No rest for the wicked, right? Right?!" He guffawed.

Oh yes, she would go and see him, if only to set him straight!

Before Sofia could say 'scumbag', she was alone with the sponsors. Makaroff sauntered off to work the room with Gugu and a bodyguard in tow. An awkward silence ensued. The sponsors didn't appear to know what to do with Sofia.

"So tell us, what it is you do," a woman in a grey business suit said, trying to sound interested.

"I live on a game farm up north, close to Botswana."

"Oh really, that must be so... rewarding..."

The small-talk dragged on until Errol made an appearance and put a glass of champagne in Sofia's hand. "I'm sorry folks, I have to abduct this beautiful, young lady here..."

He flashed his most charming smile, handed out business cards and, without much ado, steered her toward a quieter spot.

"Pretty dress, by the way," he said, liking what was in the dress even more.

"Gee, thanks..." Sofia had never been so happy to see him but standing so close to him now, made her feel uneasy. She discovered to her horror that she could still feel him, still felt a connection!

"Pleasure." Errol snatched a couple of canapés from a platter, a waiter in a striped waistcoat was offering to guests. He gave one to Sofia with a gallant gesture. "I thought we were going to meet here at seven."

"I tried to phone you. Couldn't find parking," she apologised and nibbled on the canapé. Goat's cheese with red onion jam.

"No sweat, Sofia. Wasn't that THE Stan Makaroff, you spoke to earlier?"

"You mean, while you were flirting with those teeny-boppers?" She didn't like the way the words came out. As if she cared, what he did - and she didn't.

"Yes, well the life of a celebrity DJ..." Errol grinned and pulled her out of a man's way who tottered past them obviously drunk, giving Sofia a lewd look.

They moved almost underneath the broad staircase.

"Mr. Makaroff is a customer of ours," Sofia said, a little taken aback by the direct question. "Actually, I don't like him that much... did you see that guy, how he looked at me?"

"No, who?" Errol was busy looking at some big-bosomed woman in a gold satin dress who made eyes at him.

"Oh never mind. We were talking about Stan Makaroff. I don't exactly like him," Sofia repeated firmly and took a sip of her champagne.

"Oh, come on, the guy has connections and this type of vitamin C is everything in this town. Pretend to like him and you will go places," Errol said.

"Go places? I would never be anything but polite to him. He's so brash and creepy. Anyway, he invited me to their offices in Sandton tomorrow."

"I hope you're going," he said lightly.

"Why do you care?" Sofia snapped. "It's none of your business." Her blue eyes were flashing daggers. Errol looked rather confused at her vehemence. "True."

"Sorry, I'm sure you mean well," she said and caressed her bracelet.

"I just have your best interest at heart, Sofia. I'm telling you, the man has connections." Errol angled himself another canapé from a platter that a waiter carried past.

"Right as if I care about that sort of thing right now." She finished her champagne.

People started moving into the hall, where round tables had been decorated for the dinner event. Flowers, candles in glasses, white tablecloths. Somebody tested the microphones.

"What's happening now?" Sofia wondered.

"The programme is starting in about..." Errol looked at the big wall clock, inside an overdone African piece of wood art. "...12 minutes. We have time to find our seats and get a new glass of champagne." He waved one of the circulating waiters over and grabbed two glasses off the tray, he was carrying.

Sofia took a sip from her champagne flute. "Not bad, keep it coming."

She noticed Errol staring at her but before she could do

anything, he'd taken her face with both hands and kissed Sofia right on the mouth. Sofia nearly spit her champagne out. That would have been even more awkward! At first, she was angry, then unsure, whether it had been a pleasant or unpleasant thing that had just happened.

"Hey, what was that?" She pulled away, swallowed and felt light-headed from all the champagne.

"What do you think it was?" Errol quipped and bit into another canapé, while studying the crowd as if nothing unusual had happened. "I still like you, that's all."

"You can't just kiss me, Errol. It's not right," she stammered.

"Why not? It's no big deal."

"It's complicating everything and I don't want that," Sofia grumbled.

"Oh, why do you always have to overthink everything?" Errol sounded bored. "Just be in the moment."

Bleep bleep bleep. An sms was coming through and Sofia welcomed the interruption. Perhaps, it was Gugu, giving her a time for the meeting tomorrow. She looked at her phone and saw that it was a message from Tom. Good.

But her eyes widened in horror as she read the telegram-style text that ended with a crying emoji.

*Lorraine had an accident last night. She died in the hospital an hour ago. Funeral on Thursday. Will come to Joburg with Barry and Charmaine. Phone me *crying face*'*

Sofia stared at the message. What?! Tom wouldn't make fun of stuff like that, so it had to be true. The horror must have clearly shown on her face.

"What's wrong?" Errol asked concerned.

"Sorry, something has happened. I must go," Sofia said and set her glass down on a nearby table. She still felt a little sussled from all the champagne and confused by the kiss but now she had to get her act together and drive home.

"Don't you want to finish your champagne?" Errol asked.

"It's urgent. I'm sorry, I don't mean to stand you up but there's an emergency. I have to go." It didn't matter. Nothing here mattered anymore.

"Yes, what else is new?" He was alluding to their break-up, of course, but Sofia didn't have time to play that game now. All she could think about was that she had to phone Tom. Away from this place. Away from Errol.

Sofia had spare keys but the dogs were in the front garden and made a hell of a din, yapping and howling when a security car drove by at low speed. Guarding the house was their job after all. This surely had woken Astrid up. The drive from Sandton had sobered up Sofia and she remembered to take the dogs to the back before driving in.

Errol is not so bad, Sofia thought as she walked past the rows of white roses. The Labradors were sniffing her feet all the way to the front door.

Maybe she should give him a chance, so they could at least be friends. Errol had wriggled a promise out of Sofia, to go for breakfast with him the next morning before he left town. She felt bad for dropping him tonight and it was the least she could do before going to the Makaroff Tower in Sandton tomorrow. There was still the small matter of test results to be discussed and their son Damian to be saved.

The house was dark and quiet.

Everybody must be asleep by now. Sofia checked Astrid's room. The bed was untouched. Astrid wasn't downstairs, either. So there were just the children in the house. She mustn't wake them up. Astrid had probably just popped out to get milk or something from the 24/7 shop.

"Come here, Loki, Freya! Here are some treats for you." She called the dogs in a soft voice and threw a few dog biscuits in the air. Loki and Freya caught them with ease. "Now out with you into the back garden," she whispered and closed the kitchen door. They would, no doubt, dig up some plant or something in frustration until Astrid returned from whatever she was doing.

Sofia dialled Tom's number. Voicemail. Great. She got hold of him at the third attempt. 'Where have you been? You can't just drop me a message like that and then disappear...'

'I am in the kitchen, talking to Karen about some menu

changes. I'll go to the house now.' Tom sounded tired.

'Since when do you worry about menu changes?'

Tom cleared his throat. 'Staff shortage and you are not here.'

There was another voice in the background. A woman's voice.

'I see,' Sofia said and felt some stupid, hot jealousy creep up her spine.

'Hi Sofia, how's Joburg?' It was Karen, the chef, butting in. 'Dreadful thing that happened with Lorraine Pienaar, really. The town's all abuzz with rumours. Wish, I could come to the funeral but I can't just close the kitchen for a few days. Oh before I forget: remember to bring that spiral cutter. I rely on you.'

Sofia swallowed.

'Hi Karen, I'm still looking for that thing. Any idea where I can find it?' They chatted about the vegetable cutter and what had happened to Lorraine.

'Alright, you guys. I'm going to the house now,' Tom said and walked out of the kitchen. 'Calling it a night.' Sofia could tell that he was tired, dragging his feet on the gravel. Brutus the dog growled at the hissing cheetah in the background.

'That's so sad! Do they know what happened to Lorraine?' Sofia asked.

'Not too sure. I can't get much out of Barry right now. A car accident by the looks of it. She must have fallen asleep at the wheel or something and went down a cliff,' Tom said.

'What? That doesn't sound right. What cliff, where was she?'

'In Joburg. I think Barry said somewhere in Northcliff but why she'd fallen asleep... no idea. Maybe I didn't understand him properly. Oh dear, maybe she was drunk. Those two can drink anybody under the table.'

'Let's not jump to conclusions. There could have been another car or something...'

Sofia had no idea, how close to the truth she was. They spoke of the upcoming funeral arrangements.

'You said the funeral's on Thursday. Where? Oh, I see... When will you be here, Tom?'

'We'll leave at lunchtime on Wednesday, so sometime in the afternoon.'

'Can't you give me the time?' Sofia insisted.

'No, Barry will pick me up. He's in a bad way, Sofia. Talks incessantly when he's not too drunk. Says, he never stopped loving Lorraine. Drinks like a fish.'

'That's bad. And you let him drive?'

'What am I supposed to do?'

'Well, you can drive and let him sleep it off on the back seat. So what? Maybe it'll put him in a bad mood. If he can't keep it together and has a death wish, he shouldn't drive at all. Please, Tom.'

'Alright, I'll speak to him. Will give you a call when we arrive. Could you book us into a B&B somewhere? I don't think Astrid will appreciate it if all three of us descend on her house.' Tom yawned and she could hear Jethro growl in his enclosure. If she could just be there with him!

'Possibly not," she said. "I can't even ask her because she's not at home. The kids might also be upset if they hear that somebody died.'

'Alright then, let me get a move on here and some sleep would be good, too.'

'Yes, that would be good. Have a safe trip. I love you.'

'Love you too, babes. See you soon.' Tom hung up.

Sofia had a terrible night. She didn't dream often but she dreamt a whole storybook about her mom and what she'd looked like the last time she saw her. Mom was wearing the same dress and argued with Dad. Her parents didn't see her, didn't listen to her and she wanted to speak to them.

She dreamt about Lorraine being half-drunk at the cocktail party, saying something terribly important that Sofia couldn't understand. Lorraine's dress slipped and Sofia felt embarrassed on her behalf. Then there was a boy in a coffin who looked like Damian. He was lowered into the ground. Running away, running, falling, getting up and running again...

She woke up feeling as if she'd been through the mill. It was eight o'clock in the morning and Tom was coming on Wednesday. She had to phone the Dragonfly Bed & Breakfast in Linden down the road. Then she had to meet

Errol for coffee at nine. *Come on now, pull yourself together*, she scolded herself and had her first cup of coffee in the kitchen.

*

"So, this Tom of yours is coming on Wednesday?" Errol said with a hint of sarcasm. "Well, let's make the best of it, then. Wouldn't want to cause any trouble between the two of you, would I?"

"Oh please, don't start..." Sofia groaned. Gugu's message regarding the meeting had just come through. 'See you at 10:00 at the Makaroff Tower. Ask for me downstairs.' 'Okay' Sofia messaged back.

"Come on, Sofia, I'm not being serious," Errol said, checking out the waitress.

"Really?"

"Really." That sounded reassuring. Not.

It felt like déjà-vu to her, sitting here at the table with Errol. They were bickering like an old married couple.

"I'm too tired to squabble with you. Tom has to take care of Charmaine and Barry. She will probably cry the whole time and he has to make sure that Barry's not blind-drunk during the ceremony. He always gets loud when he's drunk."

Sofia sighed in memory of such similar behaviour.

"Where is the funeral?" Errol asked. "In the country?"

"At some church in Melville. Lorraine lived in a garden flat there. Then the guests meet at some restaurant in Melville. Not sure, which one yet. Don't really know my way around Joburg that well."

"I could come. I have GPS."

"Why would you want to come, Errol? I don't think you're invited; you didn't even know Lorraine. And Tom will be there."

"I know, Sofia, I'm so sorry about your friend and I shouldn't be making jokes."

"Yeah, you and your jokes... and she wasn't really my friend. We were on different wavelengths, I guess. But Lorraine was okay when she didn't have too much to drink."

"Sounds rough," Errol said and studied the menu's

breakfast section. "Yes, but that's life. Let's talk about something else. Mmm, English breakfast sounds good."

"That's life?" Sofia asked and gave up.

"Do you want breakfast?"

"No thanks, just coffee for me."

Errol ordered an English breakfast for himself and filter coffee for Sofia. "So, you haven't heard anything from Cape Town, then?" Sofia finally asked.

Errol studied the other sections of the menu. "Ah yes, I did actually..."

"You did and you don't tell me?" Sofia got irritated with his off-hand manner. There was only the small matter of their son's health at stake!

"I'm telling you now." He looked at her over the edge of the menu.

"Errol! Out with it. What did they say?"

Sofia leaned forward and he reluctantly put the menu away.

"They said that five people got tested: my mother, my brother..."

"So five instead of seven...okay...yes, and...?"

"A distant cousin of mine seems to be a match but they need to do more tests, apparently. Don't remember why but that's good news, right?"

Sofia's face lit up.

"That's great news, Errol. When will they do that?"

"Soon. There's a little problem," Errol said and playfully rolled his eyes.

"What problem?"

"Well, the guy's on the bones of his backside and wants some kind of - shall we say - compensation for the privilege of donating part of his liver."

"You mean..." Sofia's head was reeling. It all came down to money?

"Yes. He's a distant cousin and he doesn't even know the boy and won't do it for free. He's just that kind of person."

"Fine family, you have there! What did the Daniels say? I mean that's blackmail," Sofia was skipping closer to outrage.

"They're prepared to pay half," Errol assured her and looked away.

"Only half... and what about the other half?"

"I thought maybe you could ask your... boyfriend. He does have money, doesn't he? Being the owner of a safari lodge and all..."

Sofia was flabbergasted. "And how must I explain this to him? What I need the money for?"

"You'll find a way, I'm sure. Think about our son, Sofia."

"It's not right. It just isn't right." Why was Errol so calm about this? By now, Sofia was ready to blow her top.

"I know but what can we do? I don't have money and you don't have any." Errol shrugged his shoulders. "So, you have to ask your boyfriend."

"I've saved up a little. I don't need much. How much does he want anyway?"

"Fifty thousand Rand." Errol sounded unsure of the sum.

"What?! Is he insane?" Sofia shouted. The other patrons and the waiters stared at her. She had to get a grip of herself.

"What must I do? Either we pay him or he doesn't want to do it," Errol shrugged his shoulders. How could he be so calm about this?

"And this guy is your family?" She hissed.

"Distant family."

"Some family. Disgusting. Can't you get your mother to talk some sense into him?" She became more desperate by the minute.

"They've already tried. Ah, breakfast is here." He tucked into his eggs and bacon.

"There must be something we can do!" Sofia felt defeated. "I'll try and make a plan and then let you know."

Errol stared at her, chewing. "Okay, I get it, you'll let me know. Don't you want to drink your coffee?"

"Coffee? If I drink more coffee, I'll explode!"

Just when she thought they could be friends for the boy's sake, his cousin had to try and blackmail her! Unbelievable! And Errol seemed okay with it. Maybe she had judged him too soon, thinking he wasn't so bad after all.

In Cape Town, she had found out quickly that Errol would never commit to a relationship. He had too much fun to care and she'd broken it off with a phone call. The guilt about Tom and then the horror when she'd found out that she was pregnant. Sofia didn't want to remember.

"Are you going to speak to your boyfriend or what?"

"I said, I'll let you know. I have to think about the whole thing first."

"Well, don't think for too long," Errol growled and looked at her as if there was not much to think about.

"I won't... Oh shit!" Sofia stared at her watch.

"What?"

"It's late. I must go to the Makaroff Tower now. Gugu sent a message through. Have to be there at 10 o'clock."

"You still have time to get there. Remember connections - vitamin C - is *very* important in the city."

"Oh, get your own damn vitamin C," she hissed. "And you can get the bill."

"Oooh, why so snarky?" Errol asked mockingly.

"Oh stop it already. You just drop that bomb on me and I'm tired and probably late for my meeting with Gugu, so excuse me for living." Sofia started to walk to the parking lot.

"Don't forget about my cousin..." Errol called after her.

"I won't!" She didn't even turn around. Sofia felt angry now. Anger was better than despair. Why did everything have to be so damn difficult? With some luck, she would be able to dish the story to Gugu. Her friend was level-headed and full of good advice and that's exactly, what Sofia needed right now.

"Gugu, I'm on my way to Sandton." She held her phone close to her ear while steering the bakkie. "Can I talk to you alone when I get there? Privately, I mean, not when Makaroff's around."

'We can talk *now*, Sofie.'

"No, I'm driving."

'Hey, be careful,' Gugu sounded concerned. 'I'll say that you're running a bit late because of the traffic. That should give us 20 minutes or so.'

"Good, thanks."

The Makaroff Tower in Sandton was impressive. All glass and chrome. A revolving door, a huge reception desk and a big screen overhead that changed every few minutes, showing laughing miners and young couples and people counting money. Sofia sat in the reception area, brooding.

"So, what's up?" Gugu plunked herself down on the soft couch next to Sofia without warning. She looked stunning in her designer suit, her hair done up to the side. Sofia explained and Gugu whistled unladylike, putting a small notepad on the couch next to her.

"Wow, you're not kidding. What the hell is Errol thinking, hitting you up for Tom's money? Putting you under pressure like that? I mean, it's his son as well. Can't he just take out a loan? Can't the Daniels take out a loan?"

"Yes, it is his son as well," Sofia said and looked up wistfully, "and I'll pay for it for the rest of my life."

"Oh come now if there's a problem, there's a solution. If I didn't believe that, I wouldn't be doing my job very well."

"That's why I had to talk to you. So what do you think?" Sofia held her breath.

"Sounds like a shakedown to me," Gugu mused. "Maybe I watch too many crime series but what if Errol's getting a cut."

"He wouldn't dare!" Sofia flared up again.

"Sofia, try to think this through. Do you trust Errol?"

"Not as far as I can throw a cat." There, Sofia had said it out loud. In fact, she'd had an overdose of Errol already, after only a few days. She had enough of his carefree manner, while she was worrying herself half to death over their son's health. Gugu put a calming hand on Sofia's arm.

"Don't get so upset. If you ask me - follow your intuition. And you should tell Tom everything, as soon as possible. Do you hear me? Before somebody else does." Gugu's eyes were compelling her.

"You're right," Sofia sighed.

"At the moment we only know what this Mrs. Daniels and Errol are telling us..."

"And this doctor in Cape Town."

"Right. What was his name?" Gugu took her notepad.

"Dr. Bezuidenhout from Bellville."

"Dr. Be...zuiden...hout... Bellville." Gugu scribbled on the notepad. "Look here, I'll do some digging, find out who these people are, which hospital Damian is in and so on. Then we'll know more and you can make a decision based on that."

"You would do that?"

"Sure, I would. I'm good at stuff like that."

"Thank you, Gugs!" Sofia gave her friend a kiss on the cheek. "What would I do without you?"

"I sometimes wonder about that myself," Gugu laughed. "Now we should go before Mr. Makaroff throws out his toys."

She walked elegantly in her high heels toward the lift. Sofia followed her in flat tekkies that made a little squeaking noise on the polished porcelain tiles. Gugu greeted a stocky man in a dark suit. "How is it, Alwin?"

"Fine, just fine. I'll have the files ready by this afternoon."

"Thanks, Alwin."

Sofia thought she had met the man before and smiled. They passed an abstract painting in all colours of the rainbow. The face of a man, sticking his tongue out. Sofia was in the mood to do exactly that to Stan Makaroff.

If he thought that they would have a nice little meeting about his high-flying hunting plans, he had something coming.

The lift door opened and the two women stepped in.

CHAPTER 7

Stan Makaroff's office was right on top of the towering building and it was large. Artworks, polished wood and large windows with a view of a South African New-York-City skyline dominated the carpeted space.

Gugu led the way through milk-glass doors into the office. They left the harsh sounds of the hallway behind and crossed the reception room on Persian carpets. The secretary could have passed for a tall supermodel with a perfect figure in an expensive poison-green shift dress and her artful hairdo. Holding a wad of papers, she walked from one of the smaller offices back to her desk. How can she type with fingernails like that? Sofia wondered.

The woman gave Gugu and Sofia haughty looks from under false eyelashes. "Mr. Makaroff will be with you in a moment. He is still conducting interviews," she said in a fake British accent. "Please have a seat." The secretary waved at the waiting area with its modern chairs and couches in primary colours that didn't look very comfortable.

Gugu's cell phone rang. "Yes, yes... I'm not at my desk right now but I'll check why the attachment didn't arrive. No, we'll stick to the deadline, don't you worry. Yes I'll do that, now now."

"Work?" Sofia asked her and sat down on a Plexiglas chair that reminded her of a bridge. It was surprisingly snug.

"Sorry Sofia - this is important. A media briefing. I'll be right back. Mr.. Malakoff shouldn't take long now. Wait here so long and... read a magazine."

"I didn't come here to read magazines," Sofia grumbled and surveyed the usual selection of gossip, fashion and travel magazines on the glass table.

"Humour me, please. I won't be long." Gugu addressed the poison-green secretary. "Portia, could you get Ms Helenius something to drink, please?" Gugu pulled rank with the secretary.

"Certainly, Ms Mbatha." She looked at Sofia a little less haughtily. Stan Makaroff's PR manager walked back to the lift.

"Coffee, tea?"

"A glass of water will do, thanks." Sofia picked up a gossip magazine. No doubt Gugu had her own fancy-shmantzy office on a lower level. Sofia leaned back as far as her s-shaped Plexiglas chair allowed and studied the abstract painting on the wall. What was that supposed to be? She tilted her head to have a better look. Female shapes at different angles, maybe, in shades of red.

Portia placed the water on the table and began to work away on her computer, while Sofia stole a glance at the closed door to Mr. Makaroff's office. A massive hardwood door, possibly teak, with shiny lettering on it: Stanislav Makaroff, Managing Director.

Two Asian men in dark suits were sitting on an electric-blue couch, waiting as she did. They must have been here before her. That meant, they would go in first. Great. It felt like waiting for a dentist appointment. The men smiled and nodded their heads in greeting and Sofia did the same.

She picked up a magazine about travel in Africa and paged through the colourful pages. A holiday in Namibia sounded fascinating... the 10 best beach destinations in Mozambique... would she ever make it to Mozambique? Sofia checked the wall clock. How much longer now?

What a waste of time to wait for Mr. Makaroff. Why was she here again?

Sofia fought the urge to get up, sneak out across the soft carpets, to press the lift button and leave the building unnoticed. Just that Gugu would probably get into trouble and also... Makaroff was an important client for Shangari. She could hardly treat him with the disdain, he deserved. Okay, she would at least wait for Gugu to return. Sofia had come more for Gugu anyway, wanted to see her, speak to her. But here she was, sitting in a stupid waiting room, waiting.

There were so many things she still had to do. Sofia ticked off a mental list: buy stuff for the lodge, confirm with the Bed & Breakfast in Linden, confirm the restaurant in Melville. She thought of Errol who had told her about his cousin wanting money before donating a piece of his liver for Damian.

A stitch went through her heart. It wasn't fair. Why didn't Mrs. Daniels make more of an effort to save her son? Sofia felt heartsore just thinking about it. The heavy door to Makaroff's office opened a crack and closed again. What was going on in this office?

The two Asian men began to speak to each other. "Kun pôot waâ a-rai ná?"

"Chúay kǐan long hǎi nòi dâai mǎi."

"Kam nán òk sǐang waâ yàang rai?" They tried to pronounce English words. "Oonly until toomollow." They smiled at her and she smiled back, being polite.

Sofia had no idea, what they were talking about. Were they Chinese? She couldn't tell. One of the men had a folded t-shirt next to him on the couch and Sofia read 'Explore Thai...'. Thailand it was then. The men had another laugh and carried on speaking in their own language. Sofia felt gloomy, so she read the travel magazine and learned about the ins and outs of travelling to Namibia's unspoilt nature reserves. The door opened again and she caught a glimpse of two very young women in skimpy clothes, sitting in front of a massive desk. Sofia couldn't see their faces but she could tell that they weren't at ease, sitting stiffly on their chairs. The desk was made of the same wood as the heavy door to the office. More artwork on the wall inside and carpets, of course.

Makaroff was on the phone. His voice sounded imperious. "Yes, two hundred big ones by tomorrow. No, no. It has to be tomorrow...oh, for goodness' sake..." The teak door closed again.

Makaroff's bodyguard was now standing next to the poison-green secretary called Portia. They chatted in hushed voices and Portia nodded. All Sofia could understand was '...his wife wants it that way...'

Whatever was being said, was none of Sofia's business. She didn't know Makaroff's wife. Come to think of it, Mrs. Makaroff had never even come to Shangari with her husband.

The secretary made a phone call and spoke behind her hand in a rather secretive manner. This piqued Sofia's interest; not that she had any intention of eaves-dropping. "Wonder, how much longer, he's going to take..." she said to the Asian gentlemen who smiled broadly and didn't seem to understand.

I'll give him five minutes, Sofia thought, *then I'm out of here in a flash.* She took the supplies-list out of her handbag and compared it to the mental list, she'd ticked earlier. Perhaps she could find some of the exotic stuff that Karen wanted right here in Sandton City...

"Hey, Sofia?"

"Yes?" Sofia looked up with a puzzled expression.

"Are you lost in thought, darling?" Gugu asked.

"About time you came back, I'm ready to climb out of my skull," Sofia moaned.

"We can wait in the lobby at the in-house coffee shop. It's going to take Mr. Makaroff a while longer, and he has to see these gentlemen here."

She nodded and the long-legged secretary nodded back. One last smile was exchanged with the Asian men, then Sofia stood up.

"I don't know what he wants to discuss with me anyway. It would have been rude not to accept his invitation but if he wants to talk about the damn hunting business, he can jump in the lake. Maybe I should just leave."

"What happened to giving him a piece of your mind? If you can stay a bit longer, we'll talk downstairs at the coffee shop. I'll stick you for lunch. You look hungry."

"Actually, I am, but I still think it's a waste of time..."

A group of employees, ready to go on lunch, entered the lift and didn't speak until they'd reached the ground floor.

Sofia played with her Tanzanite bracelet and wished she could be anywhere but here inside the Makaroff Tower.

"Listen, I'm really sorry, he's being such a jerk," Gugu whispered when they stepped out of the lift. "I had no idea, he was going to say those things yesterday. Normally, I have a pretty good idea, what he's planning but he can be so fickle."

"Look we can meet up later if you like, and have dinner at Cresta Shopping Centre. Whatever it is that he wants, he's not going to get it from me, anyway."

Sofia's rubber soles squeaked on the polished floor as they passed the rainbow-tongue painting and walked toward the coffee shop in the lobby. They had their own coffee shop in the Makaroff Tower!

"Will you be at the funeral?" Gugu asked suddenly.

"Yes, of course, I'll be there. Tom, Barry and Charmaine are coming to Joburg tomorrow afternoon and I still have to confirm the rooms at the B&B... and the restaurant in Melville, they've booked for the wake. I'm dog-tired and it's probably just as well that Makaroff doesn't have time to see me."

She heard footsteps approaching on the polished tiles. Squish, squish. Like a pair of slip slops.

"Well, well, well... if it isn't Lois Lane. You are not running away from me, are you, young lady?" Stan Makaroff laughed in a creepy sort of manner that made Sofia cringe. "I'm glad you stopped her from leaving Gugulethu. I guess we'll have a cuppa right here."

"Glad to be of service, sir," Gugu said.

Sofia turned to greet the tycoon. She was forced to switch gears again and chit chat with this unpleasant man.

"Well... yes sure we can have coffee," she shrugged her shoulders and put on a winning smile. "Mr. Makaroff, you caught me just in time..." They shook hands.

Gugu's eyes opened wide as if to say, 'sorry, I wish I'd let you go sooner.' Sofia's eyes accepted the apology.

"Lucky me," Makaroff said and gestured for his bodyguard to wait nearby. "I'm glad you could make it, Sofia. Sorry, you had to wait. I'm always so terribly busy. Let's sit down. Gugulethu, please join us."

Makaroff was wearing shorts and slip slops as if he was on his way to the beach! The white shirt and dark red tie didn't match his beach getup down under and Sofia couldn't help staring.

"Ah, I see you are wondering about my unusual attire." He laughed and walked ahead to a table that was set apart from the others. His table. Everyone seemed to make a wide berth around them.

"No, not really, I mean it's your business after all..." Sofia said. If you were rich and influential, you could go barefoot in a potato sack if that pleased you.

"Ah yes, that's right. Nice of you to notice. Dreadful business, having to wear suits all the time. I'm wearing a shirt and tie only because I have a Skype call in about an hour. Otherwise, you'd see me in a t-shirt."

The bodyguard pulled out chairs for Sofia and Gugu.

"Let's sit. I can give you about... let's say 20 minutes," Stan Makaroff said as if she had asked him for a meeting and not the other way around.

Gugu Mbatha was ready to object. She had a press release to prepare and a photoshoot before the TV interview but she knew that Stan Makaroff would insist or be miffed for the rest of the afternoon. It was easier to comply than risk his mood. She'd have to do the press release during the photoshoot, then.

"It's quite warm in here," Sofia said and took off her cardigan.

"That's Joburg in winter for you: freezing at night and during the day it gets boiling hot. Must be my Russian genes but I like it cool." Makaroff bellowed with laughter and Sofia smiled good-naturedly.

"Well, what must I say? My Finnish genes are also objecting to the heat. South Africa couldn't be more different to our climate at home. Especially during the winter months."

"Yes, but one big plus in favour of Africa is that we have safaris here, right?!" Stan Makaroff said. "Where else can you go and observe wild animals?"

"Have you never heard of Finnish reindeer-safaris, Mr. Makaroff? They are quite popular in Oulu in Northern Ostrobothnia. Different to the safaris here for sure but quite an experience."

The waiter who served lunch at a nearby table, slightly bowed in Makaroff's direction and signalled that he would be with him now.

"We have something in common then. Finland and Russia - practically neighbours. Excellent. Let's drink to that. Benny!" The waiter was at the table at once. "Benny, bring the usual for me... and what may I order for you, Sofia?" His slip slops made a squishy tapping sound under the table. Tap tap tap, tap tap went his fingers on the table.

"A glass of water for me, please," she said to the hovering waiter and took out her cell phone before placing the handbag on the floor. No messages.

"Still or sparkling?"

"Bring me sparkling," Sofia said, felt the blue stones on her bracelet and thought of Tom. She couldn't wait to see him. Suddenly, Makaroff didn't matter anymore - she could handle him. The waiter looked at Gugu. "Oh… bring me the same," she said.

"But the two of you have to eat as well! You cannot go through the day without proper fuel. Take it from the converted. Two Tramezzini Roberto for the ladies, Benny." Stan Makaroff ordered, what he thought best and they didn't mind. The waiter scuttled off, ignoring a lifted hand at one of the other tables.

"Toasted tramezzini with chicken mayo filling," he explained. "I hope, you're not vegetarian."

"No." Sofia tried to get the ball rolling. "Mr. Makaroff. May I ask why you invited me to your office? Why am I here?"

"Oh so direct, I like it. What do they say? Feisty women make good lovers." Stan Makaroff grinned like a naughty little boy. He was trying to put her off balance!

"I doubt that," Sofia said. Why didn't Makaroff come to the point? He began to grate on her nerves. "So? What did you want to talk about? I thought, I'd made it clear that..."

"Lois Lane, let's not get off on the wrong foot..." He said and blathered on about wildlife and the bushveld for a while.

"Ah, here's our food. Excellent."

Makaroff was distracted again. Good. The tramezzini smelled delicious. Sofia realised that she had been running on caffeine all morning and was actually starving. After a few bites, she began to feel better.

She'd wait until Makaroff had eaten, then politely make her getaway. Yes, that's what she would do. Her cell phone hummed. Gugu had texted her: *Must be something he really wants! Smile and don't say anything he can construe into an agreement*.

Sofia texted back under the table: *Okay :)*.

Makaroff wiped his mouth and slurped his vitamin water, signalling the end of lunch with gestures of his free hand. Benny jumped to and picked up his plate.

"Mr. Makaroff, I don't want to be rude and I appreciate the tramezzini..."

"Oh, did you enjoy the tramezzini? One of my favourites."

"Yes, I did. Thank you, but there is so much I have to do by Wednesday and if there's nothing else..."

"How inconsiderate of me. It's the funeral of our unfortunate Mrs. Pienaar. I am sponsoring the flowers, by the way. Poor woman," he said and seemed to be picking with his tongue at his teeth.

Sofia crossed her arms and looked coldly at the man in the red tie and shorts. "Yes, her husband is distraught and needs any help he can get to organise the funeral. That's why I still have to confirm the bookings..."

"I will make it short and sweet, Sofia." Makaroff looked deeply into her eyes. "So very blue. How astonishing." The man knew no boundaries!

"Mr. Makaroff, please come to the point." She uncrossed her arms and leaned back, away from the impudent face.

"We have a meeting in 15 minutes, sir," Gugu cut in. "The photoshoot and the TV interview. The crew should be here by now."

"Good, good," Makaroff said and tapped his fingers on the spotless bistro table. "15 minutes then. Let's get right to it..."

Before he could launch into his opening line, they heard a commotion outside the entrance. "Rhino Killer... Rhino Killer!"

There was much yelling and running around. Sofia turned in her chair and saw that large red letters were splattered all over the massive tinted windows. Red paint, like blood streaking the glass, dripping down into the geraniums next to the entrance.

She tried to read backwards what the letters spelled out. RHINO KILLER was all she could decipher. It had happened incredibly fast. Security guards were chasing after protesters in hoodies in different directions. The culprits ran swiftly across the road, dodged hooting cars and were swallowed by lunchtime traffic.

"Can you b e l i e v e it?!" Stan Makaroff sounded rather upset. "I love rhinos."

The bodyguard planted himself protectively in front of his boss wit his hand resting against his chest. Did he have a weapon in his jacket?

"Perhaps we should postpone this meeting..." Sofia suggested.

"Yes... yes of course. I'll see you at the funeral?" Makaroff said, trying to recapture the mood.

"Yes, you will." Sofia shook hands with the tycoon and wondered if he really loved rhinos.

"No time to talk now. Gugulethu, are you coming? 5 minutes." Makaroff sounded impatient now as if he'd been waiting for his PR manager and not the other way around. Squish, squish, squish, his slip slops squeaked all the way to the lift. "Right behind you, Stanislav," Gugu said. She was suppressing a smirk. No need to say anything now - the two friends would talk later. Makaroff used the key to the private lift and they were gone.

Sofia sat down. What had just happened? This must be a

save-the-rhino protest action. A flash mob in broad daylight. Cool.

She'd been out of the loop since coming to Johannesburg and didn't even check her Twitter messages. The protest action had saved her too. Sofia was free to go without having to argue with Stan Makaroff about some stupid plans he had for Shangari. Makaroff never had a chance to tell her what he wanted. Good.

Sofia couldn't help smiling. Not one of these appeasing smiles, she had gotten used to lately but a genuine smile of relief. People in the lobby began to stare at her. The protest action was not a funny thing in their eyes. Sofia looked around, checked herself and left the building.

Gugu didn't call her that day or on Wednesday. She probably had a lot on her plate. Thankfully, Grant Rankin, Astrid's husband, had not yet returned from his business trip to Mozambique. There were no awkward scenes when Tom arrived with Charmaine and a very drunk Barry on Wednesday afternoon.

It had been surprisingly easy to convince Barry to sleep it off on the back seat. He'd let Tom drive all the way without protest but wasn't all that sober even after the trip. The manager at the Linden Bed & Breakfast didn't look too happy, though, and told Tom that he was responsible for Barry's behaviour. Under normal circumstances, they did not tolerate drunkenness.

"I'm sure, he won't be a problem. Please excuse my friend. His wife just died and the funeral is tomorrow," Tom explained.

"Oh, I'm so sorry," the manager said, "I didn't know..."

"It's alright. I'll pay for the damage, should there be any. But you don't have to worry. The funeral starts in the morning and we'll be out of your hair on Friday."

They went to sit down in the quaint sitting area and ordered a round of filter coffee. Sofia consoled Lorraine's sister, while Tom chatted to a sobering Barry Pienaar. He just sat there, hanging his head, nodding occasionally.

"You better go upstairs now and sleep it off," Tom said

firmly. "We'll talk about dinner later. I must go out now and run some errands. Behave yourself."

"Sure, I'll do that, my friend. I'm just so sad, you know... just so sad."

"I know, Barry, but you have to pull yourself together. There will be people at the funeral and you can't be drunk. That would be disrespectful to Lorraine. I'll take the Brandy with me. Give it!"

Barry obediently handed the bottle of Brandy over. "Disrespectful to Lorraine? What about her being disrespectful to me? After all, I've done for her."

"Barry, don't start. She's dead. So for goodness' sake, let it rest. Sleep and take a shower, please."

"I'll also rest for a bit. It's going to be stressful tomorrow," Charmaine said and went to her room. Sofia and Tom sat in the B&B lounge and chatted a while longer.

"Pity I can't stay with Astrid and you," he said and held her hands.

"I know - but Grant doesn't like it if an unmarried couple sleeps in the same room. Even though, he isn't around. We have to respect that."

"Hypocrite," Tom liked Grant even less than Sofia did. "I'll have to look after Barry anyway. He's behaving like a little child."

"Astrid's children might also get upset about talk of a funeral," Sofia said.

"I understand but I missed you." They embraced and Tom kissed Sofia on the mouth. They hadn't felt so close in a while.

"Look, we have to get through this and then we'll talk about us, about everything," Tom said tenderly.

"Well, it's probably best if you get cracking. The restaurant wants a deposit and I couldn't get hold of the pastor." Sofia moved away a fraction.

"Yup." Tom got up and gave Sofia another kiss. "I'll see you later, then."

But that didn't happen. Tom's errands must have taken longer than expected and Sofia didn't see him until the funeral.

*

The ceremony at the small Melville church was intimate and warming, despite the cold. The pastor's words were beautiful, although he'd never met Lorraine. Everyone in attendance looked sufficiently sad, even Stan Makaroff.

Charmaine had sniffled throughout the sermon and a sober Barry had put a supportive arm around her as they sat down. During the sermon, Barry Pienaar sat with shoulders hanging and hollow eyes. New lines were carving up his grey-hued face and he was a mere shadow of the strapping vet, ready to tackle his daily challenges. He hadn't touched any liquor since this morning but the smell of brandy lingered around him. He must have still loved Lorraine, despite everything, Sofia thought.

She was nervous about Damian's health and barely listened to the sermon.

What if the little boy didn't make it? Sofia hadn't heard from Suzanne Daniels or Errol Botes for that matter, about his elusive cousin. Perhaps, Damian had recovered and a transplant was no longer needed. She would phone Suzanne tomorrow. If things were still on a knife's edge, she would have to speak to Tom about the money. No, there was no way, she'd introduce Tom to this by asking him about money! Sofia was glad when the service was over.

Barry had decided against bringing the body home to be buried in the small cemetery in Rutgersdrift, so Lorraine would be laid to rest at West Park Cemetery.

Stan Makaroff and his usual entourage had swelled the numbers during the church service. His secretary had organised magnificent flower arrangements of white lilies, carnations and baby's breath, such as the little church had never seen before. Gugu was there but hardly looked up from under the black veil that was attached to her stylish hat.

When they proceeded to West Park for the actual burial, the Makaroff party had disappeared without saying goodbye. It was probably for the best. Nobody missed Makaroff at the get-together afterwards, although some said they had seen him shedding a tear during the sermon.

It was the biggest graveyard Sofia had ever seen. But then she hadn't seen many. She didn't like places with dead people and smelly flowers and had never been to her mother's grave in Turku. Funerals always brought back memories of the accident that had taken her mother. That's why Sofia avoided funerals if she could.

This was one funeral, she could not avoid.

At the graveside, Lorraine's sister Charmaine couldn't stop weeping. It was heartbreaking to watch her wiping away tears that streaked her makeup. She wore a cheap black dress from some factory store and an awkward pillbox hat. Sofia felt sorry for both of them. The rest of the family, distant aunts and cousins, had stayed away altogether. The shame of Lorraine's actions of late was too bewildering for these staunch country folk.

Sofia felt relieved when they finally left the treed graveyard and its countless ghosts behind. She knew it was silly but she shivered at the thought of ghosts surrounding them. Tom held her hand and she felt safe again. He had dropped everything at Shangari to be there for his friend Barry. How cold Lorraine had been after the incident with the rhino poachers. Then she had broken Barry's heart by leaving him, and he had now faithfully done his duty by her.

The cars left the cemetery one by one and drove to Melville in convoy with their hazard lights on. They would meet again at the Melville restaurant, Tom had booked for brunch.

The wintry day was crisp and sunny and they decided to sit outside in the backyard, where they could munch on tasty sandwiches and cakes from great platters. It was alright, better than she had anticipated but Sofia still felt uneasy.

The mood was gloomy and the short speeches tip-toed around the elephant in the room: that Lorraine had left her husband high and dry for what most suspected was another man in Johannesburg. An unfaithful woman; but one didn't speak badly about a dead person, especially not at her wake.

A grinning couple, god-knows-who had invited, tried to

convince Sofia that their church was the most Christian of all of them and that she should come and attend a service the coming Sunday. They wouldn't take a hint. Sofia didn't need to be saved. She rolled her eyes at Tom. He came to her rescue, saying something about the workload at a safari lodge like Shangari and that they were expected back on the weekend. The couple moved on and worked the other tables one by one.

Tom sensed Sofia's discomfort. He took her by the hand and they walked up the quiet, sun-flooded street. Peace at last. They strolled along 7th Avenue and turned into one of the side roads, then stopped in front of a novelty store with unique art objects.

They laughed at a teapot in the shape of a pig and marvelled at colourful lava lamps. In Shangari, there was never enough time to go for a walk or laugh at silly objects. Tom pulled Sofia close and held her in his arms. She breathed in his fragrant scent that she loved so much. They just stood there for a while in front of the lava lamps and a fat ballerina en pointe.

"Sofia, you know, I love you," Tom said hoarsely. "No matter what."

"I know, Tom, I love you too."

"I'm sorry, we had that fight before you left. It was so stupid that I wanted to take the bakkie and follow you all the way down the road but then Karen needed me to talk to her about something and..."

"I know, Tom. There's always so much to do that we never have time for each other anymore," she said. "But it would have been a nice gesture to see you come running after me." They laughed.

"Yup, it would have been a sight for sore eyes, me waving you to the side of the road and kissing you right there in the middle of town or wherever..."

"Well, I wouldn't have minded. Especially, since it was all your fault anyway," Sofia teased him and winked.

"Oh really, my fault?" He played along.

"Yes, I was totally right about... can't even remember what we were fighting about but I was totally right."

"I just know that it made me feel miserable..." Tom moaned and Sofia snuggled up against his chest. They kissed again, just happy to be in each other's company. The tender moment ended abruptly when they heard a harsh, male voice behind them.

"Sorry to break up the party folks but Barry wants you to come and talk about your plans for tonight." They slid apart. "Did you forget about the funeral?"

"Hey man, what's it to you anyway? We were just talking," Tom said.

"Yeah, I can see that you were just talking."

"Why, what's your problem with that? Elton - isn't it?!" Tom said in a cynical tone. "I didn't know you were a friend of Barry and Lorraine's."

"It's Errol Botes. And it's a funeral, so what are you guys doing, going walkabouts and all that?"

"You know each other?" Sofia stared at the two men open-mouthed. The one so loving, the other one so harsh. "Errol, what are you doing here? Are you drunk?" He must have followed them from the little main-street restaurant.

"You know this guy?" Tom sounded suspicious.

"Yes, I do. From my time in Cape Town."

"Yes exactly, from her time in Cape Town," Errol sounded cynical. "We've been seeing quite a bit of each other here in Joburg as well."

Sofia could feel Tom tensing up with anger. What was Errol thinking, provoking him like that? Errol hadn't been at the funeral, hadn't even been invited, so why had he spoken to Barry? It had been their first close moment in a while and now it was all ruined.

"Yes, but there's a reason for that." She stared Errol down. "I'll tell you all about it later, Tom. Let's please go back to the restaurant now."

"Yes, let's do that. About time, too," Errol said.

"Look, man, it's none of your business, alright?" Tom snarled.

"Oh no? And why is it none of my business?"

Errol planted himself in front of Tom. Sofia was scared that Errol might blurt out, why the two of them knew each other and why he should care about Tom and her kissing. That would be too much - today of all days.

"What is wrong with you? Stop it, you two. You're quite right, Errol, it's a funeral and Tom and I should go back to the restaurant now," she tried to reason.

They left the shop with the curious art behind and went back to 7th Avenue. Sofia was rather upset and walked ahead of the two men. She heard a scuffle behind her and turned around.

What happened next was not only embarrassing but it didn't make sense to Sofia at all until Tom explained it back at the house.

Apparently, there had been some hard elbowing from Errol, as Tom walked next to him. Tom was stunned at first, then he got really angry had dealt Errol a blow to the chin. Errol retaliated with a blow that went into thin air but his left fist caught Tom in the ribs. Tom got so furious that he grabbed hold of his adversary's neck. He held him in a headlock, while Errol flailed his arms about and tried to push Tom off. By now other pedestrians had become aware of the brawl and intervened, holding the two men back by their shoulders.

"I'll stick you with a knife, you mampara," Errol yelled, as he was dragged away from the scene with a ripped sleeve and a swollen lip.

"Somebody is going to call the police just now," Sofia hissed and pulled Tom with her in the opposite direction.

"We can't tell anybody about this or Barry will be even more upset. A funeral and his best friend getting into a fight on the same day? Not a good mix."

"Damn this, I should have kept my cool," Tom panted. He put his jacket in order and felt his hurting chest. His ribs didn't seem broken.

"Too late for that now," Sofia said coolly.

They returned to the restaurant down the road, where a handful of guests were still sitting outside, drunk or bored by their duty to be here.

They shouldn't have worried about Barry. The grieving vet had found comfort in brandy and coke, while Tom and Sofia went on their walk, and he wasn't exactly sober. When the couple walked into the restaurant to look for him, Barry was unsteady on his feet, barely acknowledging people who were leaving. Then he started counting some money out onto the counter.

"Ah, there you are," Barry said and concentrated on the notes as if he had trouble with his eyes. "This is my best friend in the whole world," he told the lady behind the counter who shot Tom an anxious look.

"Barry, how do you know this guy, Errol?" Tom asked his friend abruptly and still somewhat upset.

"Who?"

"Errol," Tom repeated.

"Errol who? Errol Flynn?" Barry tittered at his little joke.

"Who is Errol Flynn? No, the guy who came to tell us that we must come back because you wanted to discuss your plans for tonight."

"Oh, that guy." That was all they could get out of him. They dropped Barry and Charmaine off at the B&B in Linden and drove on to Astrid's house.

"What on earth…" Astrid was astounded to see Tom so dishevelled and noticed that both of them were upset. "What happened to you? You weren't mugged or something, were you? Come to the lounge."

"No, nothing like that," Sofia said. They sat down and Astrid brought a wet cloth, so Tom could at least wash off the blood from a scratch wound on his arm. "What happened was…ouch!" Sofia applied an antiseptic that made Tom flinch.

"Here are the plasters," Astrid said and took the largest plaster she could find from the box.

Sofia took over. "What happened was that Tom and Errol brawled in the street in Melville and clocked each other - as you can see. Errol's lip was bleeding. The only thing I don't understand is why? I know he can be an idiot but why did you hit him and why did it get so out of hand?"

She shot Tom a stern look and put the plaster over the scratch. Tom squirmed. "You want to know why? He said something bad about you and needled me with his elbow as he walked next to me. Bastard. That's why."

Tom felt righteous that he had protected the honour of his woman but his woman wanted none of it. "Why didn't you just walk away? You could have been arrested. Then what?" Sofia said but her anger was beginning to dissolve. Tom had wanted to protect her back there.

"Why would Errol do such a thing?" Astrid asked.

"So, you know this guy as well? Who doesn't know him, I wonder. And how must I know why he does stuff like that? He went off at me even before that."

"That's true," Sofia confirmed. "Errol was rather harsh with Tom. We'd just taken a short walk up the road and were... well kissing... when all of a sudden, Errol stood there, telling us we weren't behaving like people at a funeral should and that Barry wanted to speak with Tom."

"You think he was jealous or something?" Astrid asked. She picked up the cloth and the remaining plasters.

"Why would he be so jealous?" Tom asked and looked at Sofia and Astrid.

"Yes, why indeed?!" Astrid said in a snide tone.

"I don't know you tell me..." Tom wiped his arm with a tissue. "How do you know this guy, anyway? You never said. Is there something, I should know?"

"Mhmm," Astrid grumbled.

"Astrid, please!" Sofia begged.

"So?" Tom prodded.

"Well, how was I supposed to tell you that? We kind of had... we kind of had a short affair. A very, very short affair, a very, very long time ago."

Sofia looked at her hands, expecting Tom to load it over her but Tom appeared to be calm.

"What, really? When was that?"

"When you were in England for all those months. But I swear, it meant nothing and was over quicker than you could say 'eye contact'."

"That's true, Tom," Astrid said. "I should make us some tea." They ignored her and Tom stared scornfully at Sofia.

"You really did that, didn't you?"

"Yes. Why would I lie about something like that?"

"Why indeed? So, you're saying... with this guy? That your love for me and all, was just an act?"

Tom was getting upset now.

"No, of course, it wasn't! How could you even say that?"

"Oh, am I not reading this right? You avoid talking about marriage, although you know how badly I want to... to marry you..." His voice faltered. "And then this... this guy suddenly appears... and you had a relationship with him, long ago. And your cousin knows about him but I don't!"

"Tom, it's not like that," Sofia pleaded.

"Oh no? What is it like then?"

"Tom, please. We need to talk about this rationally. I've been wanting to tell you for a long time but there was never the right time. I didn't want it to come out like that. I feel nothing... nothing for Errol. It was a lapse in judgement a very long time ago."

"I don't think I can handle any more surprises today. Astrid, thank you for your hospitality but I think I mustn't overstay my welcome. I need to do some thinking and I need to do it alone."

"Alone? I don't want to do this alone."

It was Sofia's turn to be upset.

"Oh dear, the cat is out of the bag," Astrid muttered and went to make tea in the kitchen. Tea was always good in difficult situations.

"Mommy? Who's that?" Her six-year-old son came down the stairs, rubbing his eyes, a soft robot toy in his hand.

"It's nothing to worry about, Charlie. It's just auntie Sofie's boyfriend. His name is Tom. They're having a bit of an argument but it's alright. Go to bed now, it's late," his mother said.

"Is he angry with auntie Sofie, mom? Do they fight like you and Daddy?"

"They are discussing something, they don't agree on. That's all."

"Okay." Charlie toddled off and up the stairs again, dragging his toy over the stairs.

Astrid placed three teacups, the teapot, sugar and milk on a tray and carried it into the lounge. "Here is some tea. Sorry, it took so long, but Charlie..."

"Thank you, Astrid." Tom looked up at her. "I'll have a cup, then I'll leave." Sofia's eyes teared up. "Why, Tom? I told you - what more do you want?"

"You just spring that on me? Something like that? What do you expect... that I take it in my stride? That I say, oh don't worry, darling. I don't mind, it's alright? How do you think I feel? Is there anything else I should know, anybody else I should worry about? Somebody coming out of the woodwork, wanting to stick me with a knife?" He took a deep breath.

"If that's what you think of me, Tom, you should probably leave."

"What am I supposed to think, Sofia?"

"Tom, I don't know if it's the right time and place..."

"When is there a right time and place for things like that?" He flared up again.

"Oh, I don't know, back at the farm?"

"We have to talk sometime, Sofia. Why not now?"

"Tom, please..."

"Alright, then come with me. We'll go back home together tomorrow. We can talk about everything at the B&B and then go home," he suggested.

"I have to stay a while longer. There's something I must do."

"And what would that be? Spend time with your other boyfriend?"

"I don't want to spend time with him and he's never been my boyfriend, Tom."

"What should I call him then?" He taunted her.

"Whatever you want but there's nothing between us, I was just drunk at that party in Cape Town and things happened..."

"Have some more hot tea," Astrid said. "It's freezing cold tonight..."

"Thank you, Astrid, but I must be going now." Tom stood up.

"You will do no such thing," Astrid ordered him as if he were a child. "You two will talk this out right here, then make up and then you can have a good night's sleep. Understood?!" Tom and Sofia stared at her in surprise and nodded.

"Good," Astrid said. "I'm glad that's sorted. Sugar anyone?"

So, Tom and Sofia talked it out right there in Astrid's lounge in front of the crackling fireplace, drinking tea.

When it came to the part, where Errol and Damian made an appearance, Sofia hesitated. How would Tom react? She was scared but she had no choice: it was now or never. She came right out with it, told him about Damian and the health problem the child faced. Tom's face turned pale. Astrid had gone to bed and Sofia was on her own.

"Are you serious?" He frowned

"Of course I'm serious." Sofia's eyes teared up. "What, Tom? I told you everything there is to it - what more do you want?"

"You have a child with this Errol? You had a lover you never told me about, while I was out of the country... and you also had a child with him you also never told me about. Anything else?"

"No, of course not. I mean... not much. Just that Damian is not well at the moment. But I'm glad, I told you all the same, even if you are angry about it."

"What am I supposed to think, Sofia? You're just bombarding me..."

Sofia was very quiet now.

"I don't know, Tom. I have to leave it up to you, what you want to think. But anything is better than living with this, living with these lies. I really don't know anymore why I didn't tell you straight away. I was probably afraid to lose you, ashamed of what I'd done... and then it was too late. It became less and less impossible to bring it up until... now."

"So why now?"

"I told you, Damian is not well and that brought it all back and then Errol was here and we tried to find a solution together. Then he told me about this cousin who is a match but wants money and..."

"...and then you remembered that there was something you had to tell me?"

"No, I was waiting for the right moment, Tom. I wanted to put the whole thing to rights. I've wanted to do this for a long time."

"Because you needed money?"

"What?" Sofia felt like slipping, slipping, the ground was tilting and she couldn't sit up straight anymore. She felt tears welling up as she leaned back into the couch. Had she lost Tom now, for being a coward all this time? A coward who had kept such a great, unforgivable secret? She couldn't blame Tom if he walked out on her, didn't love her anymore. But it hurt so badly.

"I don't want money from you. Actually, I don't think it's a good idea at all. I was going to tell Errol that. It's possible that he was so cross today because of that whole story. I don't trust him, I really don't. I mean, he should be fighting with his cousin, should convince him to do the right thing! Gugu said, she would check the situation out and let me know. I never asked you for anything, now did I? And in any case, there is only so much I can do. Damian is not my son anymore. He is somebody else's son. It's just that I feel so much pressure and don't know what to do."

She began to wring her hands and looked at the floor. At least she could bear Tom's scrutinising stares better that way.

"You made it your problem. We could have done this together..." Tom said and drank some tea. The liquid was cold by now but Tom didn't care. He saw how Sofia's translucent skin was blotched red from all the tension; her teary eyes pleading with him to forgive her.

He couldn't. Not yet anyway. Or maybe never.

"Tom, please..."

"I can't get my mind around this. I have to think. It's probably best if I go back home tomorrow and you stay here and sort out this mess. Let me know when you want me to get involved again."

"Very well, please yourself, Tom. I'm too tired for this," Sofia said. "If you want to sleep here, I'm sure you can use the other guest bedroom. Astrid won't mind, under the circumstances."

"It's best if I sleep at the B&B tonight. I know Grant won't come back just now but... I can't. I have to think," Tom said and rubbed his temple.

"I don't want any more secrets between us. It was so stupid of me to keep it a secret for so long," Sofia said. "I mean, I was afraid to lose you but this is so much worse..."

"Actually, there is something I need to tell you, as well, Sofia. It's not *my* secret, strictly speaking but rather a family secret. But I have to clear my head first." Tom felt more composed as Sofia walked him to the door.

"What, some other women coming out of the woodwork?" Sofia winked at him, as weary as she was. "Preferably, from a time before we met..."

"Well, it is about a woman but not what you think," Tom said. "You know what, I just remembered, where I know this Errol from. Barry and I met him at Sun City once, at the casino. We spent a weekend there when you were still in Cape Town, preparing to move to Shangari. I missed you and Barry took me under his wing..." Tom stared into space, remembering. "This guy came up to us, bought us a beer, asked all sorts of questions about the farms," he said.

"And it was Errol?"

"Without any doubt. That's why Barry knew him at the restaurant. Maybe the whole thing at Sun City was just a coincidence... I don't know."

"That's odd. What was Errol doing in Sun City, chatting to you about farms?" Sofia asked confused. "He's been living in Bloemfontein for some time now."

"Hmm, come to think of it, it was strange," Tom said. "Perhaps you should ask him when you get a chance."

"I don't want to speak to him again. At least not for a long time to come... and if he's trying to mess up my life, I want no contact with him at all. As hard as it is for me, I should let the Daniels take care of the problem with Damian."

"Yes, maybe you should."

"I didn't want to abandon him like my father abandoned me," Sofia said. "But I just can't do it anymore." Tom resisted the urge to take Sofia in his arms, let her cry on his shoulder. He just couldn't.

They talked, standing there in the cold passage. It was already after 2 o'clock in the morning when Tom said goodbye. He was no longer angry but he felt empty inside, betrayed and confused and in love all at the same time. Not something, he was willing to communicate.

"Take your time to sort things out," Tom said. "Speak to Gugu about this guy Errol and I truly hope that the little boy is pulling through. I have to go back to Shangari tomorrow. We have to talk again, no matter what happens and I don't know yet what will happen. I need to digest everything you told me. Good night, darling."

He gave Sofia a fleeting kiss on the cheek.

That was a good sign, wasn't it? Would he still love her after he was done digesting the overwhelming load of shocking news? Perhaps in time, Tom would forgive her for Errol and their affair and the child. "Good night, Tom."

When he was gone, Sofia sat down on the soft passage carpet and sobbed.

She cried until she felt drained of all emotion. Unbelievable, what a mess her life had turned into! Tom was right. It was her mess and she had to sort it out.

As she went to sleep in the guest bedroom upstairs, Sofia hoped that there would be at least a glimmer of love left between them when all of this was over.

She dreamt of snuggling up to Tom and laughing with him at gaily painted clay statues of overweight ballerinas in silly poses.

*

"Here is your watch... and 268.20 Rand in cash." The constable at the Brixton police station pushed a tray with Errol Botes' belongings across the counter.

"Remember, we are letting you off with a stern warning. You are lucky, the other party didn't lay charges of assault."

"He assaulted me," Errol mumbled and put the money into his trouser pocket.

"Yes sure, we hear that every day. Just stay out of trouble from now on." The constable was called to the back room and Errol hurriedly walked to the door.

Errol had spent the night in a police cell, where he'd had a chance to cool his heels. They'd made him blow into a breathalyser and was found to be over the limit. How embarrassing and it was his own fault! He put his torn jacket on and walked outside.

The look on the man's face who waited outside the sinister building with his hands in his coat pockets, was a look of disapproval.

"How could you be so careless and draw attention to yourself?" He greeted Errol in a gravelly voice. "We cannot afford to make mistakes like that. It goes down at 17:00 pm tomorrow, the shipment comes in at 16:30 pm from Sao Paulo. Handover is in the park outside the hotel and I expect you to be there with the rest of the gang. Sober."

He crossed the street ahead of Errol.

"Sorry, Bob. I will be there tomorrow, you can count on it."

"Don't play games with me, Botes. Had a hard time, explaining this crap to the boss this morning. You should have known better."

"Hey, it's not my fault that I got involved in all this."

"Yeah, tell yourself that. You could have said 'no'."

They walked side by side towards an unremarkable, silver-grey car that was parked on the other side of the road.

"I won't disappoint you. It was something private, you know but I don't want to bore you with the details..."

"Please don't. Do you have your weapon on you?" The

man asked curtly and stopped by the car.

"It's at the hotel," Errol said. "Do you think they wouldn't have made a fuss if I'd had it with me?"

"Your saving grace, man. Some of your brain cells are working, then."

"Come on, enough with the scolding. You're not the boss of me, remember?"

"Just making sure, you know what you're doing."

"I still know the rules."

The man pressed the remote and the car answered with flashing lights. They opened the car doors and Errol scooted glumly onto the passenger seat. He needed to clear his head now or he might end up dead tomorrow.

"Could have fooled me," Bob said and started the engine.

CHAPTER 8

On Sunday morning, the bi-annual 'Wild Animals of Africa' auction was in full swing just outside of Renosterspruit. Breeders from private game farms had organised the event together with an international organisation called 'Beautiful Wildlife'.

After about an hour, a bright wintry sun drove the visitors into the large, shady tent.

Everybody sat down on the chairs that crossed the tent row after row and waited for the auction to begin. That meant everybody with spare money to buy wild animals for their private game reserves and zoological gardens and those who simply came for the food. The occasional private wildlife enthusiasts attended these gatherings but the SPCA kept their strict rules enforced, where the purchase of the animals was concerned.

Visitors had been viewing the animals on offer all morning and anything from antelopes to buffaloes, rhinos and wild cats were on offer. Soon, auctioneers took turns on an elevated platform, introducing the various lots and taking offers in their typical auctioneers' chant. The animals on show lowed and stomped their feet on the sawdust-strewn ground.

As always, the front rows were reserved for VIPs, mostly politicians and their cronies, well-to-do business leaders and foreign dignitaries. Those without celebrity status and deep pockets, mostly representatives of local and international zoos, sat further at the back. Paddles with numbers written on them flew up in quick, orchestrated succession.

At one side of the tent, between two entrances that led to the car park, long buffet-tables with delectable snacks and beverages were positioned. The bar would officially open at lunchtime but the bartenders were already busy with the polishing of glasses and the cooling of bottles.

A number of corpulent wives and mistresses who accompanied some of the VIP guests, already helped themselves to the buffet. The food had been ordered from Shangari's celebrated kitchen and was excellent. They loaded their plates with prawns and slimming salads while studying each other's garish wardrobes. To all but those with a genuine interest in buying wild animals, the auctioneer's rhythmic repetitions sounded like chanted gibberish.

The ladies at the buffet tables attended such social gatherings to show off their designer clothes and killer heels. They became bored with their lavish mansions and lofty penthouses in the city and their men felt obliged to offer the occasional entertainment. This low-key event was one of their least preferred choices and most tried to stay well away from those smelly, noisy animals.

"...and fourteen... do I hear fourteen and a half? Do I hear fourteen and a half... yes, we have fourteen and a half... and fifteen, fifteen, fifteen..."

Lot 104 was fiercely contested. The auctioneer's hacking singsong and the animal sounds formed a soundtrack that made any kind of meaningful conversation near impossible. Not that meaningful conversations were the ladies' forte at the best of times.

A well-known politician in the front row grunted contentedly and held up his number. He looked around to enjoy the appreciative murmur in the audience and some applause. His dark-blue silk suit seemed a little over-the-top for the occasion but he was not the only one by far. This was a fantastic opportunity to prove one's financial worth to the peers that mattered.

"And sixteen million Rand, sixteen million Rand..."

He raised his paddle with the number 351 in an exhilarated rush of adrenaline. *Yes, everybody, I can afford it!* He thought, forgetting that his actual function in government was to mediate disputes in the mining industry.

16 Million Rand was a record price for the rare pregnant antelope. The graceful animal would have her first offspring at an exclusive game reserve in Kwa Zulu Natal; joining a white rhino, two zebras and two giraffes on a journey to her new home the following morning.

The game farmer who owned the antelope, gleefully rubbed his palms together. At last, he could retire in style, hand over the business of breeding wild animals to his eldest son and buy the house on the coast, he'd always wanted.

Barry Pienaar, the local vet, sat at the back between representatives of European zoos and wildlife organisations, wearing his khaki uniform. He had not planned on coming to the auction this year and had a difficult time staying sober so shortly after his wife's funeral. It had been a spur-of the-moment decision, more for the benefit of his new assistant than anything else. Not long now, then the bar would open and he could drown his aching sorrow in the best tipple available.

Lot 105 was introduced. A pair of sturdy warthogs in their prime. "Seven, do I hear seven? And seven twenty-five, seven twenty-five, seven twenty-five. We have seven twenty-five..."

The bidders had, of course, inspected the animals beforehand and knew them to be in excellent condition. Bidding was brisk as the numbered paddles flew up one by one. It was a mystery even to an old hand like Barry Pienaar, how the auctioneers could tell whose bid was the one that counted.

It didn't take long and a Zoological Garden in Holland received the winning bid. The modestly dressed zoo representative nodded to his colleague and there was no clapping. The proceedings paused and canned music flooded the tent. Lot 105 had been the last one before lunch. Throngs of visitors formed a line in front of the buffet tables and the bar was declared open. *About time*, the local vet thought.

"If it's not Barry Pienaar," Stanislav Makaroff cried cheerfully and patted the taller Barry Pienaar on the shoulder. Then lowered his voice. "Once again, my deepest condolences, sir..."

The vet flinched and spilled some of his beer onto his surprised assistant vet. The young man jumped aside just in time and most of the beer spilled onto the ground.

"Nicely done, my man." Stan Makaroff looked back at his bodyguard and nodded appreciatively. Barry Pienaar turned around with a glowering expression. The two men hadn't laid eyes on each other since the funeral in Johannesburg. Barry Pienaar was anything but pleased to see the man he blamed for his wife's hasty decision to leave him. Deep down, he probably blamed him for her death, too.

"What are you doing here?" The jaded vet growled.

His assistant, Janek Gelders, held a half-empty coca cola can in his hand and kept well away from his boss who was on his second bottle of beer. Barry Pienaar looked as if he was ready to throw it at this cocky man in that strange getup. Makaroff was dressed in a short powder-blue safari suit, matching sandals and a topee hat. Ridiculous.

The bodyguard crossed his arms over his powerful chest in a warning gesture that didn't fail to make an impression on the khaki-clad Barry Pienaar.

"Leave me alone." Barry Pienaar snarled the words through gritted teeth and rudely turned away from one of the richest and best-connected men in the country.

"Well now, Barry my man. You don't blame me for what happened, do you?" Makaroff said in an almost child-like tone.

"And why shouldn't I?"

Barry Pienaar turned around again and stared down at the cocky man who wouldn't leave him alone. The bodyguard cleared his throat in warning.

"Just to be clear, my good man, I had nothing to do with your wife leaving you alone in this most magical place in Africa. It was her desire to leave and she asked me for a job. That's all. I gave her the opportunity..."

Barry Pienaar lowered his beer bottle. "Sure you did, slimeball. Now if you'll excuse me, I have to speak to somebody over there."

The vet didn't feel like causing trouble in front of all his colleagues and acquaintances, but sure as hell, he would not be drawn into an amiable conversation with this spoilt jerk. Instead, he walked off with his embarrassed-looking assistant.

Stan Makaroff was not used to being rejected by lesser individuals but under the circumstances, he didn't push his luck. He nodded benevolently at Barry Pienaar's assistant and a second later, spotted an old friend standing by one of the tent posts.

The unpleasant moment passed and the disagreeable vet was forgotten.

"Oh hello, Basil," he greeted the sweating politician in his shiny dark-blue suit who had acquired the pregnant antelope for sixteen million Rand. "Congratulations on your excellent purchase!"

They shook hands vigorously and Basil Mulambo seemed rather pleased with himself. He nodded at his two cronies who had been standing near him. They left and Makaroff's bodyguard took up his position to give them some privacy.

"Thank you, Stan. I think it will greatly improve the bloodline of my antelopes at Lungani Lodge, don't you?"

"Sure it will... good choice, my man. Had an eye on the beauty myself..." Stan Makaroff laughed and rocked forth and back in his light blue sandals.

"But you don't have a game farm, Stan," Basil said.

"Exactly!" They both bellowed with laughter.

"Had a mind to buying a farm, though," Makaroff insisted. "Combining business with pleasure is not a bad idea, right?! I mean, does one need an excuse to spend more time in this splendid part of our beautiful country? Wouldn't mind starting a little something here."

"You mean, you want to buy a game farm in this area?" Basil asked and took a sip from his wine glass. The red wine did little to ease his sweating.

"Yes, of course. Love this place. Might have found something not far from here. Alas, it's not for sale - just yet."

"As if that would stop you," Basil grunted.

"You know me too well, Basil... I thought I might start something like Willem van Tonder did. You know... breeding rhinos, harvesting their horns for export to Asia. I heard he's got well over one hundred rhinos on his farm close to the Kruger Park by now. He's doing good business with hunters from overseas as well. Bloody nuisance anyway, those hunting licenses. How much does he take per rhino? 100 thousand? Not bad, I say. He just tells a dumb tourist that he needs to cull one of the animals on his farm and needs somebody to do it for him... and wham! A win-win situation, right? Gets rid of old and sick animals and it's way cheaper than an official license. It's his own farm, after all. Pity about the rhinos being poached, though."

"Yes, a real pity," Basil gave a little cough, not caring one way or the other. Rhino hunting wasn't his business. He owned one of the most expensive tourist lodges in South Africa. Nice little investment, his game lodge. The sale of rhino horn, on the other hand, was a different matter and not a good topic for today.

"Lots of work on a game farm," he complained instead. "Do-able, mind you. If you can find capable workers... otherwise, how would someone like me manage a game farm and hundreds of visitors each year? On top of that... the mansion on the golf estate, the penthouse in Sandton and a wine farm in the Cape? Not to speak of my 50-foot yacht?" The men laughed again. They spoke the same language.

"One has to enjoy one's riches, right? ...right?" Stan Makaroff guffawed. "I'm rather fussy when it comes to game farms, though. Tourists are not my thing. Everything else, I've managed quite well so far."

"Yes, you have. How's the wife?" The politician inquired in a perfunctory tone.

"Good, good. She's doing rather well."

"No children yet?"

"No, we're getting too old for that sort of thing, Basil. She has her hands full with family business as it is, you know."

"Yes I bet, she does," Basil chuckled. "But you must think

about the future. Who will take over the business one day? Helena won't want to work forever."

"We'll cross that bridge when we get there," Stan Makaroff said, waving his hand. "Plenty of time to worry about that sort of thing."

Having no children had been an issue in their marriage for a while, but then, Helena didn't want children and that had been the end of the discussion.

"Right... right..." Basil Mulambo mumbled. He had his own ducks in a row and Makaroff could take care of himself.

"Ah, let's not talk about that now, shall we? How is the new addition to your family?" Makaroff continued their pleasant small-talk.

"Ah well, Siya is still a bit weak. It was a difficult birth this time. But she's doing much better and the twins have nannies - of course," Basil said. He looked adoringly at a young, pretty woman in a frilly yellow suit with matching high-heeled Louboutin shoes. She was his idea of beautiful.

"Everything under control on that front, mind you. Have you heard from Theo?" He kept his eye on his young mistress who tucked into the salads at the buffet, chatting to a white lady with a ridiculous hat.

The two men moved closer to the tent wall and went on to discuss, in guarded terms, a somewhat hairy business. The bodyguard planted himself in front of them and watched every movement in the crowd. You never knew who may be listening, even with all this noise around.

"The situation is under control, Basil. Well almost," Stan Makaroff reported. "We have a meeting in Saxonwold Drive soon. The whistle-blower has been dealt with. According to orders from you-know-who."

"The money's in the account?" Basil Mulambo asked under his breath and Stan Makaroff nodded.

The politician fidgeted. His sulking mistress stood now alone by the buffet with a plate heaped full of treats. The woman with the ridiculous hat had moved on and chatted to some other woman by the desserts.

"Got to go and show my face over there, or Thembeka will skin me alive," Basil Mulambo said.

"Can't have that, can we? I'm glad, my wife is not on my case all the time."

"It all comes with a price tag, Stan. I can handle it. Didn't you have a thing with this Lorraine... what was her name again?"

"No, I didn't. It's all a rumour. She just worked for me," Makaroff said with a sigh. "Tragically had an accident and we buried her a few days ago."

"I'm sorry to hear that." Basil stared at his mistress who waved and began to walk toward him. He fidgeted.

"Yes well, nothing but trouble if you try to help someone," Makaroff said.

"I'll say. Well, my man, I have to go. Thembeka looks almost as fierce as the wildebeest over there."

They laughed and patted each other's back before Basil walked toward his mistress and pondered how he could best appease her. Before he could reach Thembeka, loud squeaking noises came from the general direction of the animal enclosures and a mighty commotion ensued. Chairs tumbled over and a man in a smudged suit helped an anxious woman in a silk dress onto the stage. This was apparently no easy task. Others jumped away from the aisle.

What on earth was going on?!

An incredulous Basil Mulambo soon realised why people were behaving so strangely: the warthogs from lot 105 had somehow escaped their handlers and rampaged down the central aisle in a frenzied bid for freedom.

From one moment to the next, the warthogs were pawing, snorting and squeaking madly, while thrusting their heads this way and that. Shoes, bags and hats darted through the air. Glasses broke. The two determined warthogs were a fearsome sight with their sharp, curled-up tusks slashing about and their tufty tails high up in the air.

People shrieked and jumped onto chairs or ran outside as fast as their legs would carry them to get out of harm's way.

Thembeka managed to leap behind one of the buffet

tables, losing a bright yellow shoe in the process. She let out a shrill scream and hid behind the tablecloth. Lots of people were trapped between the chairs screamed as well. Some ended up on the ground, falling on top of each other, crawling away and toppling over more chairs.

Then a shot rang out and people screamed even more. One warthog had almost managed to run the entire length of the tent. It was suddenly flung forward, stood up on shaky legs and fell again, a long bouncing dart stuck in its rump. Another shot rang out and the second warthog began to stagger around in circles, then made for its companion and collapsed twice before crumpling to the ground.

The woman with the ridiculous hat fainted into the arms of her husband when the warthog's ear brushed against her foot. It didn't take long before the tranquilliser kicked in but to the auction guests, it seemed like an eternity.

The shooter, one of the attending vets, leisurely secured the rifle and declared the warthogs safe to approach. He had been ready to leave the event and was rummaging around his bakkie when he heard screaming and crashing noises. Without a second thought, he'd grabbed his dart gun, put extra tranquilliser-darts in his shirt pocket and ran back to the tent. As soon as the warthogs were rendered harmless, other vets in the audience joined him. Barry Pienaar and his assistant helped to carry the heavy animals back to the enclosure under the watchful eye of their new owners from Holland.

Basil climbed down from a chair that threatened to collapse at any moment under his weight. His wine glass had flown out of his hand and shattered against the nearby table.

There were shards lying around everywhere and it reeked of spilled alcohol. Mulambo espied his mistress in her soiled yellow suit, as she scrambled up from behind a half-collapsed buffet table.

Thembeka spotted her left shoe and hobbled forward, plunking herself on one of the still standing chairs and put the shoe on. As she stood up, the heel broke. She began to furiously wipe the front of her new designer outfit with a wad of serviettes. Two of her fingernails were ruined, which meant that she had to book another appointment at the beauty salon! Her début at a society gathering was not panning out the glamorous way she had hoped for!

"Let's go!" She yelled when she caught sight of her approaching lover.

"But darling, calm down. I still have to..."

"I want to go *right now!*" She raged and threw down the wad of serviettes.

Basil Mulambo stared at his mistress. She was a sight to behold: bits of food on her yellow silk suit that had cost him a fortune, the heel of one of the matching shoes broken and her hair sticking out in all directions.

"I'm afraid, we'll have to wait until the formalities have been dealt with," he said in a deadpan voice, then saw her terrified face. "Okay, okay, Baby. I'll see if I can find Willem. He can take you to the car. You wait there until I'm done with the papers. Pull yourself together now."

He wiped himself down and his mood deteriorated by the minute. Thembeka was making a scene and that was not what he had brought her to this auction for.

"I could have died and you want me to pull myself together?" She fumed.

"Yes." His tone was menacing. "I do."

Thembeka recognised the tone in his voice and knew she had to calm herself, whether she wanted to or not. She swallowed and nodded in silence.

"There's my girl," he said soothingly and padded her fleshy arm. *Perhaps it is time to cut Thembeka loose*, he thought to himself. Behaving like they were married! There were plenty of mild-tempered fish in the sea...

He detected Willem, his driver, behind a row of chairs where he struggled to his feet, virtually atop a rather corpulent lady. "Arré Willem, hey Willem! Arré!" Mulambo signalled for him to come over. He instructed the driver to take his mistress out to the limousine. Then he walked off to attend to the important task of wrapping up the purchase of his new and rather pricey antelope.

Stan Makaroff had watched the surreal events from the safety of his chair. He sat numb with shock, realising for the first time in his life that he was mortal. Nothing would have prevented those tusks slashing into him, had the warthogs chosen a different path. How dangerous wild animals could be! Perhaps it wasn't such a good idea to get into the game breeding business, after all.

People around him were freeing themselves from tumbled-over chairs and his bodyguard sat on the ground in a daze. Makaroff must have kicked him in the head somehow when he sat himself down in a hurry.

The poor sod got up and dusted himself off, trying to get his bearings, readjusting his jacket over a small semi-automatic rifle.

"Are you okay, Bruno?" Makaroff asked him.

"I'm fine, sir." The bodyguard tried to sound convincing. "Not to worry, sir."

The event management had already given instruction to clean up the mess. Staff was hard at work, helping people back on their feet and putting chairs back into recognisable rows. Paramedics saw to sprained ankles and scratch wounds but nobody had been seriously hurt.

"On behalf of the... creeeeeak... creeeeeak... we wish to apologise for the... creeeeak... incident..." One of the auctioneers battled with the sound equipment. He had climbed onto the stage to make a clumsy announcement. "... and would like to invite you to help yourselves to the refreshments... Please help yourselves to the buffet and... I'm told that the bar has reopened. Everything is on the house, of course... on the house. We'll continue proceedings in about half an hour... creeeeak..."

"Mr. Makaroff!" A microphone was thrust in the tycoon's face. He was taken off-guard. "Mr. Makaroff - a few questions, please. Could you spare a minute for a short interview?"

A cameraman followed the pretty reporter's every move

and filmed the two of them. Bruno, the bodyguard, made an attempt to step in but Makaroff stopped him with a theatrical wave of his hand and smiled charmingly at the woman.

"Yes, that's my name, young lady, don't wear it out." He tried to sound funny. "Certainly, certainly, and why not? Let's go over there; it's quieter in that corner... Your name was...?"

She gave him her name and the name of the television station, she worked for. He was sure, he hadn't met the reporter before. *A rookie then. Excellent. An interview with the main television station is not to be scoffed at*, the tycoon thought in his usual supercilious manner.

She knew it was a daring move to ambush someone as important as Stan Makaroff but he didn't seem to mind and they continued the interview. "Oh good, thank you so much, Mr. Makaroff."

The reporter straightened her outfit and waved for the cameraman to come closer. "And one, two..." The cameraman held three fingers up.

"Thank you, Mark. Today, we are at the bi-annual 'Wild Animals of Africa' auction in Renosterspruit," she spoke into the camera. "I'm here with the well-known Johannesburg businessman, Mr. Stanley Makaroff." She turned toward him. "Mr. Makaroff, how did you experience the escape of two wild animals...?"

"Quite some show, wasn't it? I'm sure it's part of the scheduled entertainment to put the crowd in the mood," Makaroff cackled at his joke. He didn't correct her blunder with his name and smiled into the camera.

"To be sure, sir, Mr. Makaroff, but I'm afraid, we only just arrived and missed the entire spectacle. Please tell our viewers, what happened," the reporter said.

"As you know, Thandi, I love animals almost as much as I love children and this auction is a wonderful opportunity... "Makaroff launched into a meandering answer.

Usually, his PR-lady Gugulethu Mbatha was present but he had decided to go to the auction alone. Better if she didn't know everything about his dealings with certain individuals.

Gugu could tweak things back into shape with the TV station later. The strategy had always worked in his favour.

What was important was that his chat with Basil Mulambo had looked like a chance meeting, and Stan Makaroff was convinced that he had done a fabulous job of achieving just that all on his own.

*

A few miles north of the clamorous tent, a quiet dirt road led away from Renosterspruit and toward an unremarkable farm gate. No signage, no name. Every local knew who stayed here and that attention from the wrong crowd might have unwanted consequences. The fence was solid and properly maintained. This was important because the farm was the home of wild animals that had been found injured or orphaned in the bush.

The animal sanctuary was run by Gerda Marais, a middle-aged widow whose husband had died of cancer and left her the old citrus farm some years ago. She had transformed the farm into a home for young elephants, zebras, bucks, owls and young rhinos. New animals were joining the nursery on a constant basis. Even meerkats had to be taught to live in a communal family group before they could be released back into the wild. In a new, rather disturbing trend, the cute, young animals were sold to tourists in the Kalahari. Once they were older and less cute, the meerkats ended up in sanctuaries and even municipal parks all over the country, ready to wreak havoc.

Gerda's was one of the few sanctuaries for wild animals that took them in and prepared them for a normal life away from chic city dwellings and parks.

The farm was a smallholding, sub-divided off the Pienaar estate. A game fence and large gate separated the sanctuary from the rambling land of the much larger Pienaar farm.

As soon as the orphans were grown up enough, they would be released into the larger farm through the gate. Here they could roam the bush in virtual freedom.

The older members of each species had to teach the

younger ones, how to find food and protect themselves outside of the sanctuary. This could take a while until they were able to sustain themselves. Eventually, they found new homes in the surrounding game parks or in the wild.

Gerda Marais had been business-minded enough to enlist a number of wildlife organisations as sponsors for their upkeep. They also helped with the release of the youngsters and she was now able to employ locals to help her run the sanctuary.

There were two small lakes beyond the old-fashioned windmill. They were surrounded by tall eucalyptus trees, so typical for the area, rough bush and a small hill. Behind the main farmhouse, a grove of gnarled lemon trees was the last reminder of the glorious citrus-farming days.

The caregivers lived in a complex to the left of the main gate and the orphans were housed in three large barns some distance away from the main house. The barns served as dormitories for the young animals and as depots for food and equipment. The main house had an inviting veranda and a vegetable garden that Gerda managed to maintain.

Copious amounts of water that the sanctuary needed were drawn from boreholes inside the sanctuary. The taps were opened at feeding time and the water ran into troughs inside the enclosures. Here, the orphans also played with their caregivers and socialised with other animals. Whenever Gerda needed time to herself, she walked over the little wooden bridge to the top of the hill and took in the view on a bench that her husband had built for them in the early days of their marriage. Now her heart belonged to the wild animals in her care.

Oscar, the once sad rhino baby, had joined the sanctuary at the beginning of the year and was fast developing into a playful toddler. Thanks to a hearty diet and lots of love. Love that came from a 14-year-old boy by the name of Frans who had come back for him. Frans popped in after school to help with the feed and to just sit and hug the young pachyderm.

What was more, the boy was able to call and speak with

little Oscar, a talent that had been handed down to him through a long line of rhino whisperers. At night, a donkey named Cookie, Oscar had bonded with, kept him warm on his bed of straw and pillows inside the barn. All the little orphans had such companions, mostly sheep or donkeys and sometimes dogs. If no animal was available, one of the caretakers would stand in and snuggle up to the new arrivals until a replacement could be found. This method had proved quite successful and the animals thrived.

Orphaned elephants and rhinos were ready for a 'soft' release at the age of four or five. The gate at the back of the sanctuary was opened to allow them to venture into the bushveld and find their own kind. Wild elephants, living on the Pienaar farm, could often be seen close to the back fence, where they waited for the young elephants from the sanctuary to join them.

The boy and the young rhino sat together, leaning against a rock inside the enclosure at feeding time. "Here, here not so greedy Kleintjie," Frans tried to slow down the feed. He was holding a large bottle with one hand and patted the young rhino's head with the other. "You're getting too big for this, aren't you?"

The rhino nodded a little but maybe just to make the milk flow quicker.

"I know that you miss your mommy... I also miss my mommy. She's far away but she'll be alright without me. Kurtie is almost twelve and he's taking my place at home, now..." he chatted to the rhino in a soothing voice. Frans felt only a little homesick, but he was too old for that sort of thing. Obakeng and Frida were taking good care of him and he was happy right where he was; free to think and feel his surroundings in Shangari.

After the feed, Oscar rested. Then he wanted to play, nudging Frans with his head and the budding horn. The boy was soon running ahead, calling the young rhino to follow him, while hiding behind a thorn bush. "Come here Kleintjie, come here." He threw a ball and Oscar pushed it on the ground with his mouth.

"Howe boy, he's going to think his name is Kleintjie, instead of Oscar," one of the workers, washing down the young elephants, called over.

"He knows his name," Frans answered curtly.

"Oh, and how do you know?"

"I just know."

"Okay then." The men laughed and carried on with their tasks.

After a short month, Frans had left the desolate Khoi-San village down south and came back to Shangari. He'd missed his friends and school and little Oscar. So he had returned to live in the Shangari compound once again.

His mother hadn't been all that happy with his decision but at last Francina had relented and packed a modest bag for her eldest son. She'd let out a sigh. Frans had grown up so much, since his Xnau initiation ceremony that made him a proper Koisan. "Now you're leaving me too," she'd said and had cried for her slain husband, Cornelius.

The boy felt sorry for her. His mother looked so sad and lonely, with her crumpled, tear-stained face. It was difficult to hold back his own tears at her suffering but he was a man now and had made his choice. The plan in his head was something he could not share with his mother or anyone else, so he didn't even try to explain. Oom Obakeng would understand. He'd understand what he was planning to do, would teach him how to do it.

What Francina understood was that her eldest son wanted more than to do piece jobs on the surrounding farms and waste his time on weekends with drinking, playing cards and fufi like most of the adults in the village. Frans would succeed in life and she had no right to hold him back.

She had given him a little money and a letter for Baas Tom. It was no more than a dirty piece of paper with some scrawled writing on it but the meaning was clear. She politely asked the owner of Shangari to please let her son stay in their old house in the worker's compound and to look after him, to please send him to school. He could come home for the holidays and help out with the younger children. Baas Tom had promised to help and she knew that he would stand by his word.

Like any good mother, Francina wanted the best for her children and if her eldest son could go to a good school, she would not stop him. Francina pulled her large cotton doek into her face to hide the tears and patted her son's arm as he climbed into the truck that would take him north. During the long drive, Frans day-dreamed. The village was a dire place and not much to his liking. So windy and dusty, especially now in winter. His heart cried out for the savannah and the whitewater rushing past Shangari, and also the animals in the park. Frans had walked up the gravelled footpath, his mother's letter in his fist and his bundle on his back. Brutus the Ridgeback had waited for him by the lodge and accompanied him to the barn.

He'd passed the enclosure, where Obakeng was busy feeding the three-legged cheetah. Later, he would take Jethro for a walk on a long chain and parade him in front of the tourists. The cheetah was quite tame by now and the visitors were allowed to ruffle his fur and scratch him behind the ears. This life of leisure was not so bad for a predator with no chance of survival in the wild. Obakeng had given Frans an encouraging nod and carried on with his task.

The boy had found the owner of Shangari Safari Lodge in the barn, where he worked on his boat. The mysterious boat that gave rise to rumours among the children in the area. Would Baas Tom take it to Bokspits one day and sail it in the desert sand? Or was it supposed to serve as a monument in front of the lodge building for tourists to gawk at and take photographs?

It was the first time that Frans had stolen a first-hand glance at *The Boat* and he'd given it a quick once-over, after handing his mother's letter to Baas Tom. It wasn't as big as he's imagined but he liked the smell of the wood and the smooth surface of the bulky body.

Frans wondered what it would be like to stand on the deck

of such a boat or to hang over one side, stemming his feet against the hull, letting the sails carry the boat through wind and swishing waves. He had seen people do this on TV. An amazing sight.

Tom Rutgers had read the letter and scratched his head. Tom Rutgers had read the letter and scratched his head. There weren't enough hours in a day to get through the work at the lodge, even without the extra burden of an orphan. But he had given his word to Cornelius' widow. He looked at the boy in front of him, dressed in threadbare shorts and a pretentious Virgin Active t-shirt, his green baseball cap in hand. Tom knew he couldn't let Francina down just because he was so busy.

This bright, young man was part of the family, although his father had passed away. And who knew? One day, he might become a doctor or engineer or even run a gym in town.

"Another family has moved into your old house," he said and Frans looked close to tears. "But I will speak to Obakeng and his wife. I'm sure, there is space, now that their granddaughter got married. If not, there is still a guest room at the farmhouse, you could move into but I think that might be a bit boring for you."

Frans' face lit up as he said, "Thank you, Baas Tom, I'd love to stay with Obakeng and Frida if they will have me. I know them well and also the other children in the compound. Jennifer and Rynhart and Thabo. We go to the same school and I like to make wire cars..." He took a deep breath. Tom Rutgers had never heard him speak so much at once and looked closely at the boy before him.

"...and I promise, I will go to school and if you want to send me to university, I will also do that and become a vet one day." He studied a hole in his right tekkie, exactly where his big toe was.

"Oh, you're ambitious, laatjie," Tom laughed. "That's good, Frans. Keep it up. I want you to study hard, get good marks and behave. If I hear any complaints, you must go back and stay with your mother at her village."

"Oh no, I will give you no problems, I promise," Frans said vehemently and looked Tom in the eye.

"Good, I wouldn't have it any other way. If you need anything, you come and talk to me or tell Frida and Obakeng. I will phone the school principal tomorrow."

"Thank you, Oom Tom! There is just one very small thing. A very, very small thing," Frans whspered and kneaded his cap.

"Yes, what is it? Do you need new books or new clothes?"

"No nothing like that, only for next school year, Oom. But I want to go to Gerda Marais after school, please. Oscar needs me. And auntie Gerda said I can do my homework on the veranda." Frans used the term Oom for uncle.

Tom thought for a while. "If you promise not to fall behind with your studies and do sports and afternoon activities at school, I won't mind it one bit."

"Oh thank you Oom, I will study so much. I'm going to catch up nicely. My teacher, Mrs. Hardy says, I have potential." The boy was now grinning from ear to ear and Tom Rutgers had to smile at his eagerness.

"I'm glad to hear it. But as I said, I want you to keep it up. Go now and find Obakeng for me, Frans. I will discuss the matter with him."

Tom Rutgers turned his attention back to the wooden plank, he had been busy dressing when the boy had shown up. He lovingly stroked the smooth, rounded surface and thought, how he would take Sofia sailing in this boat one day.

"Yes, Baas Tom. Dankie," Frans said and skipped out of the barn; toward the vegetable garden where Obakeng was bending over the carrots, pulling them out one by one with great care. The gardener looked up from his work and shook his grey head, smiling.

Brutus bounded ahead and Frans threw sticks that the dog fetched right up to the wall of the workers' compound. Then Brutus loped back to the barn, sniffed and dropped himself on the ground next to Tom and took a nap.

Frans was happy. He could go to school, be with Oscar and stay at Shangari with Oom Obakeng and Tannie Frida.

That's all he needed right now and it was all he needed to devise his plan. The plan he would carry out in his own good time one day.

*

In Johannesburg, Gugu Mbatha pressed her cell phone to her ear and turned the wheel of her red Suzuki Jimny sharply to the right. She had left her office at the Makaroff Tower in Sandton in a hurry and there was no time to slow down. She zoomed past a bumbling truck, only to be slowed down again by a fully occupied mini taxi struggling up the steep road. Her hands trembled with nervousness.

"I must speak to you face to face, as soon as possible," she urged her friend. "Then you'll see for yourself."

"Okay if it's that important." Sofia was mildly alarmed. "Let's meet at the small shopping centre in Linden. At the coffee shop there, you know which one."

"Yes, I do. Can you be there in let's say 15 minutes?"

"Okay, I think I can. Anything else?"

"Turns out, it was a good thing, I made inquiries about your ex."

"About Errol? Oh, why is that?" Sofia asked surprised. She hadn't spoken to Errol since the funeral and whenever she'd tried to call the GP or Damian's adopted mother in the Cape Town, the phone lines were engaged.

"He has no extended family for starters, only an aunt and a couple of cousins in Grabouw. Then I spoke to the *real* Suzanne Daniels in Cape Town."

"What? What do you mean, the *real* Suzanne Daniels? Who did I speak to, then?" Sofia was flabbergasted.

"I don't know who you spoke to, Sofie. It's anyone's guess who that woman was but Damian is not sick in hospital and not in need of a new liver. He's happy and healthy and thriving. Apparently, he likes drawing colourful pictures. His favourite colour is yellow and they just got a new puppy. A black Labrador."

Sofia had been so tense with worry, she felt like crying when she heard this. She stopped walking and turned away

192

from the crowd, heading for the large chain store. Sofia wiped a tear away and pulled herself together.

"You mean... you mean, Errol planned this? A shakedown? No, he wouldn't do that to me..." *He wouldn't dare*, she thought heatedly. But how could she be sure, what Errol was actually capable of? She'd never thought he would be so jealous of Tom, either.

Gugu twisted the rear mirror into a better position. "I don't know if Errol knew but this cousin of his turns out to be a real tsotsi. Maybe the woman's his girlfriend. Hang on a sec."

Had that dark car with the tinted windows been following her since Jan Smuts Avenue - or was she dreaming? Why would anyone be following her? She'd been so careful. Nobody knew about Lorraine's letter but her.

"Are you there yet?" Gugu almost yelled into her phone.

"Just got here. I'm walking toward the coffee shop right now," Sofia said and wiped away another tear. "Are you saying, it's possible that this cousin acted on his own and somehow used Errol to get to me? Aalio, Kusipää. But that doesn't explain, why Errol hasn't phoned me. It doesn't make sense. Maybe I should go to the police. "

"I'm not sure yet, Sofie. Better wait. I'd be surprised if Errol instigated this but I thought you should know. We'll talk about everything when I get there. Damn!" Gugu hooted at the mini taxi. "Any slower and you'll roll backwards!"

"Don't rush like that, Gugu!" Sofia was close to the first tables and chairs on the pavement. "Okay, you can tell me all about it when you get here, just drive safely."

The Victory Gardens shopping centre would be quite busy in about an hour when parents fetched their children from school.

"Yup. Got to get off the phonenow. This is really...!" Gugu shouted. "Oh man..."

Sofia heard the engine roaring through her phone. "Don't you want to tell me what's the rush? You sound scared." Sofia walked into the coffee shop and sat down at a table by the large window, facing the parking lot.

Her friend didn't answer. A waiter bustled toward Sofia with a broad smile, holding out an oversized menu. "Anything I can get you?"

"Yes, a coffee, please. I'm waiting for my friend."

"No problem." The waiter shuffled away.

Gugu Mbatha checked her rear mirror again. Hadn't she seen that dark car back in Sandton? It was not exactly an unusual car. "You still there?" Gugu said into her phone.

"Everything okay with you?" Sofia asked.

"Not sure... I'll be there now. This car's been driving behind me all the way from Sandton; I think... maybe it's a different one. There is more and we have to talk about all that stuff, I told you - and I mean all of it. Lorraine's letter that I told you about. I'll give you the skinny just now," Gugu spoke into her phone one last time, then she threw it on the passenger seat next to her.

She stopped at a red traffic light and her eyes widened as she looked back. The dark car was close to hers but she couldn't see who was inside.

Yesterday, Gugu had phoned around and googled, only to find out that Errol had lied to Sofia about their son and made up the medical emergency. As if that wasn't bad enough, a letter had arrived together with the other mail. She had been too busy at the office to open her letters. So she had taken the whole pile home with her.

Judging by the postal stamp, it had been sent two weeks ago from a post office in Johannesburg. That in itself wasn't unusual, given the state of the South African post office but - the letter was from Lorraine! That it was written by a dead woman was kind of creepy and according to the date, Lorraine had sent it a couple of days before her fatal accident.

Gugu began reading the letter and what she read sounded too bizarre for words. She'd nearly spilled the red wine that she had with her takeaway dinner when she got to the second page. That's why she needed to meet with Sofia, so they could read the letter together and talk about it face to face.

Sofia ordered coffee and a piece of cheesecake, she would

share with her friend. It shouldn't take Gugu more than ten minutes to arrive. 30 minutes passed. Sofia tried to phone and got her voicemail.

Was she stuck in traffic and didn't want to answer her phone? She decided to be patient. While she waited, Sofia had enough time to mull over the story Gugu had told her before dropping the bombshell about Errol's cousin.

Imagine! She never thought Errol would sink so low.

He'd practically asked her for money. Tom's money. The other news was that Lorraine had mailed Gugu a letter before she died, explaining the events that had plagued her conscience for a long time and probably had led to her death. The fact that Lorraine had died under mysterious circumstances lent a chilly note of truth to the document.

Well, Sofia didn't know the details yet but Gugu would be here any minute and would show her the letter.

It was odd that Lorraine had sent an old-fashioned letter, knowing full well that it would take ages to arrive. Then again, Gugu had said that an internal e-mail could be traced, and also a call or message on her phone. A letter was unlikely to arouse suspicion...

The queue at the traffic light seemed to take forever and Gugu switched on the radio. Not the news yet, just music. Stupid music! She switched the radio off again. Gugu hadn't felt this nervous in ages.

Being Stan Makaroff's PR person was not an easy job, mind you. Gugu Mbatha was aware of the fact that much of his wealth stemmed from shady operations. She didn't know the exact details, that was the attorneys' job, but often enough she had grappled with the half-truths she was expected to fabricate in order to make her boss appear squeaky clean.

It was called spin-doctoring. Yes, she was good at spin-doctoring and received an ample salary to match her efforts, but until now, she had never guessed at the extent of it. The letter changed all that.

Seeing Lorraine's allegations written in black on white, Gugu couldn't turn a blind eye to her employer's transgressions anymore. Career or not, deep down inside she felt ashamed that she had put her talent to helping someone like Stan Makaroff. And it didn't end there.

It was not just Stan Makaroff but his wife and mother as well and politicians and attorneys and who knew who else.

Gugu had met the two Makaroff women once before at a private function at the sprawling mansion in Bryanston. The image of two snakes had sprung to mind. Two snakes with faces to match, cold and calculating. Their manner was loud and rough around the edges, despite the designer clothes and expensive jewellery - the mark of the nouveau-riche. The Johannesburg social scene teemed with the nouveau-riche, ever ready for the cameras, but the Makaroff women avoided the public like the plague.

Now, Gugu learned that they headed smuggling rings that operated in the border areas. Anything from cigarettes to drugs and cars, she had read. Okay that was possible but human trafficking? Young women held in bordellos?

That had to be fiction! How they were supposed to be smart enough to pull something like that off. Gugu couldn't get her head around that. How did Lorraine even know about these things? But then, she had no reason to make it all up. Gugu had only read the first two pages. She had taken another sip of red wine and read on. Lorraine had been involved and even named others who were involved, some of them well-known public figures.

Gugu had put the last page down and poured herself another glass of wine. This was outright, shameless crime and this dangerous information was staring at her from the page with the crumpled corners. She couldn't just forget about the things, she'd read.

Stan Makaroff had used, what Lorraine called 'romantic persuasion', to get her to make the former dairy-cottage at the farm available to the smugglers. He'd paid her well, she wrote, which had made her over-confident and a little greedy. Okay, very greedy. Bigger and brighter things beckoned her, so she went to the big city...

For about 10 seconds, Gugu had gotten angry. Why would Lorraine do something like that? Why would she send her of all people a letter and not go straight to the police or to the press? It wasn't fair to burden her with these secrets and she had no way of proving that they were true.

They hadn't known each other well. Their paths had crossed only a few times after the woman had moved to Johannesburg and only once before at Shangari. Gugu's level-headed nature fought its way to the fore again. She couldn't help but read on. It seemed that Lorraine had tried to tell someone. Not the police because she didn't trust them. She had made an appointment with an investigative journalist in Northcliff and never made it to the meeting. Now Lorraine was dead. Silenced.

The letter ended: '*...I'm writing to you because I believe that you are trustworthy and because you are friends with Sofia. I know that Sofia and I had our differences but the two of you will figure out what to do, in case something happens to me. I can't go to the company lawyers and would advise against it. But Witbooi is a good man; you can trust him. If you must contact a lawyer, choose an honest one. If I don't survive this and you finish what I've started, my efforts won't have been in vain. I have a feeling I won't survive this, as exciting as it was. But hey, you never know. If I do, we will discuss a way forward soon. If not, it's in your hands.*

Best regards, Lorraine Pienaar.'

Gee thanks. There was her answer... that's why Lorraine had shared all this with her: she trusted her, despite Gugu's position within the Makaroff Enterprises. She also wanted her to share the information with Sofia and work out some sort of a plan. Nobody else knew about the letter, yet.

That's when she had decided to phone Sofia in the morning and ask her for a meeting. To tell her as much as possible about what she knew and to show her the letter. They would talk about all these bizarre accusations and find a solution together. That's what she would do! They were good at finding solutions. When Sofia had been in trouble after leaving Errol Botes, the heart-throb radio DJ, they had found a solution together, hadn't they?

*

Sofia still waited over another cup of coffee. She had not quite digested all those crazy things, she had heard Gugu say over the phone. And there was more? What could that possibly be?

Perhaps she should write it all down before she forgot the details. She wrote on a serviette, then a second one. Another ten endless minutes and there was still no sign of Gugu Mbatha. Perhaps, she'd had an accident, Sofia worried and finally decided that one hour and fifteen minutes was simply too long. Why didn't Gugu answer her phone, goddamit?

Traffic must be bad, Sofia thought and waited some more but Gugu didn't pitch. She ate the other half of the cake and tried to phone her again. Voicemail. Strange. Sofia left messages but her friend remained elusive.

Sofia began to feel upset.

Gugu had talked about a car following her. Maybe something had gone wrong and she was no longer safe, either!

Somebody could have tapped her phone or checked Gugu's messages. She deleted all the phone call records and messages on her phone. *Don't get all paranoid on me, Sofia Helenius,* she thought. But it was better that way, just in case.

She should tell Astrid... and perhaps even get in touch with Tom. Astrid might still be at home. The kids had sport this afternoon. She also had to tell Tom what was going on, right? All this affected him as well, but then, Tom was still angry with her and it was better not to phone him. Sofia waved the waiter over, folded the two serviettes and put them into her handbag. A shadow appeared next to her table and she got a mighty fright.

"Sorry, I thought you were ready to pay," the waiter said sheepishly.

"Yes, yes. Thanks." Sofia took the bill and rummaged through her handbag for her credit card. It was underneath the serviettes with the dangerous words. *Oh come on*, she reprimanded herself, *pull yourself together!* Why should they be onto her? She wrapped herself into her jacket, took a deep breath and walked toward the parking lot. School was out and cars were queuing for parking spots.

Sofia pressed the remote and her bakkie answered with a series of short beeps. *See, nothing to worry about*, she thought, *you watch too many detective stories.* She would discuss the whole thing with Astrid and then decide what to do. Out of the corner of her eye, she saw two men in dark suits and sunglasses hurry in her direction. She looked again. Dark suits were quite an unusual getup in this part of town and at this time of day.

Sofia was suddenly on her heed. What if they were looking for her? She glimpsed weapons that were barely concealed by the men's flapping jacket-fronts. One of the men seemed to hold a gun inside his suit pocket. Sofia froze. This was no coincidence, they were coming for her!

She walked faster around shopping trolleys and women with small children, holding their hands. What would these men do to her? Grab her, force her into some car with tinted windows or shoot her in front of all these people? It didn't seem likely but her instinct screamed for her to be careful.

Sofia quickly climbed into the bakkie. She fumbled for the key, dropped it, picked it up, started the engine and reversed out of the parking space, nearly hitting a small sedan that waited for her spot. The driver shook his fist at her and she waved back apologetically, then gestured that she needed space to get out.

"Hurry up, hurry up, hurry up!" Sofia begged. The car reversed a fraction, hemmed in by another stubborn driver, trying to get past. At last, both of them moved. She checked her rear mirror and saw the two men standing between some cars to her right, apparently waiting, uncertain what to do. The locks of her car doors snapped closed as Sofia drove as fast as she could around a bright green car and sped toward the exit. The men in dark suits were making an attempt to run after her but it only took her another second and she was through the open gate, out in the street, taking a van's right of way, not looking back.

Sofia still hoped that everything was a mere coincidence and the men were just bodyguards, protecting some highfalutin celebrity. She drove on, not caring to find out. On her way to Astrid's house, Sofia kept looking in the rear mirror and got a huge fright when a black luxury car rudely overtook her at a roundabout on a quiet Linden street. The black car drove over the island in the middle of the roundabout and turned away from her.

Sofia started breathing again. She rushed on toward Astrid's street and passed the Dragonfly Bed & Breakfast, where Tom, Barry and Charmaine had stayed. She turned into a side road, then took a couple of turns around the block to make sure, nobody was following her. Then she drove back to Astrid's street.

To her relief, there was only an old car coming from the opposite direction and passed at slow speed. Harmless.

She drove past the neighbour's lollipop trees and nervously rang the bell at Astrid's gate. Of course, the metal plate sparked again.

"Hello?"

"Damn, you should get another bell!" Sofia barked into the intercom.

"Excuse me?" Astrid said.

"Se olen minä. It's me, Astrid. Open up, please."

The gate opened way too slowly and closed behind her with a hum. Safe! When Sofia finally stopped in the driveway next to the innocent white rose bushes, she was buzzing with nerves.

What was going on? Where on earth was Gugu and why had these armed men tried to come after her in the parking lot?

CHAPTER 9

A car roared down the dirt road along the Kruger Park's game fence, swirling up a cloud of dust. Blinding headlights made a couple of bucks jump up from their sleeping place behind the tall fence and a large, drowsy bird alighted in a nearby tree.

Hidden behind the thorn bushes, Sanele stopped and threw herself on the ground without a second thought. Her face was touching the cold sand and she hid as far as the sparse foliage allowed. Sanele had bravely overcome her fear of snakes and wild animals, the horror of being found by her tormentors and punished for running away; needed to get away from this place, from the groping hands of strange men on her body, their sweat and their stinking breath.

How far had she come in those three, four hours since she'd left?

Sanele had lost all sense of time. She didn't know the area, didn't know any landmarks or directions, had just followed the road. It was the safest way, to run next to the road along the fence, always ready to hide in the bushes whenever a car approached. A lion complained in his sleep and from another direction came hacking laughter. She knew it meant nothing good but the animals were all behind the strong fence and couldn't get to her.

Sanele waited until the noises subsided, then she stood up, shook off the sand and started walking again as fast as she could. She felt tired. How had she managed to run so fast earlier? Maybe some spirit had helped her through the sand and thorny brush, clawing at her flimsy clothes; the sequined miniskirt and the thin boob tube, she was forced to wear for 'business'.

Had it not been for the man's jacket, she had stolen from the plush, red sofa downstairs back at the club, she would be freezing cold by now. It was so much colder here in winter than it was in her subtropical home province. Especially at night.

Not that she felt the cold that much. Her senses were heightened, blood pumping hot and fast through her veins. She knew what she was doing was dangerous. Very dangerous. Back at the club with its loud seductive music, the gold-framed mirrors and the scent of lust in the air, Sanele had thought of nothing else but that she had to get away from all this. As far as possible. When her chance finally came, she had taken it.

Sanele buttoned up the big, dark-blue jacket, while she hastened on, not taking any time to rest. The sturdy fabric surrounded her like a protective invisibility cloak. Made her feel invisible.

They had given the girls pills as always before the main business started at dusk. Before the men came from far and wide to take advantage of her young body and the bodies of the other girls. They slept in the rooms upstairs, mostly during the day. Four girls to one room.

The air was always musty because they weren't allowed to fully open the windows to let fresh air in. All the windows at the club had burglar bars outside to foil any attempts to escape. Guards were sitting on dirty chairs by the house wall somewhat away from the entrance, their weapons at the ready behind them, trying not to scare off the customers. This was necessary for the girls' safety, they had been told.

The girls were quite diverse. Something for every taste. Some were plump with big boobs and buttocks, others lithe and sinewy. Some were light, some dark, some beautiful and others ugly - and all of them were unhappy. The pills made it easier to forget who they were and what they were doing. They took the edge off. At least for a while.

Sanele was one of the beautiful girls. She knew that because men had told her many times now and she could see a glint of envy in some of the other girls' eyes. It wasn't easy for her to look in the mirror or to put on makeup and make herself look prettier. She was ashamed of what she saw, was ashamed of her beauty. Her skin was soft and her body firm and slender. Most likely from doing all the housework and walking down to the river to fetch water twice a day at home.

Home. She would never return home. Her father had sold her to those men. To those stinking pologolos.

Sanele knew that her hair was soft and didn't break just above her scalp. It was long enough to be braided into cornrows and not elongated with extensions that the other girls liked to wear. A hairdresser came once a month and they all piled into the room that was used as a salon. The cornrows were fairly cheap. Why should she spend good money to make herself more beautiful? To attract more of the unwanted male attention? Aikhona!

The sequined skirt under the big jacket got caught on a spindly branch and ripped even more. Sanele swore under her breath and hurried on. Her feet hurt but she didn't care. It was a small price to pay for freedom.

Every week, a shrewd clothes merchant would show up at the club, on Wednesdays when business was slow. He sold skimpy clothes to the girls, taking the little they were given as pocket money.

Sanele bought as little as possible and always the cheapest stuff. She had no illusions that she would ever make enough money to buy her way out of this miserable situation but she tried to save at least some of her measly pay. Just in case.

The men gave her a little cash now and then when they were particularly satisfied. She had found a way to hide it behind a broken tile in the corner of the toilet cubicle upstairs. Her place of refuge.

Money was important. If she ever managed to run away, she would need money. Everything cost money outside in the real world: transport, food, clothes. Her savings would not take her far but it would help.

Would things have been different if her family were not so poor? It hurt to remember but she couldn't help thinking about it now that she had taken her life back.

The memory fuelled her hatred and the will to move on through the rough shrubs and the sand biting at her naked legs.

He had taken her for a walk, her father, wanted to show her something in the bush outside the village.

Her father had been drinking as usual but he was far from drunk. She had been happy that he wanted to spend some time with her. Maybe he wanted to ask, how she was doing at school. Father didn't spend much time with the family and if he ever found his way home from drinking at the local shebeen, it was to lock the children out of the one-roomed hut to have his way with their mother. Grunting or yelling or sometimes beating her because there was no food waiting for him on the table.

Sanele loved to learn and wanted to go to school but at the age of twelve, she was needed at home, to help with the younger children, with the washing and the cooking if there was any food. It was hard to keep up with her studies, but somehow, she managed.

Father would find odd jobs to bring some money in. If it hadn't been for his habit of drinking and gambling away the money he earned with a game or two of fufi, they could have lived a fairly normal life like the other villagers. His drinking ensured that he lost his employment after a few months or weeks. Her mother bore her unhappy life with the stoic endurance of a village woman.

She didn't talk much, especially not about her husband. It was her God-given lot. So Sanele had never questioned her, had endured and waited for womanhood to arrive.

Some of the girls in Sanele's age group had found a good man with steady work who didn't beat them and gave them money. Her friend Lettie, however, had disappeared one day.

They later learnt that she had been kidnapped, raped and then married off to her rapist in another village down south. The young man and his family had come to an agreement with Lettie's parents. It was common practice in rural Kwa Mashu but Sanele had wept for her friend, had wept for the bright young women, they had wanted to become, successful in school and their chosen professions.

Lettie had dreamt of becoming a nurse and Sanele a lawyer. Someone who was respected and admired, like Thuli Madonsela, the Public Protector of South Africa. The girls had talked much about their plans for the future - then.

'We can get a bursary from the government and study at university,' Sanele had said while braiding her friend's hair. 'We'll have our own house and enough money to buy decent clothes and eat pap and vleis every day.'

"With your marks, it will be easy to get a bursary,' Lettie had told her.

'You just have to work harder, learn to speak good English. You are smart, Lettie," Sanele would answer but she wasn't sure that Lettie believed her.

'Yes, smart. But how do we get to the city and who will help us there? We need money for everything. We can't live off fresh air.'

'I know - we could go to a church. They will help us. They work with God,' Sanele had suggested. 'We have to put ourselves into God's hands. That's what the pastor always says and he should know. He has a nice home and all.'

Their dreams had burst like bubbles on the day that Lettie disappeared. She was caught in a forced marriage and Lettie's family had agreed to it.

One day, she didn't come to school anymore and the kids were talking about, how she had been abducted and raped and taken to the neighbouring Eastern Cape. It was all down to a tradition called Ukuthwala. A tradition that did not consider what the girls wanted or whether they were in school and still growing up to become women. Nobody had asked Lettie for sure because she would have told Sanele.

The whole thing had made Sanele angry. Her beautiful, smart friend had no say in the matter and now she was gone, had in an instant disappeared from her life.

'We must accept our fate as women. It's the way of tradition,' her mother had said and avoided her daughter's gaze. Sanele could not accept this. The man had hurt her friend but he wasn't punished for it. On the contrary, he was allowed to marry her! That could not be right.

'Why must we accept everything? It is wrong,' she had baulked at her mother's resignation. Sanele could never talk to her about anything. Why did she even try?

Her mother had enough of a burden to carry with four children to raise and a drunkard for a husband. Sanele did not agree with her mother. She was cut from a different cloth; strong and feisty - a survivor. She wanted education and a good life. Her marks were so good that her teachers had no reason to beat her. Her father was rarely at home and her mother didn't have the strength to give her a good drubbing when Sanele was too strong-willed for her own good. She would have taken that life back in a heartbeat.

The frequent beatings, she had endured after her father handed her over to the strange men in exchange for a wad of bank notes, had made her feel small and unimportant. Defeated.

Not that she hadn't been beaten before. But there had still been hope that all that would change one day once she was out of school and studying at university in town. Being a grown-up, studying and making something of herself. For a while, it had been easier to let the men have their way with her.

Her hopes and dreams had been dashed, and if her own father didn't want his daughter around, how could she expect mercy from this lot?

The big boss who owned the nightclub in the middle of nowhere, was a harsh and ugly woman with straw-like blonde hair and lots of makeup. Sanele had never seen her without those buttons plugged in her ears, speaking to people on her cell phone, while she was in a conversation with somebody right in front of her. The person underneath all that makeup, the unnatural lips and the false eyelashes, was as scary as a tokolosh. Sanele knew that inside the bony chest beat a cold and calculating heart.

The boss collected money for the family business and

smacked the girls who didn't earn as much as they should.

'You are lucky, I don't send you to the miners up north,' Helena had yelled at one of the girls who had crumpled to the ground. 'I'm giving you a nice life here and the least you can do is pay me back by working,' she had yelled. Sometimes, she would even smack the guards and the manager if she was in a bad mood.

They weren't nice to the girls afterwards. This woman controlled Sanele's life and she hated her with all her heart. She couldn't understand why this Helena-woman seemed to be so important in the world out there.

'Her husband is a rich businessman in Joburg,' one of the girls had gossiped one day. She was a fat fair girl, they called Mafuta.

'They are real tsotsis but they know many people in government,' Mafuta had told them.

The fat girl sounded almost proud of these achievements as if she had anything to do with it! Mafuta had been at the club the longest. She was already 18 and knew all this from Vuyo, the man in charge of the club who called her to his room often.

The girls at the club sometimes watched TV. On a holiday for example when the men went to church with their families. It would have been a sin, to spend their money on sordid entertainment at the club on such days.

'There, that's big boss's husband,' Mafuta announced on one of those occasions, while they were waiting for their favourite soapie to come on.

Sanele watched closely. A short, stocky man in a blue suit gave an interview in a large tent. He laughed and joked with the reporter, waving his arms around.

'Yes, that's my name, don't wear it out. Let's go over here; it's quieter in that corner...' *So that's what a rich businessman looks like*, she thought; *and that's how he talks to a pretty reporter.* They were talking about some warthogs that had rampaged around the large tent, scaring fine and rich people. But not him. He didn't seem scared. How could he be? He was married to the scariest woman in the world!

Before Sanele could quite grasp what was being said, another segment showed him sitting among nursery school children, reading to them, laughing with them.

'The Sandton businessman who is well-known for his charities, visited the Lebogang Centre for Orphans in Alexandra yesterday, marking the tenth anniversary of the institution he founded 10 years ago...'

Sanele tried to imagine him doing to his wife, what the customers did to her. She couldn't. Big boss was so harsh and unlovely that she probably wanted to smack any man who came near her. If he was so rich and powerful, why didn't this man take himself another, nicer wife like the president so often did?

Helena was too nice a name for that crude woman who spoke in such a loud voice. Although Sanele had never practised speaking English properly, she knew from watching television series at the church hall on weekends that the woman spoke with a heavy Johannesburg accent. She listened carefully to how the big boss spoke. It was important that she learned how to speak English. Should she ever find her way out of the mess, her father had landed her in. Sanele hated it how these odious people had disrupted her childhood a year ago; hated, what she had become. She had hardened herself, swallowed the tears and began to plan her escape. The other girls were like her mother: so passive and accepting.

After a while, men asked for Sanele more often. That meant, she became valuable to the big boss and to Vuyo. She would have loved to trade with someone else any day. Some of the men were rich, many of them big and burly and arrogant and demanding. And they wanted her!

"Sanele is so pretty, she's getting more johns than any of us," one of the girls had said one day. It made Sanele cringe.

"With some luck, the lack of sleep will turn her ugly soon."

"You can have them. I wish I could get out of here," she had said more to herself than the other girls.

She had made one other girl so jealous that she snitched on her, telling Vuyo that Sanele wanted to escape. The punishment had been painful and she wasn't able to look at oranges in nets for a while without trembling. The other girl had been punished as well for her jealousy. Such an attitude could cause problems in the long run. Vuyo liked them docile, following orders without backchat and jealousy. It was with some satisfaction that Sanele saw the other girl suffer. It was her own fault. But Vuyo wasn't finished with her yet.

"If you try and run away, I'll kill you," he had said grinning coldly. Vuyo had lost no time in giving her a little demonstration of what fate awaited her. Later she had sat on the toilet, pressing a wad of toilet paper to her bleeding breast.

Sanele had buried her grief deep down inside. Her grief for not being able to breathe freely or to go to school again.

She wanted to yell at Vuyo, call him names, kick him, but she didn't dare. Even to be with her family and work hard day in day out was better than this life. That's what she had been used to. She had been able to go down to the river and sit by herself or study. Here, work meant something sleazy.

Outwardly, she had submitted to slavery but inside, her hatred burned hot and her desire to make something of herself one day kept growing. She wanted to breathe freely once again, find someone to love, perhaps.

This dream of a better life spurned her on to make a break for it when the time came. Sanele didn't remember when her sense of hope had returned, but hope was suddenly back, patting her on the shoulder as if to say: 'Hey, I'm still here. Pay attention to me.'

She had to plan carefully, needed to become more cunning. When the other girls gossiped about celebrities, their looks and makeup and made fun of certain johns, she said nothing. Soon she was known as The Mute. What the others didn't know was that she was secretly hatching a plan to escape and needed all of her strength not to lose her courage. She would do it on her own, had no time for those stupid girls who just gave in.

It would not be her destiny to be shipped to another country like merchandise one day and she would certainly not die in this hellhole, so close to the Mozambican border. The other girls had spoken about the names of the nearest villages in the area. Now Sanele wished she had listened to them.

She stumbled on through the sand. Everything had seemed so unreal at the club. Maybe it was because of the pills, the girls were given. She had dutifully swallowed them until a couple of days ago.

Sanele had faked putting the pills into her mouth, then let them disappear into her hand. She ground them to dust on the floor when she was alone in the toilet stall, wiping all traces away. The pills had made being unfree a little easier but she needed her head to be clear. The blaring music in itself had been like a drug but Sanele had learned to steel herself even against it, shutting her ears...

Some of the wild animals made growling noises and Sanele shuddered. The Kruger Park was on the other side of the fence - that much she knew. Even if she had been right there, inside that park, she would have done the same. She longed for freedom and would rather die of hunger or thirst in the bush or whatever came her way than to be a slave forever.

Another car, a bakkie, rumbled along the dirt road, much slower than the first one. Sanele flew down onto the ground and the bakkie passed. She waited awhile, just to be sure.

The bright cones of the headlights grew smaller, then disappeared completely. If she only knew where she was going! Luckily, there was no moon out tonight. Well, a sickle so thin that it hardly counted. That also meant that she didn't see enough of her surroundings and had to skirt the trees and bushes almost by instinct.

A line on the horizon grew a tad lighter than the starry sky above. The first light of morning. She had to walk faster. Today, daylight would not be her friend. Sanele concentrated on listening out for noises close by and saw the large spider web with its yellow and black occupant just in time before walking into it. Disgusting. The thought alone made her shudder again.

Like a spider in its web, that's how Vuyo was. A sweaty,

big fat spider that didn't seem to have a life outside of the boring, hateful club in the middle of nowhere. Whenever there was trouble around, he would pounce on the troublemakers and restore peace. His kind of peace.

That's exactly what had happened last night. One of the not so well-off patrons had become unruly with Thulesa, a stupid girl from Venda, who didn't seem to know anything about manners or cared much about what happened to her.

The man was a regular at the club. They called him Whatso and nobody seemed to know why. He'd wanted Thulesa to do something, he was not willing to pay for. And Vuyo did not tolerate this under any circumstances.

There had been a screaming match and the other patrons somehow got involved. A mirror broke when one of the guards pushed Whatso. Sanele had come down the stairs with her john who still acted all lovey-dovey. He tried to fondle her and she tried to get away from him, almost slipping against the bannister. Disgusting.

She wanted to slap his face and kick the man in the soft parts, yelling at him, to keep his hands to himself. Instead, she smiled sweetly and kept descending the stairs. Soon, the argument downstairs distracted him. Good.

Sanele didn't care what the brawl was all about. It wasn't the first time that men pulled knives on each other or screamed in a drunken stupor.

Then it hit her like a ton of bricks: This was the chance, she had been waiting for!

Her senses were no longer dulled by the drug as she walked back up the stairs to the toilet cubicle. Sanele fetched the money she had stashed away under the broken tile and stuffed it into the bra under her boob tube. When she came down the stairs again, her mind was alert. She moved at leisurely speed, dropped down to her knees and crouched behind the sofa.

Nobody reacted. She waited a while, watching the men yell at each other. Fists began to fly. *Good, let them smash each other's heads in,* she thought roughly. As usual, they were drunk and over-estimated their prowess.

Music was blaring and nobody thought of turning it down. The girls stood around, cheering the men on, picking a winner. Sanele grabbed the large, dark cotton jacket that was hanging over the back of the sofa as if she had never done anything else. She'd put on the jacket and was out of the back door before anyone noticed.

A van stood parked outside and she took cover behind it. It was the van with pictures and writing about hair products on it. A familiar sight at the club. Sanele didn't see anyone and could only pray that nobody had seen her.

The man with the loaded AK-47 who usually guarded the back door, had probably gone inside to watch the brawl and gloat or help subdue the unruly customer. The girls sometimes saw him from their windows on the second floor, how he shot at small animals when he got bored. The promise of violence kept the imprisoned girls in line. Sanele felt sorry for the animals and would have loved to look after a soft little hare or meerkat.

Now the guard was gone and she took her chances.

She must have had help from some spirit or maybe from Jesus himself because she was suddenly running as fast as her feet would carry her. She ran and ran and nobody followed.

Then a car had come racing down the dirt road. It had been too dark for her to see the driver, didn't really want to look too closely.

Maybe it was one of the patrons, getting away from the fight. Or maybe it was Vuyo or one of his guards, chasing after her. Who knew? It was the first time, Sanele had thrown herself on the ground and got a mouthful of sand. The car had rushed past, trailing a cloud of dust. Sanele had felt invincible with all that adrenaline rushing through her veins and safely hidden inside the big, dark jacket. She got up and kept running, spitting out the sand. It seemed so long ago, that first car.

When the dust, thrown up by the last bakkie had settled, the girl stopped and scanned her surroundings. She could see faint lights in the distance. Houses? A farm or a village maybe?

Then a horrible thought: What if they didn't want to help her? Sent her back to the club? She would kill herself, would put an end to it. She never wanted to go back to that life, so she had to take the risk!

It was another hour before she reached the buildings. They were grouped around a yard with a chapel to the left. A chapel? A dog barked and Sanele pressed herself against the nearest wall. It was rough and cold and real. The pale stripe on the horizon grew wider.

Sanele saw a handful of people walk out of a door. Men. The men carried torchlights and soon found the wild-eyed girl, standing motionless, pressing herself against the wall.

"Don't be afraid," an older man, with a ring of grey hair around his head, said kindly. He seemed British. "They already came looking for you. Come inside, child."

The other men murmured and urged her on to come inside. Sanele hesitated, clutching at the big jacket, holding it closed in front of her, hiding her body. The men seemed kind but could she trust them?

There were quite a few of them, some of them white, others black and some even looked Asian like the Chinee. She had no choice, had to follow them inside. She moved slowly, trying to assess this new situation for as long as possible but she was tired. She hadn't thought things through and what would happen, once she had reached safety. Was it safety she had reached?

If these men didn't mean well if they touched her, she would scream and bite and kick. All those things she had never dared to do with the men at the club.

Then she would run again or they would kill her. It didn't matter either way.

As the door closed, Sanele decided right there and then that it was better to die fighting than to live another moment in slavery.

*

"... according to police reports, a group of four men,

213

suspected of human trafficking, were taken into custody near the Kruger Park last night. Eleven South African girls, between the ages of twelve and eighteen, were freed by the police from a private house in the area, where they had been held captive as sex slaves. One of the girls, aged 13, managed to escape and was found by Jesuit monks at a retreat near the entrance to the Kruger Park. The girls were taken to a place of safety by emergency personnel and their families have been notified. They are treated for injuries and have been given ARV drugs as a precaution. It has, however, been alleged that some of the girls were sold to their captors by their own families. Investigations are underway and further arrests are expected. It is unclear at this stage, whether the arrested men are part of an international human trafficking ring operating in South Africa with links to government officials... In international news: a bomb blast near a mosque in Baghdad, the capital city of Iraq, has killed 47 worshippers..."

Gugu Mbatha closed her eyes. *How horrible*, she thought and switched off the radio. Imagine, teenagers as young as that, forced into the sex trade. Human traffickers with possible links to government officials.

Unthinkable. And what about HIV and other STDs, they had no doubt been exposed to? She hoped that some kind souls would take them in and send them to proper schools.

How privileged Gugu herself had been, growing up in the posh Johannesburg suburb of Bryanston, cocooned in her parents' love and by extended family, attending one of the best schools in the country and able to study a subject of her choice in Cape Town. She'd never been short of food or clothing or anything else she'd wished for. Her parents had attended parents evenings and netball games and concerts. She owed them her self-confidence and easy-going nature.

She heard plates being taken out of the cupboard.

Aunt Doris was pottering around in the kitchen, preparing breakfast for the two of them. She owned a quaint but comfortable home in Soweto, where Gugu had spent the last two days.

Aunt Doris worked part-time in a nursery school and took care of the flowers in her little garden. Gugu hadn't visited since aunt Doris' grown-up children had moved away; always too busy with her own life, she hadn't seen her aunt and cousins for quite some time now, although they lived in the same city. Her parents stayed in a retirement home on the coast. She would definitely make a plan and visit them soon.

"Come on let's eat, Gugu," her aunt said and let half of the scrambled eggs slide from the pan onto her plate. Gugu sat down at the table covered with a red wax cloth and picked up her fork.

"Take some toast, nana... oh, I forgot, the Rama is still in the fridge."

"Let me get it, auntie," Gugu said and went to fetch the margarine.

In her mind, she tried to make a plan for the day. Should she lay low, sit around listlessly in the lounge and read a book, listen to the radio again or should she make contact with Sofia or the police? It wasn't an easy decision, considering recent events but Gugu itched to get out of the house.

Her active life had come to a grinding halt since she had made her way to Soweto.

Sofia must be worried about her by now. Everything had happened so fast when she noticed the men following her. After threading in and out of afternoon traffic, Gugu had turned into a completely unknown area. She'd parked the car and grabbed her bag and the brown envelope with Lorraine Pienaar's incriminating letter. She had managed to escape by waving down a taxi Joburg-style in the main road. But in her haste, she had left her cell phone behind. It had probably fallen on the floor.

Gugu had been virtually across the road from the shopping centre, where she had planned to show Sofia the letter. When the dark car with the tinted windows had overtaken her at the traffic lights, her instinct had kicked in. She couldn't drag Sofia into this!

Anyway, she was here now in safety with aunt Doris.

Gugu picked at her food, which didn't go unnoticed.

"Hai, nana! Eat your eggs," her aunt said. "You need your strength for the day ahead."

Gugu had heard that somewhere before. Ah yes, her boss Stan Makaroff had said that to Sofia when they had met at the Makaroff Tower last week. The tramezzini Roberto. She didn't want to think about Makaroff or what was in Lorraine's letter. Lorraine who had died under mysterious circumstances after a rather unlikely accident.

'... if you must contact a lawyer, choose an honest one. If I don't survive this and you finish what I started, my efforts won't have been in vain...'

Lorraine had written this at the end of her letter.

A lawyer? Like who? The lawyers Gugu knew where working for Stan Makaroff: Alwin Goldsmith, Preston McOrman, Tilly Sebald... They all had cushy offices in the Makaroff Tower and were utterly devoted to the company.

Gugu could not contact any of them under the circumstances and whether she could trust them was a good question. They worked for Stan Makaroff after all and received big salaries. But the person she could contact was her old friend Sofia. Best from the public phone on the little square, where the minibus taxis stopped.

"Sorry, auntie, I'm not hungry."

"Poor thing, you've had quite a scare and now you're forced to sit around idle all day, wondering what to do."

"Yes, you are right. I should go into town."

"You must do, what you must do, Gugu," her aunt said. "I'm going off to work now. If you must go, that's fine. You can take what you need. Leave a note, then I know you're alright. Lock up before you leave. You still remember how to get to the bus stop? Next to the taxi rank on the square."

"Oh auntie, you're the best. Yes, I do remember the taxi rank," Gugu said.

"Good." Aunt Doris carried on eating her breakfast.

The brown envelope was tucked safely under the mattress in the room where she slept.

Her aunt lived alone and didn't keep much company. She was out most of the time, working at the nursery school. Still, if you lived in a township, your neighbours were always curious. They knew where the keys were hidden in case of an emergency. When she'd arrived unannounced a couple of days ago, Gugu had told her surprised aunt about the trouble she was in.

Aunt Doris had understood at once and said: 'Don't worry, child. During the struggle, we had to hide people now and then. Those were difficult times and the police went from house to house, to do searches. I will tell old Mavis next door that you are visiting for a few days. Everybody in the street will know and not ask questions. You will be safe here.'

Gugu had hugged her, so glad that she had family she could rely on. There was a knock on the door. She quickly sneaked into the bedroom and heard her aunt talking to one of the neighbours.

"Zinzi, I must go to work now. No, really. Aikhona. When I come back, I'll look for the can opener you left here when we had that braai. My niece is still sleeping. I don't want her to get a fright when she wakes up and sees you."

"Hai, you always work so much, Doris. I hope your niece is helping out with household chores."

Zinzi tried to catch a glimpse of the visitor inside the small house. The girl must be having a tiff with her boyfriend or maybe she'd lost her job. Why else would she come and stay with her aunt now after such a long time? Looking all posh and high and mighty with her expensive hairdo and nails and clothes and all...

She peeked into the house again. With some luck, she'd be able to tell somebody that Gugu was all teary and dishevelled-looking and Doris was waiting on her hand and foot. Nosy neighbours were one of the downsides in such a close-knit community, but on the other hand, there was no chance that your body would be found only weeks after you dropped dead at home.

"She is helping me just fine, Zinzi," aunt Doris said,

expertly changing the subject. "How is your husband doing? Has he come back yet?"

Zinzi didn't want a reminder of her deadbeat husband who couldn't hold down a job. He'd recently disappeared with some flapper after winning a sum of money at the casino. Bhentse emfene.

"He'll be back. You'll see, he will. Nobody makes pap and vleis like I do." Zinzi mumbled but had suddenly lost her taste for gossip.

"Yes, I know. You are a great cook. A great cook, madala. I have to go in two minutes, Zinzi. He is a fool, this man... but I must go now... can't be late or the parents will complain that their children are all alone at the school. I'll see you at church on Sunday." The door closed with a thump.

"I'm giving you hassle, auntie," Gugu said with a sigh and walked back into the kitchen. "The neighbours will want to know why I'm here."

"Nothing I can't handle," aunt Doris said. "I just want you to be safe. It would be better if you look for another place to stay, nana. My fancy niece seems to attract more attention than I thought. Don't open the door to anyone, while I'm gone, child. When you go out, wear some of my clothes, so you won't attract attention. You can always give them back later. Take a duffel-bag from the wardrobe in the spare bedroom and put your own clothes in."

"I'll do that, I promise. I will take a taxi into town. I'm sure that I can stay with my friend... you know."

"Perhaps you should if it's safe. You better take the bus to Eloff Street, child. Most people take the taxi because it's faster and somebody might recognise you. Put the key under the flower pot. You know the third one from the left. I'll check as soon as I get back home. Do you have enough money for the bus?"

"Yes, I did take my purse with me. Thank you, auntie."

"Good. Let me know how things go as soon as you can. Just don't phone me right away. You never know."

"You are so right. I love you, auntie." Aunt Doris gave her

a tender kiss on the forehead and was out the door.

An hour later, the rising sun had warmed the air a little and Gugu was on her way to the taxi rank three blocks up the road. First, she would phone Sofia and make arrangements with her. She had a scrap of paper with Astrid's phone number in her pocket and some change for the public phone. It was a pleasant feeling, how the coins were warming her hand.

Everything seemed perfectly normal in the bustling township streets. School children were walking to school, noisily telling each other stories. People hurried to the minibus taxis that would take them to the train station or straight into town. They were always worried that they might be late for work if there was another strike by drivers or municipal workers or if the minibus taxi broke down.

Some people bought a banana, a couple of tomatoes or an umbrella from one of the many street vendors on the sidewalk. They chatted, hands in their pockets and their breath escaping in clouds of vapour.

A bus roared past and a sleepy woman bumped into her, mumbling an excuse or a curse.

Gugu had put on a heavy salt & pepper coat, plain shoes, a shawl over her shoulders and a headscarf. She thought it made her look ordinary like any regular traveller with the old brown duffel-bag slung over her shoulder. Nobody even as much as gave her a passing glance and she began to relax, breathing more deeply, moving more naturally.

There was a short queue at the public pay phone outside the local Spar, even at this early hour. She waited, checking her surroundings from the corner of her eye. When it was her turn, Gugu put the warm coins into the slot and dialled Astrid's number. She was in luck. Astrid had taken the children to school and a yawning Sofia answered the phone after the fifth ringtone.

"Yawn... sorry, Rankin residence."

"Miss Helenius?"

"Gu...?"

"It's me, Gertrude, madam. I'm coming into town today

for a fitting at the BIG SHOPPING CENTRE. I'll meet you at the usual place in two hours? The dress turned out just the way you wanted. Perhaps we can discuss the changes over a cup of COFFEE at the big shopping centre. You know."

Even if Sofia was not quite awake yet, the word 'coffee' should wake her up. The BIG shopping centre was code for Cresta. They both knew that.

"You mean..."

"Yes, madam. The usual place."

"Of course, no problem," Sofia said quickly. At last, she understood!

"I'll be there in two hours. Glad you brought the dress. I can't wait to see it."

Sofia sounded a lot more awake now and luckily, she had grasped the situation. In case somebody listened in, he wouldn't be able to tell what was being said. Gugu was better safe than sorry.

"Bye, madam."

"Bye Gertrude."

With some luck, they would meet up at the Cresta Shopping Centre and a particular restaurant, where they often met when Sofia was in town.

Gugu put the change into her purse and noticed that her notebook wasn't there. Oh no, she had forgotten it at the house. She had to have her notebook!

She rushed back up the street, past school children in uniform, street vendors and people going to work. Gugu walked around the corner and heard a loud bang, almost like a truck backfiring. It was probably nothing. But as she walked on, she saw smoke and people running in the direction of aunt Doris' house, joining an already sizeable crowd.

Gugu wondered if she had left the gas stove on and something had caught fire. Maybe it was the neighbour's house... but she couldn't take the risk of going there to check. Dammit, her notebook was still in there. She hurried back to the square, forcing herself to calm down, walk slowly.

"Hey, baby! Wanna come with me?" A drunken man

reeking of cheap tipple tried to grab her arm.

"Hai sugga wena!" Gugu yelled at him town-ship style and clicked her tongue, giving way to her tension. The man staggered off, trying his luck with another woman who screeched and clapped him soundly.

Soon, Gugu boarded the bus to Cresta and sat down with a sigh of relief. The bus happened to take its route past aunt Doris' house and everybody was stretching their necks to get a better look.

There was no doubt about it: Her aunt's house was on fire! Thick smoke filtered through the crack under the front door. Gugu stretched her neck along with the other passengers. She saw flames licking through one of the windows and Zinzi daringly making for the flowerpot and the key to aunt Doris' house. About a dozen neighbours were already lined up, throwing water at the flames in a rehearsed order.

It would take ages for the fire brigade to arrive and the help the neighbours were the only hope of extinguishing a fire. Gugu sat back in shock. She knew that her aunt wasn't in the house but the mere thought that Gugu's presence could have caused somebody to set the house on fire was painful enough. *I have to send her money as soon as I've sorted my life out,* she thought. She wished she could get off the bus and help but who knew what kind of thugs were lurking around, ready to pounce?

A black luxury car with darkened windows pulled up next to the bus. Luxury cars with darkened windows were no longer an unusual sight in the townships. Local politicians or crime lords liked to show off their ill-gotten wealth but something made her look closer. A semi-automatic rifle was visible at the lower end of the back window. The car had pulled out of her aunt's street.

A terrible thought crossed Gugu's mind: that someone inside the car might be watching the crowd, trying to find her. She moved back from the window and drew the shawl in front of her face. The next moment, the bus had crossed the intersection, with traffic lights changing to red a second later.

The black car stayed behind, probably to have a better look at the crowd around the house, while Gugu was on her way into town.

*

Sofia put the phone down in a daze. *Gugu is alive and well,* she thought with relief. She looked at her watch and couldn't believe the time. It was 8:32 am, already. Exhaustion was catching up with her! At least Gugu was well and not being kept somewhere against her will.

Why was she pretending to be somebody else, called Gertrude?

That could only mean that she had gone into hiding somewhere and was worried about Astrid's phone being bugged. Or that somebody was listening. That meant that Sofia had to be careful as well. Should she phone the police?

No, better not. Not now. It was best to find out from Gugu, what had happened and why men with guns should be coming after her. Sofia hadn't left the house since the incident in the parking lot but now she had to get ready to meet her friend and hear her side of the story.

Errol had not phoned her again since making a scene in Melville. Sofia knew by now that the story with Damian needing a liver transplant must have been a well-planned shakedown, so she wasn't exactly eager to hear from him. Damian didn't need a transplant. He was happy and healthy with his adopted family in Cape Town. At least, she could now ponder her own situation, without having to worry about her son, she had never even met.

Astrid knew what was going on and let her be. She had a 'situation' of her own. It came as a huge surprise for Sofia to learn that her cousin had been leading a double-life that not even she was aware of.

She'd overheard a conversation and Astrid had called somebody darling. When Sofia asked who this *darling* was, Astrid had come right out with the truth.

'His name is Paul, Paul Somerset. I met him two years ago

and we started seeing each other when Grant went to Nigeria for a month,' she had confessed to Sofia. 'He is a neighbour and lives three houses down the road.' Sofia tried to visualise the road.

'The one with the dark red wall and the number 47 painted on it in huge white letters?' Sofia had asked. That particular house stood out for its colourful foliage spilling over said dark red wall.

'That's the one.' Astrid had looked surprised. 'How did you guess?'

'Oh, I don't know. Just seemed like the house you would have a boyfriend in. Maybe I'm psychic,' Sofia had joked, to mask her surprise.

'Hmm, really? Don't be cross, Sofie.'

'Why would I be cross? It's your life and you know that Grant isn't exactly my favourite kind of person. I'm just surprised. Can't really blame you... at all. Grant isn't a model husband in my eyes even when he's around. He leaves you alone way too much, so good for you. But you should have told me when I got here.'

'I couldn't, Sofie. I was ashamed of the affair but now I'm going to leave Grant,' Astrid had said matter-of-factly.

'You are?' Sofia was speechless. This was the exact opposite of what Astrid had told her before. Where was the Astrid who was resigned to a loveless marriage and content with her lifestyle?

'I've stuck it out as long as I could bear it. To hell now with feeling grateful that he rescued me from that dance club back in England! He seems to have lost every interest in me and the children, lately. It's just work, work, work all the time. Paul and I decided to take things to the next level. That's why I'm going to move out and into the house with the dark red wall.'

'I see,' Sofia had said. 'When are you going to do that?'

'I thought I'd wait until Grant is back from Mozambique. I have to talk to him. It's not fair to just leave him... and not fair to the children - although I've already had a few talks with them.'

'They know?' Sofia had asked. 'How did that go?'

'Tough, really tough. But I think they understand. Charlie takes is harder than Jessie. He is still young and feels closer to Grant. I'm a bit scared of the great show-down. Not sure, how Grant will react. He has a bit of a mean streak when it comes to his possessions.' Astrid emphasized the word 'possessions' that left no doubt about the meaning. 'The children will come with me, of course.'

'Of course,' Sofia had mumbled. 'That might not be so easy, though.'

'I've already consulted a lawyer,' she'd said.

That's how quickly things could change. Astrid wanted her to meet with Paul Somerset, the new man in her life, tomorrow. She would prepare a Finnish lunch and introduce the two of them.

Sofia felt nervous about the meeting.

The whole messy situation she was in and her longing for Tom didn't make things easier. She wondered if her cousin's taste in men had let her down again. What if this Paul was as uncouth as Grant Rankin, Astrid's current husband? Sofia would be pleasant with him and tell her cousin later, what she thought of him.

There wasn't much more she could do anyway. If Astrid decided to shack up with this man, then that's what she would do but Sofia was sick and tired of secrets and complications. She was no longer a teenager and would give it to Astrid straight this time. Tomorrow, then.

Today, she needed to meet Gugu at Cresta.

In two hours, she'd be seeing her best friend and they would put at least one problem to rest. Together. From now on, that's how she would approach this whole ugly mess: solving one problem at a time.

CHAPTER 10

It was a busy time at Cresta Shopping Centre. Shoppers were rushing to and fro and large areas were cordoned off due to building works. This didn't make it any easier for Sofia to find Gugu in the crowd and she almost didn't recognise her friend when she finally saw her.

A black lady in an old-fashioned grey coat and loafers, with an equally old-fashioned headscarf tied under her chin, sat at a table and waved at her.

Sofia looked around but it was clear that the lady meant her. The old-fashioned lady with the slicked-back hair under the headscarf waved for Sofia again to come over to her table at the busy restaurant. Sofia hesitated and squinted in her direction. Never! This couldn't be her Gugu - the usually so fashionable socialite who wouldn't be seen dead in anything but designer clothes and killer heels?

Sofia approached the table. "Hello, Gertrude."

"Stop staring already, Sofie. People are going to notice us," Gugulethu Mbatha, the PR maverick said.

Sofia suppressed a giggle and sat down. "Great disguise, Gugs. Did they have a fashion-sale at Mr. Pinky's Hefty Hideaway?"

"Really? You're laughing and drawing attention to us?" Gugu Mbatha had made it undetected to the restaurant and she'd be damned if the wrong people would recognise her. Sofia swallowed the urge to laugh.

"So, are you going to tell me, why you stood me up on Thursday? And where the hell have you been? I've been worried sick," she hissed. "I thought some Mafia-heavy got hold of you and gave you concrete shoes."

"You're not that far off the mark," Gugu said.

"What?!" Sofia cried and a woman turned half-way around.

"Oh my word, keep your voice down!" Gugu urged her in whispered tones.

"You have to tell me what happened on or I swear I'm going to pop."

"Can't risk that happening," Gugu managed a weak smile. "I'm glad you are still here in Joburg. I really needed to speak to you." She lost no time and told Sofia about the dark car that had followed her. How she had gotten away by turning into a side road and into a driveway, half-hidden from sight by cocos palms and overgrown hibiscus bushes. It had been all down to her instincts warning her - screaming at her. Hide!

The property turned out to be some private business with a few parking bays outside. So she had parked her car under a large flame tree next to five other cars and walked up the driveway and back to the main road.

"I left my cell phone in the car, that's why all the calls went to voicemail," Gugu explained. "You can take me to that place later and I will pick up my car."

"If it's still there."

"I sure hope so, otherwise I'm toast," Gugu said and carried on with her story.

A minibus taxi had happened to stop at the traffic lights to let out some of the passengers. Gugu didn't have to think twice. Going into town was as good as any plan. She had changed minibus taxis in Fox Street, in downtown Johannesburg, and before she knew it, Gugu had knocked on her aunt Doris' door in a nice suburb of Soweto. Luckily, her aunt was at home.

"That's where I've been hiding out ever since."

"So you think that whoever was in that dark car with tinted windows was after you, trying to kidnap you or take you to some storehouse in Jeppe and blow your lights out?"

"Well, they certainly scared me," Gugu admitted. "When the car passed me, that guy just stared at me with a creepy grin on his face and I'm sure I saw a gun." Gugu rolled her eyes. "That's when I panicked."

"I wonder why he stared at you like that. Just to scare you?"

"Who cares? Fact is, I didn't feel safe and I had that envelope with Lorraine's letter with me and the photographs she sent... and I was on my way to meet you. I couldn't drag you into this. It was better to bolt and what better place to hide out than Soweto. Poor aunt Doris. I can't believe they set her house on fire. She doesn't deserve this."

"Are you sure, it was your aunt's house?" Sofia asked.

"Sure, sure," Gugu sighed. "Whoever caused that fire must have been looking for me and tried to smoke me out."

"Maybe your aunt just left a candle on..."

"Sofia, please! It wasn't a coincidence. And what about those guys in dark suits who followed you at the shopping centre? Was that a coincidence, too?"

"I don't think so. I think I also saw guns." Sofia stared into the distance, remembering how she'd felt. "That's why I ran."

"There you have it. Somebody is playing games with us. It's almost like 'Men in Black', just that they aren't after weird aliens, but the two of us. What possible reason could they have than to get hold of the letter Lorraine sent me? Bummer. How did they even know about Lorraine's letter... and the photos?"

"No idea. There are photos on top of the letter? Speaking of which... I haven't seen that mysterious letter yet."

"Sorry," Gugu apologised. She took the brown envelope out of the duffel-bag and pushed it across the table in front of Sofia. "Here, read it."

Sofia took the envelope just as the waiter showed up at the table. "Can I get you something to drink?" He asked cheerfully and put two menus down.

"Yo, where did you come from?" Gugu seemed a little jumpy and Sofia stared at her in warning.

"Sorry, Madam, would you like something to drink?"

"Bring us two moccachinos, please," Sofia ordered. "And you can take the menus. We won't be eating anything today."

"I thought he was one of them..." Gugu breathed a sigh of relief when the young man left with the menus.

"Keep it together, Gugs," her friend said. "Let me read the

letter now, then we can brainstorm." Sofia took the pages out of the envelope and read through the letter. She looked up with a shocked expression when she got to the names. "She can't be serious."

"That's what I was thinking. But why should she make it up?"

"Maybe somebody from the office was following you," Sofia suggested.

"Could be. It's not exactly a 'happy family' I'm working with, no matter what Makaroff is trying to show to the world."

"Right."

"I don't know. How could I not have guessed that something was fishy? I mean, I've been his PR manager for a little over a year now and I had no clue." Gugu rested her weary head in her hands and mumbled. "It's my own fault. I should have stayed with Woolrich & Co. Not as glamorous, but at least, things were above board there. But no, I had to go for the higher salary..."

"That's of no use now," Sofia said a tad too harshly. "We must think about this carefully... make a plan. I don't want us to end up like Lorraine."

"You think it wasn't an accident... with her?"

"It's not exactly far-fetched if you ask me. Apparently, she knew details about his dealings that Makaroff certainly didn't want to get out."

"You think he knew that she was going public about all that stuff?" Sofia asked and didn't wait for an answer. "You gave me the skinny over the phone and I wrote it down on serviettes, while I was waiting for you in Linden."

"Why did you do that?"

"So I wouldn't forget. I mean, I wasn't sure what had happened to you... I had a look at the serviettes a few times since, in case I need to talk to the police," Sofia said. "They wouldn't have believed me anyway and I guess we won't need them anymore, now that we have the letter - and photos as proof."

"Wow, you thought you would have to identify my body, instead of seeing me in aunt Doris' clothes..."

"Well yes. What was I supposed to think? No wonder,

Lorraine was a bit cuckoo... to live with all of that..." Sofia said. "We must put the letter in a safe place until we have a strategy."

"What about the reporter, Lorraine wanted to visit that day? If somebody followed her and staged the accident, they must have known what she was planning."

"Did Lorraine give the reporter the proof or did she have it with her, and they took it with them?"

"You think the reporter is involved? Oh dear, that wouldn't be good. Maybe Lorraine didn't have anything on her and the crooks are none the wiser," Sofia said.

"We'll probably never know but here's to hoping."

"Maybe the reporter had nothing to do with it."

"Maybe she didn't. Damn, I should have known that Makaroff's a major crook," Gugu blurted out. She straightened her headscarf and played nervously with her bag. "I never guessed, he would try to get us all rubbed out."

"Well, his armed bodyguards should have been a dead giveaway, for starters," Sofia said in a mocking tone.

"Yes, but let's not overreact. Maybe Makaroff really isn't behind it."

"Who else would be behind it? And talk about overreacting... if he really wants to hurt us, he won't be fooled by your clothes either."

"Thanks, Sofie." Gugu looked anxiously around.

"Do you see any bodyguards?"

"No. What are they supposed to look like? Lots of muscular guys here. Lots of Makaroff's associates have bodyguards. You should've seen how many bodyguards those Indian brothers brought with them every time they met. Testosterone City." She giggled, then let her shoulders droop. "Sometimes I had to accompany him to their supa dupa mansion. Totally over the top. And I helped him."

"You have to get over it, Gugu. It's not as if you were running operations for Makaroff. So are you going to show me the photos or not?" Sofia pointed with her chin at Gugu's bag or rather her aunt's bag by the looks of it.

"I should never have trusted him," Gugu mumbled to

herself, as she took the pictures out of the envelope under the table, hiding it with her coat. Some of the pictures fell to the ground. "Oh no."

She pushed her chair back and into the waiter who had arrived with the two moccachinos, they had ordered. He managed to balance the cups on his tablet and Gugu apologized. "I'm so sorry, there's not much space here. Just put the cups on the table."

"Do you need some help with that?" he asked, trying to be helpful.

"No thanks," she said a little too quickly and the people at the next table looked up, mildly surprised. "No thanks," Gugu repeated in a firmer voice and even managed a smile. "Thank you, it's alright."

"Are you sure, you don't want some cake with your coffee?" The waiter asked in a friendly way. "We have different cheesecakes - I can recommend the one with blueberries - and red velvet, carrot cake, chocolate mousse..."

"No, we are not hungry," Sofia said with an even bigger smile and waved her hand, rejecting the offer. "Not right now."

The waiter smiled back and was called to another table to take a payment.

"You've got to keep it together, Gugs," Sofia whispered. "Let's drink our coffee."

"It's just nerves. Maybe coffee isn't such a good idea. I should have ordered chamomile tea instead. I mean, look at this stuff. Darn, there are some coffee stains on the letter now."

She wiped the paper sheets with Sofia's serviettes and put the letter on the table, face down. Then she picked up the photographs that were still lying on the floor and knocked her head against the table-top as she came up. The cups wobbled dangerously and Sofia steadied them from across the table.

"Ouch. Enough already," Gugu complained. "Can this get any worse?"

"Here, give me that." Sofia took the letter and read it again. She flipped to the second page and kept reading. Her eyes widened. "Missed the bit about how the girls are being trafficked," she said and remembered the girls she had seen at Makaroff's office.

Were they being trafficked or had they been drug mules? The mere thought made her feel ill. The third page wasn't much better. There was no doubt about it: this was highly sensitive information. And Tom wouldn't like it one bit. "Show me the pictures," Sofia held out her hand.

"Not up here... what's wrong with you?"

Gugu handed her the pictures under the table and nearly dropped them again, she was so nervous.

"No way. That blows the lid off," Sofia gasped as she looked at them one by one on her lap. "And nobody knew about this?" She took a few sips of her moccachino. "Needs some sugar," she said and poured some brown sugar from a little paper bag into the steaming liquid.

"That's what I thought. Somebody must have known... apart from Lorraine and the other dirtbags who were involved."

"Okay, so what should we do?" Sofia asked. They spoke in hushed tones now.

"What can we do? Tell the Corruption Unit and spend the rest of our lives in witness protection?" Gugu whispered. "There must be another way."

"I'm sure the police must already know what's going on. They are probably investigating Makaroff and his empire. They will need more proof." Sofia tried to think of a solution. It was not easy to find a way through this maze.

"Lorraine writes that we cannot trust the lawyers at the Makaroff Tower. And there will be corrupt policemen for sure who are part of their network."

"Afraid you're right."

"Then let's wait with going to the police," Gugu said. She pushed the letter and photographs back into the envelope.

"We can't wait forever."

Sofia thought of the one policeman, she could really trust. But did he know the police in town and who they should approach? Witbooi also didn't seem to think highly of the Special Commission on Poaching and their results to date were not very encouraging.

This was not a decision to be taken lightly and safety came first, especially now that they had Lorraine's letter.

The two women left the shopping centre and took a detour to find Gugu's car. To their surprise, they found it untouched in the same spot, Gugu had left it days before. "Can you believe it?" Sofia said. "In the middle of Joburg!"

Astrid's house was not far. Gugu would be safe there for now.

*

"Welcome! Tervetuloa!"

"Hauska tavata." Pleased to meet you. The handsome, dark-haired man shook Sofia's hand. Astrid had just introduced him as Paul Somerset. Her boyfriend. They were standing in the hallway but nobody seemed to mind.

Gugu was upstairs, watching TV. She had decided to stay out of sight, while Paul was in the house.

Astrid thought it best to introduce her beau to Sofia, while the children were still at school. They hadn't met Paul yet and only knew him as the nice neighbour who waved whenever he happened to see them in the street or at the shops. He often worked with the plants outside and mowed the lawn on Saturday mornings.

"Hi, nice to meet you, Paul. I'm Sofia. Sofia Helenius. You speak Finnish already?" She said. The ice was broken.

"Just a little phrase here and there," Paul Somerset answered. "But I'm learning." Astrid was beaming at him.

Paul seemed nice, self-confident and had a sophisticated air about him. Everything that Grant Rankin did not have. Grant, Astrid's current and often absent husband, looked down at everybody from a dizzy height.

They were expecting him back any day now. Sofia didn't look forward to it, especially now that she knew Astrid's secret lover. Apparently, Grant was about to conclude the deal in Mozambique. So this was their last chance to get acquainted without interruptions.

"Not bad for starters," Sofia said and addressed him in

Suomi. "Mistä olet kotoisin?"

"Ooh, I think that's a bit over my head. What did you ask?"

"She said: 'where are you from?'," Astrid explained.

"I see," he said. "I'm originally from Pretoria. One of the few Englishmen there, I suppose. I moved to Port Elizabeth for a while to study and now I live in Joburg."

"You must be speaking Afrikaans fairly well then if you're from Pretoria," Sofia laughed. "I stink at it, although I try my level best to learn the language."

"I wouldn't have been able to survive in Pretoria without speaking Afrikaans. Especially, since I went to school there. Garsfontein High School. Good school, actually. Played rugby there, learned how to braai and get drunk."

"I'm afraid I don't know one school from the other but I hear that Garsfontein is a nice area with big houses and it's quite affordable," Sofia said.

"I suppose you could say that. I have a flat in Garsfontein and most of my childhood friends still live there. I prefer the cooler weather in Joburg. Pretoria is too hot for my liking and the constant wind at the coast hurts my ears."

They chatted for a while until Astrid walked ahead of the others into the dining room.

The cousins had prepared lunch for the three of them. Finnish fare. Kaalikääryleet, steamed cabbage leaves stuffed with beef, onions and spices, served with traditional lingonberry jam on the side. How Astrid had procured the lingonberry jam was a mystery to Sofia but blueberries were easily available in South Africa. So this morning, Sofia had thrown herself into making Mustikkapiirakka or blueberry pie, while Gugu was still asleep. The wonderful aroma still hung in the air.

"Didn't I tell you that she's swell?" Astrid told Paul as they sat down at the table. Astrid poured some juice for them and put the jug back on the table.

"You did indeed." The nice man in his casual jeans and University of Michigan sweatshirt gave her a big smile.

Sofia still felt that it was a bit sleazy to sneak around

Grant's back but Astrid seemed so happy and excited that she didn't mind, playing along. And who was she to judge her cousin anyway?

Astrid had told her the whole story and her true feelings about her crumbling marriage had finally emerged. Sometimes, these things needed a bit of time to come out and Sofia didn't regret staying in Johannesburg longer than she had intended.

"So, what do you do, Paul? And how did you guys meet?" Sofia asked.

"Hey, what's up with the third degree, Mom?" Astrid joked. "Go easy on Paul; he's only just met you."

"Can you blame me for wanting to know who my dearest cousin is going out with? The last time you didn't ask my advice, Astrid... and see what happened," Sofia winked at her.

"Then let's not make the same mistake again," Astrid said and Paul laughed. Sofia began to like him.

"Well if you must know, I'm an architect and started my own business a few months ago. I buy slightly run-down houses in nice neighbourhoods like Northcliff and Parkview and turn them into mansions; the upper crust of Johannesburg cannot resist buying property at a good price. The house flipping is going quite well. I'm making ends meet," Paul said modestly.

"Surely more than just making ends meet," Sofia said.

"I guess it's more than just making ends meet," he admitted. "I'm financially sound." Astrid dished up the Kaalikääryleet and they began to eat.

"So... how did you guys meet?" Sofia repeated.

She already knew more or less the answer but wanted to hear his version of events. "Couldn't distract you from that one, now could I?" Paul grinned.

"Afraid not. Astrid left me a bit in the dark, so you are my last hope of finding out the whole truth." Sofia took a sip of her juice.

"Well, I'll put you out of your misery then," Paul said and Astrid rolled her eyes at him in jest. "We met at a yoga class."

"You do yoga? I didn't even know that Astrid did yoga," Sofia said. "That's unusual for a man, isn't it?" Astrid had only told her that they had met at the gym.

"I'm a man of many facets, I'm afraid, and I have a weakness for the gym. I like staying fit and what better way to do that than yoga. Nothing hectic, I might add. I'm fine with basic hatha yoga three times a week."

"I can't wait to hear about the other facets, too," Sofia said.

"While we eat..." Astrid scolded. "You've hardly touched your food, Sofie."

"It's my favourite dish," Paul said and Sofia liked him even more. They talked and they ate until Astrid decided it was time to go to the lounge.

"Come, guys, we can have the blueberry pie and some coffee there," Astrid said at last. "We can leave the dishes for now." There was plenty of food left for Gugu. What Sofia really wanted was to speak to Gugu...

Paul sat down next to Astrid and held her hand. Sofia felt like a parent who needed to keep an eye on things. "So tell me more about your hobbies, Paul."

Astrid went to the kitchen. "I'll make us coffee."

"This is delicious pie," Paul said. "Almost as good as the kaalikääryleet..."

"Thank you, Paul."

"My hobbies... what can I say, I like gardening and going to the gym. Mainly sauna and yoga and I swim a mean 10 lengths. Otherwise, I'm a homebody. Give me a good movie and I'm happy."

"You like to sauna, eh? Then you'll fit right in with us. Finns are crazy about doing sauna. Actually, all Scandinavians are. We even have a sauna at Shangari, although it doesn't get very cold there in winter. Not like here on the Highveld." Sofia helped herself to some pie.

"So I've heard. Tell me about yourself, Sofia. I know where you come from - from Finland - so that question is settled - but I hear that you live in the North West Province on a game farm with your fiancé. That must be pretty amazing."

Astrid poured more coffee for herself and Paul.

"Well, it's a safari park and lodge, actually. My boyfriend

Tom owns it. We are not engaged yet... but who knows," Sofia felt a pang of homesickness. "It's amazing to be out in nature with wild animals and a lodge to run. I admit that I can get a bit lost in the limelight of the big city."

"I don't believe it for a second. Astrid tells me that you lived in Cape Town for over a year or so. Now if that's not a big city then I don't know what is."

"Oh, what else did she tell you about me?" Sofia winked at Astrid and munched on her piece of blueberry pie. "I must be careful what lies to tell you next." Paul seemed to think that she was talking about him and Astrid.

"Are there so many lies?" he asked.

"Hmm, maybe."

"Come on now. Sofia is just joking, Paul. Another piece of pie?" Astrid intervened.

What's wrong with me, talking about lies? Sofia thought. She had so many lies and secrets to deal with right now - many of them her own - but she couldn't allow letting lies creep into every normal conversation. Astrid is going to figure out that something's going on if I keep talking nonsense like that. They were here to meet and have a pleasant conversation, so she had better pay attention to her choice of words.

Sofia had told Astrid, what a scumbag-trick Errol had tried on her and Tom but Astrid was too happy in love to notice that there was more. Much more. That there might be somebody watching the house right now.

This was definitely not the time to tell her or Paul the whole story. Sofia hadn't even mentioned her experience with the men in dark suits, she had escaped from in the parking lot of the shopping centre. As long as everything was under control, there was no need to let her into the secrets, she shared with Gugu.

They needed time to figure out their next move. Somebody might be watching Astrid's house. It wasn't a good idea to rush things if they wanted to stay safe.

Although Sofia felt tempted, she couldn't tell Astrid what was really going on.

They had told her a white lie, namely that Gugu had builders at her flat and needed a place to stay. In her usual friendly manner, Astrid had extended her hospitality to Gugu without question.

When Grant came back from Mozambique, Sofia and Gugu would move to the B&B down the road and book in under false names.

She would settle the bill upfront, just to be sure. As far as Tom was concerned... Sofia had resisted the urge to phone him. They normally discussed everything but she hadn't heard from Tom, either. It was possible that he was busy with the lodge. Or maybe, he just didn't want to talk to her...

"Sofia?"

"Yes?" She looked up.

"You were lost in thought, dear cousin." Astrid looked at Sofia, thinking that she understood why. She knew about Errol and Tom. Sofia smiled at her. *Let her think that it was the thing with Errol that bothers me*, she thought.

"If you don't eat your Mustikkapiirakka, we won't have sunshine tomorrow."

It was true; Sofia had left half her pie uneaten. "Sorry, I've got a lot on my mind right now," she apologised and picked up her cake fork. "Can't risk bad weather, can we?"

The phone rang and Astrid went to the room next-door to take the call.

"Oh hi, Grant..."

"Oh dear," Sofia said to Paul. "As if things weren't awkward enough already."

"I hope not on my account," he answered.

"No, I actually like you, Paul. A big step up from Astrid's husband I must say. It's awkward that I'm here, while this is going on. The separation and all."

"Thank you I guess - and I understand that these are not the easiest of circumstances."

Astrid came back into the room. "Grant's coming back on Saturday morning."

"Speak of the devil," Sofia said and Astrid glared at her.

"He gave me the flight details from Maputo over the phone. Okay, at least it won't be a surprise visit then. I've still got two days of peace and packing our things." Astrid sighed.

"Yes of course... should we rather get out of your hair and stay at the Dragonfly B&B down the road?" Sofia asked innocently.

"It's better if you are not here during the showdown. It would be nice if you could come with me to the airport, though. I've already arranged for the kids to stay over at a friend's house this weekend."

Red spots appeared on Astrid's neck.

She must feel really stressed about everything and having me and Gugu here in the middle of all this, Sofia thought.

Astrid composed herself. "You know what? I'll introduce Paul to the dogs in the back garden. It's high time they get to know him since they will stay with us. Could you be so kind and take the dishes to the kitchen, Sofie?"

"And later I want to hear more about this safari lodge of yours," Paul Somerset tried to add a carefree note.

"Ah I see, you're fishing for a free holiday, aren't you?" Sofia laughed and picked up the plates and cups from the dining room table.

"I would love to come and visit your safari lodge one of these days. When all of this is finished and klaar."

"I'll see what I can do, putting in a good word in for you and Astrid," Sofia said.

When Paul Somerset left that afternoon, Sofia thought that the visit had gone rather well. Astrid seemed happy, humming a song as she began packing up the last of her belongings, before fetching the children from school.

Sofia and Gugu moved into the Dragonfly B&B and spent the rest of the day hatching a plan, eager to resolve their burning problem.

CHAPTER 11

The dirty water in the harbour basin lapped up against the wall of dock 17 in slow and regular waves. A couple of ducks were riding the waves, pecking at breadcrumbs, while a cargo ship with its stack of colourful containers anchored below one of the large cranes.

It was business as usual at the port of Maputo and it was hot.

Ships moved languidly in their appointed straits past warehouses that lined the docks along the waterfront. Tfhe ships' crews waited patiently for the dock workers to remove the cargo or load containers as the scorching sun went about its daily course across the sky.

Every movement slowed down in the sticky heat of the afternoon until an orange sun moved closer toward the land.

Outside a run-down warehouse on dock 17 lay a rickety boat moored to the wall, bouncing merrily up and down to the rhythm of the waves. The pasty blue paint was peeling off the hull and the engine needed replacing but the 'Santa Maria' was no different to other small boats in the harbour and, most importantly, she didn't draw attention to herself.

The smells of rotting fish, algae and waste of all kinds mingled with that of motor oil in the noon heat.

Large metal sliding gates had been tightly shut until a handful of South African men arrived. They pushed the gates open. Just wide enough to carry packets from the warehouse into the car and other packets from the van into the dark warehouse.

It was a miracle that the sliding gates still worked. They were half-eaten by rust and wobbled dangerously on their runners, which didn't seem to bother the men. Rats lived inside the hall; in dark places behind the metal shelves, with the occasional squeaking often the only sign of life. Now, a clutch of anxious girls huddled together on wooden crates.

The warehouse had seen better days when it had served as storage space for a small sugar company. Nowadays, it stood deserted and ignored by the port authorities. A perfect place to conduct business. The kind of illicit business that everybody knew about around here but ignored as much as possible.

Until this morning, Grant Rankin and two of his sidekicks had been waiting in a hotel in the centre of Maputo. They enjoyed the fruits of the country, so to speak, while arrangements were being made in South Africa. Who could blame them for wanting a little entertainment? Their job had its perks and Mozambique wasn't a bad place to wait around for a delivery.

The hotel ranked among the most beautiful and luxurious in the country and the pool area was the ideal place to relax with a cool drink in hand. There was also a casino, where they could gamble until the wee hours of the morning, then sleep until midday. They couldn't complain about their pay or treatment but waiting two weeks for arrangements to be finalized, that was a long time to wait and the men itched to see some action. Three days ago, they had relaxed by the pool ringed by palm trees and a view of the Indian Ocean.

"Why is it taking so long, man? The merchandise was supposed to arrive beginning of last week - at the latest," one of the men drawled in a heavy South African accent. A half-naked beauty, prostrate on a lounger next to him, was playing with the trinkets he had given her the day before.

"How must I know," Rankin growled and sat up. "We don't get paid to ask questions. I'm going inside, it's nearly dinnertime."

"Alright, alright, man, no more questions. Just getting bored. Come on dolly, let's cool down in the pool," he said to his playmate and showed off his stomach muscles.

The pretty young woman smiled lazily and rolled off her lounger. "Iwe! Biggi chofista. Esse gajo é numa boa mesmo," she said and gave Rankin admiring looks. *Look! What a big show-off; this dude is really good.* Then she lowered herself seductively into the turquoise water of the pool.

Another two days went by and no merchandise in sight. Finally, the men were called to action through the usual channels. It was a bit unusual that they were not supposed to drive the usual Maputo-Johannesburg route but take a plane instead, but what the hell. They dismissed their female companions and readied themselves for the task. The merchandise had arrived and the exchange would take place the following day. Afterwards, the goods would be taken to South Africa and they could leave Mozambique at last. Grant Rankin decided to phone his wife to let her know about the travel arrangements.

"Hi darling, I'm still in Maputo and the deal has finally been concluded. Yes, yes... I'm flying home on Saturday morning. No, not by car, this time. Do you have a pen ready? Okay, flight number XLM4338. Yes, eight. Time of arrival is 8:45 am. Yes, that's it. I'll see you then. Don't be late. Bye."

He hung up, rather pleased with himself. Astrid was the perfect wife, beautiful and well-tempered. She had given him two adorable children and looked after the home, while he was away on business. They were content.

He brought home the bacon and fat bacon it was, mind you. His lifestyle also allowed him the occasional bit on the side. What more could a warm-blooded man like him ask for?

Grant Rankin's job wasn't easy, especially when merchandise had to be moved at the drop of a hat. He took great risks, keeping the business running and the staff under control, securing merchandise and greasing palms at every turn. Rankin felt that he deserved every bit of luxury he could get.

The hot, lazy mood at the warehouse persisted into the afternoon. A small group of young women sat dazed in the dark hall, handing around bottles of water, resigned to their fate. The sailors ignored them and waited outside on the dock, leaning against drums and bales.

Another load was on its way and waiting for merchandise

was nothing new to the crew of the 'Santa Maria'. They had their part to play and the South Africans theirs. That's how it had been for a long time and they were all profiting from their dirty business. It was better to just see it as work. Work, like the work the men on the docks did or the other sailors who worked on the container ships. They were hired to do a job and that's all there was to it.

The crew were well-paid and there was always time for their pleasures in between gigs. And there were many pleasures to be enjoyed around the harbour. All they needed was to bring home enough money for their families at the end of the day. Getting drunk on cassava beer in the docks was good, betting on cockfights and gambling their money away was better - and the bordellos in the harbour; well they were the cherry on top. The girls here were more enjoyable than the ones they were used to at home. They cost more money and money they had. All that made the rugged seamen feel like they owned the world.

The female merchandise was off limits of course. They knew the rules. Everything was good as long as they played the game. They were well aware of the fact that it was a dangerous game but some of them had never seen things go out of hand.

The girls meant for shipment had to be treated well, despite the fact that they were juicy girls in skimpy clothes. Marks on their skin or missing teeth diminished their worth and the seamen were paid less. This meant a substantial loss of income. Sex was out of the question since all merchandise needed to be handled with care. 'You break you buy' - and none of the sailors could afford them.

Over the years, one or two of the women had thrown themselves overboard in high seas but the men had learned their lesson and, unless the girls felt violently seasick, they were kept below deck at all times. This time, they had been waiting longer than usual because of some new deal that was being forged overseas. New suppliers had to be tested and new girls that had to be groomed. At least that's what they had heard through the grapevine. When the crewmen were needed, they had to be ready, drunk or not.

They'd received the message through the usual channels yesterday. Since then, the boat and its crew had been ready; ready to depart Maputo Harbour for another part of Africa. What happened from there, they neither knew nor cared about. Waiting was nothing out of the ordinary. Sometimes, they had to wait even longer; days sometimes. The boat would be leaving at dusk as usual and the South Africans ensured that certain eyes were shut and certain ears were closed.

The sailors knew the drill: no questions were asked, which meant no problems for them. They remembered all too well, how Grant Rankin had taken care of things before whenever there had been a deviation from protocol.

A captain by the name of Anibal, from the Portuguese Islands, had taken over from old Batista who had questioned the rough handling of some of the girls. As so often, he was to take them up north in exchange for a shipment of white powder that was wrapped in plastic. The parcels were stuffed then into suitcases, destined for Johannesburg. Sometimes there were art objects or something else inside thick layers of bubble-wrap to disguise the shape. The men took everything, they were given. As long as it paid off.

Sometimes the freight consisted of blue tablets but what did they care. Those things were decided on at a much higher level and that was all they needed to know.

Batista had broken the code of the trade by questioning the actions of his superiors. Could have taken a shine to one of the young broads.

Batista had suddenly disappeared and nobody dared ask what had happened to him. They had been told that he'd fallen in love with some prostitute and that her pimp had knifed the captain to death in some bordello. They knew that Batista was an avid Christian and had a bunch of children at home. He always talked about, how he wanted to send them to good schools, so they would have a better life someday. What would become of them now? It was useless to ask questions. What were they supposed to do? Go to the police? The punishment for snitches was even worse than death.

Rankin informed them about the obvious delay. "We are still waiting for another shipment. A friend of mine asked me to take some of his stuff out of the country. Should be here any minute now."

Anibal knew about these 'private' shipments, of course. As long as he was cut in, he did as he was told. "No problem, boss. As long it's not too big. Have to wait for dusk anyways." He scratched his untidy beard.

"It's not too big," Rankin assured him. "We are not dealing in elephant teeth here, are we?" The men laughed and settled back into waiting mode. Grant Rankin was using the network to do his own little business on the side. He'd be a fool not to. It didn't make a difference. Didn't hurt anyone, as long as Stan Makaroff didn't hear about it.

A car approached. Rankin looked nervously around one of the shelves, stacked with a variety of storage boxes. He took out his gun and held it flat against his chest, ready to use it at the slightest provocation. The car passed.

If the guns came out, the crew usually hid as far away as possible. When it was over and they were ordered to get rid of the bodies, they had complied. The younger sailors knew that from the older experienced ones.

In the past, they had used stones for weights and wrapped chains tightly around the bodies, then thrown them into the sea. Only a nasty red colour belied the innocence of the gentle waves. The propellers of passing ships and the occasional shark took care of the rest. Batista had had a problem with that but cassava beer was a wonderful remedy. Them brew let them forget such gruesome deeds - until they felt the drunken need to brag to the younger lads.

A van back-fired down the road. It had to be the minivan, they were waiting for. Grey and inconspicuous and covered in dirt. Rankin thought it a bit odd that Goldie hadn't phoned him personally to say that the driver was coming late but then he simply ignored the misgivings he'd had all day. He scolded himself for being so nervous because nerves were the last thing he needed in this business. It would be a routine handover as usual and money in the bank. Ka-tching. Everybody knew their place in the network. It would be over in less than half an hour. A moment later, Grant Rankin wished he had listened to his instincts.

The van stopped close to the warehouse. The car doors flew open and shots were fired, even before the armed agents jumped out of the vehicle. Grant Rankin was on his knees, hands behind his head before he knew what was happening. The lack-a-daisy smugglers were no match for well-trained Mozambican and South African Special Forces in bullet-proof clothing and assault rifles at the ready.

One of Rankin's men was dead, even before he had a chance to draw his weapon. The other one had run over to the screeching girls and pushed them into a corner. Then, not knowing what else to do and unable to protect the merchandise, he ran out the back and tried to close the wobbly sliding gates by the dock. The crew had already jumped on the boat and one of the sailors was fiddling with the rope but the police had not come unprepared.

"Drop your weapons. On the ground, hands behind your head!" The sheer force of the megaphone left them stunned but they knew they had to get away.

The agents fired shots from behind a nearby wall and approached quickly from the back. Bullets ricocheted off the steel doors at every angle and slammed into the crumbling walls. Some found their targets. Two of the sailors and Rankin's last man dropped to the ground and lay lifeless in expanding pools of blood.

The rest of the crew was soon overpowered and ordered on the ground with their hands folded behind their heads. A police boat hove to and more policemen jumped onto the dock to arrest the survivors. The prostrate men swore in their respective languages, as they were hauled up and pushed into an armoured police vehicle. They joined the handcuffed and profusely sweating Grant Rankin.

"You and your 'private business'. You ruined us," the captain snarled at him. "Ninja mulungo. É pah!"

"Don't blame me. How was I supposed to know? I paid the bribes like always. Fickle Mozambicans, that's the problem. Greedy bastards!"

"Você é maloucopah!" Anibal kept swearing.

"Shut up!" One of the agents yelled into the back and for a moment, it looked as if Grant Rankin's head was going to burst with rage.

The others glared at the two men. The most powerful men they knew, sat in this police vehicle like naughty schoolboys with their hands on their backs; helpless like the rest of them. The hardened seamen were shocked and angry, their comfortable lives suddenly turned upside down. Families would suffer without their breadwinners and Mozambican jail was not something, they wanted to think about right now. All that because Rankin had not been careful enough!

The arrests were celebrated in the press as a major breakthrough against the international smuggling ring for the organised crimes units in both countries. A triumph for the organised crimes units in both countries who were sure that their State Intelligence was on a par with international standards.

The suspects could not be named or shown on television since investigations first needed to be completed. More arrests were expected soon, while cumbersome legal proceedings took their course. In South Africa, a brief segment appeared on the 7 o'clock news and an article on page 4 of South Africa's largest newspaper. Nobody mentioned the anonymous tip-off the police had received, as the governments celebrated themselves. The kidnapped girls were returned to safety and the drugs were destroyed.

The rhino horns that had been intercepted before the sting at the harbour, were sent to South Africa for testing. Swiss bank accounts were frozen. What came as a surprise were the arrests of Stanislav Makaroff and his wife at their Bryanston mansion that looked like a medieval castle.

"Absolutely baseless allegations," Makaroff growled into the microphone, "I'm innocent until proven guilty. I'll have my day in court!" before he was whisked off. "An insult to any innocent, hard-working citizen in this country. I have no further comment."

The cameras followed him to a police van, where he joined his wife Helena.

Stan Makaroff was out on bail a week later. He laughed off the charges that were levelled against him and his wife while being filmed on the golf course or handing out bowls of soup to the homeless. Allegations of rhino horn smuggling, drug smuggling, human trafficking, racketeering and a list of other serious charges. But Stan Makaroff kept denying everything.

The image of bodyguards towering over him, as he walked to the court building and his lawyers in black robes, dragging their bulging black trolleys over kerbsides, dominated the TV news for weeks, while the court case dragged on.

Only his PR manager was missing from the picture. Gugulethu Mbatha had disappeared. Of course, the police were in the possession of Lorraine's letter by now and knew her whereabouts but kept the information under cover.

Reporters from all over the world camped outside the court in Johannesburg to catch a glimpse of the accused and possibly get an interview and their defence team. Stan Makaroff was a rich man and could afford the best.

Experts speculated during panel discussions about possible links to certain business people and politicians but allegations still had to be substantiated. The heads of lowly officials began to roll, although they had only followed orders. The heads of lowly officials began to roll, although they had only followed orders.

In Zimbabwe, the Wildlife Management Authority sacked its boss, after he was found guilty of stealing rhino horns worth millions that had been in safe storage for nearly 30 years. The Zimbabwean police were also investigating a South African connection and the court case was expected to begin soon. The Kruger Park received a trained special unit to fight poachers and smuggling rings and things were beginning to happen. Sofia and Gugu watched the 7 o'clock news in the lobby of the Dragonfly B&B.

"Strangely, I believe that Makaroff is telling the truth about the rhino horn smuggling. He is ruthless when it comes to his other business but he's also very much into wildlife and the bushveld. I just can't imagine him orchestrating the poaching of rhinos in South Africa," Gugu frowned.

The business news came on.

"Don't forget, that he tried to talk me into raising lions, only to have them hunted with bows and arrows by paying nut cases from overseas," Sofia reminded her.

"I know... he's so odd and talks a lot of rubbish but to my knowledge, he's never done anything like that for real. One day, he's into this, the next day, he's into that. But killing rhinos for their horns... I don't think so."

"Maybe you're right. There's enough other stuff, he's definitely involved in," Sofia said. "I can't wait for him to get punished by the courts."

"He's probably going to appeal the sentence as soon as it's handed down."

"What else is new? But we did good." The two of them high-fived. "Are you going back to work? I mean with the Makaroff case all over the media and his illegal operations flying open one by one, do you really want to be associated with Makaroff Enterprises? You might even be called as a witness."

"Don't forget that his former friends are turning their backs on him. I've already tendered my resignation. I was thinking of leaving even before I knew the truth."

Sofia turned up the volume when the weather came on and a freak winter thunderstorm was forecast for Johannesburg. She missed Shangari and she missed Tom. He had phoned her at last and begged Sofia to come home.

If things went according to plan, she would be leaving on Sunday and Gugu was coming to stay with her for a while.

CHAPTER 12

Errol Botes pressed his hand against the gun in his shoulder holster. He hoped that there wouldn't be a shoot-out again like last time, especially not here at the airport. But he had to be prepared.

Errol had taken up his post outside the arrival terminal on the tarmac by the luggage carts. Here, he watched suitcases and bags being thrown onto the revolving conveyor belt. He had been out in the cold since dawn, watching the luggage handlers work together like clockwork, while trying to ignore the sniffer dogs. In his parka and beanie, he could have passed for any of the other workers and they barely paid attention to him. He walked toward the glass doors and had a peek at the long line of passengers that slowly emerged from the sky bridge that connected the aircraft with the building.

The flight from Maputo had just landed. By the time, the passengers had gone through passport control and were on their way to the luggage carousels, the dogs would have finished sniffing the suitcases and bags from Mozambique. With some luck they would pick out the suitcase with the drugs.

According to their information, the drugs were definitely being smuggled on this flight and it was Errol's job to guard the operation.

Once the offending suitcase had been found, marked and transported onto the conveyor belt, he would move into the arrival hall, in order to support the others on the team.

They had already pin-pointed a beautiful young woman in a red coat and shiny boots up to her knees and an older, balding man in shorts as the possible suspects. Shorts in winter... brrr... Errol stuck his hands into his pockets and walked back to the conveyor belt.

It was unclear who would meet the mule and transport the drugs out of the airport. Intelligence on the Johannesburg contacts was sketchy, plus the Mozambican police had arrested most of the South African smugglers during a sting in Maputo.

Grant Rankin, the South African kingpin in Mozambique was among them at last. That meant, someone had to take over from him. They hadn't informed Grant Rankin's Swedish wife yet and the news reports had been kept as neutral as possible on the identity of the South Africans involved. No pictures or names had been released to the media. If she had anything to do with the drug smuggling, they would know soon enough. She was en route to the airport right now and Errol knew that his ex-girlfriend Sofia Helenius was Astrid Rankin's cousin.

He hadn't contacted her in over a week to make her believe that he'd gone back to work at the radio station in Bloemfontein.

Partly, because he was ashamed of his stupid, drunken behaviour in Melville and partly, because he didn't want to get involved with the surveillance detail anymore.

He felt bad for misleading Sofia. Making up stuff about a dodgy cousin wanting 50,000 Rand for donating a piece of his liver and shit like that. Errol wasn't particularly good at thinking on his feet. Unfortunately, his boss had insisted.

The others hadn't done such a great job either. Sofia had been spooked by the undercover cops tailing Gugu Mbatha to a small shopping centre in Linden. She was Stan Makaroff's public relations manager, from the Sandton office tower and her best friend. They were undercover cops like himself, albeit from a different unit.

One day, he would tell Sofia that his DJ image was just a front. That he was only doing stints as a DJ to get closer to the drug dealing network in the cities. One day, he would tell her the truth.

It had been his job, to keep an eye on Sofia and Astrid Rankin and the possible network in Johannesburg, while he attended the conference at the Sandton Convention Centre. It had been tougher than he thought. To top it all, Errol was in the dog box with his superiors. For being so stupid to jeopardise his cover with his jealous antics in Melville after Lorraine Pienaar's funeral. He had been unable to explain, why he had gotten so drunk and was reprimanded for it. He wanted to kick himself afterwards, but by then, it was too late for regrets.

At the request of the Special Commission on Poaching who already had a tail on Sofia Helenius, he had had revived their relationship and gotten close to her while she was in the city.

The senior detective of the Commission - one Captain Combrink - wanted to find out, whether she and her boyfriend Tom Rutgers were somehow involved in the poaching and rhino-horn smuggling ring. Their units had joined forces but communication wasn't their strong-suit. They hadn't been able to establish a connection with the local drug syndicate.

The unit had a point, though: how could the poachers simply disappear without a trace after the hit at Shangari and Lungile Farm? A local hide-out was the logical explanation. The smugglers were especially careful and secretive in their arrangements and there had to be an insider in the area somewhere, to keep things running this smoothly.

Unfortunately, that's where Errol had come in. He couldn't deny that he still held a torch for Sofia but he was the last man a woman should be involved with; especially not a fine woman like Sofia Helenius.

He hadn't known her that well in Cape Town, just wanted to add a notch on his belt. Errol was used to bedding beauties back then, but when he started falling in love with her, the affair had become intolerable to him. He'd been so happy when she told him about the pregnancy but there was no way he could bring himself to settle down.

Not with his job and Sofia having a boyfriend and all. That's why he had decided that it was best for the baby and Sofia if he disappeared from their lives.

Detective Combrink had told Errol about the suspicions against Tom Rutgers and Sofia Helenius and some of the other people in the Renosterspruit area.

'No way!' He had told the smug detective and explained, how he had come to know Sofia and the whole story with Damian. It would have been best to recuse himself from the case, due to a conflict of interest, but his boss had seen a unique opportunity to infiltrate the smuggling ring and wouldn't hear of it.

That's why Errol had made contact with Barry Pienaar and Tom Rutgers in Sun City first, to check them out. Then months later, he'd laid it on thick to get close to Sofia.

The cover story of their adopted son being critically ill, had been cruel and that plan had backfired. Errol Botes felt guilty for putting Sofia through all this emotional turmoil but his boss had insisted.

Personal guilt was not a good reason to throw away a unique opportunity like that. Errol didn't have much of a choice. His colleague, Robert Baldwin, had been the only one dead against the plan and claimed that personal involvement could jeopardise the entire case. And Bob was right: it very nearly had. Tailing Gugulethu Mbatha had been another investigating unit's job, and they had messed up.

There had to be a definite link to the smuggling ring within Makaroff Enterprises, but Errol was convinced that Gugu Mbatha had no active part in it. In Makaroff's criminal dealings or the rhino-horn smuggling. There was absolutely no proof. Even Stanislav Makaroff was a questionable suspect, despite his many clandestine activities. But if it was neither Makaroff nor Gugu Mbatha, then who was it?

The units had gotten their wires crossed and botched the surveillance in Linden last week. The idea with the ice-cream truck had been great at first. Just that the dogs in the area hated the music it played and howled incessantly. Some of the residents had angrily shaken their fists at the driver, so they had moved back to regular surveillance.

The other unit had lost sight of Gugu Mbatha on the main road just before the turnoff to the shopping centre, but two of their agents had gone ahead to the parking lot anyway. They had spotted Sofia at the coffee shop and when she'd left in a hurry, a suspicious-looking man had followed her to the parking lot and got into a green car.

But the surveillance team had been too obvious and Sofia was smart. She'd probably thought that some criminals were after her. The man with the green car had just been in a hurry and could not be linked to any crime.

Errol saw the dog handlers make hand signs. The dogs had found the suitcase with the drugs! He communicated in abrupt syllables with the other team members inside the arrival hall and listened to the voice in his earpiece.

The mule was the woman with the shiny long boots and red coat. They were moving in and he was needed inside. As soon as the woman picked up the suitcase from the carousel, they would follow her and her contact in unmarked cars.

Part of the unit was busy setting up a speeding roadblock. They would be informed of the car and stop it before they could get onto the highway.

In case they took the Gautrain into Johannesburg or Pretoria, another unit on standby, would get onto the train and arrest them outside the station. This would be safer. Errol had done it before and everybody knew what to do.

Bang bang, pof, pof pof.

He suddenly heard shots through his earpiece, then there were more shots and without giving it another thought, Errol Botes rushed into the brightly lit airport building.

*

"Hitto! Bloody traffic, we'll be late," Astrid moaned and took the turn-off to the OR Tambo Airport. They had been stuck at an accident scene on the R21 for almost 20 minutes and Astrid was understandably tense.

"Relax, we're nearly there," Sofia tried to calm her cousin down. She tied her dark hair up in a ponytail and switched the car radio on. '... and the rhino-poaching case had to be struck off the roll because two Vietnamese interpreters were not duly sworn in by the Specialised Crimes Court once again...'

"Oh please switch that off, Sofie!"

"Okay..." Sofia switched the radio off, scrunching up her face.

"Sorry, I'm on tenterhooks... don't want to start things off with Grant being in a bad mood. It's not going to be a walk in the park, even if he is in a brilliant mood."

"Hey, you have to get a grip on your own mood first or he'll smell a rat," Sofia sighed. "I'm not looking forward to this either way. Remember, I'm just here to support you." She regretted her decision to accompany Astrid to the airport more and more by the minute.

"I know. Thank you, cousin. Damn, why are we slowing down now?"

They had reached the access road to the airport and the cars ahead of them came to a standstill. Something was happening straight ahead of them. Sirens were blaring, blue lights were flashing and taxis were moving out of the way. The cars slowly inched forward.

"Do you see that? What's going on over there?" Astrid wondered.

"I don't know... looks like police to me."

Sofia rolled down her window.

"Oh dear, I hope they didn't cordon off the Pick-up Section in front of the entrance. There is no time to look for parking now," Astrid complained and slammed her fists on the steering wheel.

"Listen here, you get a grip, Astrid. We won't be late. They are probably still going through passport control. That can take a while."

"If you are a foreigner, maybe, but Grant is a South African citizen and that queue is usually quite fast. It doesn't look like the Pick-up Section is cordoned off, as far as I can see," Astrid said. She took a gap and tried to navigate around the cars up front. When she saw a free parking bay, she took a chance, driving past the queue.

"Do you want to wait in the car?"

Before Sofia could answer, a black luxury car with tinted windows came speeding toward them, followed by another car with flashing blue lights. People were running in all directions.

Bang bang, pof, pof pof.

Their vehicle skidded to the side and came to a halt at the barrier. "Astrid?"

Her cousin didn't answer. She'd slumped forward onto the steering wheel and sighed deeply. Sofia saw a red liquid trickling down from her head onto Astrid's arm, just a shade darker than her jacket sleeve. "Astrid?!"

The black luxury car careened off the road and hit a concrete block in slow motion. Sofia looked closer and saw that the black car had been hit by bullets, saw the holes in the tinted windshield, then all she saw were flashing blue lights.

The next moment, Errol came charging down the road toward them. Two other men followed him, their weapons at the ready. Errol also had a weapon in his hand. He stopped for a moment and stared at her. Sofia didn't understand.

Errol pointed to her collar. There was a hole with a dark rim around it. "Have you been shot?"

Sofia slowly shook her head.

"Looks like you dodged a bullet there." Errol sounded astonished. "Damn close, too."

"A bullet?" Sofia asked. "What bullet? What are you doing with that gun? Did you do that? Did you shoot at me? Do you hate me that much?"

"No Sofia, I didn't shoot, calm down... please calm down..."

But Sofia was in shock and yelled hysterically. "You shot at us, you shot at us!"

She moved away from his hand in a panic. Errol had to do something before she went into full-blown shock.

He spoke into the mike, "One bystander shot, another one going into shock. Hurry up for god's sake." Then he tried to speak soothingly to Sofia.

"Sofia, I didn't shoot at you, the drug traffickers did. I'm undercover police. They saw us and tried to get away. One handler is dead. The drug mule and the other guy will survive." It wasn't easy to find the right words.

"I don't believe you!" Sofia moved closer toward Astrid who still sat slumped over the steering wheel. Motionless. "Astrid, say something!" she cried.

She stared at her cousin and the widening blood stain on her head and arm. Blond and red, red on red... Sofia saw the life seeping out of the only sister she'd ever known. It was too much. "Help her!! Ohgod... she's shot, she's shot!" Sofia began to scream again and couldn't stop. It had to be a bad dream, had to be!

The car doors flew open and paramedics reached for her, just as she began to lose consciousness.

*

Proof against Stan Makaroff had been mounting for a few years now but proper prosecution of the well-connected tycoon had been a difficult job. Now that the wind of political change was blowing and despite the fact that police dockets and evidence had disappeared from locked rooms in the past, the special police unit was making progress at last.

The smuggling ring's contact in Johannesburg who had been injured at the OR Tambo airport shooting, was singing like a canary and the detectives were stunned. Against all expectations, they were getting more out of him than they had bargained for.

The man told them about the well-run network of safe houses in the city and the countryside that were used in their smuggling operations. They also gave the police the names of masterminds and middlemen.

Much of it corresponded with Lorraine Pienaar's letter and then the girl who had come with the drugs from Mozambique filled in some of the gaps. The special investigating unit still had to tread carefully but if everything went according to plan, those involved would spend a long time behind bars. But there was still a difference between the law and reality and not all of the masterminds had been apprehended. They needed hard proof.

*

One Friday evening in September, Alwin Goldsmith found a mysterious note on his desk:

'I've got what you're looking for. You can have it back for

20,000 Rand. Come to Shangari and wait by the woods at sundown. No police. You'll find a way.
We are watching you.'

How had this mysterious note found its way onto his desk?

Nobody had access to the office, except the staff here. Julia or Raymond? No... The attorney didn't recognise the handwriting and had no idea who could be behind this plain piece of paper. Some of the new hotshot lawyers had been retrenched along with other Makaroff employees.

Perhaps it was one of them?

We are watching you, it said. Who was that - we?

Nonsense... he dismissed the obvious threat and thought about the blatant proposal for a while. Should he ignore the note? It smacked of blackmail for sure. Well, sort of.

It's too risky, he thought and got on with his work. He had taken over the legal department again, after a blunder by his young colleague in court. It didn't look good for the Makaroff empire and there was much work to be done.

Alwin Goldsmith stuck the note to his desk lamp, pulled the green shade down and started working on the court cases. He had a lot of experience with court cases.

A motion had to be filed in High Court regarding the smuggling story... and let's see... how could this new corruption case be dragged out? High Court, Supreme Court, Constitutional Court. It would take 2-3 years at least. The Makaroff empire could still afford to drag out any lawsuit.

But the lawyer found it hard to concentrate. The small piece of paper, stuck to the desk lamp, kept distracting him.

He knew, of course, what the note implied. Why he was told to bring twenty-thousand Rand and what the exchange entailed. No, it was too risky - and why now? Why not sooner? Then again... twenty-thousand Rand was a small price to pay.

Unable to make a decision, Goldsmith picked up the phone and dialled a number. A familiar voice answered. "Yes?"

He explained the situation. "Yes, madam... yes, of course, I know it's not the best way... I agree it would be a damn waste not to try... Yes, I understand. I understand. Yes, of course, I will do that and report back to you as soon as I can."

Click. The other side hung up.

He heard footsteps outside in the passage and switched the desk lamp off. Better if nobody knew that he was still in the office this late. He waited a while and the steps faded away. The whole department was at an action cricket game, playing against another law firm, but better safe than sorry. There was another phone call Goldsmith had to make.

"It's me," he said. "Yes, who else? I have a proposal that might be interesting for you. 1.4 million... Okay, okay, let's say 1.2 million. In 100 Rand notes, used notes. Yes, it has to be asap. Well, you'll have to make time then. Where? The usual place. Yes, I'm sure, you'll find it. Sun City isn't that complicated... Yes, this weekend. Sunday. I'll let you know. Alright. Bye."

He placed the receiver back on the phone.

That was going better than expected. It's not as if Alwin Goldsmith hadn't done it before... just never under these circumstances. He rummaged through the top drawer of his desk and found the key.

It would be best if he took the private lift down to the covered parking area, instead of taking the normal route through the foyer. That way, the night watchmen would be none the wiser.

He drove his car to the lonely townhouse in Bryanston that he called home. He threw his key on the chest of drawers in the passage and went straight to the bar. After a couple of brandys, he fell into an uneasy sleep right there on the stylish couch that Gloria had picked out before she'd left him.

A few hours later, Goldsmith phoned the office.

"... the file is on my desk... worked on it last night... Raymond can do it. Not feeling well." He rasped in a phlegmy sort of way that made his assistant cringe on the other end of the line. "Coming down with something...cough, cough."

That was settled. He packed an overnight bag and counted the money in his wall safe. 24,000 Rand, 15,000 Euros and

7,000 US Dollars. No problem then.

Alwin Goldsmith counted out twenty thousand Rand onto the table. Then he put the notes carefully into a bag and wrote a note to himself that he placed into the safe. He liked doing things the proper way. Goldsmith took out the Glock pistol, he always kept inside the safe.

He dressed in shorts and a Madiba shirt, put another note for his housekeeper on the kitchen counter and left for a weekend in the country. It wasn't the first time, he'd spent an enjoyable weekend at Shangari Safari Lodge but it was the first time, he didn't fly - and today he was alone.

This is business, not pleasure, he reminded himself.

Goldsmith steered his dark blue BMW up the tar road north of Rutgersdrift and turned right by the great baobab tree. He'd cursed every small bump and ditch on the way.

Men in blue overalls waved as he drove past but he didn't see any reason to acknowledge them. The lodge was booked out for the weekend and he had to make do with a 4-man tent. He had the tent all to himself for two nights and booked under a different name.

It wasn't as comfortable as the luxury rooms he normally occupied but it wasn't luxury the jaded attorney was after. A tent would do just fine. Alwin Goldsmith alias Alan Miller wanted to keep a low profile.

He drank more brandy at the hotel bar than he should have and nearly missed the early morning safari drive as a result.

The briefing before the safari was obligatory. Get on with it, he kept thinking as he sat behind a corpulent lady with an irritating hyena laugh. Even ten minutes of this was too long. It was Nelson who drove the tourists out to the bush today.

This guy is way too chirpy! Goldsmith thought. The sun twinkled through the trees in the distance, warming the land but Alwin Goldsmith could find no joy in the beauty of the country morning. The other tourists chatted lively with each other and asked the guide questions in foreign accents. *Fools,* he thought and snorted contemptuously. He was here on business.

Since the gamekeepers had spotted predators in the hills this morning, Nelson decided to stop the safari vehicle for a few minutes by the woods. He let the tourists take a brief nature walk not far from the dry riverbed, where he could show them the baboons.

The rains had started early this year and the whitewater was surging past the beach in full force.

The tourists marvelled at the baboons and the colourful birds, they had spotted in the trees. Nobody noticed, how the glum man in the khaki shirt and a green shoulder bag, slowly trotted off into the thicket.

'Probably needed the loo', the corpulent British lady who laughed like a hyena, told the police the following day. "Barely noticed him, to be honest."

Goldsmith hid behind one of the blue Eucalyptus trees until he heard the safari vehicle drive off. *I thought, they'd never leave. Fools all of them,* he said to himself.

They didn't see the potential for business around here but Alwin Goldsmith was no fool. He knew an opportunity if it presented itself.

It didn't occur to him that it might be sheer luck that the vehicle stopped, where he wanted to get off. Over there was the spot, he was looking for. The blood had dried and long since disappeared with the spring rains. Washed away together with the memory, of what had happened here in February. He climbed onto a fairly low branch - just in case - and waited until dusk, just as the note had told him to do.

Sitting on his branch, the attorney remembered. He remembered how he and the local vet had waited here to play their part in a drama, full of greed and violence and regret that had unfolded since. It had been difficult to get the vet to participate but this insipid wife of his had played her part to perfection. Still, the man was new to this and had wanted to turn back a few times. He had grated on Goldsmith's nerves with his constant mewling and self-loathing nonsense.

Nobody could have foreseen what would happen next. They had planned it so carefully but the ranger who could call the rhinos, had seen them and recognised the vet.

The straight-laced ranger had paid with his life but the other ranger had seen nothing and had run away. Run off to his Bushman kin, apparently.

'Nobody said anything about murder,' the vet had wailed. Spineless wimp. Pienaar had been lucky to survive his constant nagging by the barn the following night. *Could have killed him just for that*, Goldsmith thought.

When Pienaar was about to draw attention to them with all this whining, he had to act. All he wanted to do was collect the rhino horns and get back into bed with the delectable Daisy de Bruin. How unfortunate that the shot had gone off and he had to run without the rhino horns. Later, he'd found out that Makaroff had been inside the barn, smoking. Damn lucky the vet had been and well-paid to boot with.

Pienaar's wife had not been so lucky.

He had asked Barry Pienaar who the new rhino whisperer was. Didn't know, apparently, but promised to try and find out. That would make the harvesting of rhino horn a lot easier in the long run. Would give him an advantage over the competition. He'd been so excited. But his plans had come to nought.

Alwin Goldsmith couldn't figure out what Makaroff had seen in this broad and why he'd offered her a job in the company. Sure, she'd been useful for a while when they needed a place to hide the merchandise but the Pienaar farm was only one of their expendable way-stations.

The heartbroken vet had refused his cooperation after she left him. What a bother. They'd found another contact for sure - money talks - but it took time. As soon as Makaroff had brought the country bumpkin to the city, she'd been nothing but trouble. Had grown a conscience or something, the moment she'd left that stupid farm and that stupid husband of hers. *Women!* He snorted, *talk about ball and chain.*

When Goldsmith had learned about her plans to conspire with the press, he'd acted in a flash and knew exactly what to do.

It had been her own fault. Couldn't leave well enough alone. You couldn't blame him for acting in the interest of all those involved. What about team spirit - Hello!

Just that the vet had never really appreciated that he was rid of his crude woman. The fool.

There were many in the organisation who could be replaced at the drop of a hat. Damn shame about his two henchmen, though. He called them his *henchmen* in an affectionate sort of way. They had always done what he'd asked of them without question and had served him well. But even they were expendable. Sipho had died at the airport and Jimmy was in prison. If Jimmy talked, he would pay a heavy price.

The vet would never talk for sure. Although, in Goldsmith's opinion, the payoff had been a bit over the top. The instruction had not come from Makaroff himself, mind you. *No, higher up than that!* The cynical lawyer thought with gloating satisfaction. He had all his bases covered and Makaroff didn't suspect a thing.

He shouldn't have accused his loyal Goldie of misconduct and embezzlement in the first place. How dare he?!

He could hold his own, could take care of himself and Makaroff was also a damn fool! He'd show him; Goldie would come out on top in the end.

Luckily, there was someone higher up then Stan Makaroff. Someone who protected him, saw his true value. Someone who would also benefit from the business transaction that he was about to conclude out here in the bush. Stan Makaroff had never even suspected how he, Alwin Goldsmith, had played him and used his networks to build his own, successful empire!

Crime was an unpleasant business but you got used to it, couldn't be prissy about the ins and outs of it. He had sacrificed his own happiness for that man.

The humiliation Gloria had endured from the sneering company wives! They were no longer included in social gatherings, not able to hold their heads up high. Things could have been worse but for Gloria, they had been bad enough - and he was still paying for her new lifestyle through his back teeth.

Damn all women! Well, except for one, maybe.

Old Mrs. Makaroff wasn't so bad if you knew how to

handle her. Ludmilla loved flattery, wanted to hear that she was still attractive and desirable - and he, Goldie, knew just how to play that game. He knew what perfume she liked, what jewellery and what TV series; and always brought her a present when he popped around to report on their poaching business.

Ouch! Goldsmith jumped off the branch and swept a few red ants off his arm and shorts. He rubbed his chest; his heart was giving him trouble lately. Palpitations. From now on, he would look out for his own interests and nothing else. There was light at the end of the tunnel.

All this went around Alwin Goldsmith's head, while he waited for dusk in the woods by the river. He waited to conclude the business he had come to conclude.

The sun sank and the sky turned a golden colour. Was there rustling in the thicket? Goldsmith listened carefully and his confidence faded. What was he thinking, coming here alone? He was vulnerable in the bush, not knowing who to expect and only his friend Glock for company.

Twigs cracked. Those were the heavy footsteps of a man! He took his pistol out from the bag. *Better safe than sorry*, he thought. Somebody was coming to meet him!

But Alwin Goldsmith was wrong. He was wrong if he thought that the spring rains had washed away the memories of the gruesome deed or that everybody but himself was a fool.

He also erred on the side of danger.

A few miles away, beyond the tall fence that separated the bushveld from the Shangari living quarters, dinner was cooked over open fires, in a compound full of gaily painted houses. In the fading daylight, the washing was taken down from long washing lines to monotonous singsong on the radio. The clatter of pots and pans mingled with the chatter of women and the crowing of small children.

Mothers called the older kids to dinner, interrupting their lively games of football and hopscotch. The children knew better than to ignore their mothers' calls. They put aside their footballs, the elastic bands, the small cars made of wire and disappeared one by one into the multi-coloured houses.

In one of those houses, painted in a bright blue colour, a man sat on the floor in a small room, on a mat made from straw. His grey head was bent down, as he sat motionless, deep in a trance. The room was bare, apart from three straw mats.

On the mat in the middle of the room, small objects were scattered in random order. Shrunken knuckle bones, plant seeds and coins. They were the tools of a shaman, a sangoma. In a flat bowl, dried herbs glowed in the twilight, giving off a smoky scent.

What the man was about to do was not something he liked doing but justice had to prevail and harmony needed to be restored. Frans had discussed with him, how the restless spirits of the rhino Ntombi and his father Cornelius could be appeased. He had agreed that what the police could not complete he, Obakeng, would now have to do instead. The police had their ways and he had his. The ancestors had spoken and he had no choice but to comply.

The man was not alone. A boy of about 16 sat in a similar pose to his right. They both wore the springbok hide of the initiated around their shoulders. It was quiet in the little blue house. Both men were oblivious to the noises outside, the music, the clatter, the clucking of chickens.

They were in a different place, saw the bushveld in the golden glory of the setting sun, saw the home of the great lion, the rhino, the zebra, the elephant.

What they saw was not peaceful or innocent. They followed with loathing another betrayal, another murder. Saw what happened with their inner eye.

The man called the great lion and the leopard. He spoke to their spirit, while the boy looked on and learned. The predators yielded. Arch enemies under other circumstances, they would act together, use their powerful force to accomplish what the humans could not.

The humans that belonged in their world were friend and formidable foe at times but never worthless prey. They lived in harmony side by side. The humans who did not belong were a different story and an evil human was waiting in the thicket by the woods.

At the bidding of the boy, all the rhinos of Shangari congregated not far from the wood by the river. They watched and waited at a safe distance, unseen. A second human approached, oblivious to the animals watching him.

What the wild cats were asked to do was not revenge for their conspecifics or the rhinos alone. Their human friend, Cornelius who had spoken to them so often and cared for their welfare, had given his life to protect Ntombi and her calf and deserved to be avenged. They all missed his gentle thoughts, his call. What man and rhino could not achieve, they could. The predators understood that there would be no place for man or beast in their world if such evil was allowed to prevail and to prey on the innocent.

The lion approached first, set his large paws in noiseless skill in front of each other. He needed to find the right angle, catch the scent. A harsh bang made him freeze in his tracks, then spurred him on. One of the humans in the thicket was on the ground. The large cat smelled blood. The man was no prey, had been a fairly good human who'd often helped when help was needed.

The other human exuded fear as he bent over the other man, taking something from him. The scent of fear almost overpowered the penetrating scent of evil. He did not belong here, brought only destruction. He was prey. The lion breathed heavily, then purred deeply.

The loathsome human had caught sight of the lion and yelled something. "Get away from me... get away!" Another loud bang. It was too much.

The leopard up in the tree snarled with all his might and the lion roared his loudest roar. He prepared to jump and glided effortlessly through the air with deadly precision.

On impact, the cold, hard metal was knocked out of the evil human's hand. The gasping man fell on the bag, he had brought with him. The bag with twenty-thousand Rand and the hacked-off the rhino horns, he had taken from Pienaar. The man's neck was broken before the man realised his fate.

Then the leopard moved in.

Jethro, the cheetah, growled with excitement in his enclosure and out in the bush, a pack of lions and all the other large cats chimed in. The two men in the little blue house felt the impact of the jump, felt the overwhelming pain of the man out in the sunbathed woods.

They lifted their heads at the same time. The man's head was grey and the boy's head dark with the knotted hair, so typical of the Bushmen. The man's face was neither young nor old and his eyes glistened in the near dark. He slowly began to smile and prodded the boy on the shoulder. The deed was done and it was time to return.

He who had received the Khoi-san name HumGau - Lionheart - during his Xnau-ceremony, quietly thanked the spirits of the great cats for their deed. The animals left the scene; there was no need to linger. The boy began to move his limbs one by one. He was still in awe of the new things he was learning, of his gift and the power of the man's skill.

"Is it done?" He asked.

"Yes, it is done," the man said gravely and held the smoking herbs in circling movements over the bones on the floor mat.

There was nothing more to be said.

*

When it was discovered the following morning that a guest from Johannesburg by the name of *Miller* had gone missing from his tent, the rangers went out to the place between the dry river bed and the rushing whitewater. This was the place, where the man had been seen last.

The morning safari drive was cancelled. They needed to find out what had happened to this Mr. Alan Miller from tent No. 213. Tom Rutgers went with the rangers to search for the missing guest. He was deeply worried, although he didn't know the man and didn't remember him arriving the day before.

The people of Shangari had found relative peace since the murders had rocked their small community in February but Tom couldn't shake a sense of foreboding. He felt his throat tighten, as they combed through the underbrush, searching for the missing tourist.

Brutus, the Rhodesian Ridgeback searched with his nose to the ground. He howled and Tom Rutger's sense of dread grew. The dog pulled on his leash and dragged him to a place by the woods, where Tom didn't want to follow.

Nelson had described the location, where he'd stopped the safari vehicle and taken the tourists on a short nature walk. They didn't have to search for long before they found what they had been looking for and it was worse than what they could have expected.

They found not one, but two men lying in their own blood. One of them was Alwin Goldsmith. His fingerprints would later confirm this fact. He was lying on his back, his face and neck mauled, his chest open. A terrible sight.

They could only assume that it was the missing tourist. He didn't have much of a face left but his pale skin, the receding hairline and the way he was dressed pointed to a city dweller.

Army-green straps were sticking out from under Mr. Miller's body. They lifted the corpse slightly to the side and found a matching army-green bag. The bag contained two rhino horns, wrapped in a dirty cloth and twenty-thousand Rand in bank notes. What was all of this doing here?

No rhino had been poached in the area lately. Not that they knew of. The other man lay on his stomach, dressed in a khaki suit. When he was turned over, Tom Rutgers recognised him at once. The eyes had rolled back in his head and a gunshot wound to his forehead had turned an ugly darkish colour, but everybody knew who the man was.

A 9 mm Glock was lying in the grass not far from the two bodies. The murder weapon that had killed Barry Pienaar. Tom's stomach turned violently.

Witbooi was on the scene within half an hour and tried to console his quietly sobbing friend. Witbooi had been speechless at first. He didn't know what he should say to make his friend feel better. Two rhino horns were lying on a blood-stained green bag. So this was poaching-related. What else could he do but call the Special Commission on Poaching and concentrate on sound police work? It was his job after all.

Tom and Witbooi stared at each other, unwilling to accept what they were seeing right in front of them.

"It can't be, Witbooi, it just can't be," Tom Rutgers repeated. "I don't get it. What was Barry doing out here? With this guy, this Mr. Miller. Did Miller shoot him or was Barry shot by somebody else? But what was he doing here?"

"I don't know, Tom, I really don't know," Witbooi said. "At least the lion didn't touch him. Why don't you sit down in the car and have some water."

They walked to the car side by side.

Witbooi radioed the police station in Rutgersdrift and turned away from Tom to wipe away a tear before giving instructions to a handful of policemen on the scene. "Search the area. Any clues. Anything," he barked.

They took photographs and fingerprints from both victims. The fingerprints later confirmed that the body of the unknown man was that of a middle-management lawyer with Makaroff Enterprises in Johannesburg. His name was Alwin Goldsmith, not Alan Miller.

Witbooi was stumped. Why would this man, a tourist at Shangari, conceal his identity? Unless he had something to do with the smuggling of the rhino horns, they had found. Had he acted of his own accord or was he a runner? Unlikely for a high-level lawyer. His next of kin were informed and the Special Commission on Poaching took over.

The coroner in Rutgersdrift found powder burns on his hands. No victim then, this Mr. Alwin Goldsmith. He had clearly done the shooting. On closer inspection of his hands, something else was found. Something odd.

The dead lawyer still held a pin in his left fist. A square pin made of blue enamel. A golden circle with a V & S inside and an animal in every corner. Before informing the detectives of the Special Commission on Poaching, the coroner called Witbooi and asked him to come to the surgery.

The station commander knew what he was looking at. It

was just like the pin, Tom Rutgers had removed from Cornelius' hand in February. Before the Special Commission on Poaching could investigate, the pin had disappeared from the evidence room together with the description and photographs of the case.

Tom could not remember what the pin had looked like. Tom could not remember what the pin had looked like. The Special Commission had not pursued the matter, since they already had a suspect in custody: Mothusi, the Khoi-San ranger. The man was later acquitted of all wrongdoing, but by then, it had been too late.

Now that Witbooi saw the pin with his own eyes, he was convinced that it was the same pin, Barry Pienaar had received at a dinner function held by the Veterinary Society in Pretoria. Barry had shown it to him, so proud of the honour.

"What do you want to do?" The coroner asked.

"Give it to me, I'll put the pin with the other evidence."

It was only a matter of time before the connection would be made.

"Sure thing." The coroner didn't think twice before handing the pin over to the station commander.

It was the second time, the blue pin disappeared.

Witbooi decided that the community had suffered enough. He dug a hole in the yard by the police station and buried the evidence. They would remember Barry Pienaar as a hero who had tried to stop the criminals.

And in a way, he had. After Lorraine's death, Barry Pienaar had tried to make amends. He knew that if he came forward, he would end up in prison. That didn't help anyone, least of all the animals he looked after. The refurbished dairy-cottage on the farm that had served as a hide-out for the traffickers was now part of his veterinarian clinic. He'd worked more closely with Gerda Marais's orphan sanctuary to facilitate the soft release of grown animals into the grounds of the vast Pienaar Farm. But still, he suffered from depression and found solace in drinking. Barry Pienaar had denied all knowledge and involvement in the crimes. The detectives clearly hadn't believed him but there was no evidence to prove their case. A contact of his had stolen the rhino horns from the evidence room at the Special Commission offices in Pretoria together with the pin that would have implicated him.

The vet had convinced the well-meaning woman that he was doing this to bring the smugglers to book since the commission had never been able to do this. He had hated himself for going along with the smugglers' demands for Lorraine's sake and wanted nothing more to do with Makaroff or his despicable lawyer. To him, they were all the same: uncaring and greedy. Still, he felt that he was being punished by God for his transgressions.

He'd decided to set up the meeting with Alwin Goldsmith; knew where the man worked and how to get into his office unseen. He was proud of himself for only one reason: that he had never told Alwin Goldsmith who the new rhino whisperer was. Barry Pienaar had planned to extricate himself from the grip of the criminals after one last deal. Just one last deal with the corrupt lawyer then he would start a new life.

He never knew just how greedy Makaroff's lawyer was; that he was running his own operation with the help of old Mrs. Makaroff. That he carried a gun and would use it. Barry Pienaar believed he could hear the roar of a lion and thought it fitting, as he lay dying on the ground in the woods by the river as the blood-red sun went down in the west and everything around him went dark forever.

Alwin Goldsmith had shot him in anger shortly before the large cats attacked. Nobody would ever find out the true reason, why a local vet had been there in the bush with a Makaroff lawyer in the first place.

*

At daybreak, Ludmilla Makaroff, the cynical dowager queen of the Makaroff empire, was arrested at her Dainfern mansion. She refused to speak to the police and her legal team fought tooth and nail for her release on bail.

There had been no clear evidence that she had known

about her son's criminal business interests or of his connections to an international smuggling ring. The new evidence changed all that. Court hearings chased one another and reporters had a field day, unravelling the many alleged crimes of the Makaroff clan.

Meanwhile, the Makaroff empire was ailing. The sheer load of criminal charges was weighing heavily on the reputation of a business that had basked so long in the sunshine of political favours. One by one the banks dropped Makaroff like a hot potato. They closed the accounts that had enabled Stan Makaroff to accumulate a fortune. The public was shocked to hear how much the empire was worth and how deep the corrupt dealings with the government ran.

This was their downfall in the end. The Fraud Unit confiscated Stan Makaroff's assets and the Makaroff Tower in Sandton was up for sale. His wife and mother were next. Despite her efforts to secure an inheritance, Gloria Goldsmith didn't receive a cent of her husband's ill-gotten wealth.

A few weeks after Ludmilla Makaroff's arrest, a tip-off led the detectives of the Special Commission on Poaching to pick up Basil Malambo in the parking lot at Sun City. Phone records and searches of the suspects' various homes had revealed the undeniable connection between the politician, Stanislav Makaroff's mother and Alwin Goldsmith.

The public was in awe for a few months until another scandal grabbed the news headlines.

*

Four years after the scandal broke, a young man by the name of Frans Grootman, helped with the release of a rhino orphan from Gerda Marais' sanctuary.

He had cared for the youngster since the day poachers had killed and dehorned his mother in a murderous attack at the Shangari Safari Park. Frans Grootman was studying to become a vet and also worked with Dr. Gelders during term breaks.

Oscar, the rhino, had grown into a strong and boisterous bull who eagerly left the sanctuary through the back gate every morning and returned at night to the safe and comfortable bed of hay in the barn. He'd been sharing his bedstead with a donkey-nanny called Cookie for a long time. Cookie now warmed another little orphan, an elephant calf called Naledi, whose mother had been shot for her magnificent ivory teeth. Frans sat on a rock by the back gate and watched the sunrise. Oscar was already outside, waiting eagerly.

"She will come." Frans smiled. "You need to learn patience, my dear friend."

Oscar grunted in response and ripped a few green shoots off the succulent new grass. A few weeks ago, the new owner of the Pienaar farm had acquired a female black rhino at an auction. This rhino showed up in the mornings to meet Oscar and to trot off with him into the vast savannah all the way to the hills in the north east.

The sun rose a little higher above the horizon.

"What did I tell you? Here she is," Frans said to the rhino bull and stood up.

"It's good to see you, Karabo," he greeted the female rhino. "You are looking particularly glowing this morning."

He laughed at her bashful reaction. "How is the little one doing?" Karabo's tummy was already by a margin thicker than yesterday.

"I'm glad," the young man said.

Frans had named the baby Cornelia after his own father. He'd call her Connie for short. He hadn't told the new vet, Dr. Gelders, about Karabo's pregnancy yet. Soon it would be showing anyway.

There were now three white rhinoceroses living in Shangari Safari Park. Oscar and his mate would be taken there as soon as the release was finalised and their offspring would greatly boost the black rhino population in the area. Oscar nodded his head as if to ask for permission from the young man to leave the familiar surroundings.

"Go and have a good day, Kleintjie. I will see you when you come back." The two rhinos trotted off toward the bush and soon disappeared among the trees.

The new owner of the Pienaar farm was Gugu Mbatha and she loved her new life in the country. The Xhosa city girl had turned her life around. Thoroughly disenchanted with the high-flying lifestyle of a PR manager at Makaroff Enterprises after the big scandal, she'd found another calling. Gugu Mbatha had left the glamour of the big city behind and decided to give the North West a try. She knew that she was taking a risk, but after an extended visit to Shangari, she had followed an impulse and bought the Pienaar farm with the help of her wealthy father.

She had so many plans and was determined to make the most of the unique location. Gugu had named the farm Tsholofelo, a Tswana word meaning 'Hope'. And hope had returned to the Pienaar farm with her.

The Tsholofelo Nature Resort now specialised in whitewater rafting and game drives. And the recent discovery of a thermal spring had led to the building of a small spa that attracted the local womenfolk.

They had given the newcomer the cold shoulder at first, but after a few months, the bookings had started to roll in from all over the country and the spa would soon outpace the rafting business. The new veterinarian, Dr. Janek Gelders, still operated from the farm with four helpers and young Frans Grootman assisted him whenever he could.

Gugu had added more rooms to the main house that had undergone a major transformation.

The hotel was not a luxury lodge like Shangari, but a normal country hotel with five rooms and twelve self-catering chalets. She'd used her contacts and expertise to build her business venture and was happy with the success.

To everyone's surprise, Gugu had struck up an unlikely friendship with Witbooi van Schalkwyk that had blossomed into love. They had moved into another Cape Dutch-style building on the farm that had been refurbished and was now a proper home.

Witbooi no longer looked the part of the bumbling, overweight commander of the Rutgersdrift police station. Trim and handsome, he commandeered a team of three raft guides and two rangers and enjoyed himself tremendously.

They'd had their wedding Xhosa-style in the Eastern Cape and a second reception at Shangari last year. Now that Gugu was expecting their first child, they could rely on her capable staff to run the hotel and spa practically on their own. Another station commander had taken Witbooi's in Rutgersdrift and ensured order in the district.

Not that it hadn't been easy sailing at first. Much like any closed, rural community, the people of Renosterspruit and Rutgersdrift had frowned upon the new addition to their fold. It helped that Gugu was now Mrs. van Schalkwyk and close friends with Tom Rutgers and his Finnish wife Sofia. The locals were warming up to Gugu since she provided work for a dozen people from the area.

Gugu van Schalkwyk couldn't be bothered with village gossip. She had never felt so happy and fulfilled in her life.

Her best friend lived across the river on the neighbouring game farm and at last, she was doing something worthwhile.

*

"Uncle Tom... uncle Tom!" Jessica called out as she ran after two-year-old Arttu who had toddled out of the house again when Frida wasn't looking.

The dark-haired little boy was trying to find his father. He enjoyed nothing more than 'helping' Tom in the barn, applying the finishing touches to the 'Shangari'. Tom and Sofia had big plans, sailing the fine-looking boat along the South African coastline from Cape Town all the way up to Umhlanga in Kwa Zulu Natal.

"Hey, you little rascal!" Tom cried laughing and Arttu ran into his open arms

"Papa, papa!" Arttu crowed and playfully chewed on Tom's nose with his four little mouse teeth.

"Hey, you can't do that anymore, Arttu. You're way too big to chew Daddy's nose." Tom picked his giggling son up and handed him over to Jessica. Astrid's daughter had grown into a lanky, serious teenager who resembled her late mother more

274

and more by the day.

Jessica and Charlie now lived with their paternal grandmother in Germiston and often came to spend the school holidays at Shangari. At first, Paul Somerset had been in the picture but they hadn't heard from him since he'd moved back to Pretoria.

Sometimes, the two children would invite their friends. Jessica's new best friends, Sanele Dlamini and Carmen Liu, had been spending the past two weeks with them at the Shangari farmhouse and the girls enjoyed themselves tremendously.

They loved the swimming pool and were often allowed at parties, where they felt all grown up in their pretty dresses. Sanele's foster parents were both medical doctors and would be joining them over the long weekend.

Arttu struggled out of Jessica's arms and sat down next to Brutus. He hugged the ageing dog and threw little twigs and stones for him to fetch. Brutus yawned and made no attempts to fetch. The family had come from Europe for Arttu's Nimiäiset, the Finish naming celebration when Arttu was six months old. Even Tom's mother had arrived for a week without her niggly husband.

"I want to go swimming with my friends, uncle Tom," Jessica said. "Can we go into Rutgersdrift later? We want to have milkshakes at the new coffee shop and go window shopping." Rutgersdrift had developed into a thriving district town, where artists found solitude and inspiration.

"Did you clear that with auntie Sofie?" Tom asked. "And how will you get to Rutgersdrift and back?"

Sofia Rutgers-Helenius was attending an international conference on wildlife preservation in Cape Town this week. She had left Tom and Frida in charge of the children and Jessica skyped with her aunt daily.

They had more time on their hands now that Stephen MacAllister, Karen's brother, had taken over the daily grind of running the lodge. Karen managed the kitchen better than ever and tried out new and exciting recipes on a monthly basis. Tom and Sofia were still involved, of course, but had an expanding family to care for.

"Auntie Sofie said no problem, we can go with Cotton. He has to buy something from the bottle store and what not. He'll take us back at about 5 o'clock." She drew circles in the sand with her big toe.

"Well if auntie Sofie says so, I guess it's okay. Just make sure, you don't wander off and don't speak to strangers."

"Don't worry, uncle Tom," Jessica rolled her eyes in teenage fashion. "Sanele will keep us on track. She'll become a lawyer just like Thuli Madonsela and knows a thing or two about that sort of stuff."

"Alright then. I'm very impressed that Sanele knows about that sort of stuff and hope she'll keep you on track. But you'll be back no later than 5 o'clock."

"I know... auntie Sofie said the same. Have you seen Charlie anywhere?" Jessica's younger brother was usually doing his own thing and was on some mission with the boys from the compound.

"I think he and Thando went on a safari drive with Nelson and the Dutch tourists," Tom Rutgers said.

"Okay." Jessica kept doodling in the sand with her toe.

It had been a hard time for Jessica and Charlie at first with their Dad in prison and their mother gone. They had gone for counselling and were doing much better now. Sofia and their grandmother Rankin shared custody of the two children and things were as normal as could be. Charlie was struggling somewhat with bullies at school and hadn't made good friends yet, but with every visit to Shangari, he seemed to become more confident.

They turned around and saw Frida huffing and puffing down the path.

"How! There you are, boytjie..." she panted.

Frida picked the toddler up, bundled him into a thin receiving blanket and put him on her back then knotted the corners in front of her bosom. The little boy waved to his father as he was carried African-style back to the farmhouse and Jessica followed Frida.

"Bye Arttu! Bye Jessica! See you guys later." Tom enjoyed having the children around. They often watched how Obakeng fed Jethro, the tame cheetah, and liked helping out with the orphans at Gerda Marais' sanctuary. Even Arttu wanted to run with the big boys if he got half a chance.

Tom Rutgers walked toward the barn and closed the large doors. He would have drinks with the Dutch tourists as soon as they came back from their game drive in about an hour.

"Mr.. Rutgers," Obakeng addressed Tom outside Jethro's enclosure and the cheetah was purring at the sound of his voice. "Mr.. Rutgers, I have to go away for a while." He looked openly into Tom's eyes.

"Oh? Where do you have to go?" Tom asked.

"I must see some relatives close to the Kruger Park," Obakeng said. "I will take Frans with me. He is on study leave until the end of July. We will only be away for a week but we have to leave tomorrow."

Tom Rutgers studied Obakeng's face. His expression was inscrutable and Tom knew that the sangoma did not ask for permission; he was telling him about his plans out of respect. Obakeng and Frans would be going, whether it was convenient for Tom or not.

"Well if you have to go, you have to go," he said. Obakeng helped Tom with the barn door and cleared some sawdust from the tracks on the ground.

"The others will take over my tasks while I'm gone. Dit is baie belangrik," Obakeng said. It's very important.

"Alles is reg, Obakeng. It's alright if you need to take care of something. I'll see you when you come back. Do you have enough money for your trip?"

"Yes, Mr.. Rutgers, I just got paid. We will stay with relatives there and I won't need much money," Obakeng said and slammed the barn doors closed.

Tom Rutgers knew that a strong anti-poaching unit had taken over the fight against the slaughter of Africa's rhinos in the Kruger Park. With some luck, the unit would branch out into different regions around the country.

The specially trained rangers were not only tested for their combat skills and integrity but also for their specific abilities with animals.

Obakeng's family had been part of Shangari for a long time and Tom could trust the loyal man who possessed the special gift of communicating with wild cats. Given the last lion attack at Shangari four years ago, he could only guess what the important matter in the Kruger Park might be. The attack had resulted in the devastating death of the local vet and that of a man who was clearly involved in the crime. There had been no poaching incidents at Shangari since.

Tom was not naïve enough to believe that his childhood friend, Barry Pienaar, was entirely blameless, but he missed him nonetheless. He wished things could have been different. If Obakeng and Frans had anything to do with it, poachers and smugglers in the Kruger Park would have a very tough time from now on.

"I wish you all the best with your plans," Tom said.

"Dankie, Mr. Rutgers." Obakeng smiled.

Tom Rutgers knew better than to ask pointless questions about the actual reason for their trip. He and the ageless sangoma had always understood each other, even without words.

The End

ABOUT THE AUTHOR

Evadeen Brickwood grew up with two sisters in Germany and studied cultural sciences and languages. As a young woman, she travelled extensively and many of her books are inspired by her experiences abroad.

Feeling adventurous, the newly qualified translator moved to Africa in 1988 and worked for two years as a secretary and language teacher in Botswana.

The author eventually settled in South Africa, where she got married and raised two daughters. In Johannesburg, Evadeen Brickwood studied computers and management of training and worked as a corporate software trainer and a professional translator & lecturer at WITS University.

In 2003, she began her writing career with youth novels in the 'Remember the Future' series, about adventures in prehistory. Book 1, 'Children of the Moon', has been published twice in South Africa and won the 2017 Book Talk Radio Club Award for Best Science Fiction Novel in England.

The author now self-publishes and other books in the series are released on a regular basis.

Her works also include the novels 'Singing Lizards' and 'A Half Moon Adventure' and the 'Charlie Proudfoot Mysteries' series. Four of her novels are available in German language editions.

About Writing This Book

Rhino poaching is a despicable crime and like so many others, I'm appalled by the greedy demand for the ground-up keratin powder and the slaughter of our irreplaceable animals. The smuggling of rhino-horn is just part of a host of crimes I'm trying to address in this book and rhino-poaching is only part of the story line.

South Africa is a wonderfully diverse country with incredible nature and city life. And the people who live here are just as diverse. I witness on a daily basis, how people with different backgrounds interact with each other in South Africa. Incredible kindness and wisdom as well as senseless animosity and greed exist side by side and to address all of this in one book would be an impossible task. That's why I wrote about the things I see and what I would like to see as a writer of fiction.

You shouldn't expect a report on crime and the usual whodunit approach. That's the job of the media and they are doing a great job already. Since I am part of the creative crowd, I tried to find a different, creative approach. You'll find an array of emotions, relationships gone wrong and gone right and how greed and violence can destroy lives and one's sanity.

I prefer non-violent solutions, and wouldn't it be fantastic if we could somehow turn this country into a beacon of peace and prosperity for others to follow its example? If it's possible to contribute just a tiny bit to this utopia, I'll gladly do it with this book.

Evadeen Brickwood

Discover other novels by Evadeen Brickwood

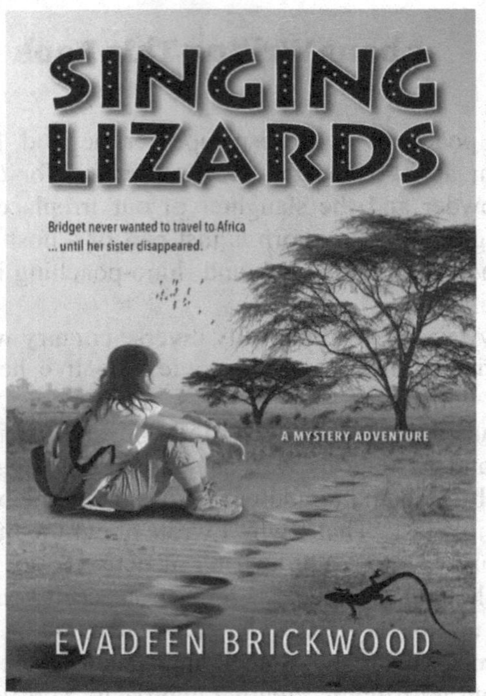

An Adventure-Mystery set in Africa

Bridget Reinhold is not exactly the adventurous type but when her sister Claire disappears in Southern Africa, nothing can keep her in England. Bridget launches herself into the search in the country of Botswana and encounters obstacle after obstacle. Soon, her mission is plunged into turmoil as everything seems to be going wrong. Just coincidence or is there something not so normal at work?

An Adventure-Mystery set in Pakistan

As if growing up in the seventies wasn't hard enough! Isabell Bertrand is a feisty teenager and too rebellious for her parents' liking. A novel treatment with hypnosis is supposed to help with her attitude and she begins her session with Dr. Albrecht, a hypnotherapist. He takes Isabell back to her early childhood and then further and further back in time. She can barely believe that this exotic beauty dressed in silk saris could have been herself once. Did she really have to decide between two men back then? Years later, Isabell is invited to a wedding in Pakistan and a host of unwanted memories return, leading to unexpected consequences.

All of Evadeen Brickwood's books are available on most online platforms and at good bookstores.

The e-books can be purchased at major online stores, such as Amazon, Kobo, Tolino, Kindle, Apple i-Store, Neobooks etc.

The author's websites are:

http://www.evadeen.wixsite.com/novels
http://www.evadeen.wixsite.com/youngbooks
http://www.evadeen.wixsite.com/charlieproudfoot

She is also on social media, incl. Facebook, Twitter, Instagram, Pinterest, google+ and Goodreads.

www.ingramcontent.com/pod-product-compliance
Lightning Source LLC
Chambersburg PA
CBHW010443100726
47904CB00008B/2455